Secrets, Lies & Grace

Things aren't always as they seem.

Julie McCullough

ACKNOWLEDGEMENTS

Writing a novel is never an easy process, but when you've gone through the shock and grief of suddenly losing a beloved sibling, then the final breakdown of your marriage, you feel like forgetting the whole idea of completing the book.

I almost did, but that intense flame to reach my dreams burned bright, so instead of giving up, I used my writing to help me back on to my unsteady feet.

I thank my children, Dylan and Ayla, for their patience in my spending so much time at the computer AND for showing this ol' girl some simple computer 'stuff' that I wouldn't have otherwise known.

This book took two years to complete and I am proud of it.

Thanks also to my wider family and friends, both personal and on Facebook, who answered my research questions, gave me writing tips or advice, shared news of excellent upcoming writing courses or workshops and, most of all, gave me the love, support and encouragement I needed. I could name names but am afraid I may forget someone.

CHAPTER 1

The lonely road loomed ahead of Grace, snaking its way up the wooded range. Destination: anywhere away from the mess her once-happy life had become. Even though she now had company in the car, her own loneliness had already clawed at her shattered heart, cutting and shredding it to slivers. She really didn't care where the journey ended.

She reached for her phone yet again, shutting her mind to everything around her. This time she hit Kain's name and tapped '*Hi Kain.*' Her finger hesitated, hovering above the screen trying to figure out what to type next. But there really wasn't anything left to say after what he'd done.

He'd made it clear as the purest glass - they were over. Done. After five, beautiful happy years. No logical explanation. No opportunity for her to beg him to reconsider, to find a solution to their problems. Hell, she didn't even realised they had any problems. He'd seemed happy until . . . until a few days before the final goodbye. He changed. Became quiet, moody. Her finger tapped out the words, '*Just letting you-*'

Without warning, the car jerked left, then to the right. She looked at the driver, opened her mouth to scream, but her head smacked the top edge of the car door. Whipping pain hit her neck. She dropped her phone, grabbed the door handle with one hand and reached for the steering wheel with the other. Her scream mingled with the screeching of the tyres, stabbing her eardrums. The car rolled and tumbled, crunched and scraped down the ravine. Pain surged through her head, chest, legs, *everywhere*. She screamed until her throat became a knife's blade of pain.

The car door flew open and disappeared with a screech of tearing metal. Grace hit the ground and rolled with the momentum and landed against a rock. A flash of pain shot through her shoulder. The smell of petrol so strong she could taste it. Another crunch from the car, then silence. She spat dirt, lifted her head and looked around, trembling, fighting back a choking sob. Her car was now an upside-down mangled mass of metal thrown against a tree further down the ravine, one wheel still turning and smoke drifting upwards.

The driver! Taking hold of a sapling, she pulled herself to her knees. Sweat dripped from her face, the forest spun and shimmered but she *had* to get down to the car. She swallowed saliva and attempted to stand. Pain flared from her feet to her head.

Boom.

A surge of heat hit her like the sun had burst and she fell onto her face. A sickening, burning smell filled the air, more than just the incinerated car. Burning flesh. She opened her mouth and vomited on the ground. Afraid to look but needing to know, she looked back. A fireball rolled high into the air, past the treetops. No one could ever survive that inferno.

Flames licked at the grass around the wreck. *Get away!* She raised herself to hands and knees, crawled and scrambled up the hillside, scattering sticks and loose dirt.

Pushing to her feet, she ran, stumbling as she wove between trees and ducking low hanging branches, hoping to find the road. Her thigh muscles strained and burned. She gasped for each ragged breath. The hill levelled out and she stopped, bent over and sucked life-saving air into her tight lungs.

Grabbing an overhanging branch for support, thorns tore at her dirty, bare, bruised skin. She yanked her arm back and rubbed the fresh scratch stinging her forearm. Wiping the sweat from her brow, she stepped backwards. One of her joggers broke a stick. *Snap* echoed through the endless trees.

Lost.

Pain and disbelief tore at her fractured heart and crumbling sanity. The accident. *The driver.* Nobody deserved to die that way.

Was this some horrible nightmare? *Am I dead? Is this hell?*

She held her breath. No traffic sounds. No road. Nothing.

The summer air hung thick. Glaring sun, stifling heat, and sweltering humidity drained the life out of her.

A growl and flash of golden tan to her right froze her to the spot, froze the blood in her veins. Afraid to breathe or swipe away the bush flies settling on her face, she turned. That growl could only come from a meat eater.

Another deep growl.

Icy chills sluiced down her spine. A huge, lean dog stood behind a full-grown Ironbark tree, watching her. A breath jammed in her throat, bringing her racing heart to a brief halt. It looked like a German Shepherd. Thank God. Maybe its owner was nearby.

"It's okay boy, I won't hurt you." She shaded her eyes and scanned the bush, searching for campers or bush-walkers. *Please.* "Hellooooo. Anyone there?" No reply. The dog watched her, head low. Invisible lasers shot from its eyes, cutting through every part of her aching body. She whistled through sand-paper lips, barely audible. She leaned forward and reached out a dirty hand to the dog.

It didn't move.

Her long hair fell down the sides of her face. She was sure she'd tied it up in a ponytail before… *before what?* Bits and pieces flashed through her brain but nothing made sense.

She straightened and pushed hair behind her ear before rubbing her aching temple. When she brought her hand down, blood and sweat marked her fingers.

Invisible talons grabbed her throat at the sight, squeezing out all breath. Her life could be oozing out with that blood.

The car. What happened? Why did it crash?

She tried to remember but winced from the pain in her head. The dog walked away from the tree, its full size now exposed. Saliva dripped from strong jaws. Yellowish menacing eyes never left her face.

Sunlight beaming through the trees highlighted the tannish-orange of the dog's matted coat that covered prominent rib bones. The white-tipped tail remained motionless. This was no one's pet.

And it was hungry, *very* hungry.

Another dog, smaller and with the fairer coat of a pure dingo, came into view only metres from the first. It glanced at the other dog in front then to her. Hunger showed in determined eyes and drooling jaws. Hunger showed in a hollow, tucked-up belly. Hunger equalled desperation.

Grace's heart thumped like an angry bass drummer. *Come on, think*! They were wild, ravenous dogs and she, their food. They smelt her blood, her fear. She spun around, looking for any sign of civilization.

Nothing except endless bush – gum trees, iron-barks, wattles and lantana, *bloody lantana.* She *hated* the pest after helping her parents clear it from a back paddock.

With no climbable trees close by, Grace searched for another saviour. Two steps to her left lay a metre-long stick. With that she'd have some hope of defending herself. She edged out her left foot.

The bigger dog growled again and took a step forward. Not too much of her skin showed. *So what. They could rip jeans to shreds in seconds.* She shuddered, fighting back the tears that stung her eyes, the lump forming in her throat.

"Look", she said to the evil staring her down, "I won't hurt you if you just leave me alone, okay." She inched her left foot closer to the stick, followed by her right, dragging it through ankle-high grass.

Life was perfect then it all came crashing down . . . *but why?* Dammit, she couldn't remember. What does it matter now anyway? Her life could end at any minute. Any second.

The dog took another step toward Grace, lowered its head and growled again.

A louder rumble came from the west. The sun disappeared behind black clouds. Another rumble. Thunder.

Neither dog moved a muscle, ignoring the approaching storm.

Tears slid down her cheeks. As if the dogs weren't terrifying enough, now she also had to contend with a storm. Her legs weakened, threatening to crumple, but that would definitely be the end. She'd be ripped apart, eaten by bloody wild dogs, her bare bones left to bake in the relentless Queensland heat. Kain will never know how much she still loved him.

"Stuff you, Kain Burrows." She shouted until her lungs hurt and her throat burned. "I loved you and now look where I am."

Kain was her life, she couldn't imagine being without him. She, ready to get married and start a family and *he* decided he needed to go out and find himself. *Find himself?* Who the hell is going to find her in this God forsaken place?

She imagined him running through the bush, calling her name, finding her, assuring her what a big mistake he'd made and that he still loved her. That was the part that hurt the most. When he'd told her he no longer loved her. The part that grated her heart into little pieces, like these dogs wanting to rip into her body and tear it to bite sized pieces.

Grace shot her hand down and grabbed the stick, grasping the end with both hands and raised it high. Searing pain speared through her right shoulder. More tears flowed. She dropped her right arm with a defeated cry.

Jumbled images continued swirling through her brain. She remembered feeling tired then the hitchhiker standing by the side of the road, with nothing in her hands. The hitchhiker in the car. What was her name? Sally? Susie?

Lightning shot to earth, immediately followed by the sharp crack of thunder. Thunder that seemed capable of splitting anything in two. Again, neither dog flinched. The storm was building fast and heading toward her. She *had* to keep it together.

It was too much. "Damn you friggin' things! Why can't you just run away and hide?" Gritting her teeth, she swung the stick around her head. "Go on, get out." She screamed, hoping to frighten the dogs but they didn't budge. Instead, her parched throat now burned like she's swallowed a red-hot ember. Water. She needed water. She dropped her throbbing right arm and held the stick in her left hand.

That scream was familiar, but why? She wanted to scream out longer, louder, harder but when she opened her mouth only a hoarse croak came out.

That same scream had filled the air when her car left the road and surged down the side of the range. But she wasn't driving. She'd seen Sally's (or Susie) head hit the steering wheel.

Phone. Grace felt all her pockets, including the one in her black blouse. All empty. There seemed no hope of escaping the dogs.

More pain flowed through her right shoulder and arm. *No, wait.* Against her better judgement she'd been texting Kain to tell him she was going . . . going *where?* She shouldn't have even bothered the courtesy of letting him know.

"*Why* can't I remember?" Anger replaced fear. A large stone caught her vision. She bent, grabbed it in her right hand without thinking. With a painful grunt, she hurled the stone at the menacing dog.

The stone hit its front leg. A sharp yelp. Another louder growl sent more slivers of fear through her body.

The other, smaller dog, mouth open and tongue hanging out, trotted forward stopping beside the larger dog. Long white teeth showed. Teeth that could soon be tearing through her skin and muscle, ripping out her innards. Tongues that would lap her blood. Icicles of fear sped through her veins and dropped into her stomach.

The breeze dropped. Bird songs fell silent. The storm, imminent. The growls fell silent. Even the thunder fell silent. The only noise, her sharp breathing, her heart pounding and her blood pulsating in her ears.

Both dogs ready to go in for the kill. A loud clap of thunder. Grace screamed and jumped. Sweaty hands quivered, her chest tightened. If the dogs don't eat her, lightning will strike one of these trees above her. Either way, she'd die.

She dropped the stick, turned and fled. One of her shoes slipped off. She didn't stop but dared look back. Both dogs lolloped after her, gaining ground, mouths open, pink tongues exposed. A blinding bolt of lightning lit up the bush. The ground shook as the thunder continued on with its deep rumbling. Rumbling like a volcano with colic.

Grace pushed onward, swiping low branches, jumping fallen logs and rocks, hoping like hell she wouldn't trip. Her jeans caught on a snag. Her right arm ached as it swung about. A painful stitch ripped into her side.

But all was quiet behind her. She halted, bent forward and gasped for each agonising breath as she turned around. Both dogs had stopped. They could have caught her if they'd continued running.

The wind picked up. Large raindrops hit her head and eerie darkness descended. The heavy clouds approached at top speed. More thunder clapped and rumbled after each flash of lightning.

The raindrops hit faster and heavier, soon washing away her tears and her blood.

The larger dog howled, came closer, crouched. The smaller one stood back. Their coats ragged and pathetic as the rain pelted them. Grace brushed wet, clingy hair from her eyes.

"I love you Mum and Dad." She needed to say her goodbyes out loud. "And you Sophie, little sis." She sucked back a sob and gulped in a breath. "Steve, I love you too, big brother where ever you are." The ground tugged away at her strength, but she remained standing. "And you, Kain, I'll always love you, no matter what."

The larger dog sprang. The smaller one circled left. Grace opened her mouth to scream but her brain had gone mute. Everything now in slow motion.

No more energy to run and nowhere to hide. Pain disappeared. Only numbness remained. Spittle sprayed from the dog's mouth. Nano-second images of her life flashed by. Her body seemed weightless, her hands turned to ice. Stomach acid rose, burning her oesophagus and throat, that was about to be torn out. Feet cemented to the ground.

A short, high-pitched whistle shot passed her head. Lightning flashed. A sharp *crack*, but not a crack of thunder.

Almost upon her, the dog jerked and crashed to the ground, skidding along the grass. Its skull exploded. Bone, blood, fur, and brain matter splattered in all directions. One eye disappeared but the other remained open, watching but seeing nothing.

Grace jumped back, clasping her hand to her mouth. The dog had been about to kill her, now it lay at her feet, mutilated. Dead. She gasped to get air down her throat, constricted from fear.

The other dog bolted away. The gaping head wound of the dead dog filled with water. Enlarged teats along its belly tugged at Grace's heart for a second. She shuddered, bent and dry retched. Her body trembled, both from cold and shock. The rain continued pelting down. More thunder growled overhead, drowning out the dull roar of the wind and rain.

Spinning around, she saw a man as yet another flash of lightning lit up the surrounds.

On a small ridge, black hat, long dark coat, rifle raised to his shoulder. He stood, amidst the whiteness of the pouring rain. She hadn't heard the shot. He had saved her . . . or maybe he'd been aiming for *her*.

Adrenaline and fear fused and reignited. No fight, just flight. Again, she turned and ran. The torrential rain stung her face and arms. The wind howled like a demented monster, sending branches crashing around her.

A white flash. A bone-jarring *crack* echoed through the forest. Branches from a large tree exploded to her right, the shower of sparks hurting her eyes. Blinding pain hit her back. She screamed.

Everything spun and blurred. She crashed to the wet ground. Kain's cheeky smile flashed through her mind right before she plunged into blackness.

CHAPTER 2

Kain's mind drifted to the lonely uncertainty his life's road had taken. All movement stopped.

"Come on Kain, what the hell ya doin'? We can't leave the wall like that. It looks like shit. Turn the sander off." His boss's angry words cut through the humid air.

"What?" Kain jolted back to the present and frowned at Eddie. He turned back to the gyprocked wall he'd just been sanding. "What's wrong with it? It's done." He bent and hit the off switch on the whirring sander. Within two seconds the room was silent.

"Done? Looks like crap." Eddie bent and picked up a piece of sand paper, reached and sanded the wall above his head.

"Sorry Eddie." Kain offered no excuse.

"You've completely missed this bit. Dunno how if you're using the machine. You're getting a bit slack these days, Kain. You used to be so neat and fussy with your work. What's goin' on, man?" Eddie stopped sanding and looked up at Kain. "It's like you've completely lost interest in your work. You want out?"

He stared at Eddie. An old man with greying curly hair and pot belly, although Eddie was only in his early fifties or so. Questions and worry reflected in Eddie's eyes. Would Kain look similar in twenty odd years' time? Middle age. Something he hadn't allowed himself the luxury of thinking about lately.

"Well?" Impatience dripped from Eddie's voice, nostrils flared, eyes grew angry. "We don't have time to stuff around on this big job. If our job isn't done when the painters are ready to start, the shit hits the fan. We're only half way through the thirty-six units yet. You crook? You wanna take the rest of the day off?" His voice emanated like a coarser version of the sandpaper.

"Huh?" Kain blinked several times and shook his head. He'd recently had his wavy hair shorn down to a number two and was still getting used to not feeling it about his ears and neck. "Shit, I'm sorry Eddie. I don't know what the hell I was thinking. I'm all right. Let me fix that." He grabbed another piece of sandpaper off the floor and rubbed the small area he'd just missed, to a smooth finish.

Eddie stepped back. "Now that's the enthusiasm I'm used to from you, Kain Burrows. Get into it, mate. I'm just going into the next unit to check on the other boys. That new bloke, Chris, seems to be workin' out okay don't ya think?"

"Yeah." Kain glanced at Eddie but hadn't really heard what he'd said, his mind already two steps ahead. He looked back at the stark wall and rubbed harder. Fine dust floated about his whitened hands as they worked.

Eddie left the room and Kain's thoughts ventured far away from his daily job. Yes, he had slackened off a bit in the past two weeks but thought he'd been covering it well. Hell, he'd been plastering for over ten years.

Grace. Her smile – the way it dimpled her cheeks – made him grin. Her shocked and shattered face when told he no longer loved her stole his grin away. The tears had immediately welled in her beautiful green eyes. Eyes that, until that moment, had looked at him with so much love. Eyes that lit up with a sparkle every time she laughed, which was often. Eyes that could see the good in everyone.

God, he missed her. It had been a week since that fateful day, with no choice but to break it off. His life without her no longer held any meaning, but there was no room for Grace. She'd be better off without him. His life had changed direction into unknown territory – doctors and hospitals.

His stomach lurched and simmered, for what lay ahead in these unchartered waters. A journey he needed to travel on his own. He couldn't, *wouldn't,* drag her through the certain hell. That would be too cruel and she'd be devastated in the end. The end? Where and when would that be? He flicked his head to shake the depressing thoughts.

A spark of energy surged through his veins. Determination took over his depressed soul like a light switched on. It's all good. It will be fine, albeit one hell of a challenge.

"Bring it on. Hit me with the best you got, God, or whoever deals the cards in this life. I'll jump every hurdle you throw at me."

Kain stepped back and admired his finished work. He found several more small areas that needed redoing. In no time the job was all done.

"Hey mate, you look like the cat that swallowed the budgie." Joe walked in, his happy-go-lucky laugh filling the room. "Ready for lunch?"

"Yep, sure am. Let's go." He dropped the sand paper and followed Joe out the door.

"Where you two headed?" asked Eddie.

Kain and Joe strode past him, toward the stairs leading to the ground floor.

"We're going for a countery over at the pub today," said Joe. "Wanna come?"

"Nah, you two can go. I've got some leftover lasagne. Bloody beautiful. Don't be late back and don't get pissed."

"We'll try not to," Joe shouted back with a wave and a laugh.

Ten minutes later the two men had ordered lunch, bought beers and seated themselves in the designated out-door smoking area. Kain took a sip of his light beer.

Joe lit a cigarette, inhaled loudly and turned his head to exhale. He downed a third of his beer, leaving a frothy line on his dark moustache. "Ah, that's better. Second and third best things in life, eh?" He licked his moustache, raised the hand that held the smoke and pointed to the beer with the other. "Hey, I notice you don't smoke much anymore. Givin' it up?"

"Yeah, trying to."

"What? The misses been naggin' about it? Speakin' of which," added Joe before Kain could answer. "How is that lovely lady of yours? Don't think you've even mentioned her once this week. She throw you out or something?" He aimed a playful punch at Kain's upper arm.

"Piss off, Joe." Kain laughed at the bitter irony. "No she hasn't actually. It's been my choice not to smoke. It's not that hard since I never smoked much anyway."

"Well, what's ya secret to givin' up? No way I could." Joe took one last drag before stubbing the butt out in the ashtray.

Loud laughter erupted at a nearby table. Kain's attention drew to the commotion. Several men of various ages huddled around a mobile phone.

"Geez, that wanker needs to be strung up by his balls," said one of the men.

"Yeah," chuckled another. "If he had any."

Kain turned back, wanting to ignore what he was hearing. "What was that, Joe?"

"I said, what's your secret?"

Kain almost choked on his beer. He swallowed and coughed several times. "What the hell are you talking about? What secret?"

"Steady on, mate." Joe held up one had in a truce mode. "I'm talking about how you're givin' up the fags. Geez, anyone would think I was trying to get classified information from the bloody Red Army or something. Keep ya shirt on."

"Sorry Joe, I didn't mean to snap. I just got a bit distracted listening to these blokes over here." He indicated with his thumb toward his shoulder. "No secret." Kain shrugged. "I have other things going on that are more important than smokes."

"Fair enough. Hey, how 'bout you and Grace come over tomorrow arvo for a barbie and we'll shoot some pool. I finally got the table re-covered. It hasn't had a proper game on it yet. Sue's not into playing pool that much. You two haven't been over for ages and the ladies can catch up while me and you let our hair down . . . well . . . " He grinned and nodded toward Kain's head. "You haven't got any to let down any more, but my lovely locks can still bounce." He patted the bottom of his wavy brown hair, pursed his lips and kissed the air.

Kain laughed. That felt so good. "You're an idiot, Joe."

"I know. Well . . . ?" Joe's leaned forward with an I'm-not-taking-no-for-an-answer look. "Do yous wanna come or not? There's a spare bed with your name on it so you can have a few drinks."

"Sounds good mate, but . . . " What to tell Joe? He won't be happy about the breakup. "I . . . I'll have to check with Grace and get back to you."

One thing Kain knew about his friend Joe, he was bull-headed and stubborn and he would not give up inviting Kain and Grace to his house. They'd spent many fun times there in the past - playing pool, darts, cards, drinking and generally enjoying the get-togethers.

Joe stood. "All right, well ring me tonight, but you'd better not say no. My shout." He walked inside to get another two beers.

You have to tell him. The nagging voice in Kain's head grew louder. How he wished there was an easy solution, but his mind was blank.

Their meal number blared through the speaker above the doorway. Kain picked up the meal ticket along with his now empty glass and headed inside. Joe met him partway with two full beers.

"Food's ready." Kain placed his empty glass on the bar and took one beer from Joe. They walked through the public bar where several patrons sat enjoying a good chinwag.

Full plates of fish, chips and salad awaited them from the servery. They picked them up and moved to the outdoor eating area.

Families, couples and small groups patronised the alfresco dining area, enjoying the scrumptious food, beautiful clear day and views overlooking the bay.

"Great place." Joe pointed to a vacant table for two. "Over there. You can never get sick of looking out at that." He nodded toward the Pacific Ocean, not more than half a kilometre from the Pacific View pub's hilltop location. "Good ol' PV. When I win lotto, I'm gunna buy this place. Hey, you and Grace can come into it with us. Whatcha reckon?" He sat down and sprinkled a generous amount of salt and pepper on his meal before handing the glass shakers to Kain.

"Yep, gotta love it all right." Kain put the shakers on the table without using them, took his cutlery from its paper bag and began his lunch.

In silence they ate. Kain knew he had to say something to Joe about Grace, but just couldn't find the words and Joe seemed to want to ask him a question or say something to him. Or was his mind just imagining things?

The silence continued and awkwardness grew to discomfort. Half way through the meal, Kain put his knife and fork together on the plate. The loud beating of his heart drowned out the din around him. His swallowed some beer to refresh his dry mouth, and drew in a deep breath hoping it would calm his bouncing nerves.

Joe placed his forkful of food back on the plate. "You got something to tell me, mate? You've been acting weird for a while now. What's goin' on?" He took a swig of his beer.

Kain opened his mouth to talk but then a large, red-headed woman in a skin tight blue dress rushed past, bumping him with her bag. She left a lingering invisible cloud of sickly perfume. He screwed up his nose. The woman sat at a close-by table, her hair reminding him of Grace's. It didn't take much of anything to remind him of Grace.

"You're late, Samantha," said her friend at the table, putting down her phone. "You look a bit flustered. What's happened?"

"Well," began the late arrival in a loud voice. She huffed like she'd just run a marathon. "I was called out to the range earlier to do a story."

The other woman started to speak, but the loud one continued at full-on pace. "There was a bad car crash and someone was killed."

"Oh no." Her colleague's hand flew to her mouth. "That's terrible. Any name?"

"No, not yet. The car rolled down a steep slope and burst into flames. Apparently the body is burnt beyond recognition. It was not a pretty sight." She screwed up her large nose. "Or smell."

Kain turned back. He didn't want to hear of other people's bad news. It was shocking and horrible but he had major battles ahead and Grace being well and safe was really all that mattered. Joe was a good mate, and after hearing that terrible news of a life gone in an instant, confessing to Joe may not be so hard after all. *Toughen up mate. Eat a spoon of cement.*

"Joe, umm . . . Grace and I have separated."

Joe splattered the mouthful of beer over the table. His eyeballs nearly popped out of their sockets. "What? Bullshiiiit!" He coughed and his shocked face reddened. "Piss off Kain, you two are made for each other. What the fuck is goin' on, mate? When did this happen?"

Kain took another deep breath and pushed his plate to the side. He brought his elbows up to the table and clasped his hands together. His brain was like a race car at the Grand Prix, a million miles per hour, yet blank.

"It's true, Joe. I broke it off. Earlier this week." Should he tell him the truth and risk Joe telling Grace, or spin him a bullshit story, like he did Grace? No, Joe knew him too well. He'd feel like an absolute dick once Joe saw through his lies, and he would.

"Why?" Joe's eyebrows creased together. His gaze hardened to stone. "Have you lost your friggin' marbles?"

Kain's stomach agitated like his grandma's old washing machine. It was time to tell the truth. No more mucking around. Thinking about it was bad enough, but saying it out loud was another thing. "I . . . I'm . . . I've got a problem." Shit, that didn't sound right.

Joe's dark eyes questioned him.

"A health problem." Kain diverted his gaze from Joe's face to the table.

"What's wrong? You're the picture of bloody health, mate. Look atcha – fit and muscly, nice white teeth and those sparkling baby blues. You put me to shame, that's for sure. I'll be pushin' up daisies, ha, I should say *weeds*, by the time I'm fifty."

Kain jolted at that comment and looked back at his mate. Not the best choice of words but Joe had no idea. "Umm . . . no, I'm not." He swallowed hard and blinked back a tear. "I might not have long to live."

Joe put his glass back on the table, his hand visibly shaking.

"At best, I won't be able to give Grace the kids she desperately wants."

"What the fuck are you sayin', Kain?" His eyes glassed over and his face paled.

"I've . . . I've got cancer."

"No." Joe whispered, shaking his head. "You're too young."

"It's true. There, I've said it. The big fucking C."

"Where? What? How long have you known?"

"A little while. I just can't put Grace through the torture. I have to start treatment soon and there's no guarantee I'll survive and if I do, I won't be able to give her kids. They told me about that possibility." Kain forced in a deep breath.

Joe continued staring at him in disbelief. "What does Grace think about the cancer?"

"She doesn't know. I didn't give her the real reason. I spun her a crap story, but she didn't believe me at first. I had to be harder on her. It broke my heart to see how hurt she was." He choked back a lump. "She deserves better. I know she'd just put her own life on hold for me. That's one of the things I love about her so much. She's so beautiful and loving and caring and . . . " The words could have easily continued flowing just as the tears now were, but the sudden wedge in Kain's throat stopped them.

"What sort of cancer do you have?"

"Geez mate, do I have to spell it out to you? Don't you get it yet?"

With a one shoulder shrug Joe looked blank.

Kain leaned closer. "Testicular cancer. You know . . . cancer of the balls – B-A-double L-S, balls!"

CHAPTER 3

A magpie's cheerful warbling echoed through Grace's head. Such a beautiful sound. The melodious singing increased and she tried to smile but instead grimaced. Her shoulder, head and back throbbed with stabs of agony.

Her eyes wouldn't open but she saw red. The colour of pain? There was no other sound except for a monotonous whirring. The faint odour of dirt and sweat teased her nostrils. Engulfed in darkness, pain and fear were her only companions.

She tried to move her hand, but . . . nothing.

Images swirled in fog then the fog swept away. With arms outstretched, Kain approached from the rugged, thick bush. Relief washed over her aching body. He'd save her. All will be well. His face wore a happy smile and his eyes burst with love.

"Kain . . . thank God you came." The words distant, raspy and hoarse. "Kain." He turned and walked the way he'd came. "Come back. Please Kain, come back." He continued walking through the bushes until he was out of sight. "*KA-IN.*" Why didn't he answer her? She tried to shout again. She tried to scream. Nothing. Her voice had gone. She wanted to cry, but no tears wet her eyes. Everything numbed.

Kain returned, but with a different face. Eyes yellow and teeth large, like the dogs that attacked her. He headed for Grace, saliva dripping from parted lips. His walk turned to a run. When almost to her he reached out, but not with hands. Hairy paws with long claws scraped the air. Dripping dark blood, they enlarged and retracted.

Run! Her legs wouldn't move. She pushed harder, but not so much as a toe wriggled. She tried to put her hands up to shield her face. Nothing.

She couldn't move any part of her body. She opened her mouth to scream, but again no sound left her throat. This was it. No strength left to fight.

She closed her eyes tight and welcomed death.

Another voice, but not Kain's. He was gone. Gone forever.

"Wake up. Hey . . . wake up."

Grace finally forced open her heavy eyelids. Blurred visions shimmered and danced before her - a monster that spoke like a man. Dark eyes stared at her.

"Don't be scared."

Grace blinked several times. The vision became clearer. A scream swelled in her chest but only a loud gasp leapt from her throat. He was on her left, she jerked her head to the right and tried to bring her battered body with her. Pain shot through her stiffened neck, but she had to get away. The rest of her body didn't budge. It seemed glued to the mattress, frozen, or was she tied down? Nothing but a pale, blank wall in front of her.

No hope of escaping.

She focussed on a dirty smudge on the wall. Tears welled but she was determined they would *not* flow or show. What happened? Where was she? She remembered Kain coming toward her. No, that was a dream, a *horrible* dream.

"You want a drink?"

A drink? Her throat scratched like a desert storm had whipped through leaving dusty sand particles in its wake. She didn't want to look at him but she had no choice except to respond. She was injured and, so it seemed, trapped.

Dreading what she would see, she turned toward the voice - her abductor. Or was he her saviour? A gloved hand passed a blue cup toward her. "What . . . what is it?" The croaky words hurt her parched throat as if she'd just swallowed a strip of sand paper.

"Water." He moved the cup closer to her face.

Grace heaved herself to a half-sitting positon. The single bed felt comfortable but she couldn't help noticing the once bright and colourful cover was in need of a good wash. *A stupid thing to think about right now.*

She reached for the cup with her right hand, but shoulder pain forced the hand back to the bed. The stab of pain jolted her memory. Running from the dogs while thunder crashed around her.

She shuddered. She needed that water. Without it she'd die an agonising death and she'd barely escaped the hungry dogs, but her head fell back to the pillow. Just too much effort.

Another gloved hand reached beneath her pillow and lifted her as the cup came toward her mouth. She glanced past the hand to the opposite wall, then to the floor, anywhere but his face. She concentrated on opening her cracked lips, ready for the water. Or . . . could it be poison? Or a drug? Grace closed her mouth tight. The cup stopped.

Too bad if it was poison. She'd be dead either way. She opened her mouth again and the cup came closer. The metal edge cooled her lips. The refreshing liquid flowed through her sticky mouth and slid down her dry throat. The coolness refreshed all the way down to her stomach. She forced a muffled sound when some water dribbled out the sides of her mouth, down onto her neck and chest. She hated any being wasted.

"Enough?" He took the cup away.

"Nooo." Grace moved her face after the cup. "More. Please."

She drank it all in two more gulps. The last of it caught in her throat. Grace coughed. That hurt her ribs and stomach - places she hadn't realised she'd been injured.

"Are you right?"

Grace's eyes watered and her nose ran from the coughing. "Yes." She tried to wipe her eyes and nose.

He handed her a hanky. "Here."

"Th-thanks." She lay back and wiped her eyes and nose. She passed the hanky back, her eyes following until she stared him in the face. Her body jerked. Eyes blinked and a gasp broke free from her lips.

A dark beard, flecked with grey, reached his upper chest. His black hair, also sporting wisps of grey, pulled back behind his head giving no indication of its length. She tried not to look at his face, instead dropping her eyes to his ample waist area. A light blue, long-sleeved shirt strained to keep buttons closed. The shirt tucked into faded, blue jeans. No sign of the black cloak he'd been wearing when he'd shot the dog. Or . . . was it even the same man?

"You want more water?"

Grace looked back to his face. Her stomach liquefied. One side of his head was almost hairless, except for the odd strand of hair that hung down. One ear, or what would have once been an ear, now a knobbly pale stump, protruded from the side of his head. His other ear appeared normal. His puffy eyes, beneath sparse eyebrows, looked dark brown but she couldn't be sure. They were almost slits, surrounded by scarring covering his upper cheeks, nose and most of his forehead.

She needed to ask what had happened, but he'd just asked if she wanted another drink. Right now, that was more important. "Yes, please."

Carrying the cup, he walked out of the room in slow but determined strides on long legs. The 'clomp clomp' of his boots faded.

Holy hell! Who was he? His face and head wouldn't leave her mind. In an attempt to clear the images, and find out where she was, she gazed about the room. A slow turning, dusty fan whirred from the mouldy ceiling. A large, brown wardrobe on the opposite wall to the bed, a matching, high-set dutchess stood against the wall to her left with two vertical pieces of matching wood, no doubt where a mirror should be attached.

On the opposite wall was a slightly open window of clouded glass, with bars. *Bars?* They certainly didn't look like average security bars. The magpie sang again, not far from her window. Thick, cream curtains moved in the breeze. A breeze carried the beautiful sound to her ears.

Under different circumstances she would find it relaxing, but those bars sent a cold tingle up her spine and into her brain. They were *not* normal. Stifling a grunt, she pulled her body to a sitting position and dropped her feet to the bare, wooden floor. She needed to see outside the window and if those bars were real. Were they to keep people out...or to keep people *in?*

The approaching footsteps grew louder and he entered the room. Hopefully he couldn't tell what she'd been thinking. He handed her the water and she drank it before passing the empty cup back to him. "Thank you so much." She screwed up her nose at the sour, sweaty smell of his gloves. She wiped her dripping forehead and wiped her damp hand on her shirt. At that moment she probably didn't smell much better. A shower would be wonderful.

"What's your name?" she asked without thinking.

Part of her terrified of what this grotesque human may do to her, while the other part was curious, itching to know more about this scarred, hulk of a man. This enigmatic man who was a top shot and, somewhere in that solid chest, hopefully carried a heart as big as Uluru.

He stared at her. No emotion showed but he seemed to be thinking hard. "Seth." He sounded like he was clearing his throat. "You want a cup of tea? Some food?"

"Where am I? How did I get here? How long have I been here . . . Seth?" Grace hoped that was, in fact, his name and that he hadn't just moved phlegm. "I'm Grace. I remember my car rolling down a slope and the dogs. There was a storm and I was running."

He scraped his shoe and the floor and folded his arms, looking impatient. "I saved you from the dogs and carried you here. Food?" His voice also impatient.

"Oh yes please. A cup of tea would be nice and -" She tried to recall when and what she'd last eaten. She wasn't hungry but if he prepared some food it may give her time to get to the window and escape. "Yes, some food too, please."

"Not long." He turned and went out.

Grace added frustration to her list of thoughts and feelings. Did he mean she hadn't been there long or that he wouldn't be long getting her some tea and food? From another room, presumably the kitchen, a tap ran briefly followed by clattering and clanging.

Taking a deep breath, she pushed both hands down on the side of the bed and urged her body up to her feet. She gritted her teeth until the pain from the extra effort subsided somewhat. Now on her feet, Grace looked down to discover she wore only damp, dirty socks, no shoes. A flash of a shoe dislodging while she ran sped through her mind but was gone in an instant.

She brought her right hand to her chest and turned toward the window. Only several metres away, it seemed so much farther. A sharp pain hit her back and she tensed. But she put one foot forward, took a deep breath and reached around under her shirt to find, what felt like, a wound dressing. So many sore areas. She needed a doctor.

Grace frowned, which made her head hurt. *Must stop frowning.* She reached up and touched her temple. Her fingers found a padded dressing there as well. She shook her head and looked out the door, but could only see bare wall on the opposite side of a hallway.

Other noises continued from another room. He must be getting her food. *The window. Forget about the food. Just get to the window before he returns.* She clenched her teeth, focussed on those bars and pushed her battered body forward. Leg muscles hurt, like she'd run a marathon.

At the window, she reached out and grabbed one of the bars. More to steady herself, but she also pulled it, let go and pulled on another and another. They were solid as a jail. *A jail?* Nausea overcame her. She leaned forward and opened her watery mouth to vomit.

"What are you doing?"

The abruptness of the loud and unexpected words jolted her upright. Her heart started like a hammermill and almost as loud. She closed her mouth, lest her thundering heart explode, and swallowed the bitter saliva. Her sweaty fingers grasping the metal window bars slid downwards.

"I . . . I was going to open the window wider so . . . I could get some more breeze. It's . . . it's just too hot." She pulled her hand off the bars, wiped it on the side of her jeans and stared at him. Her eyes had a mind of their own, drawn to his frightful scarring like iron filings to a magnet. Only minutes earlier she couldn't bear to look at him.

"Here." He set the black, TV lap-tray on the dutchess and came toward her, holding out a gloved hand.

"Thank you. Why do you wear gloves when it's so hot?" *Oh shit.* She couldn't believe she just blurted that out, again without thinking. Grace finally drew her eyes away from his face, like a mother dragging away an inquisitive child.

He stopped just before her and looked at his outstretched hand, then to Grace. "I have to. It's none of your business." His voice sharp, an axe chopping wood. He turned away.

She stepped back, away from him, not expecting the abrupt words. That seemed to be all she was getting on that subject but longed to ask more questions. Yes, it was worth a try, but she softened her voice. "Where are we, Seth?"

He grunted, still not meeting her gaze.

Not the response she'd hoped, but she didn't want to further raise his ire. She allowed him to hold her hand to the bed. Just as she was about to sit, she turned to him. "Can I come and sit at the table?"

He glared at her. "No. Stay here and eat."

She sat on the edge of the bed. The look and the abrasive words were enough for her to obey. He could do as he wished, and Grace would never be able to defend herself. Cold jitters of fear clawed their way up her body. Her mouth dried to an unpleasant stickiness. Maybe he wasn't the decent person she'd hoped him to be.

Seth placed the tray on her lap. Something smelt good; in fact it smelt so good it reminded her of her mum's cooking. It looked scrumptious too. Not what she'd expected him to bring in. "Thank you". She didn't look up. He was just too unpredictable.

Steam and a delicious aroma wafted off a colourful omelette containing mushrooms and other vegies and cheese melting on top. To the side, chopped tomato sat on a bed of crispy lettuce. She may not have felt hungry minutes earlier but this sight and savoury smell set her stomach juices flowing and her mouth watered, this time in a good way. Seth took the mug of white tea from the tray and placed it on the dutchess within easy reach.

"This looks really good. Did you just make this?"

"Yep. Hope you like milk in your tea. Sugar?" Seth picked up a small brown bowl with a protruding teaspoon handle.

"No thanks." Grace shook her head. "Just milk is all I have. This reminds me of the omelettes Mum used to make. We loved them." A twinge of sadness needled Grace's heart when she remembered Steve, Sophie and herself sitting down to tasty meals in their home on the farm, laughter always filling the air.

Things changed after Steve had left. She shook her head to scatter the memories and picked up the knife and fork before tucking into the food. She needed to keep up her strength.

Seth walked out of the room without uttering another word. She must have upset him. Maybe it was talk of her family. She wondered if he had a family, or anyone at all.

In no time he was back with another drink of water for Grace, but this time it was cold and in a glass. He put it beside the mug of tea.

"Thank you," Grace mumbled, her mouth full of food.

He walked out, again without saying anything.

Grace watched him disappear out the door and tried to figure out what was going on in that disfigured head. She shrugged then winced in pain, before concentrating on finishing every delicious morsel on her plate.

With a full belly, she placed the tray on to the dutchess, just as Seth re-entered the room. Weird. There'd been no approaching footsteps. He must have been standing just outside the door. In silence, he took the tray, leaving the teaspoon by her cup. She drank most of the water and started on the tea.

Then he was back. *What the hell do you want from me?* She wanted to scream at him, make him talk, but something told her to stay calm and take another approach.

"Did you dress my wounds, Seth?" She looked him in the eyes.

"Yes."

Grace nodded, before taking another sip of tea and swallowing. "What happened to my back?"

"Lightning struck the tree. Blew it to bits. One of the bits hit your back and knocked you down and out."

"H-how bad is it?"

"It's cut and bruised, but not real bad."

"Thank you for saving me from the dogs and the storm."

He nodded, pulled a folded white cloth from his jeans pocket and flicked it open.

Panic icicles rose from her feet, snaked up her spine and into every square millimetre of her body. Her throat soured. "What's that for?" Was he going to gag her or, worse, tie her up?

"It's a sling for your arm and shoulder."

"Woo back." Grace tried to lean away from him. Something was terribly wrong here. "Why don't you just call me an ambulance? I need to go to hospital." Enough was enough. Her father's strong determination channelled through. "Where the hell are we? I *need* medical help. You have no right to deny me that."

"No ambulance and no hospital." His previous firm voice rose in anger. He shot her a look that stood her arm hairs to attention. The fire in his dark eyes could ignite an inferno. "We are *here* and that's all you need to know." He threw the sling material on the bed and strode out the room, this time slamming the door behind him.

"*No.*" Grace's heart crash-landed at her feet. A silent alarm blared through every part of her body. The old key turned with a clunky *click.* Terror splintered her empty chest. A trembling ache seized her stomach. She glanced at the barred windows. She was locked in . . . jail!

CHAPTER 4

J oe pushed his unfinished plate to the side of the small table, eyes downcast, avoiding Kain. He sniffled and wiped his nose, as if it had been itchy.

"It's . . . it's all right, mate," said Kain. "I'm gunna get treatment and fight it as hard as I can. I'm not done yet." He laughed. "Did you think I was going to just lie down and die?"

Joe looked up at him. "What? You?" He grinned. "Not a chance. I know you'll fight it." He leaned closer. "You friggin' better mate, or I'll kick your arse." He picked up his beer and swallowed down the last mouthfuls. "Finish your lunch. I'll get us another beer." After grabbing Kain's not-yet-empty glass and his own empty one, Joe got up and rushed inside toward the bar.

The lunch was delicious, with the fresh fish done in crispy batter, but Kain's appetite had shut up shop and left. A weight of worry had lifted though, now he'd told his best mate the shocking news. No longer so alone in what lay ahead. He gazed around at the other diners. Old, young, middle-aged, various colours and all shapes and sizes. The din of everyone talking at once swirled and blended before burrowing into his eardrums and through his brain. The crowd talked and laughed, ate and drank. Some looked happy and some looked bored.

Meanwhile his life, as he knew it, had crashed to a halt. A long icicle coiled itself into a ball and bounced around in his stomach as he scanned the dining area. *No doubt some of these people have cancer. Some of the men probably have the same cancer as him and don't even know it yet.*

Part of him wanted to stand up, shout out to everyone, just to find out that he was not alone, but the other part never wanted to tell another soul. The two women at the nearby table didn't seem to have a care in the world. The red-head who'd reported on the fatal accident leaned over her plate and tucked into a huge hamburger. Sauce and beetroot juice dripped from her wrists. The other giggled at something on her phone.

Kain didn't have any stress either, until recently. His stomach spiralled at the fear creeping through his veins. When alone he worried and, as much as he hated it, cried. To a degree, company, especially larrikins like Joe, helped keep his mind off the cancer.

Joe placed the beers in the middle of the table before plonking himself on his chair. "You right?"

"Yeah, why?" An unwelcome tear trickled down his cheek. He swiped it away.

"So." Joe drank a good sized mouthful. "What happens now? As in treatment, I mean. Are they one hundred per-cent sure it's cancer? You're not even thirty yet." He put his glass down and frowned hard, resulting in one long bushy eyebrow.

This usually made Kain smile, even to the point of some friendly teasing about it in the past, but he didn't feel like laughing at that moment. "Yep, it's fair dinkum," replied Kain with a nod followed by a heavy sigh. A dead weight wrapped around his heart and shoulders. "I felt a lump, or . . . Grace did. It wasn't sore or anything, so I tried to ignore it, but I couldn't for long and Grace reminded me about it. I went to the doc and they sent me for an ultrasound which showed up suspicious."

Joe nodded, still frowning although less severe. "Is that all you've had? It might just be a-"

"No. Earlier this week they gave me an MRI and a biopsy. I went back to the doctor day before yesterday for the results and they," he swallowed hard, "showed it clearly. There's no mistake, Joe." He bit down on his bottom lip, attempting to stop the quiver.

The Grim Reaper laughed, evil and cold, and reached out to him with long, bony tendrils. Kain shuddered, blinked and tossed his head to disperse the terrifying vision of death.

"But there are options aren't there?" Joe's voice cracked, eager, desperate, tinged with pleading. "I mean, geez these days they can do all sorts of wonders."

"When I went back to the doctor the other day for the results and he told me it was definitely cancer, I kind of freaked out a bit and now I don't really remember everything he said. He said something about surgery and chemo but it was all a bit of a blur. I have to go back tomorrow morning and get the full picture. I just walked out in a daze. Lucky they realised and rang me later on to make this other appointment for tomorrow."

"True. Also lucky they'll see you on a Saturday. Hey, forget about tomorrow arvo, unless. . . you want to come around." Joe looked Kain directly in the eyes. "Anything we can do for you, mate, just name it, okay?"

Kain grinned. Joe may be crazy at times, but he was a good friend. The best. "Okay. Thanks Joe. I probably will. Just depends what happens at the doctor's tomorrow."

"Now, about this Grace-and-you-separating shit." Joe's stern voice could have come from a concerned father. "I reckon you're mad. For Christ's sake, Kain, she adores you. She worships the bloody ground you walk on. Blind Billy with half a brain could see that. Are you sure you did the right thing?"

"Yes. No. I don't know." His shoulders dropped. His bones dissolved to jelly. He wanted to let his whole body just slump into a heap. "I miss her like crazy but she wants kids and I can't give her any. Shit, I might not even be around by this time next year."

"Don't you think she's old enough to make that decision herself? She's not stupid."

"I never said she was, Joe." Kain's shackles rose, his tolerance dropped. "You have no idea what this is like, so don't friggin' tell me what I should or shouldn't be doing, okay." Kain skolled the last of his beer. Joe sat back in his chair, eyes downcast, lips curled downwards. "Ah, sorry mate, I didn't mean it like that."

Joe shrugged. "You're right, I don't have any idea what it's like. I'm just trying to help. You're miserable without

Grace and I'll bet a million bucks she's just as miserable without you. She's such a caring, loving person, I bet she'd love to look after you and get you through this."

"Yes she is that and more." Beautiful memories swam through his mind. "I remember when we first met; she had just finished her teaching degree at uni." He laughed. "She had a flat tyre and I stopped to help her. She was all dressed up and here was me in my white-stained work clothes, sweaty and grubby. I actually thought she was a bit of a snob at first."

Joe swivelled his eyes. "You sure got that wrong."

"I know. Nothing could have been further from the truth and I soon realised she was more than capable of changing that bloody tyre herself." He smiled, but tears welled. "Little Miss Capable, that's for sure. When I got to know her a bit and she told me she'd grown up on a farm, I knew then she was tough as nails with a soft heart."

"I remember you had to chase her a bit before she agreed to go out with you." Joe chuckled.

"Yep". Kain grinned. "I asked her if she would be interested in going out that night, but she said no, she was busy. I thought it was her polite way of saying she wasn't interested in the likes of me. Luckily, she did give me her number and I pestered her for days before I saw her again. We used to laugh about those early days but what I didn't know was that her older brother, her only brother, had not long vanished without any trace. She was pretty stressed."

"That's right, I remember that. Bloody hell, it was the talk of the town for a while. Did they ever find him?"

Kain shook his head. "No, nothing. When the police gave up and closed the case her parents hired private detectives to try and find him but they came up dry too. It was like he just disappeared into thin air. I don't think her parents, or her and her little sister, ever got over it. He was living and working on the farm and one morning," Kain let out a breath and his gaze went to someplace far across the large dining area, "he simply didn't come out of his bedroom. Geez, remembering this makes me feel a thousand times worse, for breaking up."

Joe frowned again. "What do ya mean, he didn't come out of his room?"

"Well, he didn't come out because he wasn't in there. His bed hadn't been slept in, or was made up." Kain raised and dropped one shoulder. "All his gear was still there, only his wallet was gone. It's one of those mysteries that never seem to get solved."

"Had he been in any trouble or something like that? Shitty relationship maybe?"

"Grace said he hadn't been seeing anyone for awhile and everything was normal. Apparently he and his father had a bit of a disagreement the day before, about some cattle, but it wasn't serious." Kain shrugged again. "I don't know. Just sorry I never got to meet him. The way Grace talks about him, he must have been a top bloke. Sorry to bore you with all this old stuff, but it feels good reminiscing and talking about Grace."

"Every time you mention her name your face lights up, Burrows, and don't tell me your heart doesn't because I'd call you a liar."

Kain replayed those words in his mind. "Yep, you're right, Joe. It does feel good to talk about her and think about her. Sometimes I forget for a few seconds that I broke it off and I think of how much I look forward to seeing her when I get home from work, but then . . ." he sighed again. "I remember what's happening and that I moved back to Mum and Dad's."

"Do they know?"

"No, not yet. They're still away on holidays. I'm not going to ruin it for them. I offered to go around and look after the dogs and cat while they're away and sleep there sometimes. I just moved some of my stuff back into my old room."

"Yeah, they were probably enjoying being empty nesters. Seriously mate, you love her so much, why not just ring her and . . . and . . ." Joe's eyes sparkled.

"C'mon, Mr Know-It-All, and what?"

"Well . . ." Joe squinted, his grey matter working overtime. His face lit up and his cheeks parted in a wide grin. *Snap!* He clicked his fingers. "They can freeze your tadpoles these days, can't they? You can still have kids later on."

Kain took a couple of seconds to digest what Joe meant. "Hmm, I vaguely remember the doctor saying something like that. Not sure if it was a definite thing. Tadpoles are no good without their father, Joe and that's the worst case scenario. That's the main thing I don't want to put Grace through."

"Look, I know you don't want me telling you what to do, but please think about calling her. Tell her you made a monumental stuff up and you want her back. I'll bet you a million bucks you'll both be happier. What sort of lame excuse did you give her anyway?" He raised one eyebrow. "For breaking it off."

"I told her that I was feeling cramped in the relationship and that I wanted to be a free man to . . . find myself." He shook his head at the absurdity of those words. "And that . . . that I didn't love her anymore."

"Find yourself?" Joe laughed as if Kain had just told a joke. "You're a dick and a half, Kain. She wouldn't have believed that New Age bullshit. Didn't you tell her any of the test results?"

"Actually, she's right into that sort of stuff. Truth be known, she'd probably be able to suggest something in nature to help this bloody problem." He gestured toward his crotch. "No, I kept the results to myself. Hardest thing I've ever done . . . until I told Grace I didn't love her anymore." The wrench around his heart twisted tighter, squeezing until the pain became numb.

"The Grace I know would never believe you no longer loved her. For Christ's sake mate, you lavished her. Geez, that's a big word for me, so it must be true, hey?"

Kain leaned back in his chair and let his shoulders drop. Everything he and Joe had just discussed made a lot of sense. He missed her so much. Missed her laughing at his lame jokes. Missed her delicious cooking. Missed their intense lovemaking. Missed *them*.

Maybe he had been too hasty in breaking up, but would she forgive him? He didn't deserve her forgiveness, but it was worth fighting for. *She* was worth fighting for.

"All right, you win Joe Miller. I'll call her now and ask if I can go see her after work." He straightened his back and lifted his shoulders. All will be good again. "We'll battle this bloody thing together." He fished his phone from his back pocket.

Joe gave the thumbs up signal while sporting the biggest grin possible.

Typical Joe, always the clown. Sometimes, just looking at his face lightened Kain's burden.   The tightness in his chest melted away. Positive vibes breezed through his body and wrapped around his heart, just like his mother's arms. Of course Grace would forgive him and they'd have good laugh about what an idiot he'd been.

His phone rang as he brought it out of its holder. Looking at the number, he debated answering. It was Linda, Grace's mother. He rubbed his forehead as if he could pull the decision to answer from his brain. She probably wanted to get up him for hurting Grace. But she'll be okay once he explained it was only temporary.

He hit the green icon. "Hi Linda." He waited for the scolding but she was crying. "Linda. . . *Linda,* what's wrong?"

She gulped down several sobs. She sounded too distraught for this to be about their break-up. Finally she formed words. One syllable at a time, punctuated with gasps and wails. "Grace. Kain. It's Grace."

His throat swelled, shutting down his voice and breath. He had to know. He swallowed down his rising panic. "What's. . . what's happened?" Kain's stomach bottomed out, his heart rate kicked into high gear.

"She's dead. Killed in a car accident. This morning. Up on the range."

Kain's already crumbling world splintered into a million shards. His gut snagged on barbed wire. The phone fell from his ear, the room spun into a crazy swirl of colour and sound, and he slumped forward, head in hands.

"Mate, what's going on?" Joe leapt to his feet and crouched beside Kain, hand on his shoulder.

A black hole of shock, sadness and agonising hurt swelled in his chest and burst forth. He sunk to the floor by the table. "Grace is dead."

CHAPTER 5

Seth turned the key, shook his head and walked down the hallway to his kitchen. Grace just had to ruin things by asking for an ambulance. She should have realised he would take care of her and her injuries. She called out over and over, but Seth turned on the small black radio on the kitchen bench and blocked out the sound. Even with gloved hands, he easily rolled the dial, past the initial 'click' and further to increase the volume.

The DJ chatted away about an upcoming rodeo in Karisdale, the nearest town. A brief desire to attend flicked through his mind, but that wouldn't be a good idea, besides he had no interest in rodeos. Or people for that matter, especially crowds. He needed some time to think and Grace had everything she required in the room.

As he reached to flick on the silver electric kettle, he stopped and looked at his hands, hot and a sweaty in the gloves. He raised each arm in turn to wipe the beading sweat from his temples and carefully peeled one glove off followed by the other. He curled and straightened his fingers and blew cool breath on them. Not that there was much point in doing so. He could barely feel his hands.

How he wished he didn't have to wear those damn gloves so often, but he felt naked without them.

With the gloves on, he could hide, or so he believed. He couldn't do much to hide his scarred head, except wear a hat, but he could certainly hide his hands. He didn't have to look at his own face and head, but his hands, with the scarred and twisted fingers, sickened him.

Both his ring fingers stopped at the second knuckle. He had no idea what had happened to the ends or if he'd been born that way. He couldn't recall ever being told. The rather rigid gloves hurt at times, as they forced some of his crooked fingers to align straighter. It was always a relief to remove them, for the dull ache would then subside.

An old song from the Eighties played on the radio. Seth had no idea of its name, but he hummed along and flicked on the kettle before getting milk from the fridge. The two-litre bottle was almost empty. Food was low. A trip to town would soon be necessary. His large shoulders slumped and a groan passed his lips.

Town! People stared and pointed, whispering to each other as they watched him with suspicion. He hated seeing fear in their faces. He hated seeing hatred in their faces. He hated seeing contempt in their faces. He just hated their perfect faces.

Luckily, he only had to go in once a month or so, unless Scott had a job for him. He froze milk and other perishables and the flourishing vegie and herb garden beside his wooden home kept him busy and well-fed, as did the variety of fruit trees growing in the house yard. Chooks in the backyard pen supplied eggs.

Every day, he was thankful that no-one else lived on this quiet dirt road. The birds and native animals lived alongside him contentedly. He didn't need humans, but there was something about Grace that drew him to her. A different feeling. A comfortable, yet inexplicable feeling. Finding her running through the bush a few hours earlier had shocked him, to say the least. He could never have imagined anything like that.

The kettle, gurgled, spewed out steam and turned itself off. When its noise settled down, Seth listened, turning his head to the left so his good ear faced toward the hallway. All was quiet. Good. She must have gone to sleep.

He took a tea bag from the opened box on the bench, and placed it in the large mug he'd picked up from the sink tray. He poured the hot water in and went about making his cup of tea, his mind returning to Grace.

He'd gone out with his rifle to track the dog or fox, or whatever predator it was, that had broken into the chook pen the previous night and taken two hens. There were plenty of wild pigs and other food for them; they were *not* having his chooks. Before he'd left, he'd mended the hole they made into the pen.

Several large cross-breed dogs had been spotted in the area in recent weeks, so he was sure they were his target. Not far from his house, he'd seen the large one and the smaller accompanying dingo. He'd followed them through the bush, awaiting the chance for the perfect shot. The silencer on the rifle put his mind at ease, knowing no-one would hear the shots and come sniffing around to investigate.

He also preferred to keep his phone on silent. The storm had brewed up quickly and was upon him in no time. Not unusual in the semi-tropics of Queensland. The storm looked wild, so he'd been about to return to the safety of home, when he'd seen her running toward him, her long dark hair clinging to her head and shoulders. He'd thought it was a hallucination, a mirage.

Seth stirred his tea, placed the teaspoon on the sink and took a sip. He walked out to the front verandah and sat on the old comfortable chair. It should be tossed in the dump, but he couldn't part with it. The stuffing puffed out of the arms and seat and it was now a dirty brown, almost black in patches, but it was comfy. Easing his large frame into the chair, he should have relaxed immediately, the chair normally did that for him, but something niggled at him. Grace.

He didn't know what to do with her now. When he'd seen her, wet and bedraggled, about to be attacked by the dogs, he'd had an overwhelming need to save and protect her. *But why her, when I hate people?*

But she'd turned and fled in the opposite direction. She should have been grateful and run toward him. When lightning had struck the tree, shooting out branches and sparks, he thought she would be killed. That hurt his heart, bringing forth tears as he'd run down the slope toward her, lying among the fallen branches. Thank God she was alive.

He'd scooped her up, cradled her limp, wet and bloodied body in his long arms and returned to the house as fast as possible. He'd run through the pouring, blinding rain, but had to rest when a stitch stabbed his side. Grace was tall, so none too light, or he wasn't as fit as he'd thought. The trip home took much too long. He hadn't realised he'd travelled so far in pursuit of the predators.

Now, here she was, resting in his house but wanting to get out and go to hospital. He should do the right thing, but . . . No, he couldn't risk it. If he took her to the hospital he'd be bombarded with questions and probably accusations, knowing the people of Karisdale. He'd only been in the area a couple of years, but was still regarded as the monster or weirdo.

Young children screamed and ran when they saw him. Once, he'd tried to talk to a young boy who'd wanted to run away, and tell him that he was not going to hurt him or anyone. He needn't have wasted his time. The boy's mother appeared and screamed at him to get away from her son. Then, he presumed it was, his father appeared and punched Seth, calling him a *fucking child molester*.

Rage had exploded inside him that he hadn't known was possible. He'd drawn his fist back to retaliate and looked the man in his eyes. Seth wanted to smash those defiant eyes. Nothing but fear showed in those eyes - a father simply protecting his innocent and defenceless son. At that moment, Seth decided he wouldn't bother with people anymore so had dropped his arm and walked away.

With Scott's help, he'd moved here to be on his own, away from staring eyes and hatred. He knew nothing else in life. Since the 'accident', any life he'd had was gone, wiped completely from memory. At times he'd experience a fleeting glimpse or feeling, but didn't understand it. Strange and jumbled dreams often woke him in the middle of the night, but he had no idea if they were just that, or distant memories returning to haunt him.

Sometimes, he'd sit in his white utility in town and watch couples walk by holding hands, laughing and generally showing each other love. A silent tear would slip down his cheek and his heart would hurt. He'd never know that love or the affectionate touch of a woman's hand, let alone her lips. No woman would, or could, ever love him.

He remembered the pain. The burning pain on his head and upper body. He'd put his hands up to stop the pain but the liquid had melted parts of them too, peeling the skin away. Loud voices had shouted at him, one had even laughed. He would *never* forget that sound. He'd screamed so loud that his lungs and throat hurt, but the laughing continued.

The kicks and stomps. The *crack* of finger bones.

He couldn't remember the faces. It had been dark and he'd been asleep. At some point he'd woken up lying in long grass, the hot sun beating down on his aching body. Next thing, he'd found himself looking down at his battered, peeling and burnt body lying in the swaying grass. The pain gone, replaced by peace. He'd looked around and saw the bright light. He'd tried to reach that light but everything went black again.

Seth shook his head to clear those horrible memories. It was pointless wasting time worrying about the past. He couldn't change it, couldn't remember it and didn't wish to relive it. He now lived his life in this little piece of paradise.

He had Grace to take care of and she couldn't remember much either. That gave them something in common. He smiled at that thought. She had no rings on her fingers or anything that identified her in any way. A small tattoo on the back of her shoulder had startled him for a moment. Familiar for some reason, yet strangely odd. He'd never seen anything like it before that he could remember. It resembled a flower, but also human-like. It had unnerved him for some inexplicable reason and he'd been pleased when the dressing covered it.

He drank the last of his tea and placed the mug on the small table beside his chair. The sun hung low in the western sky. Several Pretty-faced wallabies came out of the coolness of the bush to feed on the short, green grass alongside his drive way. Yep, he wouldn't leave this place if he was paid to.

If I was paid to? Scott came to mind again. Short, stocky Scott. Sometimes bald, depending if he had to suddenly change his appearance. Scott - the only person to treat him with any respect and dignity and that wasn't much. He'd brought Seth here, still recovering from the beating and acid burns. Scott gave him a phone, let him live here and paid him to do odd jobs for him. He owed Scott big time and, at times, wished it was all different, but he accepted his lot in life. He had no idea if he'd even still be alive if it weren't for Scott and the Scotchman dropped enough subtle hints to remind him he needed to be grateful.

Seth only knew him as Scott, maybe a nickname, so-called after his heritage. His strong accent matched only by his will. What Scott wanted, Scott got. Seth believed that Scott knew more about him and his past than he did himself, but he didn't bother questioning Scott. No point. Scott may, or may not, tell the truth.

That underlying fear of what Scott knew made him do whatever jobs Scott demanded of him. Some jobs were quick and easy while others tricky and took more time and planning, waiting for the perfect opportunity. Seth hated working for Scott. Some of the jobs sickened him to the bone, but he was more afraid of what would happen if he *didn't* follow Scott's orders.

The only way he could carry out some of the jobs was to temporarily become the monster everyone assumed he was. It wasn't so difficult then. It had been weeks since the last job. Any day, any moment, his phone would ring and he'd be given instructions, or be told Scott was on his way to see him and he knew what that meant.

He had Grace to think about now. She made his hell heavenly and there was no way Scott, or anyone else, could discover her. He got up from the chair to head back inside. The squeak of the screen door coincided with his mobile phone vibrating in his shirt pocket.

CHAPTER 6

Grace awoke. *"Seth."* She had no idea how long she'd been asleep. Seth had locked her in the room and simply walked away. No decent human being does that. His heavy footsteps had become lighter and further from the room. *Why?* He'd seemed like he cared about her, but locking her up like an animal or criminal was *not* caring. She'd called and pleaded with him until her throat burned, but to no avail.

Before long, exhaustion had taken over and she'd succumbed, pleased for some respite from this nightmare. Kain had appeared in her dreams again, this time not a snarling monster, but his beautiful loving self, smiling at her. They'd played and swam at their favourite beach. But a rip had caught him and carried him out to sea. Far, far out. He'd called her name over and over. She'd shouted and waded through the crashing waves, desperate to reach him, but he was gone. Swallowed into the dark, swirling ocean depths.

Grace inhaled deep, watching the fan above. Round and round turned the dusty blades. Her mind dulled in a foggy haze. The fullness of her bladder brought her to reality. Needing the loo, she forced herself to a sitting position.

Seth may be just standing outside her door. She shuddered. Should she call and bang on the door? No. She wasn't comfortable telling him something personal like needing to pee. Perhaps there was a bucket or container in the room she could use. Grunting and groaning, she got to her feet. Holding her right arm against her chest, she walked the several steps to the wardrobe, hoping to find a container. She tugged on one round door knob, then the other. No good. Both doors locked and no key in sight.

Reaching high, she felt along the top of the wardrobe, but only encountered dust. She wiped her hand on her jeans and tried each knob again. This time the second one came off in her hands. *Oh no.* She jammed it back on and left it alone. With a shrug, she was pleased it looked the same, so Seth shouldn't notice . . . she hoped.

The bed. Maybe there was something under the bed she could use. She eased down to her knees and lifted the bed cover that draped half way to the floor. Nothing but fluff and dust bunnies. She dropped the cover and her shoulders fell in defeat and despair.

The two large dutchess drawers might contain something useful. Using the bed as support, she pushed herself back up. The bottom drawer already slightly open, she squeezed her fingers in and pulled the front. It jammed on one side and the other side scraped out a centimetre or so. She wriggled the drawer, finally it opened. Nothing but old newspapers lining the bottom. She slammed it shut and crossed her legs, the urge to pee intensifying.

Grace yanked the knob on the top drawer. It opened enough for her to see inside, but nothing except more old newspapers. She glanced at the ceiling as if searching for a positive sign, wiped sweat from her forehead and puffed her breath out. What now?

Tears stung and her heart seemed to drain of blood. Her engorged bladder ached. The only things sitting atop the dutchess were her empty glass, teacup and the teaspoon.

She looked from the teaspoon to the door with its old fashioned, turn-key lock and took out a sheet of the newspaper from one of the drawers. The yellowed paper was old but strong enough. She picked up the teaspoon and walked to the door. Bending hurt, not just from injuries, but also from her full bladder. She gritted her teeth and placed the opened newspaper under the door. She slid it toward the hallway until only a few centimetres showed on her side. Peering into the key hole, she could see the end of the large key. *Phew . . .good. Please, don't let Seth see or hear this.*

Grace poked the handle end of the teaspoon through the hole and pushed the key out the other side. The dull *clink* of it hitting the newspaper more welcome than the singing birds. *Nearly done.*

She knelt with a crack of her knee, and pulled the sheet of paper back under the door. Her bladder ready to burst, she squeezed her pelvic floor muscles tighter. This *has* to work. The round, handle end of the key came into view. Yes.

She smiled so broad it hurt the injured side of her head. She pulled harder, but the key lodged beneath the door.

The rounded, long body of the key must be higher than the end. *No, no nooo.* She grabbed hold of the circular top part and tried to release it but it wouldn't come through. Leaning her left shoulder against the door, she gripped the key and wriggled it and tugged. *Come on, you bloody thing!* Finally, she squeezed the key through the small gap between the door-bottom and the bare floor.

She grabbed the edge of the dutchess for support, got herself to her feet. Still no sound from outside the door. Good.

Maybe Seth had left and she could find a landline in the house. Grace's shaky, sweaty fingers almost slid off the key as she pushed it into the lock and turned. The turning 'click' brought a tear of relief, but no time to wipe it away. She needed the loo more than anything else right then. Her bladder now so full it burned.

Her moist palm slipped off the rounded door knob. She opened the door. Heart beating like crazed atoms, gut in knots, Grace dared not even breathe. She stepped out of the room and glanced about for the loo.

A large, gloved hand grabbed her left arm.

"What do you think you're doing?" The voice, deep and furious, cut through the silence.

Grace looked at his stony face and gasped. His eyeballs barely visible but his stare stabbed her soul with swords of steel and clinched her like handcuffs. With no warning and no control, her brimming bladder emptied itself.

CHAPTER 7

Kain stopped his utility in the driveway of Grace's parents' farm house and wiped tears on his shirt. Grace's younger sister, Sophie's, little red car was parked by the shed. The dogs barked but didn't show, probably tied to their kennels out the back.

He inhaled deep and slow. *Grace . . .dead. No. No. No. She couldn't be.*

"My beautiful Grace." He wept. His whole upper body shuddered. He dropped his head on top of his hands which still gripped the steering wheel. His stomach rolled and the heaviness in his heart ached so much it may break out of his chest. *Why? How? If only . . .* Numerous thoughts and questions flooded Kain's mind but there were no answers to ease the pain and disbelief.

After receiving Linda's call about her beloved daughter, and getting past the initial shock, he'd rushed to his vehicle and driven the twenty-odd kilometres to the Atkinson's cattle property. How he'd arrived safely without having an accident, he didn't know, the trip now a blur. All he'd thought about during the drive was Grace and kept telling himself it must be some terrible mistake.

Wiping his eyes again, he took yet another deep breath, steeling himself to face her shocked and grieving parents and sister. They had already virtually lost one child when Steve disappeared, how could they cope with losing another?

What was Grace even doing up on the range on a Friday? She should have been at school with her students. Kain reached to the floor on the passenger side and grabbed a roll of toilet paper. He tore off a piece long enough to blow his nose. With trembling hands he screwed up the used paper and tossed it back onto the floor. Another quick deep breath and he yanked the door open.

He hesitated, not sure if he could do this. *C'mon, get your arse in there. It's probably your fault she was up there anyway.* That realisation hit him in the guts like a charging ram.

He jumped out of the vehicle and threw up on the green lawn beside the driveway. What bit of lunch he did eat now splattered on the ground in front of him like an abstract painting. Kain reached in and grabbed the half-full plastic water bottle from between the seats, unscrewed the top and took several mouthfuls. He swished around the last mouthful and spat to remove some of the sour taste.

"Kain." Linda's voice sounded weak.

He turned toward the house. Through watery eyes, he saw her on the top step of the low level Queenslander home. Grace's dad, Bruce, and Sophie were nearby on the verandah.

He wiped his eyes but sad, reddened eyes looked back at him from tear stained faces. Bruce appeared more like seventy than his late fifties. His normally proud, broad shoulders now slumped and his weather beaten face carried more lines than Kain had ever noticed.

Linda's long auburn hair was tied back in a loose, haphazard pony tail and her fair skin more pale than usual. She resembled an older version of Grace, including the same green eyes and fair skin.

Kain walked toward the steps and Sophie moved one step closer to her dad, placing her hand behind his back. She only came to his shoulder. He placed his arm about her shoulders and Sophie snuggled her dark wavy hair and head into the side of Bruce's chest. All eyes on Kain and he had absolutely no idea what he would say.

"I'm glad you came straight away. Come in." Linda beckoned him up the three steps, moved back and stood beside her husband. Bruce placed his other arm around her. Linda reached up and took hold of his large hand that draped her shoulder.

The bond between the two was obvious. Their work-hardened hands and fingers entwined in support and grief.

On shaky legs he climbed the steps, still with no words. No, he actually had lots of things to say and ask, but had no idea where to begin. Not even one hour earlier he'd been so happy that Joe had talked him into calling Grace and reconciling. The prospect of holding his beautiful Grace again, had temporarily cleared his mind of the cancer.

He reached the top step and looked from one face to the next. "I . . ." He sighed deep and fresh tears stung his eyes. "I just can't believe she's gone." The tears flowed. He didn't bother to try and stop them.

Linda came forward and hugged him tight. Her body shuddered against his chest, her sobs echoed in his ears. Her warm tears dampened his white tee shirt. Bruce and Sophie stepped closer and hugged both Kain and Linda.

All four let their grief and sadness flow. Kain had never seen Bruce cry in the five years he'd known him. This was a severe blow for the strong, proud cattleman, as tough as they come but losing Grace could break him.

Many times, while here, he'd seen the pride and love in Bruce when he'd talked to or about his daughter. One very proud father.

Everyone sensed when it was time to pull back. The small group eased apart. Kain looked about. The farm so peaceful and serene, as usual. The roses and other flowers in the front gardens flourished in beautiful colours. The shrubs along the side of the house grew healthy and strong. Cattle grazed in the lush, grassy paddocks without a care in the world. The chooks scratched and wandered about in their large pen, not far from the house. Although he couldn't see the pigs in the sty next to the chooks, they'd be wallowing in their cool mud puddle trying to escape the afternoon heat.

Grey clouds churned in the western sky signalling a brewing storm. There'd been some around earlier but not directly overhead. Storms were such a common occurrence at this time of the year.

Kain turned to Linda. "How . . . what happened?" His voice quiet, as if keeping it soft could prolong her answer.

"Sit down Kain." Bruce sat on one of the six chairs surrounding the large wooden table on the breezy verandah and dragged another out.

"Thanks." Kain sat and clasped his hands together on the edge of the table.

"I'll go and make us all a cuppa." Sophie headed to the door. She stopped and turned back. "Your usual, Kain?"

"Ah, yes please Soph." He glanced at Linda. The sadness in her eyes tore at his hurting heart. But he also saw something else there, maybe anger. Grace had most likely told them about him breaking off the relationship. Going by Linda's face, he had a sickening feeling she had. "Linda ... did-"

"Our daughter is dead, Kain. Dead!" She burst into fresh tears, bringing one hand to cover her mouth.

Bruce took his folded hanky from his front work-shirt pocket and gave it to his wife.

"Are you absolutely sure?" asked Kain. "Has someone identified her? Maybe there's been a horrible mistake." It was a useless thing to say but he was desperate for this to all be one big terrible mix up.

"They won't let us." Bruce's deep voice quavered.

"What do you mean?"

"She was burnt beyond recognition." His body shuddered, clearly imagining the horror suffered by his daughter.

Kain jolted back in his chair. The woman who came in late for lunch beside he and Joe. This must have been the accident she was talking about and the sight and smell of the burnt body. He sucked in a sharp breath. Everything spun, he dropped his forehead onto his hands on the table. A moan escaped his lips. *Why the hell didn't I sense that she was talking about Grace? MY Grace. I shrugged it off, too bloody worried about my own problems.*

"Kain". Linda's stern voice ordered him to listen.

Kain lifted his head.

"When did you last talk to Grace?"

"Umm . . ." He hesitated, taking another deep breath and trying to think of the best thing to say.

"Mate, we know you broke up with Grace." Bruce glared at him. "Why? What the hell is going on with you? Grace was heartbroken. She didn't understand any reason for it." His voice rose and his face hardened. "We think she went away because of that and *now . . . she's* gone forever. Our girl has gone for . . . ever." He choked the last word out and broke down in tears. Linda handed him back his hanky.

Kain swallowed the rising lump that threatened to choke him and gritted his teeth, trying to stifle the tears that were bursting to break out. Right now he couldn't care less if he just dropped dead himself.

Wretchedness and guilt weighed on his shoulders like two huge boulders. "I . . .I haven't spoken to Grace since we broke up, but I was going to call her this afternoon and go around and tell her what a big mistake I made and see if she'd have me back." He licked his dry, quivering bottom lip. "I still love her so much."

He brought his hands to his face, lowered his head and wept again. Wept for Grace and wept because he had cancer and what the bloody cancer had made him decide to do.

Sophie placed steaming mugs of tea and coffee on the table. Kain lifted his head and wiped his eyes. "Thanks Soph." He picked up the mug in front of him and sipped the welcoming hot coffee.

The house phone rang. Linda jumped up, grabbed her mug of tea and ran inside.

"That'll probably be the police ringing back with some more info." Sophie sat down beside her father and sipped her coffee, staring ahead through glassy eyes, at nothing.

Kain glanced at Bruce, who also stared into nothing. The awkward silence made him squirm. Maybe he should ask how the cattle were. *Don't be stupid.* As if Bruce would be interested in talking about them right now.

Linda's frantic voice could be heard inside the house. Kain had a few more sips of coffee, got up and walked down the steps. Now what? He didn't have a clue. He felt like an unwelcome stranger around Grace's family. The sickening emptiness in his stomach from losing Grace forever and worst of all, *how* she died, wouldn't leave.

Finishing off his coffee, he turned to take the cup back up to the table. Linda returned to the verandah.

"That was the police." She sat down and Kain returned to his chair.

"Well?" Bruce placed his hand on her shoulder. "What'd they say, love?"

"They didn't have much more to tell us than what we already know." She drew a deep breath. "There were skid marks and the car went off the road and rolled down the side of the range into a gully, so it must have been going pretty fast. It hit a tree and then burst into flames." Linda sniffed and pursed her quivering lips together.

Kain's heart tripped, his hands turned icy and he jumped up and vomited over the side rail, imagining Grace burning to death.

Sophie balled her fist and hit the table. The cups jumped. "Grace doesn't speed."

"The car was definitely Grace's and they found her bag with her wallet and license and everything in it. It'd been thrown out. We can collect them from the station." Linda cried, huge sobs. Bruce leaned closer and put his arm around his wife. "They also found her phone out on the ground, back up where the car must have started rolling."

She looked at Kain, now standing and holding the rail with one hand to prevent his weakened legs crumpling. He drew back at the intensity of anger and hatred in her eyes.

"She was in the middle of sending a message to *you*, Kain. The phone was still on and open." Linda brought her hand to her mouth and breathed in deep and fast.

"So . . ." Bruce leaned back in his chair and folded his tanned arms. "She was sending a *text*, while she was driving?" His gaze dropped. "Grace isn't that bloody stupid." He scraped his chair back, got up and walked to the end of the verandah. There he stood, motionless, his back to them.

"She must have been," said Linda. "She was probably so upset and confused she just wasn't thinking straight."

Nooooo. It's all my bloody fault. Kain watched Bruce. The older man stood rigid, ready to explode. His shoulders rose and fell in consistency with deep breaths.

Linda continued. "They also said there would be an autopsy done, but . . ." She leapt up, clasped her hand to her face and ran into the house.

The gut wrenching sound of dry retching could be heard. Bruce spun around, strode inside to Linda, without a single glance at Kain. Voices and more crying came from inside.

Sophie looked at Kain. "I *so* want to be angry at you, Kain, but I can see this is killing you too." She reached out to him across the table. He took her hand in comfort. But their touch was brief. After being like a family member for so long, Kain now felt like an outsider, a total stranger. An intruder.

"Thanks Soph." He forced a quick smile. "You and Grace were so close and I deserve you to be angry with me, but it won't make me feel any worse than I already do. Your parents hate my guts right now."

Linda and Bruce returned, Linda's face paler than before. With a gentle hand, Bruce held her elbow as she sat back down. He sat on the chair beside her.

Bruce cleared his throat and looked at Kain. "The police said there will be an autopsy done, but she was burnt so badly that there isn't much left . . ." He took a deep breath. His eyes watered. "So it may not show much. Going by her phone, it would be obvious to them what caused her to run off the road, but I still don't believe she'd text while driving." As if to reaffirm his belief, Bruce shook his head and lowered his tear-filled gaze to the table. "Hope to hell it was quick."

The thought of Grace burning was too much. Kain froze, stomach acid rose to his stinging throat. He swallowed it down.

"Are they going to check dental records?" Sophie's voice trembled out in a whisper.

"They didn't say, but I can't see the point. Her car, her handbag, her phone open to Kain. I'd say there's no doubt it was Gracie." Bruce bit his bottom lip, tears spilled over his eyelids.

"Kain, I want to know what happened with you two and why you broke it off with her." Linda's voice was determined. Motherly. She wasn't going to let this go. "At least have the courtesy to help us understand that. Grace didn't say much, but it seemed like she was confused . . . and very upset. You were her *life*. Her reason for getting out of bed each day. She wanted to grow old with you and enjoy the kids and grandkids she was hoping to have . . . "

The knot in Kain's belly tightened and doubled in size. His mouth dried to drought-affected dust. He should tell them the truth, but they, especially Bruce, would most likely think it a pathetic excuse. They won't understand why he needed to push her away and save her from the possible heartache of losing him. He wiped his sweaty palms on his shorts and choked down the lump in his throat.

"For Christ's sake, talk to us instead of sitting there like a friggin' stunned mullet!" Bruce's hazel eyes glared. Bruce was usually easy-going, but this man, this grieving and bewildered father sitting opposite was in no mood to muck around. The whiteness of his forehead, from his work hat, only showed the deeper creases that now trans crossed it. His jaw, firm and unmoving on the tanned lower half of his face. He tapped his long fingers on the table, waiting for Kain to speak.

Kain looked at Linda then Sophie. They watched him, anxious eyes full of questions. sadness and despair. "All right." He gulped in a breath and blew it out. "You deserve to know the truth." Telling them about his cancer was not what he wanted, but he couldn't see any other way. They'll still hate him and blame him. "I lied to Grace."

Linda gasped and looked at Bruce, whose face grew redder and angrier. The forehead lines creased even deeper. "What the f-"

"It's not what you're thinking." His own anger bubbled to the surface. "I didn't lie to her about another woman or anything like that." Clenching his jaws, he wished he could remove the knife stabbing through his heart, remove the tightness in his throat, remove the besser block in his stomach. "You know me better than that, Bruce."

"I thought we did." Bruce ran his fingers through his hair. "But I don't know what to think anymore."

"Go on, Kain." Linda's tone had softened. "Please tell us."

The pleading look in Linda's eyes eased his tense shoulders. "I . . ." Geez, why did this have to be so bloody hard? But it was nothing compared to what Grace's parents were coping with, or trying to cope with.

Heart galloping, he went for it. "I have cancer and I broke it off with Grace because I don't want her to suffer, seeing me go through it and maybe die. At best, I won't be able to have kids and I know how much she wanted them." Tears threatened. "I thought it would be best for her if she found someone else who could give her kids and be around for them and . . . her." The hardening wedge in his throat prevented him continuing. The tears came. Sliding down their well-worn track on his cheeks. He stood, walked to the verandah rail and stared off toward the distant mountains - the range that had so cruelly taken his Grace.

"Kain, is it definite . . . the cancer I mean?" Linda asked after several minutes of silence. With a noisy scrape of her chair on the wooden floor, she stood.

"Yes." He turned around toward the family. He leaned back on the rail and folded his arms, but couldn't think of anything else to say right at that uncomfortable moment.

Sophie stared at Kain through widened, glistening eyes. "Is it . . . testicular cancer?"

Kain managed a single nod.

"Have you started any treatment?" asked Linda.

"Not yet. I haven't long found out."

"Oh Kain, I'm so sorry. We didn't know." Linda wiped fresh tears from her eyes. "But you shouldn't have broken things off with Grace. She would have wanted to be with you and help you through it, regardless if you could still have kids or not. That's how much she adored you." She brought her hand to her forehead and lowered her head. "You just shouldn't have. Give our girl a bit more credit."

"Well, I think it's a load of bullshit!" Bruce raised his clenched fist and slammed it on the table. Sophie and Linda jumped. The mugs bounced and rattled. Bruce stood and walked several steps toward Kain. "I don't believe you. You're telling us this bullshit to make us feel sorry for you so we don't blame you for driving her away." He jabbed his finger at Kain. Anger and hatred flashed in his squinted eyes. "If that's the best you can do, you can just fuck off now."

Kain unfolded his arms and gripped the verandah rail each side of him. Bruce's unexpected outburst hit him like a ram rod. Bruce would react, of course, but to roar at him like he was nothing but a toxic waste of space? He didn't need yet another kick in the guts. "It's all true, Bruce. I wish to hell it wasn't but it is."

"Just get out of my sight, Kain." His jaw tightened, his voice quivered. His whole body trembled. "As far as I'm concerned you as good as killed her – my Gracie, my beautiful girl. Now get off my property." His angry red face paled to sickly grey.

"Dad!" Sophie hopped up and got between her father and Kain. "Dad, Kain is hurting too, can't you see that? He loved Grace just as much as we did. Please Dad . . ." She held her father's arms above his elbows and stared into his eyes.

Kain glanced at Linda watching her husband and daughter. Was that fear on her face? "Linda, are you okay?" Linda turned toward him. Yes, fear. Linda afraid of her own husband? Icicles rushed through Kain's body. He had never imagined Bruce would abuse his wife, but remembered angry looks and harsh words from Bruce to Linda in the past. He wanted to hug her, but Bruce would tear him away from her and, while he was at it, tear the limbs from his body.

"You'd better go," she whispered. "I'll call you." She motioned holding a phone to her ear.

Kain trudged down the steps and over to his utility. He may as well have had an elephant's weight of pain and grief sitting on his shoulders. This meeting shouldn't have ended like this. It made the whole horrible situation increase a thousand fold. Leaving with this much hostility in the air soured his mouth, but he had no choice. He reached for his car door handle.

"Yeah, go on. Run off like a mongrel dog with its tail between its legs. My Gracie was too good for you anyway." Bruce's words sliced his heavy heart into two.

He got into his vehicle, started it up and reversed around until he faced the way he'd entered. He clunked into first gear, planted his foot hard and spun up dirt and dust.

He drove off without a glance in the rear vision mirror at Grace's family. They wouldn't have been visible anyway for the tears flooding his eyes. His heart, confidence, and morale were shattered. Bruce's cruel words clawed at his brain and ate their way through his entire body and soul.

"You as good as killed her."

CHAPTER 8

Grace welcomed the lukewarm water washing over her hurting and exhausted body. A shower had never felt so good. The stale sweat, the smell, the dirt, all washed down the plug hole. If only her physical pain and the sadness in her empty heart could be washed away as easy.

She held her aching right arm to her body and attempted to wash herself one-handed with a clean washer.

Peeing herself in front of Seth had been humiliating. Pity the floor hadn't opened and sucked her down and away, but Seth had done a good job pretending not to notice.

"Would you like a shower?" he'd asked her, as if offering her a chocolate. "I was just coming to help you to the bathroom."

Grace hadn't replied. She was beyond arguing and just wanted, no – *needed,* to wash or at least change her clothes. "Yes," she'd answered simply. He'd taken her left arm and helped her to the bathroom.

She'd been surprised to find the shower cubicle clean, along with the light-blue hand basin. It was, after all, a single man living here. A tall cane basket stood in the corner of the small room, holding Seth's dirty clothes. One leg of a dirty pair of jeans hung over the side. Although a soaking bath would have been better, there was no bathtub and the absence of any mirror was unnerving, until she remembered the one in the bedroom had also been removed. He mustn't be able to look at his own face.

Several bottles of men's body wash and shampoo stood in the wire rack in the shower. Grace took out the anti-dandruff shampoo. She held it in her left hand, flicked the top open with her thumb, poured some onto her hair and lathered up. The shampoo had a manly, chemical smell, nothing like the natural herbal shampoos she used. Harder and harder her nails and fingertips massaged her scalp. The sweat and dust were bad enough, but there'd also be dried blood.

"Everything all right in there?" Seth was outside the door.

Grace stopped lathering, tensed and held her breath. "Yes . . . I'm just about finished." She shouted, save him from having to open the door to hear. His scarred and damaged ear probably affected his hearing.

She looked down at her nakedness and the water and shampoo suds flowing over her, including her nipples. Grace watched the water swirl around then disappear down the drain hole, wishing she could dissolve and disappear too. The thought of him coming in and doing God knows what, melted her stomach to liquid. There was absolutely nothing stopping him.

Once she was satisfied all the shampoo was out, she spun the taps off, slid open the shower door and stepped on to the towelling floor mat. She grabbed the clean red towel from the towel rail. Although it was painful, she wiped the excess water from her hair as fast as possible.

She wrapped the towel around herself and looked about for her clothes. There was nothing but her dirty, wet ones lying on the floor. Tears burned her eyes. She took a deep breath to give her mind time and oxygen to think. Curiosity drew her gaze to the vanity cupboard. She bent and opened the door, grateful it opened without a sound. But it contained only bathroom linen.

"Grace, I've-"

"I'm almost done." She eased the first drawer of the vanity open. Nothing unusual in there, just new toothbrushes, toothpaste, Band-Aids and other first-aid bits and pieces. But a half-full bottle of black hair dye poked out from beneath the toothpaste. Strange. After closing that drawer, she pulled the other one open. It contained a small, wooden box. Grace reached for it, but just as she was about to lift if out the click of the opening door bolted her upright.

"What are you doing? Get out!" She stood in front of the open drawer and brought her hands up to shield the front of her body. Her left hand grabbed where the end of the towel was tucked in the middle of her chest.

"Here's some clean clothes." Seth's gloved hand, containing clothing, came through the ajar door. "It's the best I could do until I can get you some more."

Grace's mind and heart raced like they were competing in an Olympic sprint. She wanted out but there was no way out, especially naked. *Deep breathe. Just go with it for now.* Her shoulders dropped in defeat. She reached out and accepted the clothes on offer. "Thank you, Seth." The door closed again.

She wanted to scream and yell and call him every despicable name she'd ever heard her father use, and demand he let her go, but that would do no good. She had to keep on his good side if she wanted to ever get out of here, besides, she needed to preserve her energy. When the opportunity to escape presented itself, she had to be ready. To grab it and run, never looking back. Physically that wasn't yet possible.

Satisfied Seth wouldn't barge in, and with curiosity gnawing, she turned back to the open drawer and the mysterious wooden box. Grace hung the clothes over the towel rack. They could wait.

The box intrigued her more than the need to dress. She reached in and lifted the box out. The weight surprised her. Heavy for its size. Grace turned it around and saw the small padlock. She shook it. Something moved and rattled inside. It seemed the perfect size for a hand gun. She placed the box gently on the corner of the vanity, hoping Seth couldn't hear any sound she may make. She took hold of the lock and tried to wriggle it without a sound. Impossible. It clunked and bumped.

"Do they fit?"

Damn you, Seth. "Just about on." The box was securely locked, but Grace had a hunch it held something important. She was determined to find out what. She shoved the box back in its place. "Do you have a new toothbrush I could use, please?" she called out, hoping to cover the sound of the drawer sliding closed.

"Yes, left side drawer."

Grace grabbed the long sleeved shirt and attempted to put it on. Her towel fell to the floor. The shirt was way too big, as expected. It hung loose, coming down almost to her knees. The pattern on the material seemed familiar. Steve used to have a shirt like this one. He used to say it was his favourite rodeo shirt. Grace lifted the bottom of it and rubbed the fabric between her thumb and forefinger as memories of her big brother came back. A lone tear fell, but she wiped it away and took the cut-off jeans from the rack.

She held up the large, long shorts. They were huge, with a thin rope threaded through the belt loops. She chuckled, but the seriousness of her predicament hit her and the laughter turned to sobs. *Come on girl, stay strong, don't fall apart now.* Her inner strength kicked in and the tears stopped. *You're an Atkinson, you're tough and you don't give in.* "Yes, dad."

She inhaled her lungs to capacity, let it out long and slow and took out one of the new toothbrushes from the open pack and adding some toothpaste.

After brushing her teeth and rinsing her mouth, she ran her tongue around her teeth. It was good to have her mouth as clean as the rest of her body. She lowered the jean shorts down near the floor and stepped into them, taking care not to place both feet in the same leg hole. Pulling them up to her waist, she gripped them with her right hand and did up the zip and button, but the rope presented a problem. One she couldn't address on her own. "Seth."

Immediately the door opened wide and he stood, staring at her. "You need help?"

"Um . . . yes, please. These pants are . . . a bit big and I can't tie the rope." She stepped over closer to him, but averted his eyes. This was uncomfortable. A strange man helping her dress.

"I'm not going to hurt you." He reached over and tied the rope into a bow at her waist, still wearing his gloves. "Is that all right? Not too tight?"

Grace wanted to comment on his ability to do intricate things so well, while wearing the thick gloves but it seemed like a touchy subject and she certainly didn't want to upset him. Something told her she could trust his words, but there was still a small amount of niggling doubt, especially since he was virtually holding her prisoner. "It's just right, thank you." She turned and picked up her towel from the floor before hanging it over the rail next to the dark-blue one already there.

Seth reached out and took hold of her left elbow and led her back into the bedroom she'd been in earlier.

"Please Seth." She stopped and brought her arm away from him. "Don't lock me in again." Looking into his eyes, she begged, trying to appeal to the kind heart she hoped was in his large chest. Was there a spark of . . . what? She wasn't sure, but something went through his mind for a fleeting moment. What she could see of his eyes, softened just for a moment before they widened. "I'm not going to run away." She laughed. "Look at me." She opened out her left arm, palm facing upwards. "Give me big boots and a red nose and I'd make a good rodeo clown."

Seth's face broke into a grin then a loud laugh. So loud it rattled Grace's ears. But he stopped and his face became sullen again, his eyes mere slits.

"I didn't think it was that funny, but it's good to see you laugh, Seth." She really had to keep on his good side. Not only keep on his good side, but she would have to dig deep into the solid, invisible shell that seemed to encase his body. There, she hoped to find a good soul and all would end well, but that was a long way off yet.

"No, stay in your room for now and I'll get you some more food and drink. It'll be dark soon."

With a gentle hand, he guided her in and toward the bed, where she had no choice but to sit. In an instant he was gone and the door clicked locked again.

Grace sighed and lay back on the bed. Kain appeared in her thoughts. How she missed him and wished he could just find her and take her home. It will have all been a silly misunderstanding and they could live happily ever after. *Oh Kain, I love you so much.* The tears flowed and she did nothing to stop them. What was the point? Lying on her left side, the pillow soon became soaked but she didn't care.

In what seemed like minutes, the door opened and Seth walked in with a tray laden with food, a cup of tea and a glass of juice. Grace sat up and wiped her eyes on the bottom of the shirt. Seth placed the tray on her lap. The food looked scrumptious, something like her mum would cook and the delicious aroma set off her salivary glands. She couldn't wait to tuck in.

One thing for sure, this man could cook - chicken, mashed potato, pumpkin and greens. "Thank you, Seth." The chicken was already cut up and there was no knife on the tray. He mustn't trust her. Grace wanted to say something, but once again, bit her tongue. She drank half the juice. It tasted a little different, but nice and sweet. Taking the fork in her left hand, she began to eat.

"I'm going out for a bit. I'll get you some clothes and I have to see someone. I won't be long." Seth turned to go out the door.

"Don't leave me here by myself, *please.*" Grace put her fork down. She didn't like the idea of being here in the middle of nowhere. Alone.

He stopped and looked back to Grace. "You'll be all right."

"No . . . I won't." The room swayed and darkened. "I think I need a sleep." Seth took the tray from her and placed it on the dutchess. "What's wrong with . . . me?" Grace slurred the last words out. While her brain could think of words, her tongue and mouth didn't want to work. Her head dropped forward, eyelids weighed down. The room went black. The 'click' of the door lock was the last sound she heard.

CHAPTER 9

Seth pulled the front door shut and walked down the steps to his utility. He shook his head, feeling like a great lump of shit. Maybe he really *was* the monster Grace feared. It showed in her eyes, in her voice. Hell knows. With no memory of a former life, and sick of trying to remember it but coming up blank, he had no idea of his true identity or what sort of person he had been. Scott had moulded him into the man he'd become. He hated drugging Grace with the strong sleeping tablets. It was wrong, but he needed to meet with Scott and also try to find Grace some clothes that actually fit.

He opened his vehicle door then stopped. It dawned on him he had no idea how he was going to achieve this task. The few shops in Karisdale that sold women's clothing would be closed for the day and besides, it would look very suspicious if he were to just casually walk in and buy women's clothing, especially underwear. He already roused suspicion wherever he went and no doubt there'd be people out searching for Grace by now. No, he had to think of some other way.

He drove along his bush-track driveway, his mind drifting from Grace to Scott and the phone call he'd received from him earlier. Scott ordered him to the Rest Stop on the other side of town at eight PM. He assumed with details for the next job. He sighed. Why couldn't his life just be normal . . . but what *was* normal?

He hated the things Scott made him do, but he had no choice. His choices in life were stolen the night he was beaten and burned with acid. That's when any remnant of his old life disappeared and his new life began. It was far from perfect, but he knew some people were worse off than him, so he persevered and gave his soul to Scott, the devil himself.

Seth turned on the radio just as the news began on the local station. News was usually of no interest to him. He reached over to change the station but the newsreader's words stopped his hand in mid reach.

"A local Anchor Bay woman was killed in a single vehicle accident earlier today, on the Range Road. Police believe she may have been texting and lost control on a tight bend. The car rolled numerous times down the steep hillside before hitting a tree and bursting into flames. The driver, believed to be Grace Amelia Atkinson, was burned beyond recognition. Police are sending out a timely reminder to ALL drivers not to text or talk on their phones while driving unless using the-."

Seth turned the volume right down. This didn't really make much sense. They had to be talking about *the* Grace he'd found and taken to his house. It didn't add up but then, "Ahh". The authorities must believe Grace died in the accident. But she was very much alive, injured yes, but far from dead. He'd heard the explosion when the car burst into flames, while out hunting the wild dogs. He'd come across Grace a couple of kilometres from where the explosion was heard. She was some distance from the site and he hadn't realised she'd been in the accident, but it was now obvious.

Glancing down at the clock on the dash, he had just over an hour to get hold of some clothes for Grace before meeting Scott. Neither task would be pleasant, but he wanted Grace to feel more comfortable. *And what do you plan to do with her?* a nagging voice in his head asked.

He sighed and rubbed one hand over his face. He had no idea why he was keeping Grace at his home when she'd have a family somewhere - a family who were now grieving. *Shit.* Was he really that much of a despicable creature that he would keep her away from them, letting them believe she was dead? *Hang on a minute!* The news reader said she was "burned beyond recognition". What the hell? If she was dead, how can she be at his house? *A ghost? Don't be an idiot.* Maybe the woman at his house isn't Grace Atkinson and maybe she wasn't even in the car that had exploded.

It was all too much for his brain, but he did know one thing – he'd have to ask Grace some questions to find out who she really was, but more importantly, what had happened to her before their lives intertwined. She seemed to be frightened, or running from something.

Over a hill, the lights of Karisdale appeared like a gathering of fireflies. It wasn't a large town, but sufficient for his needs and of those in the surrounding farming areas. Seth glanced at his speedometer and raised his boot slightly off the accelerator. He couldn't risk being stopped by cops.

With no specific destination in mind at that point, he slowed to just below the speed limit as he drove past several houses and a service station. Scott occasionally gave him fuel in jerry cans, so he rarely had to stop for diesel, which suited fine. The least amount of people who saw him or who he encountered, the better.

He cruised up the wide, main street, travelling the three blocks of the CBD before doing a U-turn and coming back the other side. Yep, all the shops bar the two cafés were shut. There was no hope of buying Grace any clothes, even if it had to come to that. He was glad that choice was taken away from him. It would have roused far too much suspicion.

Hell, he only had to drive through town in daylight to see people pointing and whispering. A few people walked along the footpath and a small group stood around out-side one of the pubs on a corner, smoking, chatting and laughing. A twinge of sadness flickered through him. It would be nice to have friends to talk and laugh among and be accepted. No one seemed to take any notice of him at night, luckily. His inconspicuous, and common, white land cruiser utility, courtesy of Scott, allowed him some appreciated anonymity. At least he could drive around unnoticed.

He turned left and headed to some of the residential areas. Probably pointless, but he *had* to think of some way to get Grace some clothes. Just as he started down one of the side streets, a large metal bin caught his eye. *The second-hand bin, yes.* He pulled into the nearest park. The street light a little further along lit up the area fairly well, but not too brightly for him to stand out. Seth looked up and down the street.

No-one was walking around, but a car drove toward him. His pulse accelerated. He turned his face toward the passenger seat hoping they wouldn't recognise him, at the same time picking up his old black cap from the passenger side floor. Making sure his pony tail was tucked into the back of his shirt, he placed the cap on his head, pulling it down far enough so he could still see out under the visor. The car continued, turning into the main street and disappearing. He took a deep breath. This just *has* to work.

Stealing a few old clothes like this was nothing compared to some of the jobs he'd done in the past, so why in the hell did he feel so nervous? *It's Grace, you clod! You like her don't you?* It wasn't that. Couldn't be . . . or could it? He had no idea, except that he wanted to protect her and have her around him. *You could get a dog for that.* "Shit. I don't know."

If only his brain wasn't so foggy at times and if that inner voice would shut the hell up for a while, he may be able to think straight. He couldn't afford to stuff this up.

Seth got out of the vehicle and strode over to the bin. He pushed the chute open, stood on tip toes and reached in, hoping the bin had not been recently emptied. Another car approached. His heart thumped louder and harder and he held his breath, not daring to look around. Hopefully, they'd think he was putting things *in* the bin. The glare of the headlights disappeared. *Phew,* it kept going as well. So far, so good.

At first his gloved hand felt nothing. Seth's raised shoulders slumped. He was about to withdraw his hand, but it touched and rustled a plastic bag. *Aha!* In one corner he could just grasp the top of a bag. He lifted it out, while holding the chute open with the other hand. It was a dark garbage bag about half full.

A grin erupted on his face. *Bingo.* He ran back to his utility, opened his door and threw the bag over onto the passenger seat before getting into his seat.

He flicked on the interior light and opened the bag. "Come on, there has to be something in here for you, Grace." There were clothes, so he upturned the bag on the passenger seat. Singlets, shorts and tops all fell into a pile. *Nooo.* All toddler clothes. Seth raked through, but there was nothing to fit a normal sized woman. His clenched fist banged down on the steering wheel and he gritted his teeth. *Damn.* Shaking his head, Seth bundled the clothes back into the bag, jogged it back to the large bin and returned to his vehicle. He may have to contend with washing Grace's clothes every day if he couldn't find anything suitable.

He started the engine and continued driving, wondering where else there could be some clothes. A light flashed in his hazy brain. "That's it. The laundromat."

Worth a try and time was running out. If he was late for his meeting with Scott . . . well, that didn't even bear thinking about. The only laundromat in town was close to one of the three pubs. He'd occasionally seen people going from one to the other, obviously spending the waiting time in the pub while their clothes washed or dried.

Going back along the main street, he saw empty carparks several doors down from the laundromat, but went around the corner and found a parking space. Better to be safe and not use the main street if he needed to make a swift getaway.

Several cars were parked close by, but no people lingered to bother him. A dog barked in one of the darkened backyards, echoing around the neighbourhood. Seth reached for the ignition to take off before anyone came out to investigate, but some shouting and cursing quietened the dog.

Again, pulling his cap down low over his forehead he got out and strode toward the laundromat. He wriggled his painful fingers and took a deep breath and stepped through the door. An unfamiliar young man sat on a hard plastic chair, reading a novel. Seth eyed him in his side vision, but the man didn't look up from his book. Warmth from the two running dryers hit his eyes. He couldn't feel much on his scarring, but his eyes often made up for the numbness.

He focussed on the dial of one of the dryers. It only had a few minutes left of its cycle. The clothes in there would probably be already dry. Wait. The young man might be the owner of the clothes in the dryers. Seth checked all machines. Three of the four washing machines were in use. *Please, let* those *clothes belong to the young bloke.*

He had no choice and no time left to hesitate. He pulled a dryer door open and reached in, bringing out a large handful of clothing. He couldn't contain his grin when he recognised women's clothes. *Grace will be pleased.*

With his other hand, he picked out several tops and some underwear then threw the rest back in the dryer. *Shorts!* He reached in again and brought out another handful. A small nod to himself and he grabbed the only two pairs of shorts he saw, in his already full hand, before tossing the rest back and closing the dryer door.

A short glance toward the man waiting, found him still engrossed in his book. Seth turned around, away from the man so he wouldn't see his face. In next to no time he was back in his utility, the clothes on the passenger seat, and starting the engine. *Hopefully, the owner of the clothes won't miss them and hopefully, the young bloke didn't take any notice of him.*

He'd better not let Scott see the clothes. While keeping his foot on the clutch, Seth grabbed them in his large left hand and reached down, placing them beneath his seat. There wasn't much space there and they'd get a bit dirty, but he'd handle that later.

That was the first hurdle over, now the next and, by far, the most unpleasant. The clock on the dash showed it was close to eight o'clock. Seth drew a deep breath. His guts had been simmering with butterflies but it started to bubble and boil now.

The butterflies metamorphosed into pterodactyls. Bit like the creek at the back of his house during the last flood. Brown gushing water, choked with debris of all kinds. Froth and foam like a rabid dog's jaws, gurgling and swirling on its aimless journey. It had no choice where it could flow, forced to follow the lay of the land.

He was that water. No choice but to follow Scott's orders and end up wherever they took him. The flooding creek took everything along with it – wood, leaves, rubbish, dead animals. Scott controlled Seth's life. Scott would end up draining and robbing his soul, taking *everything*. Of that he had no doubt.

With a firm grip on the steering wheel and steely resolve in his heart, Seth drove out of town to the designated meeting place. No way was he prepared to keep Scott waiting, even five seconds.

CHAPTER 10

"Geez, mate, I wish I knew what to say." Joe handed Kain an icy cold can of beer and plonked beside him on the large, grey lounge chair.

"Thanks Joe." Kain took the can, ripped open the ring pull and drank several mouthfuls. "I don't really know what to say either. Or think." In slow motion, he breathed in deep, let it out and blinked hard to stave off the tears. *More* tears. "I'm just glad you're home. I didn't know what else to do or where to go after I left Linda and Bruce's."

"So they blamed you for it all?" Joe shook his head, which bounced his curls about. "That's just bullshit." He opened his own can and had a drink. A loud burp followed. "Oops, pardon me."

"Linda didn't really, it was more Bruce. He was fuming." Kain winced at the memory and hit his closed fist against his thigh. "As if I would-," A sob stopped him mid-sentence. Joe reached over to the wooden coffee table in front of them, pulled a tissue from the box and handed it to Kain. "Ta." He wiped his eyes and blew his nose.

"Did you tell them about your cancer?"

"Yeah." Kain sighed, his gut knotting. "I really didn't want to, but they just kept at me about why I broke up with Grace. I couldn't think of anything else to say in the end, so I told them the truth. I thought it would make it easier but it only made Bruce angrier."

"Not good." Joe rose and walked out his front door. He lit a cigarette before turning to face Kain, who remained on the lounge chair only metres away.

"You're spot on, there." Kain dropped his head back on the top of the lounge chair and stared at the ceiling. "Bruce didn't believe me. Said I was making it up so they wouldn't blame me for 'driving Grace away'." He held up his hands and wriggled fingers from each to emphasise quoting Bruce. "God, I wish I could just wake up from this friggin' nightmare."

Joe took a deep drag then stubbed his smoke out in the ashtray on the outdoor table. He exhaled outwards into the encroaching darkness of dusk and stepped back inside. "What did the police say about the accident?"

Kain closed his eyes to stem the never-ending tears.

"If it's too heavy to talk about, mate, I understand." Joe sat back beside Kain. "Shit, I'd be stuffed if I lost Sue. I wouldn't cope at all. Can't wait for her to finish her shift later so I can tell her just how much I love her."

A stab of pain cut deep in his heart at Joe's words. How he wished he could tell Grace, just one more time, how much he loved and adored her. His eyes overflowed and he lifted his head back up. "Listen Joe, make sure you don't ever stuff up like I did. You tell that beautiful woman of yours how much you love her and you treat her like a princess." He finished his beer and placed the can on the coffee table.

"Another one?" Joe pointed to Kain's empty can.

"Not right now, thanks." Kain screwed up his face. "Yeah, the police rang while I was there." He shuddered. "They reckon she was texting . . . *me,* when she must have lost control and the car rolled. It hit a tree and . . . ah shit Joe." His sobs echoed about the silent room. He leant forward, dropping his face in his hands. Pain and sadness the only feeling within his body.

Joe placed his hand on Kain's shoulder. "Listen mate, you wanna cry, let it out. You don't have to tell me anymore." Joe rubbed and patted.

He was grateful to have Joe as a friend, but right at that moment, he felt so alone. No words, no touch, no*body* could ease his pain and loss. It was his and his alone to face and deal with in any way possible.

After several minutes, Kain wiped his dripping eyes. "Do you mind if I have a shower and stay here the night? I stopped at the pub on the way over, so I'd be over the limit and I don't want to be alone anyway." He lifted the bottom of his shirt and smelt it. "I might have to borrow some of your clothes."

"No worries. Hey listen, do you want me to ring Eddy and tell him you won't be at work tomorrow?"

"Um yes, you'd better, thanks," replied Kain. "I'd be useless on the job at the moment."

"I bet he's not expecting you anyway. I told him when I got back from lunch that you'd got the terrible news."

Joe pulled his phone out of his back pocket and flicked through his contacts. Kain got up to use the toilet.

"All good with Eddy." Joe smiled and nodded when Kain returned to the lounge room a couple of minutes later. "You'd told him this morning you had an appointment tomorrow. I forgot about you going to the doc."

"That's right, I did too, but thanks mate. Forgot about that. Ah shit, just can't think straight at the moment." Kain sat back down. "I should go and talk to the police myself and see if I can find out more about the accident."

"What are you expecting to find?" Joe drained his can and went to get another from the kitchen fridge. "Want one yet?" he called behind him.

"All right, one more." Kain smiled at his friend. No-one could ever say Joe wasn't generous or not a good host. But his mind soon refocussed on Grace and the accident. Something niggled at him. Something just didn't make sense.

"Here, get this into ya." Joe placed a plate of cheese, kabana and cracker biscuits on the coffee table, handed Kain his beer then pulled the coffee table closer.

"Geez, you got that ready quick, but I'm really not hungry." Kain waved his hand a little and shook his head. "Thanks anyway."

"Gotta eat something." Joe topped a round cracker with roughly cut pieces of cheese and kabana before handing it to him. "Here, just one."

"Anything to shut you up." Kain chuckled and accepted the offering. He munched the crunchy biscuit and its topping and washed them down with a mouthful of beer.

Joe looked at him, grinned and got a savoury from the plate for himself. Kain continued. "I was thinking, when I was having a pee, that I *will* go and talk to the cops tomorrow. There might be something they didn't tell Linda." His tense shoulders sunk, no longer able to take the strain. "Not that it will do any good now, but I just can't help wondering if there is more to all this."

Joe stopped chewing. "What do ya mean?"

"Oh, I don't know." Kain lifted and dropped one shoulder. "Bruce was right about one thing."

Joe looked at him with a blank face, yet full of questions.

"He said that Grace wasn't silly enough to text while driving. I believe that too, even though all evidence points to that being the cause of the accident. It used to really piss her off if she saw someone texting and driving."

"Yeah, but if she was upset . . ."

"Nah." Kain screwed up his face. "I still don't think she would. It's just *not* her. She'd at least pull over."

"But wasn't it on the Range Road? There mightn't have been anywhere to pull over."

"There's a few places you can pull over. People stop and look at the views all the time from different spots."

"Your mind is ticking over." Joe leaned closer. "What are you thinking, mate?"

"After I talk to the cops tomorrow who went to the crash, I'll try and get, or at least see Grace's phone, then I'm going up to the scene and have a look around. I just reckon there's more to this."

"Don't you think it might be too upsetting for ya to go to the crash site? Not sure I could handle it if I were you. Want me to come with ya?"

Kain shook his head. "No, it'll be right, but thanks anyway. I need to do this." He stared straight ahead into thin air. His fuzzy mind ricocheted all over the place, but some little thing in the whirlpool of thoughts tried to flick on a lightbulb. "I just have a strange feeling I really need to have a good look around there."

CHAPTER 11

Seth glanced about and brought his land cruiser to a stop in the rest area. Only one other vehicle nearby and it wasn't Scott's. He filled his lungs with fresh air, wondering, no *dreading,* what job his boss had in store for him. Absolutely anything was possible. He'd learned to expect the criminal, illegal, and sometimes horrific jobs Scott ordered him to perform.

Tardiness was definitely not in Scott's character. Seth looked in his rear vision mirror, but no head lights approached the rest area. Nothing but the dark and quiet of the night.

Shit. This was possibly a set up or maybe even a stuff-up. He wound down his window. Someone jumped out of the light coloured four wheel drive, parked thirty metres in front. The man, head down, and wearing a large hat, walked toward him. Seth froze a breath. Gravel crunched louder beneath each approaching step. No other sound, but Seth's own beating heart.

He locked both doors and quickly wound his window half way up, but kept his hand on the winder. This bloke could be a cop for all he knew, or worse, one of Scott's men.

Might even be one of the townspeople. Plenty of locals would like him driven out of the area.

The figure removed his pale coloured Akubra hat. Light from the one solar-powered street light reflected off his bald head. Scott. Seth wound his window back down, thawing and expelling his breath with a groan. Partly from relief and partly from dread.

"Seth." Scott's greeting - always blunt and direct. "Good tae see ye're on time."

Seth didn't miss the you'd-better-not-ever-keep-me-waiting tone in Scott's voice. He opened his door and jumped out. "G'day Scott." He shook the Scotchman's solid, but pudgy, hand and attempted to ease the tension. "You got a new car?"

"Nae, just borrowed." He let go of Seth's hand, much to his relief.

Seth hated looking at him, let alone touching Scott.

"How's things?" Scott seemed to be fishing for something. The small, Scottish eyes zigzagged as he glanced about. Maybe he was thinking 'set up' as well. Guilty mind - and Scott was as guilty as they come.

"All right." Seth nodded. A slight hint of irritation had blended with Scott's words. He never usually asked trivial things or made small talk. Surely he couldn't know about Grace. Seth knew better than to put anything past Scott. He seemed to know when Seth so much as changed his clothes.

"Everythin' aw right at the house?"

"Ahh . . . yep." Seth dropped his gaze to the ground, scratched his beard and shifted from foot to foot.

"Good. Ah dornt like surprises, do I?"

"No, you don't." Seth thought of something that may get Scott's nose off any trail he definitely didn't want it sniffing. "Been having some trouble with wild dogs getting the chooks, but I think I've taken care of 'em now."

"Good on ye." Scott's eyes burned into Seth and no pleasantries blended in his tone.

"So . . . " Seth cleared the wedge almost blocking his throat. "What's goin' down?"

Scott scanned around, looked behind then took a cigarette out of the pack in his shirt pocket, lit it and inhaled with a gulp. "We have a big job comin' up. Ah need to know if ye up tae it."

"What is it?" Seth immediately regretted those words. "Of course I am." You don't ask Scott about his jobs, you just do them.

"Cattle prices are sky high, and ah want some of the action." He took another drag of his smoke. "Ye the best horse rider ah know, so the best lad for the job. We're goin' tae take some big, fat cows tae market." A smug grin spread across his face. Shifty eyes widened and sparkled.

Seth folded his arms and took a step back. So far it didn't sound too bad, compared to other jobs he'd done for Scott. He was comfortable on a horse that was for sure. "I don't have a horse anymore, Scott. Remember I told you he broke his leg and I had to shoot him."

"That's only a wee problem. Ah have some comin' in a day or two. Ye'll come over and get acquainted with the biggest, meanest black gelding tae ever run."

"No worries." Seth imagined the horse Scott described. No horse had ever bothered him yet. He unfolded his arms and put his hands on his hips, wishing Scott would end the meeting so he could get back to Grace.

"Ah can tell ye wantin' more info, but all ah can say for now is tae be ready tae ride when it all comes together." Scott dropped his cigarette butt and ground it out with his boot. "Ah have Jimmy and Pete lined up too. Jimmy's got an axe tae grind with this arrogant farmer from a wee while ago, so he's ready tae bring the bastard down." Scott laughed. A rare sound. "Any way he can. He will nae take any more shit."

"You mean the bloke we're rustling from has upset Jimmy?"

"Yes." Scott winked. "He's got fuckin' fields full of prime beef. He won't miss a few . . . hundred."

"Righto, when do we do this?" Seth asked straight out, more worried about Grace than the upcoming job.

"Soon. Dornt get ahead of yeself. Just dae as ah say and it'll all come together, lad. The boys have a wee bit more sussing out tae do around the property then we'll go in. Ah'll be in touch." He tapped the phone through his shirt pocket, turned and walked toward his vehicle.

"So, whose cattle are we takin'?"

Scott wheeled around and rushed back. The bad vibes and daggers of fire shot from his eyes. Seth's heart rate ratcheted up a few notches.

"Listen lad." Scott shook his finger at Seth. He stepped forward, almost in Seth's face. "If ye must ask a question, dornt fuckin' yell it for the whole fuckin' world tae hear."

His shifty, evil eyes shot dirks and his words spat pure venom. "Ah thought ye had more fuckin' sense. Is your mind on somethin' else, eh?"

"No." Seth's shoulders stiffened. He hoped like hell Scott couldn't see through his lie. He towered above Scott, but still feared him. He knew just what the Scotsman was capable of, and if he didn't do the task he'd probably find himself sliced up and used for dingo bait. "Sorry."

Scott's gaze darted left then right and back to Seth. A predatory smile of pure sin crept across his face. "His name is Bruce. That's all ye need tae know for noo, okay." The smile exuded a silent, but deadly, threat. He turned and strode to his vehicle, got in and roared off.

Seth watched Scott's vehicle until the lights had disappeared around a bend. If only he'd crash and be killed, life would be more bearable. Scott had dropped a solid hint toward the house, as if he knew about Grace. If it were true, and probably was, Scott won't let him get away with deceiving him. No-one's life is valued by Scott.

Seth will have to pay the ultimate price.

Like hell. I'll kill you first, Scott, and enjoy every second of watching you die.

CHAPTER 12

G race forced her heavy eyelids open, but they weighed a tonne. Again, they closed against her wishes. *Why can't I wake up properly?* Images danced in her brain. Maybe they were dreams or maybe they were memories. Either way they tumbled and rolled through her mind, making no sense.

Her dry throat and bitter tasting mouth needed fluids. Her brimming bladder longed for the toilet. She licked her parched lips, rubbed her tired eyes and opened them wide, determined to keep them open. Looking about the basic room, her mind flashed back to having a shower the night before and putting on Seth's large clothes.

Seth. Images of the wild dogs returned, haunting even the smallest recesses of her mind. It had been only yesterday but now seemed days ago. With an all mighty effort she heaved herself up to a sitting position and dropped her bare feet to the floor. The room spun and swayed, like a boat on the rough ocean.

"Seth." she called. *"Seth!"* Silence returned her calls, except for the birds singing not far from her window and cicadas chirping out their noisy chorus in the nearby bush.

"Damn you." She forced her aching body up on to her feet. The room spun again and she grabbed the dutchess to steady herself. Her head settled and the dizziness abated but a wave of nausea swept through her stomach. Her mouth watered and she swallowed the saliva down. "Please no. *Seth.*"

Heavy footsteps along the hall preceded the clicking of the key in her door. In a second he loomed over her, larger than she'd remembered. He looked worried. For a fleeting moment he frightened her, but nature's urge overruled.

"Thank God." She sobbed, swallowed again to avoid vomiting and partially to stop the tears spilling. Grace took a deep breath. "I need the toilet badly." She expected him to say no and wasn't prepared to accept it. Enough was enough. "If you don't let me go, I'll not only pee on your floor I'll spew too."

"Come on." Seth took hold of her left arm, led her through the door and to the toilet next to the bathroom.

"Thank you." Seth's gentle tone and deliberate small steps eased some of her tension. She felt small and useless beside his tall, large frame.

Grace closed the toilet door behind her and dry retched above the bowl before sitting down to relieve herself. Once her bladder emptied her nausea settled somewhat, but she was in no hurry to leave the toilet, just in case . . .

"You all right?" His loud voice way too close.

"Yes I am now . . . thanks." *Do you really have to stand outside while I'm on the bloody loo?* "I . . . I need to stay in here a while, Seth. I feel a bit sick."

"Righto." The footsteps quietened, moving toward the kitchen end of the house.

He left her alone, at last. Maybe it was worth trying to escape. There must be a back door to this place. Once she was able to leave the unflushed toilet she opened the door, slow and careful, to keep the noise down. She couldn't sense him close by. Good. She tiptoed into the bathroom, turned on the tap a little way to wash her hands and face before swishing and swallowing a handful of water.

Back in the hallway, she looked through what must be the lounge room, toward the kitchen but could not see Seth, only hear his radio going and smell something cooking – toast maybe. She turned the other way. There was a back door, but it was closed. Her shoulders slouched, but naturally it would be locked. He wouldn't have barred windows and an unlocked back door. Seth may have been an enigma but he wasn't stupid, and for some reason he wanted her kept in this house.

Images of Kain, her parents and Sophie entered her mind. She owed it to them to get out of this place. Her parents would be worrying themselves crazy, wondering where she was or if she was okay. *Hang on, girl, you told them you were going away for a while. They won't be worrying about you yet. And Kain ... hmph, he wouldn't be worried. He dumped you - remember?*

Grace shook her head to clear that annoying, but honest, inner voice nagging at her less logical side.

The back door. Without a moment to think twice, she headed toward it. The determination and optimism in her stride and heart seemed to lessen the previous stiffness and pain in her legs. Walking past two closed doors, one either side, her focus remained on that back door. She didn't care what was in those two rooms although one would be Seth's bedroom.

As she neared the door, Grace reached out with her right hand, but the pain in her shoulder forced it back to her body. Her left hand took hold of the black knob. She turned it and tried to pull the door open, but it wouldn't budge. Locked and, of course, the key nowhere in sight.

Grace looked around the bare, back room, a small sleep-out containing a single bed, a couple of old plastic chairs. Sunshine and breeze flowed through the numerous windows. Barred, every one of them *barred* exactly like the room where she'd been confined. The coolness of the gentle breeze refreshed her moist skin. She hadn't realised how much she was already sweating, including her palms, until the air hit her. Grace inhaled to the pit of her stomach, hoping to steady her thumping heart, and wiped her palms on her baggy pants. It was no use. Her stomach rolled in time with the drummer pounding away in her heart.

She tried to run back up the hall, but it was physically impossible and quietness was essential. Her ankle clicked, breaking the silence she was confident she had. She stopped and listened. The same sounds and aromas continued from the opposite end of the house. She moved forward again, hoping her bare feet, or any other body parts, would not give her actions and intentions away. She made it back to the toilet, flushed it with Seth being none the wiser.

"You okay now?" Seth stood right behind her.

Or so she thought.

Grace jumped and spun around. This bloke was the master of stealth, his footsteps loud at times and silent at others. Was he real . . . or was he . . . ? "Yes, much better thank you." She forced a smile in his direction but avoided eye contact. "Can I have a shower please? I can't seem to wake up properly this morning." Stuff it, she'd ask him straight out. "Did you drug me last night?" This time she looked him directly in the eyes. "*Did* you?"

"I just gave you something to calm you down and help you sleep. You needed it."

"What I *need* is to go to a hospital and then be able to go home. Why are you keeping me prisoner, Seth?" Grace clenched her teeth and exhaled fast through her nostrils as determination set in. "What do you want from me?" The pressure cooker inside her body pushed against its lid. Her pulse quickened. Breaths came short and sharp.

Seth looked at her through slits. No expression on his scarred face. His mouth opened as if to speak and then closed again for several seconds. His face relaxed. "I got you something." Pride and excitement evident in those few words. His eyes opened wide. He turned and picked up a plastic shopping bag full of something. "Here, these might fit better." His cheeks puffed out in a smile and his chest expanded.

Grace leaned back, looked at the bag, to him and back to the bag. She didn't know what to say. With a loud rustle he moved the bag closer to her hand, eager for her to have it. She took the bag from his gloved hand and opened it.

Clothes. She looked back at him. "Where did you get these? When?"

"Last night. I went into town."

"You left me here alone, *drugged?*" She wanted to scream loud and long. "What the hell is going on, Seth?" She dropped one handle of the bag and reached in, pulling out some of the clothes. A pair of denim shorts and some undies hung from her hand. "These are some other woman's clothes and . . . underwear. You expect me to wear them?" She flung them off her hand onto the floor beside the bag. "Yuk. I'm not going to wear some other woman's underpants!"

"They're clean, Grace. The shops were shut so I couldn't get you any new ones." His voice and chest sunk. The smile disappeared.

Grace shuddered. "Where or *how* did you get them? On second thoughts, I don't want to know."

"The laundromat."

Her mouth dropped open. "You just went in and took someone's clothes out of the dryer?"

"Yes I did. I went to a lot of trouble to get you them, so shut up and either wear them or stay in those baggy ones of mine." His tone grew angry, or was it hurt?

Seth continued. "I've boiled the kettle and made some breakfast for you. If you keep mucking around it'll get cold." He let out a heavy sigh and dropped his gaze to the floor. "I just wanted to get you some clothes, that's all, Grace."

Sadness saturated those words. She couldn't afford to anger him either. His eagerness and excitement reminded her of a young Steve one Christmas morning. He'd handed her the present he'd managed to buy her. It wasn't much but Steve had glowed with pride, watching her open it. She cherished that ornament, not because she liked it, but because it came from his heart. Bless him. *Oh Steve.*

"I . . . I'm sorry, Seth. Thank you for getting me some clothes. I'll have a quick shower." She entered the bathroom and closed the door, listening out for his footsteps. Nothing. He must be just standing there. A short, sharp sound, like a sob, tensed her. She waited for more, but his footsteps moved toward the kitchen and faded. Silence again.

Grace wasted no time in the shower or drying herself. She picked out some shorts, undies and a top from the bag. It would be too difficult putting on a bra, so she didn't even bother and she sure as heck wasn't going to ask Seth to help. She hung her towel on the rack, tossed the baggy, ill-fitting clothes she had been wearing into the laundry basket and opened the door, expecting to find him waiting there. Again, she could not sense his presence. She walked out of the bathroom, combed her fingers through her wet hair and looked down then up the hallway. Seth was nowhere to be seen.

"Seth?" She walked toward the kitchen. The radio played and the morning culinary aromas continued. Something was cooking, but she wasn't familiar with the smell, albeit inviting. The earlier sickness had finally disappeared and her empty stomach grumbled at the thought and smell of delicious food.

Grace flickered her gaze about as she walked through the small lounge room adjacent to the kitchen. Plain and basic, just like the rest of the house that she had seen so far. Two old, single lounge chairs with stained arm rests, a low, wooden coffee table and a small television. The only thing on the stark, pale walls was a calendar featuring a picture of a buckjump rider at a rodeo. The wording below it caught her attention and she stopped. 'Karisdale Hardware and Produce Agency.' Karisdale. A long way from her home in Anchor Bay. The whole mountain range stood between the two. Maybe Seth's house was close to Karisdale. That information might come in handy. She continued to the kitchen. "Seth?"

Seth sat at the rectangle table, head in hands. His large body shuddered and shook but he made only low, gasping sounds. Grace stared, unsure what to do or say. This was not how she expected to find him. Maybe she should leave him alone. She wanted to return to the bathroom, or her room, it didn't matter. She just couldn't handle this. As she turned, her foot kicked something on the floor, sending it bumping into the wall. *Damn.* She glanced down to see a plastic cup. Hopefully he didn't hear it. She continued into the lounge.

"Grace, wait." Seth scraped his creaky chair backward on the linoleum floor and came toward her. He grabbed her elbow, turning her around to face him.

Grace trembled; frightened for what she'd witnessed and frightened of what he may now say or do. "Um . . . sorry I . . ."

Sadness and despair flowed from his eyes along with tears. He looked like a worn-down old man, though she had no idea of his age.

"Come and sit at the table."

She nodded and followed him to the chair he indicated, opposite his chair. "Are you okay?" That was a silly question, but she had no idea what to say. She'd had lots of experience with troubled school students, but this situation and this man was totally different. She was barely coping with her own inner turmoil.

"You saw me crying didn't you?"

"Yes . . . but I did call you as I came out of the bathroom. I didn't mean to sneak up on you. I'm sorry, Seth." How she wished for a trap door beneath her to open up and whisk her away from all this craziness.

He waved his gloved hand in her direction. "Don't worry about it." He let out a sigh, got up and made two cups of tea.

Grace never took her eyes off his back, except to glance around the kitchen for a moment. Bare walls and only the basic of furniture and appliances were of no surprise.

"Here you go." Seth placed a mug of steaming tea in front of her and sat back on his chair with his own cup. He took a noisy slurp, avoiding Grace's eyes.

Grace sipped her tea, but longed for food although her appetite had waned since this unexpected confrontation. Her heart rode up her throat in anticipation. As a teacher, she'd learnt to urge students to speak up and try their best to reach their full potential. Somehow, she didn't think she could use the same encouraging words on Seth. If only it were that simple.

"I've made some breakfast, but first I want to tell you something, Grace. I *need* to tell you."

"Okay." Grace nodded. At least he was talking more than he had the previous day. That was one positive sign. "Please tell me whatever you need to, Seth. I'm a good listener."

"When I brought you back here from in the bush, you talked a bit while you were unconscious."

"Did I?" She had no recollection and dreaded what he'd heard. "What did I say?" Her throat tightened with her increasing heartbeat.

"You mentioned the name Kain a couple of times and something about telling him to go to hell. You seemed angry."

His tone was flat, almost monotone, but Grace shifted in her chair and fidgeted her hands. Talking to Seth about her private life didn't feel right. She looked away, staring at nothing toward the fridge over to her left. He had invaded her personal space and thoughts without her knowledge or consent. Of course he didn't do it on purpose, but it didn't lessen her discomfort.

Seth continued. "I don't mean to pry, but-."

"Well, *don't* then. You keep me here against my will and you want to talk about my personal life?" She shook her head and drank another mouthful of tea, still avoiding his eyes. She felt like a simmering volcano of blended emotions. Angry at him, sad for him, scared of him and scared for herself, all the while angry at Kain.

"Righto. Sorry for that." Seth sounded remorseful. Air-thickening silence followed for a few seconds. He stood. "I'll get the breakfast."

Seth put two pieces of brown bread in the toaster on the bench and pressed buttons on the adjacent microwave.

Maybe she'd been too harsh on him. This whole situation seemed surreal. So *unreal.* Everything that had happened in the past week, from Kain breaking off their relationship, the accident, the ferocious and hungry dogs, to ending up here, with this . . . this frightening, yet amiable man. Surely, if he was planning to hurt her he would have done so by now.

Clunk. A plate of food appeared in front of her on the old wooden table, jumping her mind back to reality. It looked like 'bubble and squeak' – a mixture of roughly chopped vegies and ham, topped with melted cheese. The aromas hit her nostrils. It smelt divine. On the side of the plate were two pieces of toast. Seth placed the butter on the table along with a bowl of cut up mango, apple and banana.

"You want a juice?" A voice void of any emotion, he pointed to the fridge.

Oh no, he was clamming up again. "Umm, yes please . . . if that's okay." Grace looked at Seth and smiled, hoping to ease the tension. "I would love one."

Then something hit her like a freak wave at the beach. She had been trying to 'get away from it all' when she'd had the accident. Here, she was certainly away from it all. Not once had she heard a car in the distance, so the house was well off the main road. It was a beautiful, peaceful spot and now that she realised Seth was not going to hurt her she would cease fighting him, but remain alert, and let her body heal.

Kain could go to hell.

In a few days, when they would start to wonder how she was, she'd ask Seth if she could ring her parents and let them know she was okay. Satisfied with her decision, she took the glass of juice from Seth, with another smile, and drank some. It tasted so sweet and refreshing as it slid down her dry throat. The rewarding coolness hit her empty stomach, encouraging her hunger, but it could wait.

"I'm sorry I snapped at you before, Seth." She looked across the table at him. He seemed so alone and lonely. Someone who'd clearly been through unfathomable hell. A large ball of pity swelled in her chest, pushing its way to her throat. The harsh words had shot out of her mouth and now she wished she could take them back.

He hoed into his food and didn't so much as glance at her during the time she watched him, waiting for some sort of reaction. *Anything.* He continued eating like some sort of robot programmed to remain cold and emotionless.

She sighed. At least she'd tried to apologise. She nibbled the corner piece of toast before eating a fork full of food. "This is very nice. You're a good cook, Seth." *Please talk to me.* "What's your favourite food?"

He swallowed then put his loaded fork back on the plate and stared at her with an incredulous look on his reddened face. "Umm, I don't know, I eat anything I s'pose."

"Why did you look so surprised then, when I asked that simple question?"

"No-one has ever asked me anything like that before." He shrugged one shoulder. "Not many people talk to me. It feels . . ." He wiped his mouth and scratched his chin. "Strange."

"You were right before, when you said I seemed angry. I was and still am. Yep, his name is Kain and he ended our relationship after five years together just like that." She snapped the fingers on her left hand. "I was going away somewhere, *anywhere,* to get away and have some time alone to get my head around it all. He gave me some pathetic reason and . . . " the tears threatened. *Oh no you don't.* She blinked several times. "That was that."

After eating another mouthful of food she dared ask him a question, as if the food gave her some sort of invisible inner strength. "Seth, what is it you want to tell me?" Her voice softened. "It's okay, I won't judge you. I can see you've been through hell." The overwhelming urge to ask how he'd acquired his terrible scarring, burst to the forefront of her mind, more so than any other question, but it wasn't the appropriate time . . .yet.

Seth finished the last morsel of food on his plate and drank his juice. He was certainly a fast eater. He looked at Grace and his wide shoulders rose high and dropped. "Grace . . . " He took another deep breath. "Grace, please don't be scared of me. I won't hurt you."

"You keep telling me that, but why are you keeping me here like this? You must have a reason." She sensed he was thinking hard, so attempted to encourage him further. "What's really going on, Seth? What are you thinking?"

"What do you mean, 'going on'?" He frowned and tensed up, his back stiffening. "Nothing." Seth got up and pushed his chair back before clanging his plate and glass on the sink.

He stood with his back to Grace, looking out the sink window or maybe his eyes were closed in deep thought. There to be a lot more he wanted to say but she didn't wish to antagonise him by asking too many questions. No, she'd wait for the time to be just right, and she had plenty of time, so it seemed. "Sorry."

He spun around. "Look, I just want a friend. Is that okay?"

"Wh . . .what sort of a friend?" *Oh no.* Surely he didn't mean as in girlfriend. She was definitely not interested there, even though something was drawing her to him – probably just pity.

Seth sat back in his chair. "I don't mean like a 'girl-friend', just a friend - someone to talk to and eat meals with like this." A tear slipped down one cheek then the other. "I've never had a friend." He folded his arms on the table and dropped his head to them. Loud sobs echoed around the sparse room. His body shuddered.

Grace reached over and touched his elbow. It flinched. "It's okay. I'll be your friend." She rested her hand on his arm, feeling the trembling but also the warmth that emanated from his body and from his heart. "But you have to trust me too."

She couldn't help believing this was not what he was originally going to tell her. She had numerous questions to ask. Tears irritated her eyes. Rubbing his elbow and arm, her heart hurt for this alienated man, ostracised by society, but with so many tragic secrets and stories to tell, of *that* she was certain.

CHAPTER 13

Seth sat upright and wiped his watery eyes with the back of his gloved hands. "Sorry Grace." He pulled a crumpled hanky out of his jeans pocket, blew his nose then, leaning back in his chair, stuffed the hanky back.

Grace watched him. *She* wasn't afraid to look at his ugly scars. "Are you scared of me?" His lungs withheld his breath, waiting. Waiting alongside his galloping heart for her answer, hoping it would be the one he desperately wanted to hear.

"No Seth, I'm not scared of you."

She shook her head and smiled – a warm, genuine smile that washed over him, seeped through his skin and slowed his heart back to a merry trot. He couldn't recall ever seeing that in anyone, or feeling this way, before today.

"I must admit, I was at first though."

Seth nodded then shrugged. "Don't blame you. I look pretty horrible."

Grace's smile morphed to a frown.

Seth could almost hear the cogs turning over in her brain. His body tensed. "Do you want to ask me something?" Something told him he wouldn't like what was coming.

"Why don't you have any mirrors in the house?"

"I thought that'd be obvious. I don't want to look at my ugly self." He got up, walked to the doorway and leant on the side of it, facing out to the front verandah. Grace's beautiful and inquisitive face – he couldn't look her in the eye. He should never have let her see him cry. He wished the floor would open up and suck his ugly body down . . . way down. He wished life could be different. He *wished* for so many things, but they were nothing but fantasies. Useless and unreachable.

Grace put him at ease most of the time. So comfortable that he'd almost told her about Scott and what he does for him, but common sense prevailed and stopped him just in time. He knew only too well what Scott may do if Seth talked about him or the jobs he does for him, especially an upcoming job.

Grace broke the silence. "I'm sorry, it's just that . . ."

Seth turned around. "I'm sorry too, Grace, I didn't mean to snap at you." The last thing he wanted was to frighten her or drive her to escape and return home. He sat back on his chair opposite Grace. "I suppose you're dying to ask me how I got these scars."

Grace looked a little nervous. "Umm, well I couldn't help but wonder. But you don't have to tell me if you don't want to. It's none of my business."

"Truth is, I don't really know." Grace shook her head, her face full of confusion so Seth continued. "I don't re-member much about it."

He really didn't want to get into this, but knew it was unavoidable and it was so good having someone to talk to who hadn't already pre-judged him. "It was a few years ago now. All I can remember is waking up to people yelling and hitting and kicking me. I tried to get away, but they threw liquid on me. For a split second I thought it was water then the burning pain started and I couldn't see anything. I put my hands up." He lifted his gloved hands to his head. "But they threw more acid and parts of my hands burnt too." Taking a deep breath, his heart beat harder, louder. Tears threatened, but he swallowed them down. "I don't know what happened next, but I woke up some time later out in a paddock somewhere and Scott was there and . . ." *Idiot, you shouldn't have mentioned Scott.*

"Scott?" Grace frowned again. "Who's Scott?"

"He's the bloke who found me and helped me get better."

"He sounds like a good person."

If only you knew how far wrong you are, Grace. Seth now had to be careful when choosing his words. He'd already said too much. "He looked after me and . . ." He almost blurted out that Scott had found this place for him, but had stopped himself just in time. "Now I do a bit of work for him from time to time." *Shouldn't have said that either. Not being very careful, idiot.*

"What sort of work?"

Of course she'd have to ask that. What to say, what to say. Seth shrugged. "Just a bit of odd work around his property, cattle work, driving, that sort of thing." He got up, filled the kettle and flicked it on. "Would you like another cuppa? It's going to be another hot one today." Hopefully Grace wouldn't want to talk about Scott anymore.

"Oh . . . yes please. You're right, I'm sweating already just sitting here. Umm, I was also wondering why all the windows are barred."

"I did that after I moved here 'cos I was scared those mongrels who attacked me might come looking for me to finish the job."

"Did they?"

"No, thank God. Grace, I have to go into town and get some groceries and other things." He hoped the huge gamble would pay off. Could he trust her or not? "Will you stay here while I'm gone?"

Grace opened her mouth but closed it again for a moment, obviously deep in thought. "Yes of course I will," she said after several seconds. "Are you going into Karisdale?"

"Yes." Seth was surprised she knew the name. He took a pad and pen from the top of the fridge and handed them to Grace. "If you would like a few things, write them down and I'll see if I can get them for you."

Grace's face and shoulders fell. "Couldn't I just come with you?"

"No." Seth shook his head. *No way in hell.* People would stare and someone may recognise her and talk to her, then she'd surely want to go home, especially when she realised her family think she's dead. Scott could be in town or one of his men. Just too risky. "You need to stay here and rest. I'll be as quick as I can."

"All right then, I guess you're right and getting in and out of your car would be painful." She wrote on the paper with her left hand. Seth took her empty mug and made her another cup of tea.

Phew, that was close. At least she saw reason without any fuss. Hopefully, she won't ask any more questions. He placed the mug of tea on the table in front of Grace.

She looked up at him. "I can't remember much about how I got lost in the bush, but I do remember being in my car and then I picked up a hitchhiker. I must have let her drive for some reason, and then I remember the car rolling and all the dirt and dust, but that's it. Do you know what happened to my car and the other girl?"

"No, sorry."

Grace sniffled and wiped a tear from her eye. "I can't even remember her name. Oh no . . . she could be wandering around lost too and my bag and other stuff is still in the car. Could you take me there later, please Seth? I'd like to at least find my bag and my phone. I had it in my hands so it could be on the ground somewhere. On second thoughts, I'm probably better off without it. At least I can't be tempted to contact Kain and he can't contact me. Hmph, not that he would." Sadness shrouded her face.

Okay, now how to handle this. If Grace learned the other girl was burnt beyond recognition when the car exploded then she'd realise that people could think it was her by mistake. She doesn't seem to remember the explosion. He must not let her find out. "On my way back, I'll try and find the accident spot and have a look for you, okay." There'd probably be nothing left there by now, but he'd try and find out anyway, just to appease her. He'd do anything to keep his new friend happy. His only friend in the whole wide world.

"Thank you." She gave him that warm smile again. His heart swelled. He was finally doing something right and he was determined he would see that beautiful smile more often. She wrote a couple more things on the paper and handed it to him.

Seth took the list from her and read it – several women's magazines, a pair of size eight thongs and some women's toiletries. Now it was his turn to frown. "Is this all you want? I expected to see more."

Grace shrugged then grimaced before clasping her right shoulder. "I can't do much but lie around anyway, so that'll do. I can always watch TV." She sipped her tea.

TV! Seth had forgotten she may watch TV if he left her free to roam the house. She might see something about herself and the accident. Could he risk it? He didn't watch much television himself, but he was sure the local news only came on early in the night time, so it should be all right . . . hopefully.

"Could you also get today's newspaper please?" asked Grace with an optimistic look on her face.

This was proving more and more difficult. "Yep, can do." He had no intention of getting it, unless of course, it did not feature anything about the accident, but he doubted it would be missed. Then he'd have to come up with an excuse.

Grace stood and handed him her almost-empty tea cup. "I'm pretty tired again. I'll go and lie down now for a while."

"I'll help you." Seth moved toward her and reached out to take hold of her arm.

"No, it's okay. You get going. The sooner you go the sooner you'll be back." She laughed a little. "That's one of my mother's favourite sayings."

"I've heard that one too. What's your last name, Grace?" She continued walking. He watched her walk through the lounge room before turning into her room. She seemed to be ignoring him, which wasn't like her. "Are you right, Grace?"

"Yes, I'm fine. Thanks. And it's Atkinson," she called from her room.

Seth's breath caught when she spoke her surname. Oh no. She *is* the woman supposedly killed. He looked at the TV. Maybe he should take the remote with him. No, he had to show her he trusted her. *If only she knew.*

He checked his wallet was in his shirt pocket, grabbed Grace's list and headed toward the door. The radio on the kitchen bench caught his attention. He picked it up and strode out the door. He stopped and removed the key from the inside of the door lock, before closing the door. *Do I lock her in . . .or not?*

CHAPTER 14

Kain clunked his utility into first gear, switched off the ignition and lifted his foot from the clutch. He stared at the sign on the opposite side of the street - 'Anchor Bay Police Station'. The dull throb in his temples plus lack of sleep equalled him feeling like shit. The headache may have been from the beer but the insomnia came from thinking about Grace, *his beautiful Grace*, and her death.

Staring at the building behind the blue and white 'Police' sign, his thumping heart pushed all air out of his chest. Rising stomach acid found his throat. He tried to swallow it back down, but there was no saliva in his foul tasting mouth. He grabbed the plastic bottle of water from between the seats and drank several mouthfuls.

He had no idea if talking to the police would achieve anything but he had to do something. He hoped to see Linda again soon, but best to avoid Bruce for a while. *The funeral. Shit.* Grace and he had occasionally chatted about what each wanted after they died, without making any concrete plans. Knowing Bruce, Kain couldn't see him accepting any advice or suggestions, especially from himself. Hell, he'd probably not even let Kain attend. "Try and stop me, Bruce," Kain muttered. He grabbed the keys, jumped out of his vehicle, locked it and walked across the road to the police station.

"Can I help you? Oh, hello Kain." A young brunette police woman greeted him with a cheerful smile. But her smile vanished and her bright eyes turned downcast. "I'm so sorry to hear about Grace."

Kain stared at her. She sounded like she knew him. The face was familiar but he couldn't put a name to it. "Ahh . . . ." Come on brain, *think*.

"Constable Katy Jones. I'm a friend of Sophie, Grace's sister."

"That's right." Kain nodded. "Now I remember. You were at that last party Bruce and Linda had."

"What can we do for you?" Katy looked him with sad, brown eyes.

"I . . . I would like to talk to someone about the accident. I just want to know more about what happened and exactly where it happened. Can you help me Katy, or is there someone who can?"

"I'll just go and ask the Sarge. I'm not sure if we're handling it all or if the Karisdale police are. Hang on a sec." She rushed into one of the offices to the side of the main area.

Kain nodded politely to another young male officer who said G'day as he walked past, before turning around and looking at the wanted posters adorning the wall.

Some rough looking characters watched him. One felon stood out from the others. A centipede of electric zaps raced up his spine. Kain walked closer. An evil looking man stared back at him. Solid, with short fair hair and tattoos on his muscular arms. Wanted in two states. Murder, assault, armed robbery, abduction, arson, extortion – this bloke was as bad as they come. 'James William McTaggart'. The name was not familiar. 'Heavy Scotttish accent. Considered very dangerous. Do not approach. Call Crimestoppers,' etc. Kain shuddered. He didn't like the look of him one bit. McTaggart's whole body exuded fear and hate and those eyes . . . small and shifty. Those sorts of eyes belonged on some cunning little ferocious animal ruthlessly hunting its prey.

"Kain Burrows?"

Kain jolted and spun around. "Yes."

A tall, greying officer extended his hand. "I'm Sergeant Rawlings. You want to know more about yesterday's accident up on the range?" His voice began very matter-of-factly, but softened with just a hint of sympathy by the end of his sentence.

"Yes please." Kain returned the handshake.

"Come into my office." He beckoned Kain to follow him to the office in which Katy had entered. "Sit down."

Kain sat on the appointed chair and Rawlings sat behind his desk. "Thanks for this."

"So you are Grace Atkinson's boyfriend?" He picked up his glasses from the desk and put them on before opening a manila folder.

"Yeah, well we had broken up but I was about to reconcile with her when I got the . . . news of the accident." Tears stung his eyes, but he sucked a deep breath and blinked them away. "I still love her very much," he added, realising that the police don't give out information unless the person asking is closely connected to the subject. Not that he had to lie about his feelings for Grace.

"We still have the forensics team out at the site today. They did as much as they could yesterday, but it was pretty late in the day before someone saw the burnt out car. It was a fair way down the gully. It's a wonder it was seen at all." He shook his head. "I don't understand why someone hadn't heard the explosion or seen the smoke, although it's in a fairly remote area. Not that it would have helped Ms Atkinson at all. She had no hope of getting out of that . . ." He looked to the side and rubbed his hand across his mouth. "Sorry, that was a bit insensitive of me."

Too bloody right, it was. "I heard that they found her mobile phone and she'd been texting me when the accident happened. Is that true?"

Rawlings read through some of the hand written notes in front of him. "Yes, apparently so. It was found about thirty-odd metres from the car and it wasn't damaged." He looked up at Kain and raised his bushy eyebrows. "Why would she do such a stupid thing, especially on that bloody road? It's got more twists and turns than you can poke a stick at."

Kain's shackles rose along with his heartbeat. His face flushed hot. "She's *not* stupid and I don't believe for one second that she would've been driving while texting. She *hated* anyone doing that. Did they find anything else, like her bag or anything?"

"Not that I'm aware of at this stage. The Karisdale boys are out there too. One of them might have come across something."

"Where was the accident?"

"Why?" Rawlings drew back and frowned. "You're not thinking of going out there are you?" He shook his head and his eyes squinted. A silent warning?

"Yes I am, actually." Kain didn't like this arrogant attitude. "I need to see where my lady died." Even if Rawlings didn't tell him exactly where the accident occurred, he'd find it himself, one way or another.

"You'll get in the way. Just stay away for now. You can go in a couple of days."

Kain thought for a moment. "Okay, you're right. I'll wait for a few days, but can you still tell me where it was? Please." He had no intention of waiting, but he'd let the police think he would. Not his fault what the cops surmise.

"All right, but only because you look like a decent bloke who'll do the right thing. It's on the Range Road, about a kilometre west of Possum Creek, right hand side, just past that little parking and lookout area."

Kain jumped up. "Thank you Sarge." He shook hands with the sergeant who remained sitting. He exited the Sergeant's office and the police station. A small weight disappeared from his shoulders. Good thing Constable Katy was nowhere to be seen. Kain didn't need any small talk or polite references to Grace.

He wanted to sprint to his utility, but Rawlings may see him through a window so, instead, ambled across the road. His legs longed to run. His heart beat a million miles a minute and all he could think about was getting to the accident scene. In his shattered heart he believed he would find *something.* Something that would free Grace of any wrong doing and clear up some of the misunderstandings surrounding the accident. If only it could bring Grace back.

Kain sat in his utility and opened his battered, brown wallet. Grace's smiling face looked at him with much love in her eyes. He touched the clear plastic in front of the picture, stroking her face. "Nobody's going to call you stupid, Grace, I'll see to that." About to put the key in the ignition, the tears burst forth. Kain dropped the keys and held the top of the steering wheel. "Noooo, Grace, nooo. I can't handle never seeing you again." His forehead dropped to his hands that gripped the wheel. He convulsed with sobs, no inner strength to fight them. Who cared? He slumped down in his seat as the hurt and sadness flowed from his body.

Moments, maybe minutes, later he lifted his head and wiped his wet hands on his shirt. He had no idea how long he'd just cried, but it needed to happen. Lifting the bottom of his shirt he wiped his eyes and sniffled hard. "Bloody cancer. Damn you to hell." He glanced at his watch. It was almost 9.30. *Doctor's appointment. Do I go or do I head to Range Road?* "Come on Grace, help me make the right decision."

Grace was gone, but he was still here and he needed treatment. But did he really want to be here without Grace? Maybe he should just let nature take its course. If

Grace and he were meant to be together then it wouldn't matter if he died. The thought of going on without her pained him more than her death.

Then he thought of his beloved parents and what terrible grief Linda and Bruce were suffering. No way could he do that to his parents. He picked up the keys from between his thighs and stabbed into the ignition, started the engine and headed in the direction of his doctor. He'd get the appointment over and head up Range Road.

CHAPTER 15

Seth drove to the intersection of his quiet road and the main highway. He automatically indicated left to Karisdale, but flicked off the indicator. It would look way too suspicious if he were seen buying women's items in familiar surroundings. There'd always be someone who'd notice him and comment or gossip then it would be all around that God-forsaken town. No. He checked the fuel gauge. Enough to get to Anchor Bay then he'd top up while there without having to use Scott's donated fuel and arouse his suspicions. He was sure Scott was psychic at times, unless he had a twin somewhere. A twin just as evil and conniving.

He'd only ever been to Anchor Bay once that he could recall, so surely no-one would question anything 'odd' he'd purchase. No doubt they'd look at him like some sort of freak, but he was used to that. Kids will probably point and stare at him while trying to hide in fear.

The smaller, closer town of Karisdale served his sufficient needs and the people of Karisdale generally kept their distance from him *these* days. It didn't bother him as much now that he had Grace at home. He had a friend. She cared about him. That was bigger than anything he knew in his world. Maybe, just maybe, one day that 'care' could grow into something more wonderful. A little smile snaked its way from his heart to his lips. It felt good. He nodded to himself, hit the indicator and turned right.

Grace. Surely he'd done the right thing by not locking the door, which would have locked her in the house. His gut instinct told him he could trust her, or was it just wishful thinking? She seemed happy enough to stay. That Kain must be a proper arsehole to just dump her like that. *I'll never let anyone ever hurt you again, Grace. But, what if she WAS faking and she DOES take off and has you charged with holding her prisoner?* "No. No she wouldn't!" Seth said it aloud to shake off that negative inner voice. He *hated* that annoying little shit. Like some sort of wriggly worm, always appearing in his brain at the most inopportune moments. Moments that began positive but were soon turned negative by that invisible intruder.

For several seconds, he pondered the consequences of that scenario eventuating and sucked in a deep breath. He could only come up with one solution. If Grace ran off, got home and had him charged, he'd just grab his gun and end his miserable life. It wouldn't matter to anyone. No-one would miss him, well, maybe Scott, but that would only be to do his dirty work. There was no friendship or care there.

Since he and Grace had opened up to each other earlier, a tonne had lifted from his shoulders. Maybe the world was not such a horrible place after all. He kept remembering the smiles she gave him and how she genuinely cared.

A smile spread across his bearded face – something that hadn't happened for a *long* time, except for the earlier incident. A rare and new feeling – happiness. He relished how it seemed to spread calm over his troubled soul.

He soon ascended the range and began the windy descent on the opposite side. Apart from the dangerous road, he slowed to a tortoise's pace so as not to miss the accident site where Grace 'died'.

It wasn't difficult to spot, with police and other unmarked, but official-looking, cars parked about, some precariously close to the edge. The blue and white police tape swayed in the breeze, draped from tree to tree, going down toward where the burnt-out car must be. Uniformed police and other well-dressed people walked about. Some were writing things down on clipboards, while others appeared to be searching around on the ground and even up into trees and bushes. He had no idea why they'd be searching up..

Seth shook his head. The chances of being able to stop and have his own look about would be impossible if they were all still here when he returned later. But he was still a long way from Anchor Bay and by the time he'd done his errands and returned, *hopefully*, they'd all be finished and gone.

Out on reasonably flat ground and road, again Seth turned on the radio and settled back for the rest of the drive. He couldn't wait to get back home to Grace. She consumed his thoughts. He *should* have been thinking about Scott and the upcoming job, but Grace was much more important and a pleasure to think about. Her smile and those pretty green eyes. The sound of her voice. There was nothing about her he didn't like. Just to sit and talk to her again. *I know . . . I'll buy her some flowers.* Yep, good thinking.

Large signs welcomed him to Anchor Bay. He soon found a shopping centre without too much driving about and completed his shopping, including the items for Grace plus a few extras for her. No-one had whispered or stared at him. Well, no-one that he'd *noticed,* anyway. Today he was on cloud nine and no rude, ignorant person was going to stuff that up.

Seth hummed a nameless tune as he pulled into the service station on the edge of town to fill up for the journey home. Humming . . . that was new to him too. As always, he pulled his hat down low over his eyes so people would see less of his scarring, and got out of his vehicle. He may have been happy but instinct forced him to continue protecting himself.

The hot, humid air hit him with a stifling gush after his air conditioned vehicle. He gulped in a short, sharp breath and opened the cap of the fuel tank. Air conditioning was turning him into a softie. The fuel flowed into his tank. Lifting his hat, he wiped his damp forehead with the other gloved hand and long sleeve. He glanced about and did a double take at the man using the next bowser. The stranger stared at him, a look of disgust on his fat face. *Ah shit. There's always gotta be one.*

Seth plummeted head-first from cloud nine to cloud zero. "What the hell you starin' at, mate?" He wasn't in the mood for this crap today.

"You," replied the larger man. "Why don't you go and crawl back under the rock you came out from. People don't need to see your Freddy Kruger face. I bet you give kids nightmares."

Seth sucked in warm air between pursed lips. Was it worth it? Was that bundle of shit with his huge, blubbery gut really worth getting riled up about? His tank now full, he replaced the nozzle and screwed on his fuel cap, gritting his teeth. *Ignore him.* He drew in a slow, deep breath and expelled it at the same rate. *Stay calm.*

"What, can't you talk? Is your tongue as fucked up as your head and face?" The fat arsehole replaced his petrol nozzle with a loud laugh. A laugh that sounded nothing short of fake. He turned back to Seth. "Gutless wonder." He shook his curly haired head and turned to walk to the servo shop.

Seth strode several metres and stood in front of him. "What did you just call me?" Towering over him, Seth stared him directly in the eyes. Determined. Unafraid. He knew the worst kind of fear and this idiot didn't scare him one damned bit, just made him so bloody angry. *Seething* angry. Snap-his-neck kind of angry. How dare the moron steal away the good, happy feelings he'd been enjoying.

The man was huge, but he was all blubber. Sweat droplets popped out on his frightened red face which drained to ashen white. He stammered to speak. "N . . . nothing." He tried to duck around Seth but Seth grabbed his arm.

"Not so fast. I said, what did you just call me?" Seth'd had more than a gutful. In the past hour or so while in

Anchor Bay, no-one seemed to take any notice of him and now, on his way home, here was this bastard wanting to give him a hard time. Well, he wasn't going to take it.

The man's eyes watered. "Let me go, or I'll call the p-police."

Two uniformed police officers rushed over from their car parked on the roadside. "What's going on here?" one of them asked. He looked at Seth. "Let that man's arm go."

Seth dropped the bloke's arm, who immediately rubbed the reddened area where Seth had held his firm grip.

"He attacked me." The man's voice rose several pitches. He pointed to Seth. "That monster attacked me. He should be locked away. I want him charged." His voice now a high pitched whine.

Seth shook his head and looked down at the concrete. "That's bullshit." But, as usual, he'd get the blame because he was *different*. Nobody liked *different*, well, except for Grace maybe.

"Aren't you going to put the handcuffs on him? Come on, do your job." The man's forehead dripped with sweat. His face reddened again. His slightly squeaky voice quavered as the words tumbled and dribbled out of his mouth.

"Shut up," said one of the policemen, staring him down a moment and shaking his finger at him. The officer looked about. "Did anyone else see what happened here just now?"

Several people shook their heads and went about their business of fuelling their cars, but one man strode forward. "I did."

"And what actually happened, Sir?" asked the other policeman.

"Yeah." The red-faced idiot cleared his throat. "You tell 'em what this big bucket of ugliness did to me." His normal voice had returned. He straightened his shoulders and puffed out his chest, seemingly expecting everyone to have the same views as himself.

Was he right? Would this stranger take the loudmouth's side? Probably.

The witness, who'd walked over, spoke. "This man", he pointed to Seth, "was just minding his business, filling his ute, when this . . . *idiot* starting calling out to him and calling him ugly and generally putting shit on him." The witness' gaze brimmed with anger as he glared at the loudmouth.

"Go on," urged one of the policemen. "What happened then? Did he respond to the verbal diarrhoea?"

With a frown, the witness looked at the policeman. The frown died and a grin was born. "You saw and heard it too, didn't you?"

"Yes," both policemen said in unison.

One turned to Seth. "Would *you* like to press any charges, Sir? Something like bullying, verbal assault, disturbing the peace, shouting at a servo? I could go on and on."

Seth looked at the loudmouth, whose chest and shoulders had sunk and sweat now trickled down the sides of his face and front of his neck rolls, not just from the hot weather. Seth glanced further down. His chubby knees even seemed to be trembling. How he'd love to just punch his smart mouth, but he wasn't worth the effort. He shook his head. "Nah, not worth the paperwork."

"Go and pay for your fuel and if we ever find you abusing anyone again, watch out," ordered one of the officers.

The man scampered into the shop to pay, like a scared rabbit that had just escaped a cage. The blubber on his hips wobbled beneath his tight green tee shirt.

One officer raised his eyebrows and grinned at the other. "*Shouting* at a servo?"

The other shrugged. "Why not?"

"Well, I'll leave you all to it." The witness turned to go.

"Wait," Seth called after him. The man turned around. "Thanks, but why did you bother coming to defend me?"

The man shrugged. "Why shouldn't I?" He walked back to Seth. "Mate, I don't know what you've been though but it looks like hell. I've just lost the love of my life". His bottom lip trembled and he bit down on it. "And now I'm battling cancer. If I can do one good thing for someone, why the hell not? Life's too short to have that sort of shit going on. Good luck to you." He held out his right hand to Seth.

Seth looked at the outstretched hand and back up to the eyes of the stranger. They were kind, caring eyes. No stranger had ever offered to help him before, let alone shake his hand. What a weird feeling. Thinking of his scarred, deformed hands, he looked again at the stranger's perfect hand. What would he think of Seth's hands if he could see them? Would he still want to touch them?

"It's okay, mate." The hand came a little closer.

Seth clasped the hand and shook. The genuine warmth and concern emanating from the man, even through Seth's gloved hand, sent tingles up his arm straight to his heart. A marble stuck in his throat. Unable to speak, he nodded and let go.

The stranger nodded back with a sad smile, walked to his utility, got in and drove off toward the range. Unbelievable. Two people had genuinely cared about him in as many days.

Seth turned around and saw the loudmouth jumping into his old van then roaring off with a squeal of his tyres, mouthing something to himself. The policemen were back at their vehicle so he headed in to pay for his fuel. As he walked toward the door of the servo shop he looked west along the straight road that went on forever. The witness's utility was growing smaller in the distance, approaching the mountain range. Seth's eyes became moist. "You poor bugger."

CHAPTER 16

The range loomed large, dark, and foreboding. A sleeping giant who had stolen Kain's beautiful Grace.

He drove up the gradual slope, approaching the steepest and windiest section of road. His mind filled with thoughts of Grace, but he couldn't help thinking about the man back at the servo with the horrendous scars. A decent enough bloke, and he definitely didn't deserve to be abused by brain-dead morons. Sticking up for the guy had made Kain's aching heart feel good briefly, although the coppers wouldn't have let it get out of hand. The scarred man would have, no doubt, been able to stand up for himself, given his size and obvious past sufferings.

He crossed Possum Creek, looked over the side and could just make out running water quite a distance below, amidst bushes and boulders. Not long now until he reached the crash site. His stomach contained an electric beater set on 'slow' and his mouth dried to a sour stickiness.

Could he cope with seeing the burnt out car?

The news reporter at the pub said the smell was terrible. That *terrible smell* was his Grace, burnt to . . . virtually nothing. Sickening images flooded his brain. The electric beater increased its speed. His mouth salivated. He needed to pull over. *Where the hell is this parking spot that's near the crash site?*

Kain continued around the next bend. *Come on.* He gripped the steering wheel and swallowed. The saliva needed an escape. His stomach revolted, needing to purge. Then around the next bend he welcomed the sight of a parked vehicle with space around it. This has to be the site. He veered his utility, hit the brake pedal hard and shut off the ignition. Jumping out, he couldn't hold back. With a sickening moan, the contents of his stomach gushed out. Some of the vomit splattered back on his bare legs and thonged feet.

"Shit." He groaned at the mess and straightened back up. He looked about and wiped his mouth on the back of his hand.

Eerily quiet. Not even a bird sang from the trees.

Must be too hot for them. A chill speared up his spine and shot out the hairs on the back of his neck, leaving them standing. Someone or something was watching him. Spinning around, he saw a man and woman standing beside the other car. Both stared at him with looks of disgust. He empathised with the scarred man back at the servo.

He wiped his tears and the sweat from his forehead, got a bottle of water out of his utility and had a long drink, quenching his thirst. He swished his bitter mouth and poured some water down each leg to wash off the vomit.

He glanced around again. They continued staring at him. *For Christ's sake, piss off will yous!* Sighing so deeply it came out as a moan, he had three choices. He could get in his vehicle and return home, he could just ignore them or he could ask them what the hell they were staring at. But a confrontation was something he didn't need right now.

The doctor's words returned to his brain – "It's definitely cancer. We need to begin treatment as soon as possible. You have a good chance of beating it, but you can't waste time."

Right now, he needed to do what he felt was right in his coping with Grace's death, and right now that was seeing the crash site.

"Are you two all right?" Kain walked a little closer to them. Surely they were just tourists and had stopped at this spot to check out the view through the forest and across the plains. Being semi-rainforest there were not many places through this range that afforded a clear view between the numerous trees.

"Yeah buddy, we're fine." The bespectacled, fortyish woman grinned, showing a missing front tooth. "Can't say the same for you though." She sniggered, loud and exaggerated.

"Nice view through here." Kain indicated the clearing, trying to be polite, which was becoming difficult under the circumstances.

"Oh, we're not here for that view, are we, Frank?" She glanced at the tall, skinny man beside her.

"Nup, we came to see something more interesting than that." He picked at his big nose and flicked the findings on to the ground.

Kain's watery stomach contents threatened to dislodge again. He turned away but wondered what they were talking about – surely not the accident site. Surely they were not that insensitive and despicable. Were they partners or mother and son? *Who'd know these days?* His eyes drew back to the strange couple. "Okay, well what did you come to see?"

"Did you hear about the accident here yesterday? *BOOMMMM.* A car went up in flames and burnt the driver. We came for a gander at it." She giggled like a teenager and tucked her brown, shoulder-length hair under her dirty, red cap. "Did you come for a look too?"

Kain's blood simmered, fast approaching boiling point. "You what?"

The woman shrugged. "Well, why not? It's not every day you get to see something like this. I hope the body's still there. I have a fascination with these sorts of things. Ever since I was a little girl, I used to like dissecting animals and burning toads, you know that sort of thing. Mum always told me it was creepy and that I should play with normal toys, but-"

"Stop!" Kain's voice echoed around the forest. "No more. You're a sick excuse for a human being. The person who died in this crash was someone's daughter, sister, friend and . . . girlfriend. She was *my* girlfriend."

The man's eyes widened. The woman's face went sullen and pale.

Kain continued. "It's not some fucking circus for freaks like you to come and gawk at. Get in your car and piss off." The shouting hurt his throat, already tender from vomiting.

"W-well, why are you here?" the woman asked in a quiet voice.

"None of your friggin' business, lady." Kain felt like grabbing both idiots and throwing them over the side of the mountain. *Calm down.* He took a deep breath. "Just go . . . *now.*"

"Oh righto, keep your pants on." The woman's face screwed to an indignant look. "Come on Frank, let's go. The cops probably took everything by now anyway". They got in their battered old Holden and the woman wound down her window. "Spoil sport," she yelled at Kain and drove away, blue smoke coughing out of the exhaust.

Kain spun around, thumped his fist on to the roof of his ute and clasped his trembling hands. Another vehicle, similar to his, approached. He didn't want to deal with anyone else and hoped like hell they wouldn't stop. Opening his utility door, he tossed the water bottle back in and stood a moment with his back to the road.

The approaching vehicle slowed. *Oh no.* Kain rolled his eyes and his pulse rate quickened. *Bloody rubber neckers.* But the vehicle revved and continued around the next bend. Kain watched it disappear from sight. Possibly the scarred man from the servo. Kain's breathed deep in relief. At least he had the decency not to stop.

"Come on Burrows, let's get this done." He locked his utility and headed toward the area still cordoned off with police tape. No-one seemed to be around anymore, which was a relief.

Kain walked, stumbled, slid down the rough steep terrain, littered with trees, bushes, dead wood and rocks of all sizes. Trying hard to clear his mind of sickening thoughts, he focussed on getting to Grace's car.

He didn't know what he hoped to find, but a gut feeling that he would find *something* pushed and dragged him on. Gouges and scrapes on the ground indicated where the car had rolled. How it avoided the trees to get this far bewildered him. Several bushes were snapped off a little up from ground level. Kain's eyes peeled the ground and his feet struggled to keep his body upright.

A strange smell assaulted his nostrils. He looked ahead and winced. The burnt out, blackened shell of Grace's Toyota sedan, on its roof and up against a large tree trunk. Bushes, lower tree branches and surrounding grass were blackened from the explosion and consequent fire.

The sun at its summer hottest, Kain stopped and wiped the sweat from his brow. His stomach heaved again. Could he go any closer? With tears threatening, he ignored his brain's urge to baulk and pushed his body onwards, one foot after the other until he was only several metres from the wreck. He checked the number plate. The green paint had charred but definitely Grace's number.

The ripped passenger side door now leaned against the car. It couldn't have possibly landed like that. The forensics team would have put the door there, meaning it must have come off before the car stopped rolling. The odour of burnt paint and other chemicals stung his nostrils, watered his eyes and sickened his stomach even more. He pulled the front of his tee shirt up, covered his nose and took a deep breath. Should he look inside? He knew there was no way Grace's remains would have been left here . . . *or would they?*

"Oh Grace . . . " He forced himself to take the last few steps to the open passenger side door. "You died like this Sweetheart, and it was all my fault." Kain dropped to his knees and leant back on his haunches. His hurting heart shattered into splintered pieces. He looked skywards. "Grace . . . I love you *sooo* much. I'm so sorry."

Tears flowed. He bowed his head and buried his face in his hands. His body shuddered and trembled with loud sobs that echoed through the lonely bush. What was that sound? It sounded like crying. He stopped. Was a second person also crying out their broken heart? Kain held his breath and listened. Could it be Grace crying? Of course not. *You idiot.*

The bush, with its secrets, remained silent in the midday heat.

Kain stemmed the tears. Wiping his eyes with his shirt, he inhaled a deep breath, seeking courage. Then he peered into the car. Everything so charred and black it was difficult to recognise anything. He walked around to the driver's side. The window glass was scattered about on the ground near the car. That was odd. Grace loved to drive with her window down, especially out in the bush. Said she loved the fresh air on her face. If the glass was out here then the window must have been up. Kain put his hands on hips and walked back to the passenger side.

The police wouldn't think twice about that. They'd assume she'd have had the window up and the air con on, but it didn't make sense to him.

He peered inside the passenger side but saw nothing unusual or suspicious so looked into the back seat area – nothing but charred remnants, probably Grace's bags. He swallowed sour saliva to the hopelessness and dread that had pooled in his belly. No use searching the wreck any further. There seemed nothing left that wasn't now a pile of ash or unidentifiable material. Nothing left of his beautiful Grace.

His stomach chopped and churned like a boat caught in an ocean storm. He turned to head back up the steep slope to his vehicle. In the ground-burning heat, he looked about for a less steep route to ascend, and, to the right, found an easier path.

Kain trudged some of the way, but his head went from a dull ache to pounding and spinning. Heat stopped him and he sat on a large, smooth rock in the shade. He breathed in deep, wiped the never-ending sweat from his face and looked back at the wreck. *Oh Grace, I so wish things were different.* Blinking back more tears, he stood and pressed on, forcing his tired body up the steep terrain, getting away from the site as quick as possible.

Kain glanced ahead. His shoulders fell at the remaining distance still to go. *Come on Burrows, keep going.* Leaning a little forward and dropping his gaze to the ground, he stepped but his foot brushed something. Imagining a stick, he half-heartedly glanced down, but it wasn't a stick.

He picked up a lady's leather thong. Well-worn and brown with a white flower where the straps meet near the big toe. Grace didn't have a pair like this, he was sure of that. He glanced toward the road. It was too far down from the road to have been just chucked out of a car. He turned back at the burnt out wreck, thought for a moment and ran back to the blackened car.

Scraping about what would have been the roof, Kain picked up burnt bits and pieces. His hands soon blackened, but he didn't care and he did his best to ignore the smell, holding his breath intermittently. He held something up. "Aha, that's it."

He compared the thong to the item he found, a flat, charred solid piece, roughly the shape of a sole. It had to be the matching thong. Part of one strap was still there. They were not Grace's shoes. Someone else must have been in the car. Maybe she'd borrowed them from Sophie or a friend. No, she had plenty of shoes. She didn't need to borrow any. This means someone else may have been in the car.

Clutching the thongs, he scrambled back toward the road, his mind abuzz. *They said she was texting while driving – Grace wouldn't. The driver's window must have been open - Grace wouldn't. And these thongs are definitely not Grace's. If Grace wasn't killed in the car, where was she? Someone else must have been driving, but who? And why?*

Kain stopped to catch his breath, wipe his brow again and try to slow his mind of the question bombardment. He looked around – nothing but miles and miles of bush, some of it impenetrable. A car went by on the road above.

She might have got out somehow and been picked up by a car or, he looked at the bush again, she could be lost out there somewhere, hurt or . . .

What should he do first? Go to the police or go look for her. Joe. Yes, get Joe. He'd help.

For Christ's sake Kain, wake up. She's dead. Grace is dead. The police wouldn't make a stuff-up like that. He shook his head. In his brain, he knew she was gone, but his heart told him otherwise. He needed absolute proof, he was going to dig and dig until he uncovered what really happened during and after the accident. And, if Grace were still alive, he would find her.

CHAPTER 17

S eth relocked his gate and drove his driveway, unable to contain his grin spreading from east to west. Grace would be so happy with the things he'd bought her. *Yeah, that's if she's still there. Why would a beautiful, 'normal' girl like her want to stay with you?* Seth shook the nagging inner voice from his head. Always so negative. Always trying to bring him down. Always blocking anything positive in his life.

His house came into view and he homed in on the door. It was shut which meant she was still there. *Idiot, she could have closed it behind her on the way out.* "Please be here, Grace." He licked his dry lips, swallowed and pulled up near the front steps.

He switched off the ignition and gathered up the plastic shopping bags from the passenger seat. He hesitated and sucked in a long breath, his thumping heart working overtime. He wished he could remove the vice gripping his chest.

"One way or the other, this is it." He opened his door, jumped out, and ascended the stairs two at a time. Trying to keep his footsteps light, he crossed the verandah and clasped the door handle with his gloved, empty hand. Nausea rolled in his stomach, his knees weakened. He turned the door handle and pushed it open.

All was dead quiet. *Told you she'd do a runner.* "Grace," he called, but not too loud in fear of waking her if she was asleep. He scanned the kitchen. On the sink, an empty glass that wasn't there when he'd left. Could mean she's still here. He smiled, but the nagging voice returned. *Well, of course she would have had a big drink before she left.* His smile disappeared.

He placed the shopping bags on the table and walked through the lounge room. The door to Grace's room was shut. He slowly opened it, attempting to remain quiet. His thumping heart performed cartwheels at top pace. Never in his life, that he could remember, had he wanted something so much. *Please be here, Grace.*

There she was, asleep on the bed. The huge rock in his gut disappeared. He expelled the deep breath he'd been holding.

She looked so beautiful and peaceful lying there with her long reddish hair spread on the pillow, fine strands of it dancing and moving from the whirring fan above. His hand itched to reach out and stroke her cheek, but he held it back. "Thank you," he whispered. A grin relaxed his face and slowed his overworked heart. Her eyelids fluttered and a low moan escaped her slightly parted lips.

"Seth?" She opened her eyes wide, blinked several times and yawned. "You're back."

"Of course I came back." He smiled. "Are you all right?"

"Mmm, I think so." Grace swung her bare feet to the floor and sat on the edge of the bed. "What time is it?"

He shrugged. "Don't know, but my belly thinks it's dinner time."

"Is it that late? I must have been asleep all day." Grace looked toward the open window. "Only looks like the middle of the day or there abouts."

"It is. Dinner time. Are you hungry?"

"That's weird." She looked at him with a grin.

"What is?"

"Hearing the term 'dinner time' for lunch. Mum and dad say that and my brother Steve did too. It's 'dinner' in the day and 'tea' at night time at my parents' place."

"Don't you say dinner and tea?"

Grace laughed. "Nah, I guess the country girl went out of me a bit when I was at uni. I call them lunch and dinner . . . well most of the time. Sometimes the old ways still slip out though, especially when I'm around mum and dad".

"Do you want a hand to the kitchen?" He stepped closer and held out his elbow for her to take hold. "What did you study at uni?"

She got herself to her feet and waved his elbow away. "No thanks. I feel pretty good at the moment. My shoulder has stopped aching and my back doesn't feel too bad. I'll be right. I need to go to the loo and bathroom anyway. Oh, I'm a teacher."

He nodded, impressed, but unsure what to say about her profession. He didn't know anything of his former education or if he had been a 'somebody' or just a 'nobody'. Maybe it was best not to know. "Righto then, I'll go and get the rest of the stuff out of the ute." He strode off to bring the remaining shopping inside. "Yes." He raised his clenched fist into the air and descended the stairs. "She didn't run off . . . thank you Grace. Thank you."

He re-entered the kitchen with bags full of groceries.

Grace walked in from the lounge. She spotted the numerous bags on the table and her eyes widened. "Wow."

"The ones on the table are for you and these are the groceries." He heaved his load up on to the bench, removed his hat and dropped it on the floor beside the door. "Phew, hot out there again." He wiped his forehead with his long shirt sleeve. "Looks like another storm might be brewing."

"Well, I'm glad I'm not out in this one." Grace peered into one of the bags on the table.

"Oh, I nearly forgot." He rushed out the door and down the steps. Back in the kitchen in no time, with one arm behind his back. "I got these too . . . for you, Grace." He brought out the huge bunch of coloured roses.

Grace's face changed into a frown. She wasn't happy.

Uh oh, think I might have been a bit forward. "Just wanted to brighten the old place up a bit. It's not really a place for a lady, especially a lady as . . . like you." The unscarred areas of his face flushed hot. "If you don't like roses, I'll put them on the verandah. Or chuck them." He shrugged and turned away, not wanting her to see his hurt.

"I do love roses. I really do." Her frown disappeared. "I just wasn't expecting you to get so many things for me and roses too. Mum has lots of roses growing in her garden at home. I'll repay you for all this when I go home and can get some money. You got a vase?"

When I go home. Hearing those words, his shoulders sank, dropping like a pulley that had let go. Grace going anywhere was not in his hopes and dreams. Loneliness engulfed him again, shrouding him in a heavy cloak of hurt. He was no longer hungry. Loneliness. His need for a friend was much greater than his need for food. For several years, food, apart from the local wildlife, had been his only friend.

"No I don't think I have any vases." He opened the sink cupboard and took out an empty bottle. "This'll do." He filled it from the sink tap, put the roses in and placed them on the table.

"I'm not going anywhere yet." Grace shrugged then grimaced. "Ow, that shoulder is sorer than I thought. Seth, did you stop by the crash scene and try and find my bag or something?" She looked about, as if hoping to spot her shoulder bag.

Seth did drive by the scene on his way home. A car was just driving away and a man, possibly the one who'd witnessed the altercation at the service station, was there. He hadn't seen his face, but it seemed like the same bloke. Seth hadn't been comfortable with the idea of stopping for a look. "Ah, no, Grace, sorry. There were some people about so I thought I'd better not."

"Bugger. I'll have to cancel all my cards and things. Some looter has probably picked it up, or maybe the police have it." Graced took out items from the bags. "Thank you so much for getting these things for me." She dropped the white, rubber thongs to the floor and stepped into them. "Perfect."

He grabbed scissors from one of the kitchen drawers and bent beside her to cut the elastic holding the thongs together. "Hold still." He stood up, towering over her. "There you go. You can walk in them now."

"Thanks." Even though her eyes were sad, she smiled *that* smile and his heart somersaulted once, then again.

How he would love to hold her in his arms. He knew she was hurting over the break-up with Kain. She needed a hug, but did he dare offer one? "Grace . . ."

Grace stopped what she was doing and looked at him. "What is it, Seth?"

No, he didn't have the nerve to suggest a hug. "Um, what would you like to eat? I have plenty of salads and I got some chicken and some fish."

"Fish and salad sounds good. Wow, thank you again for buying this stuff for me. You even got me clothes?" Her eyes glistened.

Oh no. "What's wrong?" He hoped he hadn't done the wrong thing.

"It's just this top." She held up a white, sleeveless tee shirt with a picture of a dolphin on the front. "Kain bought me one like this last Christmas, after he'd seen me admiring it in the shop. So it reminds me of him, which makes me sad . . . but angry too. Angry that he just dumped me for no good reason. I hate him at the moment." Her sad eyes changed to eyes full of anger. "I hope I *never* see him again." She laid the top on the table. "But I do love the top and I will wear it. It's funny how you picked out one that I loved so much. If anything it will remind me not to let Kain or any other man, into my heart again."

"You're just angry now, but you won't be forever." He put several grocery items in the fridge, got a frying pan from the cupboard beneath the bench and put it on the stove. "I'll get this fish on."

"I'll bet that arsehole is having a wild old time, going out with his single mates and . . . and has probably already found someone else." Tears welled in her eyes and she tried to wipe them away, but they kept flowing. "Bastard."

He moved the tissue box from atop the fridge to the table in front of Grace. "You're too good for him, Grace."

"I'm nobody special." She pulled out a tissue, wiped her eyes and blew her nose. "I loved him very much, but . . . " She sighed deep and long. "Obviously that wasn't enough. Well, he can just go to hell for all I care." She picked up the scissors Seth had left on the table and cut tags off the new clothes he'd bought for her. "Can I throw these in the wash please?" She frowned and looked around. "Where is your laundry?"

"Downstairs. Under the house. I'll take them down now for you." He gathered them up and headed out the front door with a happy stride. Seems like he hadn't upset her at all. Hopefully, she'll forget about calling the bank and, especially, her parents.

With the new clothes in the machine, he returned to the kitchen and put the fish in the pan. Grace had put most of the groceries away and had two plates and cutlery on the table.

"Don't overdo it, Grace. You're supposed to be taking it easy." But it felt good to have her here and at ease. It was a feeling he couldn't describe. He'd never known it before. *Maybe we'll become a normal couple. Even a family one day. Idiot.* Stupid to get ahead of himself. He hit his forehead with the heel of his hand. There's so much happening in his life and most of it will be pure hell.

"It's all right. I feel better when I'm doing something. For starters, it takes my mind off Kain. It also makes me feel good that I'm doing something for you. I haven't forgotten you saved my life out there yesterday. Those dogs would've killed me." She shuddered and paled. "Wouldn't they?"

Seth nodded. "Yep, they would have. Those cross-breeds will kill anything for food. Just so glad I was there." Grace had no idea just *how* glad he was to have found her.

"That was so scary. I really thought I was going to die, and in such a horrible way." She began to cry. Huge tears rolled down her cheeks to trembling lips.

Seth dropped the tongs he'd just used to turn the fish, put his long arms around Grace and held her tight. Her slim body trembled against him with the increasing sobs. "You need to cry. You've been through hell, so let it out." Seth's shirt dampened with her warm tears. "I've got a broad chest. Plenty of room there. Cry as much as you need to. You're safe now." He stroked her head and hair with one hand and the other held her against his body.

His heart and head wanted to protect her, but his body responded in a way he hadn't felt or known before, that he could remember. He stepped back and held Grace by her elbows. *I hope she didn't feel what happened. You idiot, you'll scare her away now, for sure.* "I'm . . . I'm sorry, Grace." His face burned hot. He let her go and turned the stove off under the fish. He couldn't bring himself to look at her. He filled the kettle and turned it on, not knowing how to handle the incident.

"What are you sorry for? You were just comforting me. Did I do something to you?"

You certainly did. "Um . . . I shouldn't have grabbed you like that. I hope you weren't scared."

"Why would I be scared? I know now you won't hurt me." She grabbed another tissue and wiped her eyes. "I do feel a bit better for having that cry."

"That's good." He nodded. "I just thought . . . I thought you might be scared of me being so close to you when I look like I do. Lots of people get scared when they see me. They think I'm some sort of ugly monster. I don't know how you can bear to look at me, Grace. I hate seeing me. Hell, I hate *being* me." He swallowed back tears.

"Well I don't. When I look at you I see a beautiful and kind heart and that's more important than what's on the outside."

He looked at her and wanted to tell her how much those words meant, but the shock of hearing himself being described as beautiful and kind left him speechless. His heart swelled, his eyes swam with tears, but his tongue remained silent.

Grace laughed a happy, melodious laugh. "You look stunned. Don't be so hard on yourself, Seth. You'd make some lucky woman a great husband. You can cook, you're clean and tidy and you're very thoughtful and kind. Is there . . . a woman in your life?" Grace's cheery face fell. "I'm sorry, I don't mean to pry."

Again his shoulders slumped. Her words that had been so uplifting, now brought him crashing down to reality. *She* was in his life now. He only wanted to be with *her*. "Hmph. You're kidding. Nobody will even look at me in the street, let alone give me the time of day. You wouldn't have either if I'd just sent you off to the hospital."

"Probably. But now that I've got to know you I can see how much you have to offer someone. That's why you wouldn't call me an ambulance, isn't it? You're so lonely." She looked sad. Or was it pity in those pretty green eyes?

He nodded then put the fish and salad on to the plates, making unnecessary noise to avoid furthering this conversation. He and Grace were far from being on the same level . . . yet.

Seth sat at the table and swallowed his first mouthful. "Hmm, this tastes good."

"Sure does. Seth, I really want to ring mum and let her know I'm all right. If the police know about the accident then everyone will be worried and they'll be searching for me and I really should ring the bank. Can I use your phone after lunch. *Please?*"

Seth searched for the right words with which to respond. Everyone thinks Grace is dead, so they won't be searching for her and her things would have been destroyed when the car exploded so there was no need to call the bank. Could he trust her enough to admit all that and expect her to still want to stay? He couldn't see her staying.

If she called her mother then wouldn't her mother tell Kain? But, by the sounds of it, Kain probably wouldn't care. Seth ate another mouthful and put his cutlery down. "Grace there's something you need to know. I don't know how you'll take it, but I hope you understand why I didn't tell you sooner." His mobile buzzed and vibrated in his pocket. "Oh, sorry."

He pulled the phone out and looked at the screen. Oh no. Not right now. "I'd better take this." He got up and went out to the verandah, shutting the door behind him. "Yes Scott."

"Seth, come over tae my place noo. We need tae go over these plans for the job, plus ah want you tae get to know the horse you'll be riding."

"Ok, I'll be over soon."

"Nae, you'll come over right now."

The phone went silent. Scott had hung up. He was as unpredictable as this sub-tropical Queensland weather.

"Damn." He walked back inside.

"Is everything okay? You look worried." A deep crease marked Grace's forehead. She was also worried.

"I have to go out. I'll be back later though. I'll peg your new clothes on the line before I leave."

"But you haven't finished your lunch and you said you wanted to tell me something."

He shook his head and scratched his bearded chin with his gloved hand. How he hated being Scott's servant. "I'm sorry Grace, but it'll have to wait. Will you be all right here? You won't run away will you?" He pleaded to her with his eyes.

"I'll be here. I have plenty of reading material now." She nodded toward the new magazines at the end of the table.

"Okay, see you later." He turned to walk out the door, but took one more look at Grace, taking in her soft, natural beauty, in case it would be the last time he saw her. He would never forget her.

CHAPTER 18

K ain's mind buzzed during the drive back to Anchor Bay. So many thoughts swarming through his brain with so few making any sense.

The thongs he'd found, one good and one charred, sat on his passenger seat. They were not Grace's. But what does that, and the other things that don't add up, mean? The amount of shattered glass spread on the ground around the driver's side indicated the window was up, or possibly both windows. He knew Grace hated driving with the windows up and the idea she was texting while driving . . . no way in hell. Grace just wouldn't.

And Linda had told him the police found Grace's shoulder bag with her purse and everything in it, along with her phone. Who should he talk to first? The police? His gut instinct told him they wouldn't believe his findings or his opinion. He couldn't blame them, with all the circumstantial evidence showing Grace was driving.

Linda? He wished he could talk to her, but that would be impossible if Bruce was home. Bruce's cruel words cut deep into his heart and soul. He fought back tears and flicked his head to banish the memories of the scathing accusations.

That left Joe, his best mate. Kain sighed. Joe probably wouldn't take him seriously. Joe would tell him he was grasping at straws or something like that. But he had to talk to someone.

Kain pulled over to the side of the road, switched off the motor, took out his phone and called Linda's mobile. It was worth the risk, despite Bruce's hatred for him. He didn't dare ring the home phone in case Bruce answered.

Linda's phone rang . . . and rang. He almost hung up, partially disappointed because he felt confident she would listen, but also partly relieved that any possible negative confrontation would be avoided.

Linda answered, a barely audible, "Hello".

"Linda, it's . . . it's Kain." He held his breath, waiting to determine Linda's attitude. His empty stomach filled with a bucket of dread.

"Oh. Hello." It was flat and emotionless, not what he was hoping or expecting, after the way she'd seemed to pity him yesterday and signal that she'd call him.

"I, umm, I wondered if I could see you sometime today." The bucket of dread churned.

"What about? Bruce is home and he's in a bad state. It wouldn't be a good idea for you to come here." Her voice no longer carried the pitying tone.

"I was wondering if you've picked up Grace's belongings from the police station yet."

"Ye-s, early this morning." She sobbed.

"I'm sorry to bother you, but could I please see her bag?" Tears prickled, but he pressed on. He no longer cared who heard or saw him cry. "I also wanted to show you something I found at the crash site."

"You've been up there? Kain, how could you? You have no right. After *everything,* you go snooping around where she was *killed?*" She almost sounded like Bruce. This was not what he'd counted on from Grace's mum.

"Linda, I . . . had to, for my own peace of mind. I thought you understood yesterday. I didn't think I had a choice in breaking it off with Grace. I loved her so much. Still do." The warm tears spilled over his eyelids and down his cheeks.

"There's nothing in her bag concerning you. The only thing about you is her phone was open and halfway through a message to *you.*" The anger in her words streamed through the airwaves to his ears and heart.

He tried to ignore the blatant blame in her tone. "Well, can you please tell me what the message said? *Please*, Linda." It was bad enough that Grace's father hated him and now he sensed that her mother also despised his existence. Bruce must have really filled her head with crap since yesterday, but he wasn't prepared for a no. "I have the right to know that much. I'll ask the police if you won't tell me."

"It just said she needed to get away – from you no doubt. It also said she'd taken two weeks leave from work."

"So you don't know where she was going at all?"

"No Kain. All we do know is that she's never coming back." She moaned. A painful, lonely, agonising moan. "Our beautiful girl is never coming back and now we only have one child left. You have no idea how that feels Kain, do you?

What could he say? "No . . . I don't. I'm so sorry, Linda." He felt a sabre pierce his heart. Not just hurting for him losing Grace but also for a mother losing her adored children.

"I have to go, Bruce needs me. We're very busy at the moment. Goodbye Kain." The line went dead.

"Linda wait . . ." His shoulders fell, pushing out a sigh of defeat. He placed his phone back in its holder. He *really* wanted to show her the thongs. Then again, she probably wouldn't know all of Grace's shoes, given she'd been living with him for a long time.

Regardless of whether Linda recognised the thongs or not wouldn't prove a thing. Maybe it was *him* that wasn't very observant when it came to Grace's shoes. After all, she had heaps of them piled up in the bottom of her wardrobe. She could have bought them ages ago, been wearing them and his dopey eyes hadn't even noticed.

He picked up the good thong and scanned every square millimetre, top and bottom and found a number - seven. Size seven. His mind ticked over. Grace bought a couple of pairs of shoes not long back. She'd said she was so glad they had one pair left in size eight as the sevens were too small. She'd even mentioned the size eights where a tiny bit tight, but there were no size nines. No way would she wear a size seven.

He could go back to the house and compare sizes with her other shoes. If there were no other seven's then this could be a breakthrough. He started the vehicle and roared off toward the home he and Grace had shared.

His phone rang. Having forgotten to plug in the hands-free, he pulled over and answered, hoping to hear Linda telling him it was safe to come over, but it was Joe.

"Hey mate, are you okay?"

"Hey Joe, yeah . . . no, not really. What are you up to at the moment?"

"Nothin' much. I got out of bed and you were gone. I was a bit worried. Have you been up to the range yet?"

"Yep and I want to talk to you, but can you come around to our place now? Some weird things have happened.""Your place? You mean your parents or where you and Grace lived?""That's the one, see you in ten." Kain ended the call and headed to the house he and Grace had called home. The home they'd lived in for three happy, beautiful years.

It seemed to take ages to cover the several kilometres to the house. Every traffic light was red, and other traffic appeared to all be in go-slow mode. "Come on," urged Kain, crawling along behind a car towing a caravan. Luckily it turned off and he soon pulled into his driveway.

He jumped out of his utility just as Joe pulled in behind him in his blue, duel-cab ute. Kain clasped the thongs and waited for Joe to get out and walk over. And, as he expected, Joe's face oozed questions and one big frown.

"Watcha got there?" Joe nodded toward Kain's hand.

"I found these at the crash site. This one," he held up the good one, "was on the ground about thirty metres from the car and this one", he held up the charred sandal, "was in the car".

Joe shrugged. "Um . . . so? Are they even a pair?"

"I knew you'd ask dumb questions, mate. Yes they are. I checked."

"Well, they'd be Grace's wouldn't they?" Joe tilted his head to one side and raised his eyebrows. "Kain, you seem excited about something, but I don't get it." He shrugged again, raised his open hands in the air and placed them on his hips.

"Mate, when I was up there, I found that the driver's side window must have been up for the amount of glass that was shattered and spread all around near that side of the car."

"So?" Joe looked totally blank.

Kain resisted the overwhelming urge to grab and shake him. "Joe, Grace hated driving with the windows up, especially out in the bush and there's no way she would have been texting while she drove. Just no way. And then I find these shoes. Mate, they are *not* Graces, I'm sure of it." The words spilled out faster and faster. "I've never seen them before and they are too small for her anyway. Come inside, I'm going to match them up for the size against her other shoes. If they are too small, then . . ." He took a deep breath and smiled. A smile loaded with hope. A smile that needed no words.

"Then what?"

"Then . . . it could all mean that Grace wasn't driving her car. Don't ask me who was or why." Kain shrugged. "But, Joe, don't you get it now?" He couldn't resist a grin and expected the same from Joe. Joe's face remained blank but with eyes wide.

"She could still be alive. Come on." Kain strode up the several front steps, over the patio and slotted his key in the front door. He stopped. The smile vanished. His heart began an Olympic sprint, but an alarm wailed in his head. It was not going to be easy, seeing all Grace's things. With sweaty palms and a deep breath he opened the door, slow at first. "What the . . . ?"

Things were out of place. He was entering an unknown zone. This was more than just strange. Kain went to the bedroom he and Grace shared. "What the fuck . . .?"

Joe stopped right beside him. "What's wrong?"

"Grace's stuff is all gone." He pointed to one wardrobe standing open and empty. "Her shoes were all at the bottom of that." Going to her bedside table, he yanked open the three drawers, one after the other. "What? They're all empty. This is *bullshit!*"

"Maybe she moved her stuff to her parents before she went away."

"She told me she would stay here. Maybe she did. No, I don't think so. I'll check the other rooms." Kain headed to the bathroom, stopping dead in his tracks. The blood drained from his face and heart, his knees weakened and the hair on the back of his neck rose and tingled. "Joe, come here."

Joe entered the small room behind Kain. "What the . . .?"

Kain own horrified gaze remained frozen on the mirror.

Scrawled in dark lipstick across the glass were the scornful words, 'YOU KILLED HER. YOU LOSE. YOU GET NOTHING!'

CHAPTER 19

Grace put down the magazine she'd been reading while lying on the bed, and gazed about the stark room. Her mind wandered over the events of the past two days - so frightening, but at the same time, so surreal.

It all seemed like a dream. This sort of thing doesn't happen in real life. The physical pain reminded her that it was real. Her back injury from the flying tree branch still niggled. The cut near her temple hurt if she touched it or frowned hard. Her shoulder pain only bothered her if she tried to lift or use her arm. At this precise moment the pain was minimal, except in her heart and soul. Etched so deep in every speck of her body and mind, it would never subside.

Kain. She could curse and call him every despicable name she could think of, but as much as she tried and *wanted to*, she couldn't hate him. She'd adored him for years but, as the memories snuck out of her eyes and flowed down her cheeks, she just couldn't understand his reasoning for the break-up. It was completely out of character for him, unless . . . she didn't really know him as well as she thought.

The thought of living the rest of her life without him still too much to contemplate yet, even though he'd made it perfectly clear their relationship was finished. Well bugger him. She'd stay out here in the bush for two weeks and let him wonder what happened to her. Ha. Who was she kidding? He won't be wondering about her at all. She must let her mum and dad know that she's okay, though. She'd ask Seth again to use his phone when he returned.

"You can get stuffed, Kain Burrows." Saying it aloud helped convince herself she needed to stay strong and not allow him or his memory to get to her. "I just *won't* let myself be upset about you anymore." She gave a determined nod and sat up on the side of the bed, needing something to take her mind off Kain.

It hadn't been long since Seth had left. She had no idea where he went or how long he'd be. Grace stood and walked to the hallway. The house was quiet except for the occasional creaking of the tin roof in the hot Queensland sun. No bird sounds came from the surrounding bush, but a deep, distant rumble signalled an approaching storm. It stirred memories of being caught in the storm and the wild dogs, sending an ice cube down her spine and prickling out to her fingertips. But she felt safe here in Seth's house and she felt safe with Seth.

Seth. She stared at nothing, picturing his face. He certainly was an enigma, someone with an amazing and compelling story. Grace walked to the door and looked out across the verandah - no sign of him yet. She made a decision, but her gut feeling was against it. Should she or not? *Stuff it, I will.*

She turned and walked down the hallway until she came to, what she assumed was, his bedroom door. With her heart cranking into top gear and feeling like a naughty child, she gripped the round knob and turned. The door opened into the darkened room. The warm stuffiness and the motionless, thick curtains indicated the window was closed.

Just as she expected, the room was plain and bare but for the basics – a double bed, with one bedside table, a dutchess and a large, brown wardrobe similar to the one in her room. The bed neatly made, which didn't surprise Grace. Seth was a clean and tidy person. Nothing but small clock sat on the bedside table. She approached the bed. The clock's loud ticking matched the beat of her heart. *Should I?* She chewed on her bottom lip, pondering. *He trusts you, Grace. You shouldn't be poking around in his personal things.*

Ignoring her insistent conscious, she bent forward and dragged open the top drawer beside the bed. Underwear. Jocks and socks all folded and neat. Jocks on one said, socks on the other. She smiled. It was unusual for a man to be so fastidious about underwear of all things. Kain just tossed his in the drawer and closed it, so did she for that matter, but her father and brother Steve were neat freaks when it came to their clothes storage.

She closed that drawer and opened the one below - nothing but a few old newspapers. She went on to the third and final drawer. It rattled as she pulled it open. "What the . . .?"

Grace stood upright, pulled one curtain to the side, letting in some light, and bent to peer in the drawer again. She didn't dare sit on the bed for fear he'd know she'd been there.

Bullets of various types and sizes, ranging from the smallest .22 up to shotgun cartridges covered the bottom of the drawer. Her jaw slackened and she tensed. It wasn't what she expected to find, but then again, he'd proved he was an excellent marksman and no-one would become that competent without practise. *So . . . where are the guns?*

Grace closed the drawer and looked at the wardrobe. She took a deep breath before glancing out the window. She could just see part of the driveway where it turned into the house yard. Thankfully, still no sign of Seth. Poking through Seth's personal belongings was wrong, so very wrong, and it nagged at Grace. On the other hand, it did help her get to know him better.

She pulled the wardrobe door open before her conscious had time to get the better of her. Several long sleeved shirts of various colours hung on hangers while a few pairs of denim jeans lie folded at the bottom, alongside some newish work boots. She opened the other door, sucked in her breath and froze. Guns stood upright in the corner of the wardrobe. Even though she was looking for guns, seeing them tensed her.

She leant forward for a better look in the darkened space and counted four guns. "I bet none of them are registered." She quickly closed both wardrobe doors. It didn't matter and the guns weren't hurting anyone. One of them saved her life. Of course. Grace scolded herself for being so self-righteous.

Seth would never purposely hurt anyone with them. It had to be her father's ideals and beliefs instilled in her at an early age, coming to the forefront. Everything had to be done correctly and by the book, according to Bruce. He couldn't bend any rules for anyone at any time. "You're so damned pig-headed at times Dad, but I still love you," She smiled at the thought of one of his comforting hugs.

There wasn't much else to see in Seth's bedroom. Grace checked to ensure nothing remained out of place, reclosed the thick curtain and left the room. Part of her glad she hadn't found anything suspicious or odd, but part of her still curious and determined to find *something, somewhere* in the house on this mysterious man.

The closed door opposite Seth's bedroom was too intriguing for Grace to ignore. She grasped the handle and turned but nothing happened. The door was locked. *Damn.* Why would he lock this room? Grace groaned. She'd thought poking about in Seth's house would be easy. She leaned down, closed one eye and looked through the keyhole with the other. Of course she saw nothing but blackness. Now what?

The box! She remembered the small wooden box in one of the bathroom drawers. That *has* to contain something of interest. Forgetting the locked room, she headed to the bathroom and pulled that particular drawer open. Half expecting to find it gone, she smiled when it remained exactly the way she'd left it previously. Grace lifted it out of the drawer.

Something was different, *very* different. The box now much lighter then when she'd first found it. She shook the box but heard no sound, so went to her room and sat on the bed, placing the box beside her.

A snapping sound outside her window jolted her and her heart thudded fast and furious. Maybe Seth had fooled her and had only driven up the road a short distance before walking back to spy on her.

She really needed to stop being so paranoid, but walked to the window to check. Looking through the bars at the surrounding bush she saw nothing out of the ordinary but a rustling sound below dropped her gaze. A breath gushed from her lungs with a laugh. Two huge goannas were fighting, or mating. She soon became mesmerised by the long, dark bodies, writhing and rolling about on the grass and small twigs. The goanna's stopped and looked up at her for several seconds before one emitted a short hiss. Slimy saliva dripped from gaping jaws. Grace jumped back from the window, back to reality and the mysterious box sitting on the bed. The goannas could get back to their business.

She sat back beside the box and took hold of the padlock. Her shoulders drooped. "If only I could get this open." The lock moved a little while the loop remained through the latch. She jerked up straight. Wow. It wasn't locked. Grace sucked in a sharp breath before lifting the padlock away from the latch. Seth must have been at the box and took out whatever it was that had weighed it down. A pistol? Grace shuddered. Why would he need a gun? Just *what* was he doing?

Her heart pummelling her rib cage, Grace opened the lid of the box and peered inside. It was empty except for an old envelope. She reached in with a trembling hand and brought it out. Nothing was written on the front so she opened it. Inside was a photo, or at least a piece of a photo.

Taking the photo out, Grace frowned. The top half and one side was torn away, but it seemed like it was of two children, possibly boys, going by their boots and clothes. The photo was discoloured as if it had been exposed to heat or something similar. It was difficult to determine what colours were meant to be in the picture, but the boys held hands and perhaps that was a dog just behind one of the boy's legs. The state of the photo and its possible age made identification near impossible. Seemed like a flower bed to the left of the boys. She smiled. That flower bed looked as neat as her mother's garden beds. Obviously there was another fanatical gardener somewhere too. Or had been.

She focussed her attention back on the two boys and her smile disappeared. Who were they and what did they have to do with Seth? Was one of them Seth? If so, who was the other one? Why was the top half of the picture torn away? She looked in the envelope for answers but it was empty.

She looked in box for the rest of the photo, not expecting to be lucky and she wasn't disappointed. The box, bare. *Bugger.* She turned the photo over. Some writing on the back, albeit smudged and almost illegible. Bringing the photo closer, Grace studied the words.

Being a school teacher, she was used to seeing all kinds and levels of handwriting but this tested her. She could read "*Jon and*" but the next name must be on the missing side. Below those words, the number "19", most likely the year it was taken, with the rest of the number also being on the missing piece.

So . . . were they brothers? Is one of them Seth or, God forbid, are they Seth's children? Was he old enough to have had children before the year 2000? She shook her head. This made no sense at all. She had no idea how old Seth was, going by his face. The acid scars so bad there were no wrinkles and with his beard . . . She shrugged her good shoulder. Studying the photo up close again, the boys seemed like twins - similar in size and their clothes matched.

Whether they were Seth's children or one of them was actually him, he deserved help finding his family. Someone, somewhere must be missing him and probably just assume he's dead. A mother and father, siblings or even a wife and children - Seth must belong to someone and he should be with them. Grace stuffed the picture back in the envelope and the box before returning it to the bathroom drawer, ensuring the lock remained exactly the wy she'd found it.

She headed to the kitchen to make a cup of tea and await Seth's return. Her mind swam with questions and possibilities surrounding the two boys, but she had to think of questions that wouldn't alert him to her having seen the picture. That may not be easy, but she owed it to Seth to help him.

Hell, she owed him her *life*.

CHAPTER 20

Seth leaned on the wooden, stockyard rails and watched an unfamiliar man saddle up the huge, black horse Scott had ordered him to ride during the cattle heist.

The niggly, sick feeling that had increased in the pit of his stomach while driving to Scott's place wouldn't subside. Something told him this job was a terrible idea, but, if he refused, Scott would probably shoot him and dump his useless body out in the bush. Scavenging wild dogs would tear him to pieces. Grace came close to dying that way. His body convulsed and he shook his head to clear the sickening images. Two seconds later thunder rumbled overhead. Definitely an ominous sign.

"Seth. How's things?"

Seth spun around. "Jimmy. Yeah all right. You? Haven't seen you for a while."

Jimmy shrugged and swiped at the annoying bush flies about his face. "Can't complain I s'pose. I've been down south doing a few things. Whatcha think of this beast?" He leaned on the rail beside Seth and nodded toward the horse snorting and prancing about as the man struggled to tighten the girth belt beneath its belly. "He's a beauty, hey?

Scott tells me he's for you to ride on the job. You'll have your work cut out for you. I hear he's one mean animal."

"You mean the horse or Scott?" Seth looked at Jimmy and couldn't help a grin. He rarely found *anything* to grin or smile about but Grace's presence in his, otherwise gloomy, life lightened his mood, giving him a valid reason to smile.

Jimmy laughed and scratched his chin.

Was Jimmy being sarcastic or did he feel embarrassed? Seth waited for him to continue.

Jimmy's face turned serious again. "Well, I meant the horse, but take it whichever way you like."

Seth looked about. "Where is Scott? He asked me to meet him here."

"He had to take off. Had a call from someone telling him the cops got a reported sighting of him in this area, so gone underground for a bit."

Hmph. I'd like to put him underground. Six feet under! "Now what?" Seth hoped the job would be put on hold, or better still, cancelled altogether. All he wanted to do was spend time with Grace.

"We go ahead as planned. Scott gave me details and we can work out when, where and how we go in. I know that property like the back of my hand and the arrogant arsehole who owns it, from the time I was there. It won't be too hard." Jimmy removed his old, black cap, wiped his sweaty forehead and scratched his ginger beard again. "Geez, I hate this beard in hot weather. How do you go with yours? It's even longer than mine."

Seth looked at Jimmy and shrugged. "I'm used to it. Sounds like you haven't had yours long. It'll settle down. Why even bother if you hate it so much?" His beard was an attempt to cover his scarred face, but Jimmy's skinny, fair face was normal. How he envied 'normal'.

"I like to change my appearance every now and then." He rolled his green eyes. "It helps when you work for Scott. Bit late now to go back to the old, boring life. I like living on the edge, you know, the adrenaline rushes. Nothing like 'em, hey?"

"Whatever you reckon, Jimmy. I could certainly do without 'em these days."

"What? You goin' soft? Geez, mate, since I left my old life a few years ago and met Scott, I haven't looked back. But I have to stay one step ahead all the time. After we do this job I'll shave the beard and my head too." He took his hat off and ran his fingers through his short, ginger hair.

"Don't you miss your old life?" Seth didn't know what it was like to know an *old life*. To *have* an old life.

"Nup. Well, I do miss some people. *Some* of my family, but . . . " He shrugged, upturned his mouth, and stared off into the nothing.

"Is Jimmy even your real name?"

Jimmy's gaze shot back to Seth. He stared a moment, in deep thought. "No. Yes. It is now. No point living in the past. I aint goin' back." He jerked his head to the side. "It's best forgotten."

Seth nodded and opened his mouth to speak but before the first word had formed, it closed again.

The massive horse and it's equally large, dark shadow loomed closer. The stranger held the leather reins in one hand. His knuckles bared white, his forearm muscles tensed tight. The horse raised his head high, his dark eyes watchful, wary, almost angry.

He allowed himself to be led behind the man, as if this were part of some game the horse had yet to tire of. His jet black, but shiny, hooves sank into the dusty dirt littered with dry cow manure and the odd scraggly weed, leaving an impression with every step.

Another rumble from the heavens. The horse trembled a moment and pricked his ears forward.

"He must be scared of the thunder." Seth reached through the rails to pat its nose. Its ears flicked and flattened back. Large nostrils flared and twitched. A loud snort sent out a spray of watery snot and its head jerked high. Seth never made contact. He looked deep into the gelding's eyes. Black as coal. Cold, hard and unforgiving as steel. Jimmy's description of 'mean' seemed way below the horse's true nature. This horse looked meaner than anything or anyone Seth had ever seen . . . except for Scott.

"Which one of you is Seth?" The tall man leading the horse looked from Jimmy to Seth.

Seth raised his gloved hand and one finger. "Me."

"C'mon then. Come in here and give him a go. Scott wants you to get used to him before the job." The man fished a loose cigarette from his top pocket, put it in his mouth, took out a lighter from the same pocket and lit the smoke.

The horse raised its head and opened its mouth. A deep, back-tingling scream pierced the humid afternoon air. The reins were almost yanked from the man's hand. The horse reared high on his strong hind feet, poring at the air with his shod, front hooves, potential weapons of death.

"Whoa." The man shouted. The cigarette and lighter dropped to the ground. He grabbed hold of the reins with both hands, pulled hard and ducked to the side of the descending hooves. "Settle down now, boy." It was a command, not a suggestion. This bloke wasn't scared of the monster.

The thunderous hooves hit the ground, sending up dust. The horse screamed again, with mouth agape, the whites of his eyes glowing and teeth bared. This animal meant business. The back feet shot out and upwards, scattering small sods of dirt metres through the air behind.

"Holy hell." Jimmy stepped back from the rail. "Glad he's yours."

Seth continued leaning on the rail, studying the horse and his movements. He had to learn everything about him. This huge, black thrashing machine and he were going to have to become as one if they were to pull off Scott's job. God help them both if they didn't. Both man and beast were indispensable to Scott.

"Come on, you bastard, settle down." The horse reared up on his back legs again. The man pulled harder in the reins, every muscle and sinew in his tanned forearm straining.

The gelding jerked his head, trying to lose the restraints that held it tight, but the man refused to let go of the long reins. Muscles moved and strained in his strong arms as he dug his booted heels in the dirt. Sweat glistened on his reddening face. One hoof clipped the side of the man's head. He grunted loud and jumped to one side. Bright red blood mixed with his sweat. His old, battered hat fell to the ground. The hooves rose again and pounded down on the hat, flattening it into the dirt. The determined handler refused to let go of the reins, clinging to them as if his life depended on it.

Knowing Scott, it probably did.

Seth sprinted the fifteen-odd metres to the gate and yanked the latch board across before pulling it open. He ran into the yard.

The man was now on the ground, shouting incoherently, crouching down in the dirt and dust, his hands and forearms clinging to his head. The reins swung freely. The horse reared again before crashing both front feet down on the man's head and shoulder. He slumped to the ground with one last grunt and lay silent in the dirt and cow manure. One leg twitched. Crimson blood flowed on to the earth next to his head. Flies swarmed to the wound site, now dribbling blood.

"No." Seth tried to grab the reins, but the horse spun on its back feet and his gloved hands clasped nothing but air. The horse reared again, dropped down and trotted to the far side of the holding yard. Its shiny, black coat glistened in the scorching sun that had peeked out again between the storm clouds.

Seth watched the horse for a second until it stopped and appeared to have settled down then dropped to his knees beside the fallen man.

"Jimmy. Get over here." He waved Jimmy over without looking up.

Blood poured from the large wound on top of the man's head, soaking his curly, black hair. Seth struggled to tug one tight glove off, cursing it for getting stuck. Once his fingers were free he felt the man's neck.

"Anything?" Jimmy dropped down beside Seth. "Holy God above."

"Nope . . . ahh shit, I can't really tell. I can't feel much with these friggin' scarred fingers. You try."

Jimmy pressed his fingers to the man's neck for several seconds. "He's dead, I reckon." The redness of Jimmy's face faded to a pale pink and his jaw slackened.

Seth groaned. "Shit, now what, Jimmy? Bet this wasn't in the plan." He glanced at the horse, which stood still, hanging its head as if it regretted the incident. "Look at him now. Butter wouldn't melt in his friggin' mouth." He struggled to get the glove back on.

Jimmy closed his mouth and shook his head slowly. "Un. . . real." He reached down and closed the man's staring eyes. "Poor bastard. I didn't even know him. Don't even know his name, except for 'Stretch', but that would've been a nickname."

"Ring Scott and tell him, hey? I have no idea what the hell we're supposed to do now. If the cops come around everything'll be blown out of the water and then Scott will blow *our* brains out." Seth felt in the man's pockets for some identification but came up empty handed. "There's no wallet. Nothing at all to tell us his name."

"Scott told me not to call him under any circumstance until he all is clear again, then he'll call me." Jimmy's words rose in pitch to reach panic mode.

"Great." Seth stood and looked about, a heavy brick of worry in his chest. "Where's this bloke's vehicle?"

"Scott told me he dropped him and the horse here early this morning so there's no vehicle. I s'pose he was just going to stay here with Scott in the house." Jimmy shrugged. "Hell . . . I don't know."

"I thought you were running the operation. Was the horse pinched?"

"Pete's doing stuff too." Jimmy shrugged again. "Probably was stolen. You know as well as I do that whatever Scott wants, Scott gets - one way or the other."

"We'll have to bury him."

Jimmy frowned. "Who . . . the horse?"

"No, you idiot. This bloke." *And Scott has put you in charge?* He nodded down toward the dead man. "We'll have to do it quickly then I'll take care of that rogue." He pointed to the horse that remained motionless but alert, watching, waiting. Waiting for his next conquest . . . or victim. Seth breathed deep, determined not to let the dangerous animal frighten him.

"Where?" Jimmy threw his hands into the air, tendons standing out in his neck. He blinked in quick succession. "I don't like this." His voice cracked like a weak floorboard and ascended to a frightened girly pitch.

"Oh, for fuck sake, Jimmy, grow some balls." Seth grabbed the front of Jimmy's brown shirt, lifting him until he was on tiptoes. "Don't you get it? We're in this up to our necks whether we like it or not."

"B-but can't we just take off and clear out? Scott's in hiding and . . . *hey,* why don't we just dob him in and tell them all we know. We'll get off and he'll be in jail for the rest of his miserable life." Beads of sweat appeared amidst whiskers above his top lip.

Seth let go of Jimmy's shirt and sighed. "Jimmy, I thought you were smarter than that. If we did that, Scott would still find us from jail. He has other people working for him. He's not stupid. I've seen firsthand what happens to anyone who double crosses him. You wanna go to the cops, fine, but do yourself a favour and shoot yourself as soon as you spill your guts. If not, you'll wish you had."

Jimmy squirmed, blinked watery eyes and jammed his hands into his armpits.

Seth removed his hat. "See my ugly face and head? Scott has dropped a couple of little hints over the years that I might have deserved this. I can't remember a thing before this happened, but a niggling feeling tells me that I upset him. From what I've seen of others who've double-crossed him, I got off bloody lightly." He replaced his hat.

Jimmy stared at him, wide-eyed. "You really think he did this to you?"

"I don't know and probably never will. It doesn't matter anymore. Come on, let's see what's in the shed to dig a hole with." He headed toward the large iron shed beside the run-down farm house, fifty-odd metres from the cattle yards.

Seth slid open the heavy shed door and entered with Jimmy following close behind.

"Tractor. Good." Seth strode to the newish, green tractor in the middle of the shed. "Wonder if it has a blade?" He walked around the front. "Nope."

"It's got a posthole digger on the back." Jimmy sounded excited. "We could bury him vertically."

"He's tall. It wouldn't go deep enough . . . are you *joking*?"

"Yes . . . no. Why not? There'd be less messed up dirt to be suspicious of. What about beside the creek in the sandy soil?"

"Well, we've gotta do something. You go and drag him over and I'll dig a hole."

"Great Seth. Drag him over? What about the trail of blood he'll leave behind? And he's not going to be light. He's friggin' ten feet tall." The high-pitched voice had returned.

"For Christ's sake, Jimmy, I don't know. Stop whining. Go to my ute and get an empty plastic bag off the floor and tie that over his head. The way it was pouring out, I don't think he'll have much blood left." Seth pushed open the large door behind the tractor before climbing up into the cabin and turning the ignition key. "Come on, you have to start."

The tractor groaned, shuddered and spluttered before roaring into life. Grey smoke coughed out of its vertical exhaust. Without hesitation, Seth reversed out of the shed and drove to a small cleared area near the creek, not far from the shed. Scanning about, he found a suitable spot and lowered the posthole digger toward the ground, ready.

He needed to check Jimmy's progress. Jimmy seemed to drag the body through the gate without too much effort although his fair skin glistened with sweat and his face was now a deep red. His mouth was shut so he wasn't cursing and complaining, or maybe the flies forced it shut. Either way, the situation was bad enough without Jimmy carrying on.

Returning to his unpleasant task at hand, Seth soon had enough holes dug side by side to lay the man horizontal, but some remaining loose dirt would have to be shovelled out. Seth drove the tractor back to the shed and looked about for one or preferably two, long handled shovels. There wasn't much in the shed, so he soon spotted assorted shovels and other similar tools leaning in one corner.

Why the hell did this have to happen? Can things get any worse? Grace would be horrified if she knew what he was doing. She'd never want to so much as look at him again, let alone talk to him.

Seth returned to the makeshift grave as Jimmy arrived with the man's body stretched out behind, complete with grey plastic shopping bag tied around the neck. He dropped the two booted feet he'd been holding against his hips. They hit the ground with a simultaneous *thud*.

"Shit, he's heavy." Jimmy wiped his brow and panted, his chest heaving.

"Here." Seth handed him a shovel. "Get some of this loose dirt out."

Both men shovelled fast and hard. Within minutes the grave was ready. Seth dropped his shovel, lifted his hat and wiped his face with his long sleeve while looking skywards. "Looks like that storm missed us. Gone to the north. Good."

"Yeah, I don't fancy storms much."

"Righto, let's get him in there." Seth grabbed the man's feet and dragged him over a little further until he lay alongside the grave.

Jimmy brought the man's outstretched arms down by his sides and muttered something under his breath.

Seth knelt down beside the body and placed his gloved hands on the man's hips. "Ready?"

"Yep." Jimmy dropped to his knees and placed his hands on the man's shoulder. "Go."

Together they rolled the lifeless body into the metre-or-so deep hole. It was the perfect length and width. The body dropped down, almost out of sight, landing with a dull thud. The bagged head rustled a moment before silence.

"Sorry to do this to you, mate." Jimmy leaned over and looked into the makeshift grave. "Don't you think we should at least give him some sort of last rites or something?" He snatched his hat off and pressed it to his chest like a chastised schoolboy at assembly. His index finger lifted and traced an invisible cross.

Seth raised his eyebrows and stifled a laugh. As if *that* would get Jimmy through Heaven's gate with his history. With shovel in hand, Seth stood. "You can afterwards if you want, but I don't have time right now." He began shovelling dirt back into the hole. "Get up Jimmy, or I'll put some on you too."

Jimmy pushed himself to his feet, picked up the other shovel and helped Seth fill the hole. "Mate, I don't like this. I think things are gunna get really bad."

"Me too, for what it's worth Jimmy, but you and me have to do everything possible form now on to make sure nothing else stuffs up, okay? These things are sent to try us, but we have to be prepared for anything."

"You got a point there." Jimmy packed the sandy soil down with the back of his shovel. "You gunna ride that black tornado over there?" He nodded toward the yards.

"You bet I am. He's not getting away with this. What are you ridin'?"

"My grey mare that I used to ride. Scott said she's still here in the back paddock with the others and in good nic, so she'll be right."

Seth looked about on the ground. "Can you cover this with some of the grass and leaves and whatever, so that it's not noticeable? Then just check back along where you dragged him over and try to cover the drag mark or any blood, especially that blood in the yard. You might have to find a bucket or something to put it in and take it somewhere else on the property and bury it. Sorry to order you around, Jimmy, but I gotta get on this horse."

"No worries, I'd rather do this than ride that killer any day. If anyone can handle him, you can, Seth. Good luck." He held out his hand to Seth, which Seth shook.

Jimmy may be irritating at times but they were bonded over this unexpected death. They had to stick together.

Seth wasn't a hundred percent sure he could now trust Jimmy. Jimmy was scared. Scared people make mistakes or run to the police, hoping for protection. He just had to hope Jimmy had the guts to stay strong.

"Thanks Jimmy." Seth turned and strode over to the yards. His thumping heart could compete with the thunder. He needed to focus on one thing and one thing only at that moment. The temperature was high but his adrenaline and determination soared higher. No time to think about what just happened or what might happen when he attempted to handle the horse.

Entering the yard, his eyes remained on the animal, especially the black eyes watching him.

That horse could kill just with his eyes.

"Righto, now it's my turn." Without hesitation he walked straight to the gelding, aiming to grab the hanging reins. The beast snorted and lifted his head as Seth approached. "It's all right mate, I'm not going to hurt you so you don't have to hurt me either."

He was now only several metres from possible death.

The horse turned around. It's swishing tail and fidgety back legs toward Seth. Its feet stomped the soft ground.

"You think you're gunna kick me?" Seth eyed a stone near his feet. In one fast motion he bent and threw it at the wooden fence close to the horse. It hit the rail with a loud *clunk*. The horse spun around and kicked at the rail where the noise came from. In a split second, Seth dived to the front of the horse and grabbed the reins. Caught off guard, the horse reared up on its hind feet, but Seth refused to let the reins be yanked from his strong hands.

"Settle down now." The horse dropped his front feet to the ground, snorted and eyed Seth. "Right, that's better." Seth reached out and rubbed the sweaty neck. A deep tremble beneath his hand signalled the agitated horse was ready to fight or flee.

It's now or never. Seth drew a deep breath, reached passed its head and tossed one rein over the horse's neck, grabbing the end with his other hand then holding both ends. In less than one second, one boot was in the stirrup and he was swinging his other leg up and over the saddle.

Even though he was tall and heavy, mounting horses was a breeze. While placing his other boot in the stirrup he pulled the reins in tight. *Right . . . I'm here.* The horse jumped and pranced around on the spot, chewing on the steel bit in its mouth. The grinding sound sent prickles up Seth's spine. If that was the worst he copped, the ride would go well. "You're not that bad, are you?" Seth leaned forward and rubbed the side of its neck, but couldn't help glancing at the spot where death had just occurred. A gush of adrenaline replaced the fear coursing through his veins. "Come on, let's go for a ride." He loosened the reins a little and relaxed his thigh muscles. A slight dig with his heels and the gelding was free to move.

The horse reared up on his hind feet again, but Seth leaned further forward, his face only centimetres from the wild mane, and hung on. The front hooves dropped back to the ground before rising up again.

"Righto, that's it." Seth looked about. Jimmy wasn't far from the main gate into one of the paddocks. "Jimmy, can you open the gate for me?" Seth hoped his raised voice wouldn't stir the horse even more.

"Okay." Jimmy gave the thumbs-up signal, ran over and dragged open the heavy wooden gate.

Seth slackened one rein while pulling on the other, turning the horse toward the gate. "*YAH.*" He loosened both reins, leaned forward again and urged him into a gallop. The shout burnt his parched throat but he didn't care.

With the leap of a lion catching its prey, the horse charged to full throttle, his long black mane flying free on the wind. Seth leaned lower and let him have his head. He needed no more urging. Down through the small creek crossing they galloped, *cloppiting* over the creek stones, splashing water to the sides then up into the grassy, semi-cleared paddock beyond. A small bird shot out of the grass in front of them but the gelding didn't shy or miss a beat. Excellent.

He held the reins in one hand while pulling his hat down tighter with the other. With a blur, the ground disappeared behind them. The wind dried the tears that formed in his eyes. Tears for the anonymous man now lying lifeless in the cold ground back near the creek. Tears for Grace and, mostly, tears for the total mess his wretched life had become. Grace could never love the likes of him.

Nothing else could be heard but the *ka-dump, ka-dump, ka-dump* of pounding hooves and the roar of the wind past his ears. It was the closest thing to flying Seth could imagine. Physically, this was pure exhilaration. Freedom. But mentally, nothing but sheer hell. How he wanted to leave that hell behind. "Faster." He leant further forward, kicking the gelding, spurring him on to even greater speed. To hell with the consequences.

To hell with Scott.

CHAPTER 21

Kain planted his foot, gripped the steering wheel and roared into Bruce and Linda's driveway. How dare they barge in and take all Grace's things and leave him nothing but the shocking message on the bathroom mirror.

"Take it easy, mate. We wanna get there in one piece." Joe grabbed the dash with one hand. "I know you're pissed off and I don't blame ya, but I still don't think this is a good idea. You don't really know it was Bruce."

"It was him all right." Kain gritted his teeth. "After what he said to me yesterday, it was him. He thinks he's fucking higher than God himself. Doesn't give a rats about anyone else, except Grace. She was his favourite. No decent father should ever favour one of his kids over the others anyway." He skidded his utility to a halt beside the house yard gate and looked at Joe. "You coming with me?"

"Ah shit . . . only if I have to."

"Joe, I know you told me earlier to take some time out and think about confronting Bruce, but all I did was stew over it and get angrier. You were okay with it when we decided to come out here. What's changed?"

"*We* didn't decide. *You* did and you're not thinking straight. You're still in shock over Grace's death."

"Look, whatever you wanna do is fine, but I'm going in to see Bruce." Kain got out of his vehicle, slammed the door and strode to the stairs, taking them in one leap. "Bruce. *Bruce.*" He yanked open the screen and banged several times on the closed front door with his fist. "Linda? Are you there?" No response. He wasn't prepared to *not* see them. He walked back to Joe's side of the utility. "They're not here." He kicked hard at the dirt beside his tyre. "Shit! Now what?"

"You don't think they'd be hiding inside, not wanting to see you, hey?" Joe shrugged one shoulder.

"Nah, Bruce wouldn't hide from anyone." An approaching vehicle caught Kain's attention. "Here they come." Rage and dread swirled in his gut.

The Atkinson's silver Jeep veered to the right and drove into the shed beside the house, pulling up next to Sophie's car. Linda's white sedan sat in the third bay. Even through the tinted windows he could see the boxes and other items loaded in the back seat next to Sophie and in the rear compartment. Grace's things.

He took several quick deep breaths, trying to calm himself, and fought back tears. Tears not only of sadness and grief, but also tears of absolute anger. How dare they? He hoped he'd be able to restrain himself.

"I've never hated anyone as much as I hate that bastard right now." Kain shook his head, his heart beat quickening like a drummer's introduction.

"You gunna go to them or wait until they come over here?"

Kain didn't bother responding. He was off, determined to confront Bruce head on. His swirling gut churned to liquid, his mouth dried to bitterness but he never, for one nano second, took his eyes off Bruce alighting from the vehicle.

Linda closed her door and looked up. Her sadness flicked to fear. "Kain, *no*. What are you doing?"

"What the hell did you do that for, you arrogant . . . ?" The words choked in his throat. Tears stung his eyes as he fought for a suitable word, respecting Linda and Sophie's presence. He stopped several metres from Bruce, who suddenly seemed so much taller. Bruce's eyes or facial expression gave Kain no indication of his thoughts. He stared at Kain with a blank look. That was confusing. Maybe he was putting on an act.

Without taking his eyes from Bruce, Kain yanked open the back door of the jeep. Glancing in only for moment he recognised Grace's personal belongings, confounding his suspicions. Stomach acid rose and watered his sour-tasting mouth. "How could you?"

Too angry for any more words, he reached for the large, open box on the seat closest to him. Some of Grace's books and a large framed photo of him and Grace confronted him. It had always been a favourite of them both. "No fucking way are you having this!" He grabbed the photo.

Bruce's long, muscular arm slammed the door shut, catching Kain's right elbow. He cried out in pain, dropped the picture and forced the door back open with his left hand. The picture fell onto the concrete floor, crashed and shattered, echoing around the shed, piercing his eardrums.

Kain's heart exploded into a million pieces along with the glass. He clenched his teeth to prevent screaming. His left hand grasped the door handle, but wanted to lash out at Bruce. Thump that smug face.

Seeing Grace's beautiful smile among the shards of glass was having her die all over again, right before his eyes. He bent for the photo but Bruce's large, black boot crunched on the photo and glass pieces, before his hand reached it.

"Leave it, Burrows. Get off my property. I told you you're not welcome here, now *get out!*"

Kain took his time straightening up. His gut instinct was to attack Bruce. Punch the air out of his gut. Watch him fall and suffer. His gaze trailed up Bruce's body to meet his eyes. The throb in Kain's arm was nothing compared to the unbearable pain in his heart and head.

Bruce's eyes bore into his with nothing but contempt and hatred and the corners of his mouth turned down in a sneer.

"Believe me, Bruce, as much as you hate me right now, it goes ten-fold for me. Grace would hate what you've done. You're not a man, you're a coward." Kain may have overstepped the mark, but no longer cared. "Sneak into my place when no-one's home and take all Grace's things . . . I can't even stand looking at you."

He glanced at Linda and Sophie standing over to the side. Both had tears streaming down their cheeks. "Did you two agree with this? Soph, I can't believe you'd be in on it. Did Bruce make you do it?" He looked from one sad face to the other, but neither spoke a word, only shook their heads once or twice. Sophie chewed her nails and her chest heaved. Linda's pale face, so worn and tired she looked much older.

Kain turned back to Bruce. "What the hell did you think you were doing? I could call the police and have you arrested for this."

"No Kain, please don't." Sophie expelled a loud sob. "I . . . I'll look after Grace's things. I promise."

The sneer on Bruce's face changed to a smirk. That's it. After one quick, deep breath Kain drove both hands into the taller man's chest and pushed hard. The smirk switched to shock. Bruce, caught off guard, over balanced and fell back, landing on some bags of cement and plastic drums of farm chemicals stacked in the next bay of the shed.

Kain crouched, grabbed the picture, shook away the broken pieces of glass and wooden frame and ran back to his utility. The ladies screamed and shouted, both to him and Bruce, but his heart and head t humped and the adrenaline seared through his body. He was not stopping for anyone.

Joe jumped out of the vehicle. "Look out!"

Kain turned but Bruce was already there, grabbing Kain's right arm - on the sore elbow. The fist came from nowhere, slamming into the edge of Kain's jaw. He fell backwards on the ground, the setting sun catching his eye. More screaming and yelling but he couldn't comprehend a word of the commotion.

"That's it. No more." Joe stood between the two men with his back to Kain. "For fuck's sake, you two. You've both lost someone you love. Stop all this shit!"

Joe's hairy legs quaked in front of Kain as he scrambled back to his feet. Any other circumstances he would have laughed, but there was nothing funny happening here.

"Get this bastard off my property now or . . . I *will* shoot him!" Bruce's red face deepened to purple, glaring at Joe. If eyes could shoot bullets, Joe would be dead.

"Righto, but calm down." Joe put his hand up in a 'stop' mode.

Kain fought the overwhelming urge to attack Bruce again, to wipe that smirk off his conceited face. The image of that look returned. It would be something he'd never forget. Grace came to mind. Taking a deep breath and trying to avoid Bruce's eyes, he picked up the picture again. "Only for you, Grace." He glanced at Bruce. "For Grace's sake, I'm walking away."

"All right, you can keep it, but that's all you'll get." Bruce came closer to Kain. He poked a finger at Kain's chest, stopping only several centimetres from his shirt. "And you can forget about a funeral."

"What the hell are you talking about?" Kain was forced to look at him, but that half-smirk was back. He clenched his fists. Fight or flight? He was ready to fight but glanced at Sophie and Linda.

Sophie ran toward the front steps, sobbing. Linda brought her hand to her mouth, fresh tears filling her eyes.

"What's happened?" Questions darted about in Kain's head, but his gut feeling only had one answer.

"Yep, we've already had it. We had her cremated today. It's over Kain." The smirk changed to anger. "Now, get in your bloody ute and get the hell off my property. If I ever see you again, I'll . . ." His hazel eyes burned into Kain. "Just go!"

"No. You can't do that." Kain turned to Linda who remained standing alone and crying. "Linda?" She shook her head, keeping her eyes to the ground.

"Bullshit." Kain whipped around and headed toward his utility. Tears goaded his eyes. He knew defeat. Joe was already waiting near the passenger side door. The shoes, the shattered glass, the texting – it hit Kain. He pivoted back toward Bruce. "That'd be right. With all your money and power in this town, you, the *mighty Bruce Atkinson* gets whatever he friggin' wants, doesn't he? You don't give a shit how much you hurt anyone as long as you get your way. Well, I got news for you." Kain looked down at the picture he clutched in his left hand and swallowed hard before returning his gaze to Bruce. "Grace is still-"

"Come on, mate." Joe grabbed Kain's arm and yanked him toward his vehicle.

"Joe, what the . . .?" Kain jerked his arm away.

"Don't say a word, mate," hissed Joe close to Kain's ear. "Just get in. I'll drive."

Without looking back, Kain got in the passenger seat of his own vehicle, did up his seatbelt and studied the photo. Beautiful Grace smiled back at him and his own face was so relaxed and happy. How so much had changed in the few short months since this picture was taken. He hugged the photo tight to his rising and falling chest.

Joe roared the vehicle to life and headed down the drive-way. "Mate, I don't think it would have been a very good idea to tell them you think Grace is still alive. Either he'd flatten you there and then, good and proper this time, for being an idiot or . . . if you get their hopes up and you're wrong, well . . . he bloody well *will* shoot ya. I don't really know him that well, but I could see he was serious. Let's just see what more we can find out first, hey?"

Kain half-grunted, half-sobbed out a breath. "You're right. Thanks for stopping me, but the arrogant prick just made me so mad. That smirk . . ." He clenched his teeth and slammed his fist down on the front dash. "I'm more determined than ever to find out the truth now and find Grace. That'll make him feel about two inches tall. One way or the other, Bruce Atkinson is going to fall, and fall hard, from his fucking high horse and I want to be there to see it."

CHAPTER 22

G race walked out on to Seth's breezy, front verandah, closing the screen door behind her. The golden sun sank low over the nearby smokey-blue mountains. She frowned, but frowning still hurt her head injury. *Have to stop frowning.* "Where *are* you, Seth?"

Since he'd taken a phone call earlier and left in a hurry, apart from the prying, she'd read two magazines, tidied the kitchen, taken her new clothes off the line, fed the chooks from a bag of grain she'd found under the house and collected several eggs. Lastly, she'd prepared a stir-fry for tea but still no sign of his return.

The whole time she couldn't get her mind off the old photo of the children. Over and over she'd pondered how to delve into his history without him knowing she'd been snooping, but still nothing positive came to mind.

Several shy Pretty-Face wallabies emerged from the bush to feed along the driveway in the cool of the afternoon. Thousands of cicadas began their song of the bush with intermittent deafening bursts. The 'ark-ark' of crows in the distance carried on the breeze to Grace. She shuddered, imagining them feasting on the dead dog, even though she had no idea how far away or in which direction it was.

The cicadas stopped as suddenly as they'd begun. All was quiet except for a lonely, sad *woop woop woop* call of a pheasant somewhere in the bush down the back. When she'd been at the chook pen earlier, she'd heard the soothing sound of a small creek running close-by. She imagined the pheasant and many other animals would be drawn to it for water. She'd briefly toyed with the idea of going to the creek herself, but the memory of the dogs frightened her enough to remain in the relative safety of the house yard.

Grace watched the driveway and listened. No approaching vehicle. She sighed and wandered back inside, unsure of what to do to pass time. "I may as well have a shower and see if I can watch TV," she muttered with the slight shrug, which also invoked pain in her shoulder. But it *was* easing so maybe there weren't any broken bones after all.

The warm water sprayed over her naked body, washing away some of the tension. She made a mental note to ask Seth to check her back wound.

Seth. A wave of nausea swam through her stomach and rose to her mouth and she wondered for the thousandth time where on earth he could be. She spat watery saliva down the plug hole, raised her head and opened her mouth to the spray. Taking in a mouthful, she swished it about, spat it out, and turned off the shower taps. At least her mouth tasted a little better but her stomach remained queasy.

What has happened to him? He'd said he'd be back later, but *how much later?* What if something has happened to him and he never comes back? No. No. Not an option.

Grace dried and dressed, combed fingers through her long wet hair and wandered toward the kitchen. The new shorts and top fitted well. Surely he'd be home soon.

She stopped, gasped and her shoulders jerked upwards. Her overactive mind hit a brick wall at full speed. There he was, sitting only several metres from her, with elbows on the table and face resting in his hands, partially hidden by the bunch of roses. His hat sat on the far end of the table. "Seth. You're back." A stupid thing to say, but it'd popped out of her mouth before she'd taken time to think.

"Seth . . .?" He remained quiet, making her even more uneasy. "I . . . I've cooked dinner." The way he sat there, head in hands, something was very wrong but she had no idea what else to say. "There's plenty so I hope you're hungry." She tried to keep her voice upbeat to cheer him up from whatever was obviously upsetting him. Unpleasant vibes filled the room, chilling the air. Grace shivered.

He lifted his head from his hands and wiped moisture from his eyes. "Sorry Grace, I, um . . . " Seth turned and looked at the frying pan on the stove. "Thank you for doing that. It smells good." With a loud scrape of his chair, he stood. "I'll go for a shower."

Grace nodded, still unsure what to say. He walked past her without even glancing her way. She screwed up her face before holding her breath for a moment. Seth definitely needed that shower. Maybe he'll open up once he's feeling and smelling better, but it weighed on her mind. She switched on the kitchen light and went about setting the table for two.

No sooner had the bathroom door closed when the high-pitched humming of the pressure pump under the house signalled the taps were running. Grace let out a deep sigh. He seemed to have clammed up again, just like when she first tried communicating with him. Something had happened while he was out and her gut feeling told her it was not good. Hopefully, he wasn't in any trouble.

Grace walked out on to the verandah again and breathed in the cool breeze of dusk. It smelt so natural and clean and tingled on her skin, cooling it down. She loved this place. There was nothing like the fresh air of the bush, but her mind was abuzz – what was wrong with Seth? Would he tell her? What exactly *does* he do? Just who are those kids in the old picture?

His phone. He'd left his phone on the table. It might reveal some of his secrets. Did she dare . . .? She walked back into the kitchen, closing the screen door quietly behind her. The pump still hummed – *good*. The cicadas started singing again. There it was, just where he must have put it when he'd sat at the table. *I'm sorry Seth.* Feeling like she did the day, many years ago, when she and Steve had eaten lots of lamingtons their mother had made for a graziers meeting even though they'd been warned to have only one each, she picked up his phone and tapped the screen. Locked. Damn.

"What are you doing?" Seth's voice was abrupt, deep and angry.

Grace flinched and her heart contracted. She placed the phone back on the table and her faced burned hot. How did he get out here, fully dressed, so quickly and in total silence? "I . . . I thought I'd try and ring mum to let her know I'm okay. I didn't think you'd mind. Sorry." *Please buy that excuse, Seth.*

In silence, she hoped and prayed, not taking her eyes off his for a second. He glared at her, but with the scarring and his eyes merely slits, especially if he seemed unhappy, she had no idea what he was thinking. *I'll change the subject.* "Are you ready to eat yet, Seth? I'll heat it up." She turned her back to him and went to the stove. Invisible daggers stabbed her back. *Please don't be angry with me.* She wasn't sure if she was scared of him at that moment or just felt pity.

"It's okay, Grace." His voice had softened. So much so that it bordered on sadness. "Yes, I'm hungry, thank you."

A wave of relief swept over her and she turned to him with a smile to match her gladdened heart.

He sat down at the table with a heavy sigh.

She hoped he'd let her help him. "Only another minute or so." Picking up the wooden spoon she'd used cooking the stir-fry, she stirred it several times in the deep frying pan before turning off the stove.

"I'll dish it up." Seth got back up and took both plates to the stove. "I forgot for a second, about your sore shoulder. How does it feel now?" He took the wooden spoon from Grace and put several scoops of the colourful, steaming food on each plate.

"Oh okay, thanks." Grace sat at the table. "It actually feels a bit better this afternoon. I can move it more without so much pain now. Maybe it's not broken at all. But I wouldn't mind if you could have a look at my back and see how that injury is going."

He set the plates down on the table and sat down. "Yep, I'll do that after tea. Wouldn't the sling be easier for you and less painful?"

Grace gave a half shrug. "No, it's all right." She watched Seth pick up his fork and begin to eat. *Okay, so he hasn't said a thing about the phone or what happened today.* The uneasiness hung in the air between them like a heavy fog cloud. Grace swallowed several mouthfuls but her appetite had waned. Seth finished his meal without a single word being spoken or a glance in her direction.

"Aren't you hungry? It really was good, Grace." He stood and put his empty plate on the sink before sitting back opposite her and folding his arms.

"Oh, I nibbled at the vegies as I was cutting them up," she lied, averting his gaze. "Now I'm full." She couldn't help but laugh. "My mother used to always get up my brother Steve for eating too much after school then he wouldn't want to eat tea."

"What was he like?"

"Who, Steve?" Grace didn't expect such interest in her long lost brother when Seth clearly had serious things on his mind. Maybe it was a way of distracting himself from his woes, or maybe distracting *her* from prying deeper into his soul, which she had every intention of doing when she found the appropriate words and time.

"Yeah. You sound like you miss him a lot."

"I do." Tears threatened and she tried to think of funny things about him to stem the flow. "He was a pain in the bum at times, but we got along good most of the time. He was such a good horse rider. No-one could ride like Steve. He loved going to rodeos and riding the barebacks. One shelf in his old room is full of trophies and ribbons he'd won over the years."

"So, you don't know where he is now?"

Grace shook her head and the tears trickled down her cheeks. "No idea. We don't even know if he's alive or dead."

"Has anyone ever tried to find him?"

"Yep, Dad hired a private detective after we'd exhausted all avenues and the police had closed the case." She wiped the tears from her cheeks and eyes. A box of tissues appeared and she pulled out two. "Thanks." Seth left them within reach of Grace. "But there was no trace of him. It's like he just disappeared into thin air." She wiped her eyes again and blew her nose one-handed.

"Why did he leave? Your parents seem like pretty good people and he had a good life, by the sounds of it." Seth shrugged, unfolded his arms and placed his gloved hands on the edge of the table. He glanced at his hands and dropped them out of Grace's view.

"He and Dad used to clash all the, well, *most* of the time. They had different ideas on just about everything, but sometimes . . . " Her mind wandered back. "Sometimes I used to see Dad looking at Steve like he hated him, you know, *really* hated him. There was something deep in

Dad's eyes and heart that . . . I don't know . . . something must have happened a long time ago because it had been going on since we were kids and sometimes Dad says things that make me think he's glad Steve has gone."

"That's awful."

A long breath came out as her shoulders sagged. "I asked Dad once why did he get so angry with Steve and he refused to answer, just told me to 'leave it alone'. He said it so angrily I was never game to talk about Steve again to him." Grace wiped more tears away and forced a grin. "Sorry to blubber like this in front of you."

"Don't have to be sorry, Grace." His words so soft and caring, he reminded Grace of a giant teddy bear.

The time seemed right to ask Seth some questions. "How did your afternoon go? You seemed upset when you came home." She held her breath, but picked up her fork and casually played with her food. Silence. *Maybe it wasn't such a good idea.* Putting the fork on her plate, along with her knife, she got up and filled herself a glass of water from the sink tap. "Would you like a drink, Seth?"

"Yes please."

She got a fresh glass and filled it before placing it on the table in front of him. "There

you go.

"Thanks." His reply snappy and terse, but he drank the whole amount.

She may as well give up trying to break through his invisible shield. "I'm tired. I think I'll go to bed."

"No, wait Grace." He stood and placed his empty glass on the sink. "The afternoon didn't go well at all. I have a few things to sort out and one day I'll tell you all about it, but not yet okay."

"Seth, if you're in trouble I could help you, that is, if you'll let me." She grabbed his hand and looked into his eyes. "Can't you tell me what you're doing? How am I going to tell anyone when I'm stuck out here in the middle of nowhere?"

His eyes watered and he squeezed her hand tighter.

"I'm sorry. I didn't mean that in a bad way. It's beautiful here. You're lucky to live in such a beautiful part of the country. In some ways I'm glad to be stuck here, away from all the craziness."

"Grace. . ." His large chest and shoulders fell with his outgoing breath. "If only it was all so easy but it's not. All you need to know is I am never going to hurt you, but I can't let you use my phone. The bloke I work for checks it and," his gaze shifted away from her, "if he knew someone else was here or using my phone he'd get very angry. He's like that. To be honest, I'm a bit scared of him. I promise I'll call your parents for you from town next time I go in. I'll even go in tomorrow and do it for you."

Grace's shoulders lightened and she breathed easy. "Okay." She smiled, slipping her hand out of his much larger one.

Seth dropped his hand. "Do you still want me to look at your back injury?"

"Yes please." She wore no bra, so turned her back to him and attempted to lift her shirt over her head, but it was difficult. She couldn't yet lift her right arm.

"Can I help?" Seth's large, gloved hands took hold of the bottom of her shirt and lifted it slowly up her back to the nape of her neck.

"Um, yeah, okay." Having him help her undress brought a swarm of flittering bugs to her stomach. She gathered and moved her hair over to the front of her left shoulder and folded her arms across her chest.

Seth's words, '*I am never going to hurt you*', echoed in her ears but his breathing deepened. *Is he getting aroused? God, I hope not.* The room spun, slow like a kiddie ride at the show. Her heart thumped and beat against her wrists. She hoped Seth couldn't hear it.

"Do you want me to take the dressing off? It looks like it's about to fall off anyway."

"Y-yes please. Do you have another to put on it?" Seth pulled off the sticking plaster. Grace flinched.

"Sorry, I didn't mean to hurt you." His voice was slow and tender.

"You didn't, I just. . ." Those jittering bugs again. "Just wasn't expecting that, that's all." Her head danced in the clouds. She held her arms tighter to her chest until the light-headedness subsided.

"It doesn't look too bad, but I'll put another one on just to be safe." His finger moved with a feathery touch down her back. "Hold on." He walked off.

Kain's face came to mind. "Damn you, Kain. Everything is so stuffed up because of you." She sniffed back tears but couldn't help remembering the first time they'd made love. He'd been so sweet and gentle, taking time to caress her skin. His strong, workman hands and fingers could be firm when and where needed, but would also dance over her skin like light snowflakes.

The way Seth had just touched her back was so similar to Kain's touch, it frightened her. In one way Seth was her saviour and she wanted to crumple in his arms and let him take away all her pain, but then sense and reality kicked in and reminded her not to be crazy and that she loved Kain. Oh, how she still loved him. A dull ache brewed in her heart, the same intermittent ache since Kain broke off the relationship. Seth re-entered the kitchen with some new dressings and she wiped away the tears.

"Here we go." The tearing sound was succeeded by Seth's hands on her back again, gently putting the dressing in place.

Something felt different. Goose bumps erupted over her back. Her breath and pulse seemed to stop. It was his bare hands, not gloves, carefully rubbing over the plaster and brushing along her exposed skin. Surely he didn't really need to do that. Of course it would have been easier for him with bare hands, than trying to open a band-aid with gloves, but she couldn't shake the uncomfortable, yet mesmerising feeling. The goose bumps spread over her back and arms.

She took a deep breath, unsure what to say or do. She longed to turn and see his hands, even hold them in hers. His breathing, loud and fast, brought her back to earth and reality. "Thanks for doing this." She took a small step forward, his hands left her back and her shirt fell.

"It's my pleasure, Grace. I'd do anything for you."

She turned to face him, hoping to see his bare hands. Finally she would know why he kept them covered. But he'd already stuffed them into his jeans pockets. "Seth, can I see your hands, please?" She didn't wish to raise his ire, but was taken aback to notice something else had risen inside his jeans.

Oh no. Now, she'd find out if he was true to his word about not hurting her. If not, she hadn't a hope of getting away from him.

Seth turned away from her, his hands remained in his pockets. "You don't want to see them, they're too ugly. Just like the rest of me."

"That's not true. The acid might have made you feel ugly on the outside but it's what's in here that counts." She placed her hand on his upper back. His beating heart and warmth radiated through his shirt.

He turned around. A lone tear ran down his cheek. "Do you think you could ever love someone like me, Grace?"

She wanted to speak, but no suitable words came to mind. A tear seeped down his other cheek. His eyes bore into her, seeming to analyse and study every square millimetre of her body and mind. She felt naked, exposed with nowhere to hide. Frozen to the spot. Mute.

"I didn't think so." He looked away.

"Seth." She thawed, thinking fast and hard for the correct words. "I could easily love someone like you, but my heart belongs to Kain. Yes, I know he dumped me and it's over, but I need time to . . . to get over him. We were together for years and I thought we'd stay together forever.

Watch our grandkids grow up." She grabbed a tissue from the box on the table and wiped her eyes.

"You're just being polite and I've upset you." His gaze dropped to the floor, as if holding eye contact another second pained him. He studied the worn linoleum floor, his shoulders tense, his hands still wedged in his jeans pockets.

The wall in her heart crumbled. Grace reached out to touch him, he jerked his gaze to hers and took a step back.

"I'm sorry, Grace." The words hung in the air, quiet and lonely. More tears slid down his cheeks.

She pulled another tissue from the box and walked closer. She reached up and gently wiped the tears from his eyes and scarred cheeks. His eyes remained locked on hers. She didn't know what to say. Maybe she did feel more for him than just pity.

Kain dumped her and she was thrown into Seth's life. Everything happens for a reason, she believed that much. Her life's journey included Seth now. She loved Kain, but didn't want to walk away from Seth. He needed her and she was happy to be here for him.

"Thank you."

Grace smiled. "You're welcome."

His eyes scanned her face. His warm breath swept her forehead.

She should move back and walk away, but her feet wouldn't budge. They were nailed to the floor. His face moved closer and his breath quickened. *This is crazy – walk away, girl.*

She closed her eyes and tilted her head back. She was lost in a daze, no control of her own body. The softest lips she'd ever felt touched hers. His whiskers tickled with a feathery touch, a sensation she had never felt. Kain had always been clean shaven. Her breathing accelerated. Tingles shot up her spine and to her nipples. Seth opened his lips a little and she responded the same and brought her left hand to the back of his neck. A low moan passed his lips, followed by another louder one, and his body jerked. Several short, guttural grunts escaped his throat.

He stepped back. "I'm sorry. I shouldn't have done that." He strode from the kitchen, down the darkened hallway. The door of his bedroom opened then slammed.

The night insects buzzed and chirped outside the screened window of the, otherwise, silent kitchen. A dingo howled somewhere in the bush.

She plonked on a chair, horrified at what she'd just done.

CHAPTER 23

Seth lay on his bed, hands behind his head and stared into blackness. He kept his shirt on but had put on clean underwear. *What an absolute idiot you were.* The same words ran around and around in his brain. What must Grace be thinking right now? *Disgust and nothing but.* He'd ached for her and now it was over and finished. She'd never be able to look him in the eye again and vice versa.

What the hell had he done? Grace's beautiful face wouldn't leave his mind. Soft lips that tasted so sweet. Her fresh scent, after she'd had a shower, lingered in his nostrils.

His senses overflowed, but so did the tears, running down the sides of his face to his ears and pillow. How the hell was he going to fix this stuff- up? The afternoon's unexpected disaster with the horse was bad enough. Now this.

He shook his head and blinked hard. Grace left his mind only to be replaced by the maniacal horse, the dead man and his subsequent burial. Every moment of every scene tore through his mind in annoying intricate detail. The horse ride had temporarily taken away the sickening dread and fear brought on by the man's unexpected and horrific death. Seth had galloped that spirited, black tornado until the horse's sides heaved, caked in white foam.

Seth loved his free spirit, but not his angry heart. Most others would have shot the horse, but Seth could see his potential. In some ways he felt akin to the huge gelding – a loner with a wild heart and the ability to do whatever necessary to survive. Seth had left him in the small holding paddock by the yards and hoped he'd stay there until needed.

What the hell would Scott say, even worse, *do,* when he found out about the man's death and how they disposed of the body? Jimmy had said Scott commanded not to call him under any circumstances, until the coast was clear and he could come out of hiding. At least that gave Seth some reprieve from worrying about what and when to tell Scott.

The nagging feeling that the whole operation will end in disaster just wouldn't leave the deep recesses of his mind and gut. Maybe he was simply too used to everything going wrong. Maybe he expected it to and *deserved* the worst. *Especially after what just happened in the kitchen, you useless loser.*

Seth flicked on the bed-light switch above his head. Hopeless trying to get to sleep. His brain wouldn't slow down. He had to fix this mess with Grace, but he had no idea how. Sitting up, he swung his feet to the floor and sucked in a deep breath. He'd probably just stuff up *again* and apologise *again.* How many times does he say 'sorry' to Grace? Too many, that was for sure. *Face it, loser, she's just too good for you.*

Opening the wardrobe and taking out a clean pair of jeans, his pulse raced, but if he was going to do this, it had to be right now. No idea what he would say, but he had to think of something immediately. Grace was the best thing he'd ever known in his all too short memory. She just *had* to understand that . . . understand *what?* Hell, he didn't understand much of it himself.

These feelings for Grace were like nothing he'd ever felt before, either physically or emotionally – that he could remember anyway. He ached to hold and kiss her again and make love to her. His brain had no memory of sex but his body would know what to do. Most importantly, he didn't want to scare or upset her. *Too late, loser. She's probably heading out the door and up the track now.* No.

He pulled the jeans on and did up the button and zip. Taking an extra deep breath to slow his hyped up nerves, he wiped the tears and opened his door. Total darkness. He'd expected to see Grace's light on or, at least, a light still coming from the kitchen. Now what? Maybe he could pretend he was getting a drink of water. Yep, good idea and he *was* thirsty. He went to the kitchen and flicked on the light.

Turning the tap off with one hand, he drank the full glass before placing it on the sink with minimal sound. Seth looked around, hoping to see Grace enter, but all was quiet and he was alone. *Story of my pathetic life.* His large shoulders collapsed from the weight of the universe. May as well just go back to bed and try and get some sleep. He walked over to flick off the light.

"Are you okay, Seth?"

The gentle words were like music in the still night air. His heart pistoned and he spun around. "Grace." He had no idea what to say now they were face to face. "I . . . I was just getting a drink. I didn't mean to wake you."

"You didn't wake me." She smiled that damned beautiful smile again. "I was worried about you and . . . what happened."

"Look, I don't know what I did that for. I didn't mean to do it. I am *so* sorry." The last word choked out in a hoarse croak.

"I'm not upset with you."

"You're not?" That was not what he expected.

"I am with me though." Her gaze dropped, along with her shoulders.

"Why?" Seth frowned, unable to think of any reason she should be upset with herself.

"I was wrong to kiss you and let you kiss me. I led you on and I'm the one who is sorry." She sat at the table, but still couldn't look him in the eyes. "You saved me out there in the bush and you've looked after me and I was nothing but a bitch to do that to you. It *won't* happen again, I promise." She continued avoiding his eyes.

In other words, she's too disgusted with herself to even look at you, loser. Seth hoped that wasn't true, but he had to be realistic - a beautiful woman like this, coming from a perfect life, giving it up *for him? Yeah right, as if.* Another mule-kick in the guts, but nothing new. The only bit of happiness and decency in his pathetic life just crashed around him. He wanted to cry. Howl like a baby. But what would be the use? Grace would only feel sorry for him. No, he didn't need anyone's miserable pity. "Can we pretend this didn't happen."

She nodded toward the floor. "Yeah, I think that's best."

He feigned a shrug of indifference but would never forget that beautiful, tender moment when their lips touched, even though he had to pretend. His heart wanted to fall from his body and his shoulders slumped again.

Without Grace in his life, he had no reason to go on, especially after what'd happened that afternoon and what was likely to happen once Scott resurfaced and got this big job under way. If this job is successful, he planned to, *somehow*, escape from Scott's clutches and, *hopefully*, take Grace with him.

Grace looked at him and smiled, but her smile also showed sadness. *Of course she's sad, you fool, she's just been dumped by the love of her life.*

She held out her hand to shake his. "Friends?"

Seth took his bare right hand out of his pocket and grasped Grace's hand to return the shake. Grace looked at his exposed hand and caught her breath in a gulp. Seth snatched his hand away and shoved it back into his pocket. "Goodnight, Grace." He practically ran to his bedroom. *You idiot, now she's seen your hand she'll be even more put off by you.*

Why was he so bloody careless?

CHAPTER 24

Kain opened his eyes and stared at the white ceiling. Warm sunlight already streamed through the partially drawn curtains of his old room at his parents'. It must be getting late. Some traffic drove past and a distant dog barked, otherwise all was quiet in this suburban street of Anchor Bay.

Reality smacked him in the head. The breakup, Grace's death and her father's actions and choices, not to forget the blame Bruce fired at him. Not that he needed any more on his shoulders, he felt guilty enough but it was all too much to tolerate.

Closing his eyes again brought the demons racing to his mind. The demons who wanted him to go and give Bruce Atkinson what he deserved. The demons that repeated the scenes of the previous days - the phone call from Linda telling him his beloved Grace was dead; the sight and smell of her burnt out car and Bruce's selfish and unforgiveable behaviour, especially having her remains cremated immediately and without a word to him.

Joe had offered him a bed again at his place, but he'd declined, needing some space and time to get his head around everything. Sleep had been slow in coming, and when he finally did succumb, his brain went into overdrive with vivid dreams.

He could now only remember flashes or jumbled bits and pieces but Grace's face featured in all the contorted images. Some, she smiled and looked happy, some had her calling desperately to him but he couldn't see or find her. Some, the worst ones, had her face and body melting before his eyes. He'd tried to rescue her, but the heat of the fire melted his hands to charred, black stumps.

Finally it was morning and the dreams could pack up and get out of his head, even though the grief of losing Grace engulfed him all over again. A hard fist seemed to land in his chest, leaving the severest pain at the point of impact before branching out through his body. He breathed deep, but the ache in his fractured heart refused to budge.

Lifting his head, he reached under his pillow and brought out the large photo he'd rescued from Bruce's car the previous day. With both hands, he held it up and stared at Grace's face for the hundredth time. He had no idea how long he'd looked at the photo before turning his light off the previous night, or how many tears he cried, but his pillow remained damp.

Without a moment's warning, the tears resurfaced. Drenching his eyes and spilling down to his ears and pillow. "Oh Grace." He sobbed and let the tears flow, forming their own little cascade past his temples.

The shoe he'd found came to mind. He just knew in his heart it wasn't Grace's and she would not text while driving. His inner conscious came to life. *But what if she was so distraught from the breakup that she just wasn't thinking straight?* "No." He balled his fist and bit his knuckle. "You wouldn't do that, Grace. I know you better than that." But did he?

"*Argh!*" It was all too much.

Kain sat upright and placed the photo on his pillow. He had no idea what to believe. His head buzzed. A thousand bees flew about in his brain. Each one told him a contrasting thought or idea or showed him a different image. He clenched his teeth and thumped his temples with open palms before shaking his head fast and hard. Shower. He needed a shower. Maybe that would slow his brain down and drive out those bloody bees.

The tepid water gushed down his back as he rubbed and washed his tired eyes. He held his breath and turned so the stream hit him directly in the face. It felt good. Not that anything actually felt good anymore. Food had no taste. Sleep was not restful. Funny things no longer seemed remotely funny. Life had all changed. There was no pleasure left in anything.

He moved back and the water stream hit his pelvic area. Another memory hit him hard. The cancer. He'd actually forgotten about it for the night. He looked down at his penis and especially his scrotum, both looking like drenched, sad water rats. "This is all because of you." He took hold of his scrotum in one hand. "Grace would still be alive if it wasn't for you and your fucking cancer." His hand tightened as did his jaw. "Well, *fuck you!*"

He gripped the loose flesh, squeezed and closed his eyes tight. He twisted the handful and more tears seeped from his eyes. Searing pain overrode all other discomfort and aches, including the one deep in his heart. "I *hate* you."

He wanted to rip that cancer right out of his body, but his body had other ideas. His legs weakened and softened to jelly. The dagger piercing his groin drove deeper. Deeper. He grunted, gritted his teeth and doubled over, dropping his hand to his side.

His legs numbed. He stepped back until his buttocks pressed against the tiled wall. It couldn't hold him. Crumpling to a heap on the shower floor, his body heaved with loud sobs. He brought his knees up to his chest. No air remained in his tightening lungs. He gasped through his open mouth. Water entered along with air, burning his constricted lungs.

He gulped for air between bouts of coughing, but it brought in more water. The pain in his scrotum stopped him from moving away from the water spray. His chest burned. Why not just let it be? He'll probably die soon anyway. Kain closed his eyes, inhaled more water and awaited his fate.

Darkness closed in. A strange peace descended.

The water ceased, bar a few remaining drops dripping on his bare head.

"What the hell are you doin', Kain?"

Kain coughed and spluttered out water before opening his tear-filled eyes. Water and warm saliva dribbled down his chin. Through the diminishing pain and steam, he could see a pair of legs. Hairy legs. He looked up and squinted. "Joe?" It came out sounding more like a croak.

"This is not the prettiest sight I've ever seen. What happened?"

Several more coughs cleared Kain's chest enough for him to speak, but inflamed his throat. "I can't take anymore." He sobbed, wiping his eyes with his wet hand. "I can't face another long, horrible day thinking about Grace being dead and this . . ." He pointed toward his groin and dropped his knees to one side. "I . . ." The words didn't want to come.

He took a deep breath and looked at Joe. The tears spilled out once again. All he could do was shake his head and swallow saliva to ease his irritated throat.

"C'mon, mate." Joe's voice had softened. He stepped one bare, white foot into the shower and held out his hand. "Let's get you out of here for starters."

Kain took hold of the strong hand his friend offered. Part of him wanted to hide in shame, but an even bigger part just didn't care anymore. Joe pulled him to his feet. He let go of Joe's hand and grabbed the shower door. "Thanks mate."

Joe yanked a towel from the rack and handed it to Kain. "Wipe yourself. I'll go and make us a coffee."

Kain did as he was instructed, threw the towel back over the rack and headed to his room for some clothes. By the time he came into the kitchen Joe had two steaming mugs of coffee made and had sat at the table with one in his hand.

"Wanna sit out the back?" Joe indicated with a sideways nod of his head.

"Nah, I don't really care." Kain pulled out the chair opposite Joe at the round, wooden table. "Doesn't make any difference where I sit. Grace is *still* dead and I've *still* got fucking cancer." He took a sip of the coffee while staring at nothing on the table.

Joe sighed. Several moments of silence passed before he spoke. "Mate, I really wish I knew what to say. I can't say that I know what you're going through because I have no friggin' idea, but . . . " Silence again. "What happened in the shower?"

Kain shot his gaze at Joe. "Are you serious? Do you really have to ask?"

Joe's face reddened. "Um . . . sorry mate. It's just that I've never seen you in that state before and . . ." He stood. "I need a smoke." Without glancing at Kain, Joe headed out the back of the kitchen, through the laundry.

The back door opened, followed by the screen door. Kain pushed his half-drank coffee to the side, folded his arms on the table and dropped his head on to them. He'd hurt Joe's feelings. *Shit, can't do anything right.*

A huge black hole opened up and engulfed him, spinning him round and round, hurting every part of his body, mind and soul. He just wanted it to stop. Sleep. Sleep forever. Sleep would be so welcome, but without the nightmares. Was that possible?

Aha. His mother sometimes took sleeping tablets. Kain lifted his foggy head from the table. His neck felt like rubber, unable to hold the weight. It wanted to drop again. He shook his head, got up and went to the small cream-coloured cabinet above the fridge, where his parents kept their medications and the like. A plethora of small bottles and boxes greeted him. He grabbed some in each hand and put them on the kitchen bench. Two white bottles fell over and rolled off the side, hitting the floor with a simultaneous rattly *plunk*. He bent, swooped them up and read the labels. No, they weren't familiar.

He threw them back into the medicine cabinet and picked up another bottle from the bench. 'Temazepam'. "Yes!" He'd picked up his mother's prescription for them one time. Not daring to think of the consequences, he unscrewed the cap and peered in at the green and white capsules. More than enough to do the job. *Need a glass of water.*

The bottle was snatched from his hand. "No way, Burrows! Don't even *think* such shit."

Kain spun around. He reached out to grab the bottle of capsules from inside Joe's clenched fist held close to his stomach. But, in Joe's eyes he saw something he'd never seen in all the years he'd known the larrikin. He saw fear. He saw absolute terror. He saw love and mateship. As the tears spilled out of Joe's widened eyes, Kain was looking in a mirror. Reflecting in those tears, he saw himself and flashes of his life.

"Please don't do it." Joe's bottom lip trembled as the words quavered out. He shook his head. Gone was the fun-loving jokester for whom he was well known and loved.

Kain wanted to speak. But his brain and tongue hadn't yet connected. A heavy cloud of shame and embarrassment wrapped around him. Was he *really* prepared to put himself out of his misery? He lowered his head and slumped back into the chair at the table. Joe sat opposite. Kain couldn't bring himself to look directly at his friend. Joe's breaths came fast and heavy.

Joe cleared his throat. "Mate, I . . ." He swallowed with a gulp, bobbing his Adam's Apple. This was obviously making him very uncomfortable.

Kain forced his gaze to Joe. "I'm sorry. I don't know what I was thinking." Tears found their familiar exit along with his words.

"Maybe you need to get some professional help." Joe reached across the table and placed his hand firmly on top of Kains. "I love ya, mate, but I don't know how to help ya." He shrugged. "But you can't bloody do *that*, okay."

Kain couldn't help a grin before bringing his hand back from beneath Joe's. "You gettin' mushy on me?" A tiny part of the ominous cloud had just dispersed. He wiped the tears.

"Yes, I bloody am." Joe's words growled in mock seriousness. "If I have to wrestle you down to the floor and give you a big sloppy smacker on the lips to get you to lighten up, I bloody well will."

"You're serious, aren't you?" Kain wasn't one hundred percent convinced, but he wouldn't put it past Joe. The grin turned into a chuckle. More of the heavy cloud melted away.

"Betcha a million bucks I'd do it." Joe's grin almost split his face. The fear and terror had disappeared from his eyes. The cheeky larrikin was back.

Kain laughed. His heart lightened. His shoulders lifted and the dark cloud drifted higher. "No thanks. I think I can come to my senses without you slobbering all over me."

"Right, I'll put these away then, shall I?" Joe got up, picked up the remaining items from the bench and put them and the bottle he'd taken from Kain, back into the medicine cabinet. "We need one of those child-proof locks. Even an adult can't open those bloody things." He sat back at the table and swallowed the last of his coffee. "Okay, now what?"

"Thanks mate. I don't know what would have happened if you hadn't come along." Kain sipped his now luke-warm coffee. "Yuk, that's cold. You want another?" He got up and switched on the plastic electric kettle by the sink.

"Yeah thanks." Joe spun around on his chair and handed Kain his empty cup.

"I was in a horrible black hole before, Joe." Kain shuddered, spooning the coffee and sugar into the cups. "I just wanted out."

"I think I understand, mate. But that doesn't mean it's the right choice to make."

Kain took the milk from the fridge, stopped and stared at Joe. "Please don't tell anyone what just happened, Joe. No-one needs to know and I'd rather just forget it. It was a stupid spur-of-the-moment thing, okay? I feel a lot better now."

Joe held up both hands. "No worries mate. S'long as you're certain you won't ever think like that again."

Kain shook his head. "I won't. Promise." He finished making the fresh coffees and placed the steaming mugs on the table before sitting again. "Actually, I'm going to go back to the cops today and tell them my suspicions." He took a sip of coffee.

"What? That you think Grace might still be alive?" Joe frowned and averted Kain's eyes.

"Yes, why not? Oh come on, Joe. Don't give me that look. You don't believe me do you?"

Joe looked back at Kain. His shoulders dropped with his outgoing breath. He scratched his chin. "I don't know what to believe, to be honest. Some things do seem a bit suss, but . . ." He looked away again.

"But what?"

"I'm worried about you getting your hopes up for . . . something that might not happen, okay." Joe's brown eyes bore deep into his.

Kain placed his cup on the table and leaned back in his chair. "Mate, if there is the slightest, most *remote* chance that some big stuff up has happened and Grace *didn't* die in that crash then I want to know and find her. She could be wondering around out in that bush. Injured, scared or . . . " He couldn't bring himself to say, 'dead'. He gulped down the last of his coffee and jumped up. "I'm off to the cop shop. Wanna come?"

"Nah, sorry, I can't." Joe finished his coffee and put both mugs on the sink. "Have to do some stuff at home with Sue. She likes to get all homey on Sundays. I'll call you later, though. Sure you're okay?"

Kain nodded and gave a thumbs-up signal. "Okay. Thanks, mate. Lock the door on your way out." He snatched his keys from the kitchen bench and strode out the door.

"Be careful." Joe followed him out. "Good luck."

Kain slipped on a pair of thongs that was in his utility, pushed the keys into the ignition and roared his trusty vehicle to life. He had an optimistic feeling about the outcome of this visit to the police.

Traffic was quiet and in next to no time he was pulling up outside the police station. He took a deep breath to steady the flitting butterflies and wiped his clammy palms on his shorts before alighting.

"Anybody around?" The foyer and main office seemed deserted. The click of a door opening from a side office broke the silence. Kain recognised Sergeant Rawlings who he'd previously spoke to about the accident.

"Ah, Kain Burrows. How are you holding up?"

His tone was sympathetic, or was there a hint of pretentiousness in his greeting? Kain decided that he didn't want to focus on analysing anything, so let it go. "G'day Sarge." Why the hell was he here? Maybe this was not such a good idea. "Um . . .yeah, I'm okay . . . thanks."

He hadn't put any thought into what he'd say when he arrived here. Every minute of the drive he'd thought about Grace, his hope of finding her and the wonderful reunion they would have. Maybe he was unrealistic and just plain stupid.

"What can I do for you today?" He frowned at Kain and averted his eyes to the left.

Kain turned slightly, following the officer's gaze, wondering if someone else was behind him. There was no-one. Strange. He looked back at Rawlings. "Umm . . . it's about Grace." He took a deep breath and wiped his damp palms on his shorts again. This was not going to be easy. "I . . ."

His gaze darted about the room. They came to a sudden stop on a wall poster. The graphic picture showed a smashed car and a bloodied body hanging out one opened door. Just below the dangling, lifeless hand was a mobile phone. Kain didn't need to read the dire warning in large letters about texting while driving. He looked back at the Sergeant. "I have reason to believe that Grace *wasn't* killed in that accident."

Rawlings stiffened. Hands dropped to his side. His shoulders jerked further back, like a soldier ordered to attention. He stared down at Kain. "What the hell are you on about, Kain?" His frown deepened, as his voice had just done, furrowing his pink forehead until his greying eyebrows almost joined.

A bolt of panic hit Kain, flowing from his head to his now tingling feet. He realised how a mouse must feel a second before being grabbed by a ravenous eagle.

"Well?"

Come on Burrows. Just spit it out. That inner voice solidified his resolve. "Look Sergeant, I know you'll think I've gone mad, but I think Grace might still be alive. I found evidence at -.”

“You *what?*” Rawlings roared. “You went up there yesterday, didn’t you? I told you to *stay away?*” His pink face now a deep red, a stark contrast to the narrowing green eyes. Beads of sweat appeared on his forehead. He leaned over the counter toward Kain, placing his elbows on the counter-top. “And what sort of evidence did you find, Sherlock?”

Was that a half-smirk on Rawlings face? Kain wished Joe had come with him. *You old prick.* “I found a shoe that-.”

“So.” The smirk was real. Rawlings thin lips briefly widened before tightening again. He shrugged, but his glare burned through Kain.

“It’s not Grace’s.” Kain inhaled a deep breath of re-solve and tolerance. It wasn’t enough. Rawling’s non-chalant attitude burrowed under his skin and raised his pulse rate. The knot in his stomach blew up like a beach ball. “Can you at least let me finish what I’m saying?”

Rawlings grinned. “Okay.” He held up both hands in truce. “Sorry. Tell me what you found.”

The pathetic falseness of the apology left a bitter taste in Kain’s mouth, but he thought of Grace. Grace, who could still be alive and wandering around in the bush, dazed and hurt. Grace, who just might be back in his arms soon. He’d never let her go again. “All right, I *did* go up to the crash site.” Rawlings’ eyes rolled. “And I’m glad I did. I found a shoe that had been thrown out of the car. It’s *not* Grace’s.”

"How do you know it came from the car and how do you know it's not Grace's? Women have thousands of shoes." The sergeant stood back upright and placed his hands in his dark blue trouser pockets.

Kain slammed his closed fist down on the counter. "Look, I know you think I'm an idiot, but I *know* the shoe is not Grace's. She doesn't have *thousands* of shoes and they're not even her size." Rawlings raised his eyebrows. "It was fresh on the ground when I found it. I could easily tell it hadn't been there very long. The other one was in the car, burnt but I'm sure they matched."

"But you don't know for certain, do you?" The officer's head shook several times.

For Christ's sake, give me a break. "Yes I do, actually. And that's not all I found. There was broken glass from the driver's window around on the ground. Grace hated driving with the window up. She always left it down, unless she was on the highway. She would have been driving slow up that range so she definitely would've had it down. One time, when we were going up there she said how she loved to feel the wind on her face and smell the bush smells. There's no way she would have had that window up, going up that range."

"Mr Burrows, I appreciate you clinging to hope that your girlfriend may still be alive, but shattered glass doesn't necessarily mean the window was up. The car landed upside down. The impact could have still shattered the glass while it was down and it could have simply fallen out."

Kain's heart dropped to his feet. He hadn't thought of that. Then the sight of the glass spread out several metres came to mind. "That glass was spread around." He flung his arms out in demonstration and frustration. "If it had've just fallen out wouldn't it just be in a little area right near the window?" Tears of frustration threatened but he swallowed hard and blinked several times.

Rawlings shrugged. "Possibly. But your assumptions still don't prove that Miss Atkinson was not the driver and not the body retrieved from the vehicle. You have to come up with something better than that."

Kain wanted to bang his head against the counter. One last effort… "I know Grace better than anyone. She would *never* text and drive. She does *not* own those shoes and she would *not* have had the window up."

"From what her father told us, she was very upset with you for dumping her. She may not have been her usual self. As a matter of fact, you want to tell me why you dumped her?" His eyes squinted in scrutiny again.

"What? No!" Kain hadn't been expecting such a personal question. A blatant attack on him. Something Bruce would ask. "That's got nothing to do with it. Yes, I know she was upset and I'm so bloody sorry I did that. I want her back. I want to say sorry to her and . . . just hold her . . ." The persistent tears won out. He couldn't hold them back any longer. He wiped each cheek in turn with the back of his hand.

"What do you think happened then Kain? Do you think someone else, another female, was driving and it was *her* that was killed?"

The unrealistic absurdity of that information confronted him when he heard those words. He turned away from the sergeant and breathed long and deep. Perhaps he was just grasping at feeble, spindly straws. Straws that seemed to snap and crumble as soon as his anxious fingers touched them. *But it WAS possible.* That inner voice wouldn't let up. He turned back. "Yes. That *is* what I believe. Why aren't yous out searching?"

"There are no reports of anyone else missing. Only Grace's belongings were found in or near the car. *Her* car, might I add."

"What about an autopsy? DNA? You didn't do that did you?" The hairs on the back of his neck rose along with his blood pressure. A rhythmic thumping began in his temples. "You don't know for sure it was Grace and you can't now because that . . . that arsehole excuse for a father of hers demanded she be cremated straight away."

Kain lurched forward and grabbed the front of the Sergeant's shirt, sending papers and pamphlets to the floor. "How much did he pay for that to happen?" He twisted his hand, pulling the shirt tight. "How much? Who took his dirty money?" His spittle flew out and hit the officer's chin.

"Let go." Rawlings red angry face now a deep shade of purple.

"No. Not until you tell me." He heard a click by the officer's side. Something hard and cold poked him in the ribs. Letting the shirt go, he stepped back with his hands up. "You haven't got the guts. You haven't got the guts to answer my question and you don't have the guts to shoot me." He pursed his lips to stop them trembling, even though his whole body now quivered. "If you know, one hundred percent, that that was Grace in the accident, then shoot me now."

"Don't be stupid, Kain."

"I said, just fucking shoot me *now*." Kain shouted. He wanted to scream. He wanted to just get all the horrible feelings out of his body and heart. Most of all he wanted his soul out of his useless, pain and guilt wracked body.

Strong hands grabbed each of his arms from behind. "What the . . .?" He spun his head but didn't have time to see much. Two younger officers forced his forearms up his back. "Let me go." It was no use, he couldn't move.

"You okay, Sarge?"

"Yeah, I'm all right. Glad you two got here when you did though."

"What do you want to do with him? Charge him with assault?"

The grip tightened on Kain's arms. The room spun. This shouldn't be happening. Bruce Frigging Atkinson would just love this. No, no, just *no*.

"No. Throw him in a cell until he calms down. He's crazy with grief." Rawlings straightened up his shirt.

"Come on."

Kain was pushed toward a hallway. So many things he wanted to say, but nothing came out. It was just another twist in the nightmare that had become his life. One officer slammed him against a wall, while the other opened the barred door and grabbed Kain's phone from the top of his shorts. Again he was pushed. Pushed inside the cell as the door clanged shut behind him. Pushed to his limits.

How much more could he take?

He tried to see the officers' faces, etch them in his memory, but when he looked back they were walking out.

He turned to the stark, brick wall of the cell. The simmering volcano erupted. Lava spewed forth. Kain brought his clenched fist back and drove his knuckles into the rough, dark brick. Air gushed from his lungs with a mighty grunt. Pain like no other replaced his hand. He couldn't move his fingers. There was no feeling, only screaming pain. So many different types of pain, but they permeated every millimetre of his body, mind and soul. He collapsed on the bed clutching his injured hand and cried long and hard.

CHAPTER 25

G race closed her eyes, splashing the welcome refreshing water over her face in the bathroom basin. The sun, well and truly up and heating everything. Humidity already hung in the air. The moment her eyes closed, Seth's scarred hand with the twisted fingers overrode any other thoughts. The images played tag in her mind most of the night, thwarting sleep.

Her overactive brain insisted on reliving the events of the previous night. She and Seth had kissed. *Kissed!* What on earth had she been thinking? Maybe the sudden coolness of the water would erase the warm flush that prickled her face. She looked up, expecting to look into a mirror. The blank wall. *Damn.* Probably just as well. Her dry, scratchy eyes felt like falling out of their sockets. A touch of nausea swirled in the recesses of her stomach. Or maybe the nerves danced on hot coals, at the thought of facing Seth.

She wiped her face on the thick towel. Her tired body longed for a shower but she simply couldn't muster the energy. Putting off the inevitable would only make her feel worse. Her brain wouldn't let up. Over and over it nagged her to talk to Seth about what had happened, but her heart just wanted to forget all the craziness. Not just the previous night, but the whole past week or so. Could this all just be a bad dream? Soon she'd wake, surely. Wake up in Kain's loving arms and all would be right with the world. *Her* world.

Grace reached for the door handle. The small room began to spin. She closed her eyes and leaned forward, on to the door. She licked her dry lips, but there was barely any moisture on her sticky tongue to wet them.

She needed water. Taking a deep breath, she opened her eyes and exhaled. The dizziness exited along with her breath. Another deep inhalation, also of relief. She let go of the door handle and returned to the hand basin. Turning on the cold tap with her right hand, she cupped her left hand and let it fill with the cool water as she leaned down. It spilled over the sides of her hand and gurgled down the plug. She brought some to her approaching thirsty lips and swished the water about in her mouth, ensuring it reached every nook before swallowing. The coolness slid down her oesophagus and spread into her stomach which rumbled and gurgled when another mouthful followed. It seemed to be saying *thank you.*

Two more mouthfuls and the unpleasant sensations subsided. She stood upright and, again, looked at the blank wall. She really needed to assure Seth it was okay to have a mirror.

Now, come on Grace, go out and talk to him. Her inner conscious badgered. "Okay, okay. I can do this." *Now!*

Grace took one deep breath, opened the bathroom door and stepped out to the hallway.

The liquid in her stomach growled in protest. Her mouth went from desert sand to a slushy bog. She turned and dived into the toilet, lifting the seat just as the water, now warm after mixing with her gastric juices, shot out of her mouth. Grabbing both sides of the bowl, Grace's stomach exuded its mere contents. Tears dripped into the bowl. Saliva dribbled from her open mouth. She spat to remove the sticky, tepid fluid. Her stomach turned inside out and continued to buckle and spasm. Nothing more would come out. Stomach acid burnt her already irritated throat.

Through blurred eyes, Grace staggered back to the hand basin. Another mouthful of water, but this time she spat it out after swishing her mouth. She swallowed just a sip and washed and dried her face . . . again.

"Are . . . are you all right . . . Grace?"

The deep, but yet soft, voice froze Grace to the spot for a second or two. Seth was right there. She turned toward him, bringing the towel to her chest, clutching it below her throat. "Um . . . " Even through his scars she could see the concern on his face - the slight furrow in his forehead, the intensity in his eyes. Hear it in his words, as few as there were. The way he spoke her name - slightly softer than the other words and after a brief moment of hesitation. Like speaking her name was another question on its own.

She nodded. "I think so. I was sick, but I feel a bit better now."

Standing in the doorway, Seth's solid frame took up a large portion of the space. She wanted to get out of the bathroom. *Needed* to get out of the bathroom. Fresh air and something logical to come from this chaos, were the two things Grace needed more than anything at that moment.

He didn't seem to want to move. Dressed in the familiar long sleeved shirt, jeans and boots he just stood there, arms by his side. The gloves. He had both gloves on. That's odd. Why would he bother wearing them now, knowing she'd seen his hand the previous night?

Grace hung the towel over its rack, hoping the action would induce Seth to move aside, or better still, just go to the kitchen or where ever he needed to go. She thought she could be strong and talk to him about the previous night. *Yeah right.*

Thoughts scattered throughout her brain like a bunch of scared rabbits. Why was she so sick all of a sudden? Why couldn't she sleep last night? Why was Seth so damned *nice* to her when he was virtually holding her prisoner? *You know the answer to that.* She wished that inner voice would just shut up. Why did her car run off the road, causing the accident? Why did Kain *really* dump her? Why? Why? Why? So many damned questions and so few answers.

She turned toward him again, without a clue as what to say. He was gone. There'd been no sound at all. No heavy footsteps. A prickly chill skied full speed down her spine, shooting out pins and needles to her hands and feet. '*The Ghost Who Walks*', her only thought for a moment. She gulped in a deep breath, not realising her breathing had frozen. An elephant grip grasped her chest and her heart beat quickened.

Could he possibly read her mind? Was he superhuman? Subhuman? *More damn questions.*

Grace tiptoed forward and peered out the door. No sign of him in the hallway. Had he even been there? Maybe she'd imagined it. The house was quiet. The birds outside were quiet. Eerily quiet. She looked at the floor then chided herself. *You idiot. You're not going to see his footprints.* The toilet. She went back and flushed her sickness away.

"Okay, so I might be losing the plot," she consoled herself, "but I'm alive and . . ." She stopped whispering, unable to think what else to be thankful for at that point. It was all too confusing. "Could go a cup of tea." She nodded and walked to the kitchen, hoping the tea would stay in her unpredictable belly.

An ear-splitting clang, followed by a crash, from the kitchen jolted her as she walked through the lounge room. Her heart was now at the Olympic Record speed. She took the deepest breath her lungs could hold and lunged into the kitchen. "Seth? What the . . .?"

Seth lay sprawled on his back next to the sink, one arm out to the side and the other resting on his lower abdomen. A frying pan and saucepan either side of him. A chair lay on its side and one of the lower cupboard doors hung open.

Grace ran the several metres and knelt by his head. His eyes were closed, skin pale and breathing shallow. She placed her hand on his chest. "Seth, can you hear me?" Afraid of hurting him further, she shook him like a mother gently waking her child. He barely quivered. She shook him harder. His ashen lips parted several millimetres and emitted a faint groan. "I don't care about the consequences. I'm calling an ambulance." She grabbed the phone from his top shirt pocket and tapped the screen. Nothing. She pushed the button at the top. Still nothing. "Locked! Shit! Stuff you and all your bloody secrets." Grace dropped the phone on the floor, got up and rushed back to the bathroom for a face washer. "Wouldn't have been able to tell them where we are anyway." She sighed at the hopelessness of the whole situation.

After wetting the face washer she rushed back to the kitchen. She gasped, stopping in her hasty tracks. Seth was sitting, leaning against the sink cupboard. His knees were up, his elbows rested on them and his hands clasped his head.

Several of his shirt buttons were undone, exposing bare, but slightly scarred skin of his chest. Again, she knelt beside him. "Are you okay? What happened?" She wiped the beaded sweat from his pallid forehead.

As soon as those words left her lips, a hard rock formed inside her galloping heart. The rock expanded until it took over her whole chest. She placed one hand on his shoulder while the other took hold of his gloved hand. That 'rock' wasn't fear, confusion or hopelessness. It was an overwhelming desire to help and protect him.

"I . . . I don't really know." He opened his eyes wide and blinked several times. "I remember getting things out to cook some breakfast and . . . " His large shoulders rose and fell in a shrug. "Next thing I woke up on the floor. Must have fainted."

Grace got up and poured him a glass of water from the fridge. "Here, this might make you feel a bit better." She moved the glass closer to his lips.

He took it. "Thanks." One careful sip at a time he drank it down.

His chin rose with the emptying glass and more of his chest became exposed. Grace couldn't help but look. There were some scarring and sparse dark hairs. *Why are you perving on another man's chest? I'm NOT perving.* How she wished that inner voice would bugger off. In total disgust with it, she looked away. She was *not* perving.

Something lassoed her gaze and pulled it back to his chest. He continued swallowing his water. A birth mark? A darker scar? Or was that a tattoo? There was something on the left side of his chest. Quite small, part of it obscured by scarring.

Grace inched toward him, tempted to open his shirt a little. She could only see part of it, but the green and red colouring on his pale skin had to be a tattoo. Maybe it signified something to him. She wanted to see more, look harder, closer, but he swallowed the last mouthful and handed her the glass.

"Thank you again, Grace."

With his chin back down, his beard almost covered the shirt opening. She missed her opportunity. She just knew that tattoo told a story even though she couldn't see it properly. *I will find out who you really are, Seth.*

"You're welcome." She smiled and took the glass, reached up and placed it on the sink. Grace got up and stood the chair back upright. He was on his feet before she'd even turned around. "Be careful. Here." She pulled out the chair she'd just up righted and turned it toward him.

"I'm all right." His voice hardened. "But thanks for your concern."

He seemed distant, closed off all of a sudden. "Geez, we're a fine pair today aren't we?" She laughed. "I'm spewing and you're fainting." She hoped it would lighten his mood.

He flickered a brief smile at her and stared off into nothing.

She couldn't help herself. "Seth, what happened then? What are you thinking about now?" She expected him to snap at her or at best, tell her to mind her business.

Seth shuffled his feet and looked at her. "Grace, I . . . what the . . .?" He looked down. "Did my phone fall out of my pocket?" He reached and picked it up, turned it on and slid it back into his top pocket.

"No." He was not going to like this. "I got it out and tried to call you an ambulance."

His dark eyes narrowed to slits and his lips tightened. "You what? Grace, don't *ever* do that again, do you understand?" Precise, firm anger seeped into his voice, bordering on rage.

Every word pierced her heart. He glared at her with quickening breath. His cutting gaze and scathing tone could have sliced the air and shattered the silence. Silence that descended the room like a monstrous boulder had crashed to a halt after a landslide. It was *not* what she was expecting.

So much for learning what he was thinking or what happened to make him fall and so much for caring about him. Tears stung her eyes and she took a deep breath to help clear her thoughts. "I only wanted to help you. You could have been dying for all I knew." Grace walked to the front door. One hand reached for the screen handle but her brain told her to stop. She wanted to get away from him. Far away. It was all becoming too much, but deep down she still wished to help him. Grace Atkinson was not a quitter. She *had* to give it one last try.

Grace dropped her hand and turned to face him. *It was now or never.* "Seth, what the *hell* is going on? I have no idea where we are. You don't want me to leave. I try to help you and now you're angry?" She threw both hands in the air, but the right hand only rose so far. She winced. "Ouch. Bloody thing." She rubbed her right shoulder. "If you're going to keep me here, for goodness sake, let me in."

His scowl softened and turned to a frown of confusion.

"Let me into your mind. Tell me what is going on . . . *please.*"

He stared at her. She could almost hear the cogwheels turning in his brain. Maybe, at long last, he would open up. *Really* open up. Grace couldn't cut the connection between their eyes. To do so would lose it. His cold, hard stare softened. His body seemed to relax, just a little, but it was a positive sign.

He indicated to the chair opposite. "Please sit down, Grace." His voice had mellowed to a soft tone.

At last. Some of the tension left her body. She dragged out the chair and sat opposite. A cuppa would go well at this precise moment but she daren't distract herself . . . or him. Grace clasped her hands together on her lap and waited for some much needed answers.

"I'll make us a cup of tea." Seth stood, turned to the bench, shook the kettle to check water level and switched it on before settling back on the chair.

"Thanks." Grace nodded and smiled, the air between them no longer so thick. Maybe she wouldn't have to prise the words out of him after all. The minor distraction seemed to decrease even more of the tension.

Seth placed his gloved hands on the table edge. He glanced at them. In a split second they were out of view, down on his lap.

"You don't have to keep hiding your hands, Seth. Or your face either, for that matter." She thought of the blank walls in the bathroom and his bedroom, where a mirror should be. "I haven't, and never will, judge you on your appearance. But I can't handle all the mystery and secrets." There . . . she said it. She sucked in her lips and held her breath, awaiting his reply.

"I don't know all the answers to your questions, Grace. There are things that-." The boiling kettle stopped him. He could have ignored it but looked relieved at the excuse to get up.

Yet another distraction when he was about to tell her something. More frustration.

Seth returned the milk to the fridge and held up a packet of bread. "Toast?"

Grace would have just liked tea for the moment. Not just for the sake of her queasy stomach, but she didn't want any more time wasted. Maybe he was hungry and also needed a few extra minutes to organise his words. *His words?* What was he going to tell her? Maybe she shouldn't hear his story. Maybe it would destroy the trust that was building between them. No, she *had* to know. "Yes please."

Soon the enticing aroma of toast filled the kitchen. Grace's mouth watered, but this time from hunger, not nausea. Seth remained silent, spreading the toast and placing Grace's on a plate in front of her. He sat and chomped into his piece, crunching through the crust. He seemed in no hurry to tell her anything. Maybe he'd just told her to sit down to shut her up and keep her inside. *Who knows?*

Grace almost gave up in defeat. It was obvious now that Seth would only tell her *anything* when he was good and ready. She sipped the hot tea and bit into her toast. *No point starving.* She watched his lips move as he ate. Her mind drifted back to the previous night and her gaze dropped as her face flushed warm.

"I was going to cook a meal, but I don't feel so hungry since I fell. I'll cook you something if you like."

Grace jumped. His deep voice came as a surprise. "What? Um . . . no thanks. I'm not that hungry either since I was sick. I'll get something later if I need to." She did feel hungry, but just wanted him to open up and talk. "You were going to tell me something." She had no idea if that *was* his intention, but he needed a push. He stared at her again. Was he trying to read her mind or just trying to think what to say, or what *not* to say? His neutral expression gave away no clues.

"Grace, I . . ." The beeping phone stopped him. He took it out of his shirt pocket and looked at the screen. His face paled. "I have to take this," he mumbled, getting up and heading out the door.

His boots clomped, almost rattled, down the steps. He must have run. Grace couldn't hear his voice at all. "Damn you, Seth." She got up and went to the front door. The screen swung open in the breeze. He'd been in such a hurry he hadn't even latched it properly.

She reached out to take hold of the handle. There he was, standing over in his driveway, his back to her, still on his phone. She heard his voice but the strong breeze carried the words away. It was pointless trying to listen so she closed the door and made another cup of tea.

She sighed. *I give up.* The second cup of tea tasted and felt good as it went down. She grasped the mug with both hands and leant on the bench staring out the window above the sink. A large eagle circled and glided above the trees. The morning sun brightened the bird's shiny brown feathers. It dived, disappearing among the green canopy of the bush. Some luckless animal was probably now being carted off somewhere to be torn apart and devoured. Grace thought of the dogs and shuddered.

"Grace, I have to go somewhere." Seth was behind her. She flinched. This man was certainly the master of stealth when he wanted. Hard to comprehend when he was so large and heavy but she hadn't even heard the familiar click and squeak of the screen door opening.

She pivoted to face him, still clasping the mug. He looked scared. Was it worth asking him 'where'? "Oh." Was all she could muster. Another disappointment. No point asking any questions. Her shoulders dropped and she placed the almost empty mug on the bench beside her. Maybe there was one last glimmer of hope. "Is there anything I can help you with?"

"Um . . . no, sorry. I'll be back later." He picked up his hat from beside the door and disappeared. Within seconds his utility was roaring into life and heading along the driveway.

Grace stood in silence for . . . she had no idea how long she stood grounded to the spot. The noise of Seth's vehicle had long faded. Again the bush sounds were her only companions, but as the temperature rose with the morning, the bird songs gradually quietened.

What was she to do now? The cups of tea revitalised her. She now had the energy for that much needed shower. She smiled and headed to her room for clean clothes. The calendar on the lounge room wall caught her eye and drew her over. Just what *was* the date? Heck, she wasn't even sure what day it was, so looking at the calendar wouldn't help.

A ripple of nausea travelled through her stomach again. She placed her hand on her lower abdomen. A flicker of movement danced beneath her hand, like a butterfly fluttering about on a flower. Or maybe it was her imagination. Grace studied the calendar. Her brow creased but she ignored the pain it produced. She had no idea why she felt so different since placing her hand on her stomach, but one thing she *was* sure of and could remember . . . it had been a long time since she'd had a period.

CHAPTER 26

Seth flicked off the radio in his utility. Even with the volume turned down low, the incessant chatting and laughter of the DJ's, the loud sing-song advertisement for a local caryard and the soppy love song that followed, tensed every cubic centimetre of his body.

His gut already in knots over what lay ahead. Jimmy's words over the phone had been urgent, drenched with fear.

The need to lash out and punch all those people on the radio overpowered Seth's rational thinking. Why couldn't his life be oh-so-perfect like theirs? Why can't he ever laugh and sing like he hadn't a care in the world? Instead, the top of the steering wheel copped his frustration. His gloved, clenched fist smashed down hard. A half-grunt, half-growl flew out of his mouth, scratching and burning his throat. His temples throbbed. "Fuck you, Jimmy and fuck *you*, Scott."

Scott. The arrogant, pig-headed, heartless Scotsman. Scott, who only reached Seth's shoulder in height. Seth's hands gripped the wheel tighter. If only it was Scott's neck. His teeth clenched and his breathing deepened. Steam could start spewing form his nostrils at any second. He was a stirred-up bull, about the charge. *Wish I could snap your neck, Scott.*

How he wished he had the courage do just that. With Scott out the way he would be free. Free of guilt, fear and the onerous burden he carried on tired shoulders. Free to spend more time with Grace without being at anyone's annoying beck and call. But he would never be free of one thing – his scars. If only . . .

Seth reached up, turned the rear vision mirror and forced himself to look, not just into the mirror, but into his own face and soul. He wondered what he really looked like. How he wished he could tear off the layers of scarring and see his true face. His true identity. Who the hell was he? He slowed the vehicle over to the side of the road and let it idle. Taking a deep breath for courage, he forced his reluctant gaze to the mirror again.

A pathetic, tortured soul looked back at him, something out of a horror movie. Sometimes he'd sit up late at night watching horror movies. He felt comfortable with them, like he should be the starring character. Vague memories of the horrific attack entered his brain. He closed his eyes and pretended a bulldozer was pushing all those memories to one side, exposing fresh, clean soil, or in his case, a fresh, clean unscarred face. The thumping in his temples increased the more his silent pleas intensified. *Just let me see what I used to look like. Please.* He brought his hands up, pressing the heel of his palms into his temples and rubbed in small circles.

Was that an outline forming in that fresh, clean soil? Was that a smile? "Come on . . . *think*." Short brown hair? *Poofff.* Gone. The scarred monster now all he could see. The laughing voices of his attackers tormented his mind and assaulted his eardrums like it was yesterday. The soil was all messed up and ugly again.

He opened his eyes, dropped his hands and let his head fall back against the headrest. It was no use. There was absolutely no point in wishing for something that would *never* happen. And as for killing Scott. Who was he kidding? Scott was almost like a Deity. He had men, and probably women, who worshipped the ground he walked. Disciples. If he so much as looked at him the wrong way, one of them would make his life even more miserable. He'd be living in a deeper pit of fear and dread than he did already.

Seth took his wallet out of his jeans pocket and opened it to reveal his license. The same wretched face stared back at him. Empty. Devoid of any emotion or life, just like his heart had been before he found Grace. The day Scott took that photo seemed so long ago. He'd told Seth what had happened, what was happening and what would happen, especially if he didn't follow orders. A week or so later, 'Seth Andrews' was able to legally drive on the road. He had an identity. He had a wallet containing a licence and some cash. He had a home.

Even though he'd asked several times, Scott was adamant he didn't know Seth's real name. Probably a lie. He flung his open wallet on to the seat beside him, grated the gear stick into first and planted his foot. May as well get this over and done with, one way or the other. "All right, Jimmy. I'm comin'."

Some thirty minutes later he lifted his foot from the accelerator and hit the indicator switch left. The shady, long dirt driveway would take him back to the property where'd they buried the man the previous day. Seth's heart banged against his ribcage, like a madman trying to escape a padded cell.

He took several deep breaths but to no avail. His heart knew this was not good but his head just did as ordered. Stomach acid ascended to his throat. His mouth watered, leaving a bitter, acrid taste. He swallowed hard and rubbed his chest. "This that last job I'm going to do for you, Scott. Some way, somehow, after this I'm *out*. No more."

Even if it meant taking Grace home. She cared enough not to let anything happen to him. *Didn't she?* She may even know of a doctor that could fix his scars. He'd seen a television programme one night where they turned grotesque into 'normal'. Yes, it *was* possible. He dared to dream.

A silver utility similar to his appeared out of nowhere. With no time to veer off Seth lifted his boot from the accelerator and slammed it down hard on the brake. His heart rate shot off the Richter Scale. His body jerked forward, only held back by the seatbelt. His chin hit his chest, flew upwards, bumping the back of his head down on the headrest. A shudder and he was still, except for slight trembling caused from the idling, vibrating vehicle.

The silver ute also came to an abrupt halt. The driver got out and approached. Seth's shoulders dropped with a grunt of relief. "Jimmy. I didn't know who the hell it was. Glad it's you." The herd of brumbies stampeding through his heart dispersed to a one-horse trot. "You nearly gave me a heart attack. What are you doin' here? Thought we were meeting up ahead, at Scott's." Seth lifted his pointer finger from the steering wheel, pointed ahead of him and dropped both gloved hands to his lap.

"Sorry, mate. Didn't mean to." He lifted his broad hat and wiped the sweat from his white forehead. "Bloody hot."

"Yeah, I know that." Seth did the same thing, using his long sleeves. "Righto, what's going on? You sounded frantic on the phone but you're not now." He switched off the ignition and returned his hand to his lap. Jimmy went to speak, but the loud call of a storm bird in a nearby tree drowned out his words and shut his mouth.

It seemed like an eternity before Jimmy spoke again. "Yeah, well . . ." He licked his lips, looked about and turned back to Seth. His green eyes squinted and his brow furrowed beneath his hat. "We can't meet there. Scott just called me again and said that the cops were getting closer to sniffing out the place. So far they didn't know that it's Scott's. But he's not taking any chances. He said for us to meet at your place."

My place? Oh no. This was *not* on the agenda. *Shit!* He hadn't even thought about that possibility. How could he have been so stupid? *Too wrapped up in fantasising about Grace, that's how.* The words swum around Seth's brain. Scott said, *ordered* would be more like it, they were to meet as his place. Was his suspicious about Grace? Was he sending Jimmy in as a spy? Anything was possible. *Think fast.* "That's not a good idea either."

Jimmy shrugged. "Why not?"

"Because . . . there was a strange car sitting up in my driveway yesterday. I think someone was spying on me." He glanced through the windscreen ahead, hoping Jimmy would buy his lie.

"Shit. What did it look like?"

"It was blue. Dunno what sort it was. It turned around and took off when I walked out on to the verandah." He looked back at Jimmy. Yep, the worried expression showed he believed Seth. *You're not the brightest spark are you, Jimmy?* Sometimes he wondered why Scott kept Jimmy on. No doubt he had his reasons, as Scott did for every choice he made, no matter how misguided they often were, or cruel.

The sun disappeared behind thick clouds. A distant rumble spread throughout the bush. The breeze dropped to sticky nothingness.

"Storm comin'. Bit early." Jimmy looked at the sky behind him. "C'mon, let's get out of here. I don't want to be caught out in it."

"That's right. You're scared of storms." Seth grinned. "Geez, Jimmy, if that's all you got to be scared of, you must be . . . " He couldn't think of a word to complete that statement. If Jimmy thought storms were scary he obviously had never copped the full wrath of Scott.

"What? Yeah, a bit." Another, louder, rumble. His fair face paled to bed-sheet white. "Well . . . what are we gunna do?"

"Get in your ute and follow me."

Jimmy nodded, ran to his vehicle and jumped into the driver's seat. Seth started his utility, backed around, careful not to hit any bushes and hoping not to back into any rocks hidden by the long grass. No bumps or obstacles. He drove out the way he'd entered with Jimmy tagging close behind.

Several kilometres along, Seth indicated right and swung into another dirt road. Jimmy followed, like an obedient puppy. Over a crest and around a bend, satisfied they would be out of view of the busier road, Seth pulled over, switched off the ignition and got out.

Thunder rumbled again, deep and foreboding. Through the filtered treetops, heavy clouds grew darker by the second, swirling and churning in the heart of the approaching storm. Branches had stopped swaying, birds had stopped singing. All was still and quiet. The thick, humid air almost choked Seth as he breathed. He coughed into his fist and wiped his dripping forehead and temples. Flies buzzing about his face ignored his swiping hand.

Jimmy approached. "I don't like this." He pointed upwards with a trembling hand.

Seth shook his head. He didn't understand why Jimmy was so scared. "Get in my ute. We'll be right."

Jimmy shot Seth a worried look, bounced around to the passenger side, jumped in and slammed the door.

"Easy on the door, mate."

"Sorry." Jimmy took off his hat, wiped his forehead, leant forward and gazed upwards through the windscreen. "I see green. Hail. Shit, we should just head into town."

"Jimmy, forget about the storm for a minute and tell me more of what Scott said. What's going on?"

"Righto, well -." A sharp crack of thunder pierced the sultry air, splitting an Ironbark tree not fifty metres away. Sparks, leaves and splintered timber sprayed in all directions. Nature's fireworks. Jimmy leapt upwards and off the seat. Huge raindrops splattered the windscreen, spreading out and sliding down the glass. "Shit!"

"*That* was close." Seth had jolted with fright too, but held it together for Jimmy's sake.

"Too bloody close, if you ask me." Jimmy groaned, shuddered, pressed his back into the seat and rubbed his palms on his shorts.

"Why *are* you so scared of storms, Jimmy?"

"Why *aren't* you?" Jimmy's voice rose and cracked.

Seth shrugged. "Dunno. I suppose because a storm's never hurt me."

"Well it did *me.*"

"What happened?"

The rain pelted down heavier. The windscreen was soon awash. Twigs, small branches and leaves thwacked against the windscreen and roof. Another flash of white, immediately followed by an ear-damaging crash, which continued as a deep rumbling growl, shaking the earth.

"It's here. We're right under it now." Jimmy's face lost all blood, he shivered, his hands clenched together on his lap.

"Tell me why you're so scared of storms." Seth raised his voice above the din.

"All right." Jimmy cleared the sandpaper from his throat, returning his voice to a more manly tone. "When I was a kid, I was a bit scared of storms and the old man used to make fun of me. I tried not to let it show, but I just couldn't get over the fear." He took a deep breath. "Dad must've realised that I was still scared. One day, a huge wild storm came up. I was helping him fix a fence out in one of the back paddocks. I got scared, but he wouldn't leave the bloody fence and go home. Kept calling me a sook and a wuss."

"How old were you?"

Jimmy shrugged. "About eleven, I think. Anyway, once the rain started and the storm was nearly above us, he threw some tools in the back of the ute and told me to go and get the roll of wire that was back a bit. I ran for it, but then he took off and left me there."

"Are you for real? What sort of a father would do that to his kid? Hmph, probably something like Scott would do . . . if he had kids?"

Jimmy spat forth a short, bitter laugh. "My friggin' father. I saw him laughing at me as he drove away. He said something too, but I didn't catch it. Yeah, I could imagine Scott doing that."

"Surely he came back for you?"

"Ha. Like hell. He kept going all the way home. I ran and ran, calling and calling. Balling my eyes out too. Lucky there weren't too many trees, or I probably wouldn't be here now. Bastard."

"Does Scott ever mention family to you? Wonder if he does have any kids."

Jimmy shrugged one shoulder. "No, never heard him mention kids. He did say something once about wishing he could kill his uncle and father. I wasn't game to ask why."

"No, best not to."

Another flash and simultaneous bang.

"Shit, that one sounded like a gunshot." Seth leaned forward trying to see something, *anything*, amidst the white of the pouring rain.

Jimmy pulled his feet up onto the seat and wrapped his arms around his knees. "That's what I thought when I was running home through that storm. I thought God was trying to kill me and dad was letting him. I just couldn't understand what I'd done wrong. Why the old man hated me so much." He wiped both eyes and pursed his quivering lips together until they were as white as his face.

"You ever ask him why he did that?"

"Nup. When I finally got home, soaking wet and buggered, he just laughed a bit and told me it was for my own good. To 'toughen you up', I think were his exact words. I didn't talk to him, just went straight to bed. Mum didn't look very happy with him and she came in later and asked if I was all right and brought me a drink of milo. I wanted to grab her, hug her and disappear into her soft, safe body, away from him, but I was scared he'd just get up me more and her too."

"What about the next day?"

Jimmy shrugged again. "Nothing. Dad acted like nothing had happened. At first I thought it was a dream, but my throat was sore from yelling out, my legs were sore.

It wasn't a dream. Mum seemed to give him a few dirty looks and tried to give me more attention on the side, but otherwise nothing. I tell you what, Seth, it was bloody scary running all the way home through that storm. I'll never forget it and I'll never forgive that arsehole for doing that. It didn't fix my fear of storms, just made it worse."

"Do you get on with him these days?'

"You kidding? Nah. Things just got slowly worse over the years. Eventually I left home and I've never been back. Don't care if I never talk to him again in my life."

A large branch whacked the windscreen. Jimmy leapt off the seat, dropped to the floor under the dash and held the back of his head in both hands. Seth winced. He thought the storm was abating, but the wind seemed to have picked up again. The rain pelted the back screen. The storm had changed directions. *Ping. Ping.* Small hailstones hit the vehicle from all sides. Not good, but nothing to do but sit it out.

"So, I take it 'Jimmy' isn't your real name then, if you work for Scott?"

Jimmy removed his hands, looked up wide-eyed and brought his rear back up to the seat. He wiped his palms on the front of his shirt. "Bloody hail. I copped some of that running home that afternoon too. It cut my head a bit. At least this is small and round. What? Umm . . . " His gaze wandered away, through the misted windscreen. "No-o it's not. Yes it is . . . now. "

Seth didn't push any further. He didn't care what his real name was or wasn't. He just cared about getting this job done for Scott. "Look, the hail's stopped already and the rain has eased a bit. Can you tell me what Scott said now?"

Jimmy sat up straight, sucked in and blew out a sharp breath. "He thinks the cops are closing in. He wants this job done in the next few days. He's already got a few wheels in motion. Apparently, the old bastard we're pinching them from is a bit preoccupied at the moment, so now's a good time. I've got to go see Pete and the other blokes later today. We have to get the cattle to his contact up in the Gulf so they can be shipped straight off. Scott gets his money then he's clearing off."

Seth's heart danced and his eyes widened at the sound of those last words. It wasn't only the dark clouds outside that lifted. "What do you mean, he's clearing off?" Should he dare hope Scott would be out of his life forever?

"He said he'll have enough cash to get right away. Start a new life somewhere. He didn't say where, but he did say he wasn't coming back. Ever."

Seth smiled. Maybe, just *maybe*, his miserable life really was about to turn around for the better. With Scott out the way ... The smile spread until his cheeks hurt. The possibilities were endless. "I, for one, will be glad to see the back of him forever."

"Don't get too excited, Seth."

Those five words hit his guts like a medieval rammer. Jimmy's tone was lower than flat but overflowing with warning. A cold, jagged hail stone dropped all the way through Seth's spine. He swallowed hard. "What do you mean?"

"He reckons he's taking you with him. Dead or alive."

CHAPTER 27

Kain dragged his eyelids apart. Someone called out to him. Joe. He sprang from the cell bed and rubbed his eyes. Joe stood beside Rawlings outside the door, with a what-the-hell-have-you-done-now look in his eyes. A rattle, a couple of clinky clicks and Rawlings pulled the door open and stepped inside the cell.

"You can go, Kain. No charges . . . *this* time." He shook his finger at Kain and his eyes filled with anger. "I know you're going through hell, but that doesn't give you the right to come in here and demand something then assault me. Or anyone else for that matter. Here's your phone. Now get out and don't let me see you in here again."

Kain's gaze darted from Rawling to his phone being offered. He touched the back of his hip. It was bare. "How did you get that?"

"One of the officers confiscated it when they put you in here. Take it."

Kain stepped forward and reached for his phone. His inner rage still present, but reduced to a simmer. He breathed deep and fast, trying to calm his activated nervous system. "Thanks." He glanced at his phone, attached it on his hip and stepped around Rawlings. "Let's go, Joe." He headed to the door but his conscious got the better of him. He stopped and spun around. "Sorry about earlier, Sarge. I didn't mean to grab you."

Rawlings nodded once. "Just don't come back."

Kain nodded back and exited the police station with Joe by his side.

"Mate, what the hell happened in there?" Joe sped up to keep up with Kain's fast strides. "Hey, slow down a bit."

"The usual." Kain slowed his walk. "Hurry up, Joe. Rawlings wouldn't listen. How did you know I was still there?"

"I tried calling you a few times and got worried, so I rang here to see if you'd been. He told me you were in the lock-up. Of all places."

They stopped beside Kain's utility. He took his keys out of his shorts pocket. "Ouch." He looked at his right hand. Dried blood covered several areas of missing skin on the knuckles. He flexed his fingers. "Don't think anything's broken. Bastards locked me up."

Joe looked at Kain's hand and shook his head. "Did you hit one of them? Please tell me you didn't."

Kain tensed. "Joe, I don't need the third degree from you, okay. Had enough bullshit for today." He opened his vehicle door.

Joe slammed it shut, narrowly missing Kain's leg. "Hold on, mate." The jovial sparkle that normally accompanied Joe's easy-going banter had disappeared. "Look, I know you're going through a nightmare, but, for Christ sake, *stop* being such a hot head. Look at the trouble it gets you into." He grabbed Kain's right wrist and held it up. "You didn't punch anyone with this did you? You punched the wall. Was that before or after they locked you up?"

"After." Kain pulled his wrist away and turned his back to his best mate. Joe was right. Joe was always right. He did jump into things too soon, but he couldn't help himself. He rested his elbows on the vehicle roof and clenched his hands together under his chin. His chest expanded as he took the deepest breath possible. He had no idea what to say. He had no idea what or how to feel. He had no idea what to do next. Someone had just thrown him into a washing machine and turned it on, tumbling him this way and that.

Joe sighed with a slight groan. Was that unintended or was it to remind Kain that he was still there and he also had no idea what to say or think?

A floodlight lit up Kain's brain. He dropped his hands and turned to Joe, whose eyes were almost as sad and droopy as his moustache. "I'm sorry, Joe. It just pissed me off so bloody much when the cops weren't interested in what I found. I still think I might be right. Something is just *not* right with all this. Thank you for coming and getting me." He grabbed Joe's hand to shake it. "*Ow.*" Kain let go of Joe's hand.

"Sorry, mate."

Kain grinned. "The intention was there."

Joe slapped Kain's shoulder and chuckled. "It's all good. You know I'll always save your arse, Burrows. But what now? You're face has changed in the last minute. What are you thinking? I can see the cobwebs stirring in that brain."

"I'm going back up to the crash site and gunna search for Grace. I just *don't* believe she died in that crash. Will you come with me?"

"What? Now?" Joe's eyebrows joined as one. "Mate, the day's half over. By the time we get there, it'll . . . " He shrugged. "Where do you plan to search?"

"All around the area." Kain's shoulders lifted with his hopes and pulse rate. Adrenaline shot up his chest and raced down his limbs. "C'mon, Joe. I'll go get a few things from home then pick you up from your place. Let's go. No time to waste." He jumped into the ute and roared off.

Thirty minutes later they were driving toward the range. Kain kept glancing at the speedo. He didn't need a speeding ticket on top of everything. No way was he going back to the cop shop. Next time they would not let him off so easily.

"Mate, I still don't know if this is the right thing to do. We should call the SES or someone like that. That countryside is so hilly and rugged. Us two will be like two little ants in a jungle," said Joe.

Kain's mind raced, heart pistoned, eyes remained glued to the road ahead, hands clenched the steering wheel. "No point. They wouldn't believe me either."

"At the risk of you snapping my head off, you're doing it again."

"Doing what?"

"Jumping in all gung-ho."

"No mate. I'm right about this. I know I am. I just *have* to be." Grace's grieving family came to mind. Linda telling him Grace had been killed. Bruce's cruel words, blaming him. Grace's shattered look when he'd told her they were over. Each image, a rock being pelted at him. The images wouldn't stop. The rocks would never stop. The images and memories would stone him to death. "I've got no choice but to prove I'm right, Joe. Don't you get it?"

"Not really, but I'll help you as much as I can. How much further?"

"Just up a bit and around a couple of bends." He pushed his foot a little harder.

Kain pulled up in the same spot as previously. No other cars or drongo rubber-neckers were around this time, thankfully. He jumped out, grabbing a backpack from the floor as he went. "C'mon, Joe. We can't wait. Grab that other pack. There's water, matches, rope and a few other things in there. I've also got a map of the area. Is your phone charged?"

Joe looked at his phone and picked up the back pack with his other hand. "Yeah, it should be right. Lost a bar though."

"Shit, me too. Hope we don't lose any more. That's all we need, no reception in the middle of the bush."

"Did you tell anyone where you were going?"

"Don't be stupid. No-one believes me, remember? Don't look so worried, Joe."

"Sorry mate, I just got a nervous feeling about this."

Thunder rumbled to the west. "Hmm, I don't like the sound of that," said Joe.

"It'll go around us. Most storms don't go over the range anyway. Come on, don't worry about it."

Kain locked his ute and had a long drink from a plastic water bottle before returning it to the backpack. "We'll start down near the crash and go from there." He walked toward the edge of the ravine.

"Umm . . . mate I don't want to go too close to it. This is starting to . . ." Kain glared back at him and Joe sighed. "Righto then, lead the way."

No words were spoken between the friends as they walked, slid and half-stumbled down to the crash site. Nothing had changed from when Kain had first visited. The burnt out, lonely car shell remained on its roof against the tree trunk. The sickly smell still lingered. Kain's stomach rolled like a ship in a storm. He swallowed hard, hoping to keep everything down where it belonged.

"Shiiiit." Joe stopped dead, his eyes glued to the wreck for several moments. "Oh, Gracie." Tears spilled over his eyelids and down his red, sweaty cheeks. He wiped them away before lifting his cap and wiping his forehead. "I can't look at this." He turned away, sat on a rock and took out his water bottle.

Kain walked around the site and scanned nearby bush. Which way? Which way? Surely, if Grace was injured and had wandered off, it'd be easier for her to go downwards instead of scrambling up the steeper slope. He looked upwards, frowned and nodded. Yes, he had to go with that theory. If she'd gone up she'd have ended up on the road and someone would have picked her up, for sure. *Picked her up?* No! No, no, no. He couldn't dwell on that notion. No, she had to have wandered off.

Kain switched his gaze a little further down the valley. A slightly darker green area snaked its way around bends and rises in the bushy landscape. A creek. He walked over and placed his hand on Joe's shoulder. "You right, mate?"

Joe nodded and returned his water bottle back to the pack. "Yep. Which way?" He stood and slipped his arms through the back straps. "Let's go."

"I reckon we head toward the creek. I don't think she would have gone back up there." He indicated behind them with his thumb. "We'll walk about fifty metres apart, okay?" Jo nodded and they set off.

Twenty minutes later they neared the creek and verged closer. Bird songs came alive and the welcoming sound of the water cascading over rocks increased. A small mob of Eastern Grey kangaroos jumped up from their shady resting spot and bounded away into thicker bush up another slope. The big daddy stopped and turned back toward the men. He stood up on the tips of his toes and tail. His eyes, even at a distance, pierced the air between them like lasers.

"Bloody hell, I hope he doesn't get any ideas," said Joe. "Look at the size of him. He'd make stir-fry strips out of me and you. Don't spose you have a gun in that pack? We haven't got a hope in hell of fighting him off if he comes for us."

"No, I don't." Kain stopped. "But I do have my fishing knife. Just keep walking toward the creek. He should go away . . . I hope."

Joe walked several more metres then looked back, but continued walking. "Phew, he's gone."

"Look out!" Kain grabbed Joe's arm and yanked him back, almost throwing him off balance.

"What the . . .?" Joe looked down. "Farrrrk." A huge brown snake, thick as a man's forearm, slithered away into longer grass. Another step and Joe would have trodden on it. "Geeez, mate. I nearly shit meself then." Joe placed his hand on his chest and sucked in a deep breath. "The old heart's jumpin',"

"Too close for comfort." Kain's own heart contained a crazed mule trying to kick its way out of his ribcage. But they couldn't waste time dwelling on what *almost* happened. "Come this way and let's fill our water bottles." He shuddered. If his poor Grace was wandering around here injured, it would be a miracle just to survive the wildlife. "*GRACE,*" he shouted, loud as he could. Again and again he called, but no reply.

The beautiful cool water refreshed Kain's sweaty face. He took a drink from his cupped hands. "Nothing like fresh mountain water."

Joe was busy on his knees, bum in air, dunking his whole head under the water. He lifted it out and flicked his head back, flicking the water everywhere, including on Kain. His head remained upward, letting the water run down his back. "Ahh, that feels better." He stood and placed his cap back on his drenched head. "Now where?"

Kain looked about. He really had no idea, but refused to let panic overrule his intentions. He didn't want Joe knowing he didn't have a clue. His mate was already sceptical. They just had to press on and hope for the best. "It's pretty rocky and deep here. If she did come this way I don't think she would have crossed here. Let's go a bit further and see if it gets easier to cross."

"Sounds reasonable." Joe nodded and followed Kain.

"We'll just spread out again, just in case. You wanna go up that way a bit and I'll stick near the creek."

More thunder, but quieter.

"See." Kain nodded toward the sound. "I told you it would go around us."

Further on they trudged, carefully treading through long grass, stepping over dead logs and rocks, ducking under low hanging branches and veering around large tree trunks. Flies hung about their heads, refusing to be swiped away.

"Don't spose you put any repellent in the pack?" shouted Joe. "These flies are giving me the shits." He waved his hand about his face for the hundredth time.

"Nope, didn't think of it, sorry- Ahh, shit." Sticky thread clung to every exposed part of his body and probably his clothes too. Where was the friggin' spider? *"Joe."* He picked, brushed and whacked at himself.

"What happened?" Joe panted, stopping beside Kain.

"I walked into a web." He continued to pull at the stubborn web and throw it off. "Can you see the spider? Hurry." He shuddered. "I can't *stand* spiders."

Joe picked up a stick and walked behind Kain. "There it is. Hold still." He swiped Kain's backside. "Got it." He stomped the luckless spider to mush. "It didn't bite you, did it?"

"No, I don't think so. Can't feel anything." Kain looked at Joe then the ground and what remained of the spider.

He shook his head in defeat. "Shit Joe, I don't know what I'm doing. I don't know if we're going the right way. We might never find her." He crouched and brought both hands to his face. He wanted to cry, howl his lungs out to the mountains. Instead he took a deep breath, wiped his eyes and face and stood.

"Looks like the creek is veering away from the road from here on," said Joe. "We may as well keep going like we have."

Kain nodded. "May as well."

The sun hung low in the western sky when they came to a sandy, narrow creek crossing. Kain took off the back pack, had a long drink and pulled out the map. He studied it for several minutes.

"I reckon we've come about six k's from the site. We're further away from Range Road now. It veers the other way. There's a couple of other dirt roads around here, but they probably don't get used much. Let's cross the creek and go that way for a while." He pointed ahead.

Joe lit up a smoke and headed toward the crossing. "Just hope we're not going around in circles." The water trickled over sand and a few scatted rocks. The men were able to step or jump from rock to rock without getting their boots drenched.

"Let's just spread out wide again and see what we see." They pressed on, taking turns at calling for Grace. Their relentless calls echoed about the endless rugged terrain. The only replies were the odd bird call, insects and the like.

Over several ridges and through gullies they continued.

"I need a rest for a minute, mate." Joe looked about and found a suitable log to sit on.

"Okay, me too." Kain plonked down beside him.

"Phew, did you fart?" Joe screwed up his face.

"No. Piss off."

"That's rotten. Something's dead! Oh shiiii . . ." Joe stood.

Kain sniffed. "Yeah, I can smell it too." Hope turned to stone and bottomed out in his stomach. "Grace," came out a hoarse whisper. He jumped up and followed the sickening smell. Joe followed, sniffing fast.

They split up. Soon Joe shouted. "Over here."

Kain raced over, jumping some recent fallen branches of an ironbark tree. His legs jelly, his heart a thrashing machine. The only thing he expected to see was the decomposing body of his beautiful Grace. He sucked in a breath and fought back the tears, preparing for the worst sight imaginable. Through tears that had escaped their ducts he stopped and stared toward the ground.

Tufts of golden red fur lay about a larger body, or what was left of it. Exposed bones and darkened innards fed thousands of maggots. Blow flies buzzed about, settling on the remains.

"A dog?"

Both men stepped back.

"Wait." Joe pointed to the dog. "Look at the skull. If I'm not mistaken, it's been shot. A powerful gun too, by the size of that hole. Not much of its head left. How long do you reckon it's been dead for?"

Kain shrugged. "Dunno. A few days by the looks. Strange place to find a shot dog. Must be a wild one. Still, it's odd." Kain held his breath. "Let's go downwind of it for a while. I feel like spewing now. I thought . . . I thought . . . " He couldn't say the words.

"You don't have to say it, mate. I thought it too. Thank God it wasn't."

Down the slope they stopped for a drink.

"It's going to be dark soon. We're gunna have to head back. I don't fancy camping out here at night. Too many predators." Joe shuddered.

"I know you're right, but I hate to go. Feels like I'm leaving her behind. Ahh, I don't know what to do for the best." Kain looked about the ground. "What the . . . ?" He ran several metres and picked up what had caught his attention.

"What is it?" Joe rushed over.

Kain broke into a grin and his heart lightened. "It's a shoe."

Joe shrugged and frowned. "So?"

"It's Graces. I know it's Graces. See that little green bit around the air hole?"

"Yeah".

"I coloured that in one day, when we were mucking about out on the back lawn. She's here, Joe. She *is here!*" Kain's grin grew to a chuckle, followed by a laugh then a loud, "*Yes!*" He punched the air. "*Woo hoooo.*" The echoes of his triumphant discovery call carried throughout the bush. "She *definitely* didn't die in that accident."

Joe's eyes widened. "Well, who the hell did? They found remains of *somebody.*"

Kain sucked in a breath, his euphoria waning. "Good question. I have no idea. Just another thing that doesn't make sense in all of this. We just need to concentrate on finding Grace for now."

"Let's look around a bit more. *Grace,*" Joe called as he scanned the bushy area.

Kain called and called, continuing the search.

"Now what?" asked Joe. "My throat's sore." He stopped for a welcome drink.

Kain clutched the shoe to his chest. "I don't know. I want to look at that dog again." They headed back toward the putrid smell. "I wonder where the other shoe is?" Kain's eyes scoured the ground as he walked. "What's this?" He stopped and bent toward a small sapling.

"Whatcha got?"

"This." Kain held up a small, jagged piece of denim material. "It was caught on this sharp bit sticking out. Jeans. Grace nearly *always* wore jeans. It's fresh too." Tears stung his eyes, mixing with sweat dripping from his forehead. "Mate, *now* do you believe me?"

"Sure seems like you're right." Joe slapped Kain's back and walked toward the dead dog.

Kain joined him, picked up a stick and poked around the dog's skull. "Phew, hard to hold your breath long enough." He exhaled out his mouth, brought up the sweaty front of his tee shirt and sucked in another breath through the material.

"Well, it certainly didn't die of natural causes." Joe stepped back several paces and coughed.

"No. Something has blown half its head away. Bloody big dog too." Kain dropped the stick and joined Joe.

Joe's face contorted between a frown and look of disgust. "So, we've got a shot wild dog, Grace's shoe and *probably* a piece of her jeans, but no sign of her or . . . the person who shot the dog."

Kain called to Grace some more, turning about as he yelled, projecting his voice in every direction. His throat dried then burned and the calls became raspier. No reply. He looked at Joe and tried to keep his heavy shoulders up. "My gut instinct tells me that whoever shot this dog has Grace. Or, at least, knows where she is."

CHAPTER 28

Grace plonked herself on a kitchen chair, straightened her back and gazed ahead at nothing. Was it possible? Could she be pregnant? She'd stopped taking the pill a few months earlier due to side effects but they'd used other methods . . . carefully. Although there was that *one* time - when lust took over and there was no time or thought put into birth control.

She stared at the blank wall trying to remember what she was doing when she last menstruated. Her temples began to throb. She rubbed them in a circular motion with her finger tips. Then it came to her. It was during a school excursion, of all days. How long ago *was* that? It had to be weeks before they'd broken up. Before *Kain* had broken off the relationship. Her mouth filled with sour, her heart filled with hurt, her eyes filled with tears. It didn't get any easier with time.

So . . . what if she really was pregnant? She placed her hand on her lower abdomen. A smile gushed its way from her heart to her lips. A baby. Visions of holding a newborn fluttered and pirouetted in her head. The beautiful little bub, perfect in every way. A cheeky little boy or a cute little girl. What would she name it? 'Kain' would be his middle name.

Kain.

Grace gritted her teeth and the now familiar dagger stabbed at her heart. What would he think? "Hmph, bet you wouldn't even care." He's probably out wooping it up with some of his single mates. Could even have another woman by now. "Nooo". Grace sobbed at that horrible thought. All the evidence pointed to it, but she just couldn't believe the Kain she knew and loved could be that callous. But his words circled and landed in her head like a flock of vultures, wanting to pick her heart to pieces. *"It's over Grace. I don't love you anymore." I don't love you anymore.* Just the mere thought of those icy words, and they duplicated themselves driving that dagger right through her heart.

She placed her hands on the table, dropped her head to them and let the anger and hurt wash away. She sobbed loud, wailed louder but what did it matter? No-one could hear her. The tears wouldn't stop and she didn't care. She dragged herself to her feet and trudged to her bedroom, nearly having to drag her heart along the floor behind her. It was lead, weighing her whole body down.

The soft mattress welcomed her tense body. Her head rested on the pillow and some of the heaviness left her body. Grace breathed deep several times. The tears and sobbing subsided. Now she had to think. *Really* think.

If she is pregnant the whole ball game has changed. This will change her life. And Kain's. No, she won't tell Kain. At least not yet, even when she does finally go home. He can get stuffed. He doesn't deserve to know. Okay, maybe one day she'll tell him, but she'd wait and see what his attitude is first. If he's running around with other women, no way would she tell him he was going to be a father. Maybe he will have left town when she goes back. It won't be an issue then. The dagger twisted with a serrated edge, slow and painful. No, that notion just too much to bear.

So, telling Kain was not an issue right now. Getting her hands on a pregnancy test kit was.

Seth. Should she tell him and ask him to buy a test for her? Somehow, she didn't think he'd be too keen. No, she couldn't tell Seth she may be pregnant. Their conversation had been awkward and frustrating enough when he'd left. God only knows how he'll be when he returned.

The vomiting and general nausea. Of course. It now made perfect sense. She'd put it down to her situation. The sadness and anger of the break-up, shock and possible concussion from the accident and finding herself here with Seth. Naturally it would upset anyone's system, emotionally *and* physically. Too many coincidences for any other possible outcome. Unprotected sex, late period and nausea. Not forgetting the overwhelming maternal feelings suddenly kicking in.

Grace placed her open hand on her stomach again. "Okay, little one. You and I have a tough road ahead of us, but we'll be fine. Mum, oh, I mean *nanny,* will be thrilled." She smiled, knowing Linda would adore her grandchild. "And your poppy will love you too. Probably be teaching you to ride a horse before you're even out of nappies. And your Aunt Sophie. She'll fuss like an old mother hen over you. And your Uncle Steve . . . " The smile faded to darkness and heaviness again swamped her body. She looked at the open window. "Where *are* you, Steve?"

Grace held her breath and listened. Thunder in the distance but another sound lightened her mood. An approaching vehicle. Seth? She dragged herself off the bed and went to the front door. "Oh good." Seth's dusty white ute pulled up at the front of the house. She smiled and placed both hands on her abdomen, both protecting and loving the new little life it contained. So innocent. So pure.

All will be right with the world.

CHAPTER 29

Seth switched off his ignition and stared straight ahead. Jimmy's words spun around and around his brain. *"He's taking you with him. Dead or alive."* Like hell. He'd kill Scott with his bare hands before he'd be taken prisoner. Life under Scott's rule was already bad enough.

"Seth. *Seth.* Are you okay?"

"What?" He jumped, throwing his mind off the destructive path it approached. "Oh Grace." He emptied his lungs through clenched teeth and pressed his chest to steady the heart palpitations. Staring at her, standing only a metre or two from his vehicle, she looked so worried. "Yes, I'm okay." He nodded twice and got out of the vehicle.. "Are *you* all right? You look upset."

"Umm . . . no, I'm fine." Her eyes darted this way and that. "Did your meeting go okay?"

She still couldn't look him in the eye. Something wasn't quite right. It was a strange question for her to ask. He waited for her to return eye contact before answering. Finally, after uncomfortable silence, her gaze met his. "It was all right." What a lie. It was far from *all right.*

But Grace needn't know anything about the impending job. Hopefully, she'd never need to know. Once it was all over and Scott was out of their lives, one way or the other, life could be good . . . and *normal,* whatever that was.

"I turned on the kettle before I came downstairs. Do you feel like a cuppa? Another storm in the distance." She turned and headed back up the steps.

She didn't even wait for his answer. So unlike Grace. "Ah, yes please." Seth followed her up the stairs, trying to keep his mind off Scott's threat . . . or was it a promise? Hell, was Jimmy even telling the truth or just playing with him? Who'd know. Nah, Jimmy wouldn't do that. He was just as scared of Scott and there'd been no hint of a lie, or even a joke, when Jimmy had delivered those ominous words.

Jimmy may be terrified of storms, but not even the wildest storm possible could instil fear in Seth like Scott does.

Seth slipped off his boots outside the door, and dropped his hat on the floor just inside. He wiped his sweaty brow on his sleeves. Grace was already pouring the milk into two steaming mugs of tea. A quick stir with a teaspoon and she handed Seth's over.

"Thanks." He took the tea and sat at the table. She seemed to be stirring hers forever. The slow, rhythmic whirring, chinking noise. He glanced behind him and noticed her head upright as if staring out the window instead of at what she was doing. Was she angry at him? Probably. He hadn't been very communicative before he left. Of course he knew she wanted answers, but it was for her own good not to know anything. She just has to realise that. Knowing he made her angry saddened him. He shrugged, unsure what to say.

Grace stopped the stirring and turned around, sipping her tea. Still no eye contact. She looked directly at the opposite wall, her face pale and emotionless, her eyes sad.

"Grace, have you been vomiting again?" That must be it. She's not well. Maybe he will have to take her to a doctor. No, please don't let it come to that.

"No. Not since the morning." Her face brightened to a faint smile. She sat opposite and looked at him. She actually smiled. Phew. One of the tonne weights, that had been sitting on his shoulders, melted away.

"That's good. Do you feel okay?" He sipped his tea and wished the other, heavier weight would also disappear. Not a chance of that.

"Yes. I'm . . . " She stared down at her cup. "I'm good." She nodded. "Would you like me to prepare something for dinner?" Grace jumped up and opened the fridge. "There's plenty here."

Food was the last thing on Seth's mind. He couldn't eat anything even if he had to force himself. "I'm not that hungry. But thank you. Can I get something for you?" How rude of him to expect her to cook her own meals, let along his as well.

"Umm, no thanks. I'm not hungry either. I might go and sit out on the verandah in the cool. I love the late afternoon." She put her cup on the sink and disappeared out the front door.

This was getting uncomfortable. Seth had no idea what to do or say to Grace, but he had to do *something*. He was so close to possibly being able to have a life here with her. He couldn't risk upsetting her now.

Scott. Bloody Scott. He just needed to forget about him for now and concentrate on Grace. He downed the last of his tea, put the cup next to Grace's and went to join her on the verandah.

The sun's golden rays were low on the horizon, peeking through the last of the storm clouds. An artist's palette of pinks, oranges, purples and all colours in between spread across the western sky. Even though it hadn't rained at Seth's place that day, the air was clean and crisp.

Grace sat on the top step, not moving or making any effort to turn and look at him. A slight breeze blew in, cool and fresh, sending wisps of Grace's hair dancing about her head. Surely she must have heard the screen door open and close.

"Grace." He was almost afraid to say it too loud. She didn't move. "*Grace*?" A little louder.

She flinched and turned toward him but just stared with that far-off look in her beautiful eyes again. "Sorry, Seth. Were you calling me?"

"No, I . . . I was wondering if you'd mind if I sat here on the verandah too. You seem a million miles away." He sat in his old faithful chair. It was a familiar comfort.

Grace turned her head away again. He persisted. "I'm sorry about earlier. Having to rush out like that. I know you have a heap of questions for me and I *will* answer them one day, but there's things going on that . . ." He sighed.

He had no idea how to word this properly. "Even I don't know what's happening." That didn't come out right. He shook his head. *Useless fool.*

Grace turned her whole body to face Seth, bending one knee toward him. "It's okay, Seth. We all have our secrets." She shrugged, then winced and touched her right shoulder.

What on earth did she mean? He wasn't expecting to hear something like that, but best not to question her cryptic comment. "How is your shoulder?"

"Not too bad." A cute little smile lit up her face. "I'll live." Silence for a moment before she continued. "Seth, when are you going into town again?"

"I don't know. Why?" He remembered he'd promised he'd call her parents and tell them she was okay. No doubt she hadn't forgotten.

"I just need something, but I *have* to go with you to get it."

Seth raised his eyebrows. That was also not what he expected to hear. She seemed to have forgotten her earlier request. Good, best to leave it that way. "What do you need? I'll get anything for you."

If he could just keep Grace calm and happy enough to stay here for the next few days, all will be good. Having to deal with taking her to town could mess everything up, something he didn't need right now.

"It's . . . it's personal. Sorry." She did look sorry and sad and worried.

It didn't soften his fears at all. Maybe she was making this up to get a chance to escape. She must have been thinking about it while he was away with Jimmy.

Jimmy. Those words. Again, they haunted every crevice of his mind.

His phone vibrated. He pulled it out of his pocket, looked at the screen and stood. Speak of the devil.

"Hey Jimmy." Seth glanced at Grace, who watched some pretty-faced wallabies emerging from the bush. He stood and walked into the kitchen. "What's happening?"

"Just been with Pete. He's sussed out the property and Bruce and worked out exactly where we'll go in. Where the prime cattle are kept."

"When is this happening?" Seth's gut felt like someone had flushed a toilet in it.

"Tomorrow night. We have to have the cattle over to the yards for loading on the trucks by early the next morning. Scott wants them on the road just after daylight. We'll meet at Scott's place tomorrow arvo. I'll call you tomorrow. Get ready, mate. This is it." A 'click' and the line went dead.

Tomorrow night. Tomorrow night he would know his fate, or meet Satan.

He looked through the screen door at Grace. She wacked her arm, probably a mozzie. Bloody things. Blood sucking parasites.

Okay, now to think. It's too late and impossible to get himself out of the looming situation. Scott would kill him. He had no choice but to prepare.

Seth strode to his bedroom, lifted the end of his mattress, reached far under and took out a long key from a hole
in the mattress underside. He dropped the mattress down
and went to the locked door opposite his room. Glancing
along the hallway toward the front door, Grace remained
sitting at the top of the stairs. With a trembling hand, he
pushed the old fashioned key into the hole and twisted.
Another glance to the front. All was well. Seth pushed the
door open, flicked on the light and immediately spied what
he was after. He picked up the sleek black pistol.

Scott had no idea Seth owned this gun. Scott thought
he knew everything about Seth. Thought he had the *right*
to know everything. "Well, you're in for a shock this time,
Scott. You're not taking me *anywhere.*"

CHAPTER 30

Kain dropped his backpack on the floor and grabbed two beers from his parents' fridge. He handed one to Joe, ripped off his ring-pull, downed several large mouthfuls and burped. "I still can't get my head around this. Grace is still alive. She *must* be. She *has* to be."

"Certainly seems like it." Joe wiped the beer froth from his moustache. "But *where* is she? I mean, I'm no psychic, but the amount of times we yelled out, if she was around there she would have heard us. I just don't think she's out in that wild country."

Kain drained his can, threw it in the bin by the stove and got another from the fridge. "She must have got thrown out the car. The front passenger door had come right off and the burnt body was in the driver's seat. She was texting me so *no way* she would have been driving. It all makes sense now, Joe." His gaze wandered off and he sighed. "Grace, where are you? And whose burnt remains were in the car?"

"Listen mate, I'll just ring Sue and let her know where we are then we'll have to work out what to do next. Don't worry, I'll tell her to keep it to herself."

Kain nodded. He'd heard Joe, but his mind was already racing ahead. First thing tomorrow he'd head out again, this time more prepared. He'd find Grace, wrap her in his arms and promise never to let her go. Promise never to be so stupid again. Promise to love and cherish her for the rest of their lives. Heck, he would even propose to her. They can adopt kids or use a donor father. What does it matter, as long as they are together? He'd start treatment immediately and all will be wonderful. His chest expanded and his heart filled with optimism and love for Grace. His cheeks widened, unable to contain a big fat grin.

"Kain . . . are you listening?"

"Huh? What?" He shook his jam-packed head and looked at Joe. "What did you say?"

"I said, Sue's excited and wants to ask her brother, Anthony – he's one of the head honcho's in the local SES – if he'll come with us tomorrow. He knows heaps about the area up there from searches they've done in the past. You've met him at our place before."

"Yeah, I know him. Sounds good." Kain got two more beers from the fridge.

"What about Eddy?" Joe ripped his can open. "And work?" He glugged down several mouthfuls. "Eddy won't be expecting you tomorrow, but he'll be pissed off if I don't turn up."

"Oh shit. Work." Kain groaned.

"I'll ring him in the morning with an excuse. I'll think of something." Joe scratched his chin. A frown indicated the cogwheels of his brain had cranked into action.

Kain's phone rang, flinching his already tense body. He grabbed it from its holder on his hip, without checking the number. "Hello. Kain speaking."

"Hello Kain, this is Doctor Burns."

"Oh." Kain's heart jumped a beat then raced to catch up. He'd forgotten about the bloody cancer for most of the afternoon. "Yes, Doc."

"Kain, I know it's an unorthodox time to call a patient, but I have been reviewing your file and test results. It is *imperative* you start treatment immediately if you are to beat this. Can you please come in first thing tomorrow? I'll be here by 8 AM and will see you then, before my normal appointments commence. We can get things underway."

"Ummm . . . " This definitely was not in his plans for tomorrow. *Shiiit.* Finding Grace was the main thing that mattered at the moment, the *only* thing.

"Well, Kain, will I see you then?"

"Yeah, righto Doc, see you then." He tapped the screen and replaced his phone.

"What now?" Joe looked worried.

Kain shrugged. "Just the doctor asking me to go see him tomorrow morning."

"Sounds urgent."

"Nah. He just wants to do more tests, that's all." Kain placed his can on the table and went to the toilet, more to avoid the chance of his best mate detecting the lie he'd just told. At this point in time, all he could think about was Grace.

A minute or so later and he was back, sitting down at the table. "Okay, I reckon we should ask Anthony. We do need some help, but *no coppers* and none of Grace's family are to know anything at all, okay. Especially Bruce."

Joe nodded and shrugged. "It's up to you. I'll call and brief him then you can talk to him." He got up, pulled his phone out, took his smokes out of his pocket and headed out the front door.

Kain filled the water bottle in his backpack and threw in some muesli bars and dried fruit from the pantry. He opened the fridge and stared into it for minute. Food was absolutely the last thing on his mind but he had to keep his and Joe's strength and stamina up for the wider search tomorrow. A plastic bag of red apples caught his eye. He snatched the whole bag and dropped it into the backpack. *What else?* Yes, the first aid kit.

When he got back from the bathroom with the kit in hand, Joe stood by the table holding out his phone. Kain put the kit in the back pack and took the phone.

"G'day Anthony. Kain here."

"Hey mate, I hear you need some help tomorrow."

Kain told Anthony everything he knew and suspected about Grace's disappearance including what they'd found in the bush. Anthony agreed to be at his place at daylight the next morning and the men ended the call.

"All good?" asked Joe.

"Yeah, mate. Anthony'll be here at daylight. You too?"

"Shit yeah."

"Thanks Joe. This means the world to me, you know that don't you? He reached out to shake Joe's hand.

Joe stared at Kain a moment, his eyes watering. "Of course I bloody do." He ignored the hand and grab Kain in a manly hug. "We just might put an end to this night-mare tomorrow, mate." Joe let go of Kain and his eyes shifted from happy to downcast.

"What's that look for?" The good vibes slowly died away, leaving Kain's chest hollow.

Joe's gaze darted about the room, he shuffled his feet and folded his arms. "Look, I'm going to say something and I know you won't like it but don't get angry, okay."

Oh no. There always seems to be a damper put on anything positive. Kain took a deep breath and stood back against the bench with folded arms. "What?"

"Well . . . I *do* believe Grace wasn't killed in that accident, but . . ."

"You think she could still be dead anyway, don't you?" Kain's face heated up. "No. No. No." He wasn't about to entertain that dreadful thought, even for one second. Grace being alive was the only thing keeping him going. "Mate, we are *not* going down that road, okay? I don't want to hear that shit."

Joe nodded. "Okay."

"So, are you with me?"

"I'm in."

The two men hugged again and slapped each other's back.

Kain wiped the tears that had unwittingly seeped out. "Righto then. You best go home to that gorgeous lady of yours. Thank her from me, won'tcha? I don't know how, but I'm going to try and get some sleep. If we don't find Grace tomorrow, we'll find her the next day." A wave of hope, relief and fear all combined, rolled through his stomach, chest and limbs.

"Okay, see you at daylight." Joe waved, gave the thumbs up signal and was gone.

Kain showered, put his phone on charge and went to bed, unable to eat or focus on anything but what they'd discovered today and what he believed they would find tomorrow.

He picked up the photo of Grace, from the bedside table, stroked her face and let the tears fall. "I'm coming for you, Grace. Hold on sweetie. Just hold on. We'll find you." He kissed her face, clutched the photo to his chest and turned off the bed light.

Minutes later, memories and dreams and hopes all blended to make one beautiful scenario of him and Grace together. But what was that sound? Kain's eyes shot open. Wind? A slow moving car driving past? It increased. *Rain?*

He flicked on the light, grabbed his phone and brought up the weather app, something he'd taken no notice of in days. "We don't need this tomorrow...What? Bullshit. *Nooooo."* The weather forecast stated a stationary Category 3 cyclone sat off the coast, and may possibly head for Anchor Bay and surrounds.

CHAPTER 31

Grace rubbed her bleary eyes and stepped from the toilet to the bathroom. The lull of gentle rain on the roof through the night must have finally put her to sleep. She'd tossed and turned for hours, her mind in absolute tangles over her possible pregnancy and what it will mean to everyone's lives.

At first the rain had been barely audible above the whirring fan, but soon the beautiful, comforting sound was loud enough to send her to dreamland. Seth had remained quiet which didn't bother her. She'd headed to bed, leaving him sitting on his verandah chair.

'Dreamland' had been a hectic, chaotic place. She had multiple children, all running and dancing around her, calling her 'mummy'. Some looked like Kain. Some looked like Seth. Some had no faces. She wondered if they depicted the two in the old photo hidden in the wooden box, and why.

She shook her head, rubbed the side of her neck that had stiffened through the night, turned on the cold tap and placed her hands in the cool running water. Grace looked up and jolted. She stared at herself! A mirror now hung on the wall above the basin. Leaning forward, Grace peered at her reflection. Who was the woman watching her? Her hair dull and lifeless, her face pale, her green eyes puffy and sad. A wide sticking-plaster stuck to her temple. The scabby end of the injury extended past the side of the dressing.

The tap. Grace jerked back to reality. She cupped her hands beneath the flow, leaned forward and splashed the cold water over her face, giving extra attention to her eyes.

One more splash over and she felt half alive. She wiped her face and hands and headed for the kitchen.

A few seconds of nausea brought her hand to her stomach, but the discomfort passed as quick as it had come. The house was quiet. Gentle falling rain was the only sound apart from her footsteps. No birds sang. No sign of Seth.

The empty kitchen was quiet and lonely. His hat was not in its usual spot just inside the door. She touched the side of the electric kettle. Warm. Grace walked to the verandah and looked below. No ute. Seth was gone.

A brief up-beat moment of relief was followed by a drop of her shoulders. She was alone. Solitude was good, and needed sometimes, but this morning her heart pained for company. She hadn't even heard his vehicle start up and leave.

With nothing she could do about her loneliness, she walked back to the kitchen, filled the kettle and flicked it on. Leaning against the sink, she gazed out the window. The dark green tree tops swaying in the wind were in stark contrast to the white/grey rainclouds moving across the sky. The distant mountains, usually seen through a gap in the closer trees, were obscured by falling rain or low cloud. Was Seth out there among those trees? Why was he always so secretive and elusive?

The bubbling kettle brought her back to the here and now. She took a mug from the sink, dropped in a tea bag and got the milk from the fridge. A minute later she settled herself in Seth's favourite chair on the verandah, watched and listened to the relaxing rain.

Kain. What was he doing right at that moment? *Forget about him, Grace.* That inner voice refused to leave her, even in moments of peace. Much harder to forget about him now when she might be carrying his baby.

She looked at her stomach. "This is not the way things were supposed to be." Hell, only a few weeks ago she was daydreaming about their wedding and their forthcoming children and their *grandchildren.* A tear threatened but she blinked it back and swallowed it down. No. No longer was Kain going to upset her. He could go to hell.

Grace stared ahead and tried to piece together the dream fragments, but the two faceless children kept appearing. It must mean something. She downed her tea, pushed herself up with some effort, from Seth's low chair and took her cup to the sink. She had her mind set on the bathroom and that little wooden box.

She brought the box to her bed, sat down, opened it and peered inside. Her pulse rate ramped up a notch or two, knowing she was prying into Seth's mysterious personal life. She looked at the window and listened. She must remind herself he could come home at any moment. Knowing how he had a knack for seemingly appearing from nowhere, she'd better stay on her guard. No approaching vehicle. Good.

The picture was just as she'd left it. Two small children but with no identifying details and only part of a date on the back. Grace studied the back and front again, but nothing came to mind. She knew no more than when she first discovered the secret picture. Did she dare keep it out so she could show Seth when he came home and ask him point blank who the children were? A dark wave of negativity washed through her entire body at that notion. No, not a good idea.

Grace stared at the picture a few more seconds, returned it to its envelope and the box before returning the box to the bathroom drawer. "Well that was a waste of time." Sinking optimism dropped her shoulders.

She walked out of the bathroom and Seth's bedroom door caught her eye. Maybe it was worth snooping in his room again. She gripped his door handle and opened the door. Her heart rate upped the ante. Nothing different or unusual caught her attention. Grace closed the door and wiped her sweaty palms on her shorts.

She looked at the closed door opposite Seth's room and sighed. "If *only* I could get in there." She grabbed the door knob and rattled it with a teeth-clenching grunt of frustration. The door opened a little. Grace snatched her hand back as if she'd touched hot coals. Her jaw dropped open sucking in a gush of breath. She placed her hand on her galloping heart and took a slow deep breath. Had Seth slipped up? Or had he left it unlocked on purpose . . . for her?

Grace had yearned to get into this room for days but now the door stood open and nothing stopped her from entering. Nothing tangible but something foreboding lurked in the midst, stopping her from entering. Something dark but invisible.

Dozens of visions and possibilities swirled about her brain like a swarm of angry moths, darting this way and that. What if there was evidence of Seth being a psychopathic killer in this room? What if he led a double life and this room contained . . . women's clothing? *Don't be stupid.* She stomped on *that* angry moth. What if the room contained a dead body? Multiple bodies? *You'd smell them.* Of course.

She had to find out. Bugger him. If he can keep her here against her will, be evasive and elusive, then she has the right to find out things for herself. Pressing the door with her index finger she pushed it open, very slowly. She listened. Listened for any sign of Seth returning plus any noise coming from within the room.

What if he had another woman, just like her, locked away in here? The only sound, her heavier breathing and the thumping of her heart, like a boxer-in-training punching the life out of a speed-ball.

It took a few moments for Grace's eyes to adjust to the semi-darkness. She reached around, flicked the light switch as her eyes continued to scan the room and its scant contents. A full garbage bag stood in one corner and several boxes, haphazardly stacked on top of each other, sat just inside the door. The musty closed-up odour hit Grace. She stopped breathing and brought her tee shirt front up over her lower face before sucking in a fresh breath. *Okay, toughen up, girl. You might only have minutes before Seth returns, so stop wasting time on trivial stuff. Get in there.*

An invisible urge pushed her into the pungent room. The smell reminded her a little of Steve's room when he was a teenager. Dirty, sweaty clothes lying about the floor, door always closed, curtains drawn.

She opened the flaps of the top box. A few old novels, newspapers and western novellas. Nothing startling. She lifted it with her left hand, plonked it on the floor and opened the second box. Looked like a bunch of old mail. Grace picked up an unopened letter addressed to a name she'd never heard. She leafed through the letters. All addressed to Jeffrey Simms. That name meant nothing to her. Who was he and why was his mail here in Seth's house, in a *locked* room? Some of the envelopes contained cards, some had windows, but all were unopened. Satisfied there was nothing else in that box she placed it on top of the first and dropped to her knees to open the third and final box.

Several lidded jars stood in that box. Grace frowned and picked up the largest, having to put in some extra effort for the unexpected weight. It contained stones – mainly white quartz and purple amethysts. Another bottle contained rounded smooth stones, possibly from a creek. Another held darker, flatter stones, while the last bottle, the smallest, was half full of what looked like gold pieces stuck in stones. Maybe it was fool's gold – iron pyrite.

Either way, it didn't matter to Grace. The stones meant nothing either. It just showed that Seth fossicked for and collected stones. Nothing unusual about that, especially for a man or boy. Especially someone living out in the middle of nowhere.

She and Steve used to scratch around parts of their creek too, looking for unusual stones. Grace liked to give any pretty ones she'd find to her mum while Steve took his to school for his science teacher. Grace's heart saddened but her brain signalled a smile to come forth at the memory.

Steve had a *huge* crush on his high school science teacher. When she was transferred at the end of grade eleven he was shattered, sad and moody for weeks. No-one but Grace knew why. He'd told her he'd break her knees if she told anyone. She knew he wouldn't but it was his way of emphasising how badly he wanted it kept secret. "Oh Steve." Even after more than five years, her heart ached for her big brother.

Remembering she may be time limited she replaced the boxes exactly how they'd been and approached the garbage bag. Before she took hold of the twisty-tied top, she turned and looked about the room, particularly behind the door. Nothing but old cracked, faded lino on the floor surrounded by bare walls in need of a decent wash.

Grace poked several parts of the bag with her foot. It sunk in each time. Must be clothes or some sort of material items. She picked it up, wondering if she really needed to look through clothes or sheets or whatever. Hunger pains started to nibble at her stomach. Won't be long and the nibbling mice will become growling tigers. Nah. She dropped the bag. It landed with a clunk that echoed around the sparse room.

She had to see what was in the bottom of the bag. She parted the dark curtains and returned to the bag. Careful not to let the paper come off the twisty wire, she undid it and placed the twisty on the window sill.

All she could see were clothes. Mens jeans and shirts and jackets. Grace upended the contents on the floor. If Seth comes in . . . too bad, she'd deal with that if and when it happened. The clothes spewed out into an untidy pile. Nothing hard appeared. She shook the bag. It was empty so she tossed it behind her and raked through the clothes.

Her hand touched something cold and hard. She thrust her hand in, rummaged about and picked the treasure out from among the clothing. It was a leather belt and she had hold of the large, silver buckle. Grace stepped closer to the window and studied the buckle.

It was tarnished and in need of a good polish. The leather belt dull and stiff, like it hadn't been worn for years. An engraved galloping horse covered most of the buckle's front.

She turned it over. The air gushed from her lungs and the room spun. She looked away for several seconds then back to the buckle. Inscribed on the back were the initials S. B. A. Same as her brother – Steven Bruce Atkinson. Steve did have a belt with a horse on the buckle, but she couldn't be sure it was exactly the same as this. Seth could easily have the same initials. What if it *was* Steve's belt? What was it doing here? This opened up a whole other tin of caterpillars.

The rain started again. A drizzle soon turned into a downpour. She wouldn't be able to hear if Seth came home. No, she really didn't want him to catch her snooping. She shoved the clothes back into the bag and tied it shut before returning it to the corner. Wanting to keep the belt out, but unsure why, she rushed into her room and placed it flat beneath her mattress before returning to the forbidden room.

There was nothing else to look at, but the newspapers returned to her mind. Why would he keep newspapers locked away? She reached into the top box and took them out. She needed to sit, so closed the curtains, switched off the light, closed the door behind her and headed to the kitchen.

The hunger pains could no longer be ignored. Grace put the papers on the table and made herself some toast. While waiting for it to pop up she gobbled down a banana from the fruit bowl on the bench. The rain eased to a drizzle again. She glanced at the clock. Almost eleven AM. No wonder she felt so hungry.

Once she was settled with toast and vegemite and a glass of juice she sat at the table and opened the first newspaper. Front page contained a large heading circled in red. 'MAN KILLED IN ANCHOR BAY BANK HOLD UP'. She recalled that happening several years earlier. A customer was killed and, to her knowledge, the robbers had never been caught. Grace turned each page, quickly reading all the headings on each one. Nothing else caught her attention.

She put that paper aside and looked at the next one. The front page headlines jumped off the page at her. 'HORSES AND DOGS SHOT ON LOCAL PROPERTY'. This time two black lines crisscrossed the article. What on earth does this have to do with Seth?

Her appetite flew out the window at top speed. Grace dropped the last bit of toast back onto her plate. She pushed the plate to the other side of the table and homed back on the article. These horses had belonged to neighbours of her parents. Two of the five shot were the kids' ponies. The dogs were the farm's working dogs. The family had been devastated, especially the kids. No-one was arrested. She glanced at the first paper. Was there some sort of connection?

Around that time her father had received anonymous threats, but he would never say what about. Grace had assumed it was to do with Steve's disappearance. Though Bruce would stubbornly refuse to talk about it, his facial lines etched deeper. Even her mum was kept in the dark, something that clearly irked Linda for ages afterwards.

The third paper's front page was about wild storms damaging homes. She licked her finger and flicked over a page. Nothing outstanding there either. Next page over brought forth a frown. A large portion of one page had been torn off. Grace searched through the rest of the paper, hoping to find it, but to no avail.

She added that one to the first two and opened the fourth and last newspaper. An article on the third page was circled in red. 'MAN BEATEN AND LEFT FOR DEAD ON CREEKBANK'

This article was only vaguely familiar to Grace. It must have happened when she and Kain were away on holidays. She read it through. A man, believed to be one of the king-pins in a local drug cartel had been tortured and left for dead on a creek bank in the mountains. He had been taken to hospital, but had died soon after. Just before he passed away he'd uttered two things – 'Scottish' and 'big ugly man'.

Grace's brunch blended and churned in her stomach, like a rip in the ocean. It frothed and bubbled until her saliva turned to water. She swallowed hard, jumped up and ran to the toilet clasping her mouth, hoping she'd make it in time.

After flushing her meal down the loo, she washed her face and rinsed the sourness from her mouth. What did all this mean? *Big ugly man.* That could only be Seth. Did he bash and torture the man? Grace shook her head as she walked back to the kitchen. No, surely not. The Seth she had come to know and . . . *and what?* She dismissed that thought. Seth wouldn't hurt people like that or shoot peoples' beloved animals. No way.

She gathered up the newspapers and took them back to the box. Leaving the room, she noticed her hands trembled. One thing was certain – she was more confused now than ever. She went to her room and took the belt out from where she'd hidden it. Sitting on the edge of her bed she studied the back of the buckle again. Smaller writing on the bottom caught her eye. It was barely legible. Grace grabbed the bottom of her tee shirt and buffed the buckle like cleaning sunglasses.

Her face froze as the words jumped out at her. '*Race the wind*'. Steve's ex-girlfriend had given him a silver belt buckle after he'd won several events at the Mt Isa Rodeo back in 2008. She'd had those exact words engraved on the back of the buckle. The blood drained from her head, taking all sense of logic with it. Her stomach hardened to concrete. This was *Steve's* belt. It had to be! How? Why? When? A billion questions tore through her brain.

She rushed back to the room and emptied the bag of clothes again. Grace held up a pair of jeans. Dark stain splatters covered most of the leg fronts. Blood? She gasped and dropped the jeans. A gush of adrenaline burned beneath her ribs and spread throughout her body. What should she do? She grabbed the clothes and stuffed them back into the bag. Her shaky hands couldn't hold the twisty. It dropped to the floor. Grace picked it up and tried again. Success this time. She threw the bag into the corner and bolted out of that room back to her own.

Steady now . . . think. She had no answers to the flood of questions. Okay, analyse the evidence. Seth has Steve's belt, that's for sure. Seth has some sort of connection to those horrendous crimes. *Doesn't prove he committed them.* There's blood-stained jeans in that bag. *Could be paint.* Damn that argumentative inner voice, but Grace prayed it was right.

"Seth, you couldn't kill anyone . . . just *couldn't.*" She thought about how gentle and caring he had become with her. How sad and lonely he really was. She just knew that under that tough, scarred exterior was a lonely, kind hearted soul who wouldn't hurt a bug.

Grace picked up the belt and clutched it to her chest, closing her eyes. What if . . . ? What if Seth really was the terrible monster who committed those sickening crimes?

If he could do that, he could have . . . *nooo.* Grace's eyes burned then spilled tears. He could have killed Steve. The rain pelted down, roaring on the tin roof and drowning out the sob from Grace's irritated throat and heavy heart.

CHAPTER 32

Seth took the map from Pete's hands and spread it over the ute's bonnet. "Right, so let me get this straight. He tapped an area of the map with a gloved finger. "There's a hundred and fifty prime steers in this paddock on Cedars Road and we're rounding them up late this afternoon?" Seth gritted his teeth. "It's pouring rain and Scott still expects us to carry out the job?"

Pete nodded and put one hand on his hip. "Yes, that's the orders."

"Jimmy, why the hell doesn't he hold off until the rain clears? Have you talked to him this morning?"

Jimmy scraped one boot in the dirt and cleared his throat. "Just a quick call earlier to confirm that Bruce is going away for a day or two and to go in, get the cattle and get out. He's booked them on a boat to Indonesia. No ifs, buts or maybe's."

Seth shook his head. "How does he know what Bruce is up to, when *he's* not game to come out of hiding?"

"He has a contact, plus I've been sussing the place out." Pete's deep, gravelly voice matched his stern face, neat moustache and broad shoulders.

Seth wondered if he'd been a drill sergeant, but didn't bother to ask. There were more pressing issues at hand. Getting this job done and getting back home alive. Hoping Grace was okay. He should have left her a note instead of just leaving while she was still asleep. She'd looked so beautiful and peaceful he didn't want to disturb her. Then worrying about what lay ahead drove the note idea completely out of his mind until he had almost reached this meeting point - an old abandoned shed, not far from Scott's property.

"I took a few of lick blocks over two days ago and placed them near the back entrance to the property, not far from the Kendall farm boundary and back yards," continued Pete. "Then dropped some molasses on them yesterday and again early this morning. The steers are starting to gather and camp around there. They're not too stirry. Most seem pretty quiet. Old man Kendall doesn't use those yards much. His wife is in hospital at the moment, so he won't be around his backblocks. This really worked to our advantage. Scott expected it to be much more difficult."

"Once we get them into the yards, then what?" asked Seth. "This seems a bit too easy." He straightened up and stepped back. The rain eased off to a sprinkle.

"We leave them there until four AM then we drove them from Kendall's yards along that old stock route to Butterfly Creek," replied Jimmy. "That should take about an hour or so, hey Pete?" Pete nodded. Jimmy continued. "There's a bit of a clearing just inside the national park.

Rosco is organising semi's to pick them up from there and head west to the gulf. Scott will be in one of the semi's."

The mere mention of the Scotsman's name sent a zap of electricity through Seth. The sooner this was over, and he was finally free of Scott, the better.

Jimmy seemed to be emulating Pete's authoritive voice, but he just couldn't match it. Seth could have laughed if the whole thing wasn't so serious. More questions begged to be answered.

"What's the state of this stock route we have to use?" He threw his hands in the air. He was just *over* Scott and his jobs. He just wanted a normal life. Hell, *any* life would be better than the one he'd been living for as long as he could remember. "Is there yards at the end? A loading ramp?"

"Calm down Seth." Pete's voice hardened to a warning. "I've checked it all out and the temporary yards, including a loading ramp, were erected yesterday. I did most of it myself. The fences along the route are good. The creek crossings are okay."

"Hmph. If this rain keeps up they won't be."

"Seth, what the hell is your problem, mate?" Pete's brown eyes glared. The veins in this neck stood out and his face reddened. Even in the dull light of the shed on a rainy day, Seth could see he was not one to be mucked with. Seth could look down on Pete's cropped, brown hair, but something about him reminded Seth of Scott. Best to keep calm and go with the flow. It'll all be over soon.

Seth raised his hands in a truce. "Sorry, Pete. It would be a disaster if we got half way along and got stranded, that's all." He shrugged and turned his head toward the open side of the shed, more to avoid Pete seeing the anger Seth knew his eyes conveyed. "Looks like it might be clearing up a bit. I can see some blue sky out there." He pointed toward the west.

Pete and Jimmy turned their heads. "Good," they said in unison.

"Supposed to be a cyclone out off the coast a bit," said Pete. "Last I heard they think it might head south."

Jimmy shrugged. "Dunno. I don't listen to any news, or read the papers. Too depressing."

"What about the horses? How are we getting them over to where the steers are?" Seth couldn't help but think of the poor bloke the black gelding killed. A slight quiver rattled his body at the thought of climbing on that beast again.

"Rosco will bring his smaller truck over to Scott's place this afternoon and we load them on and take them over," replied Jimmy, placing his hands on his hips.

"And our vehicles?"

"Best meet here again this afternoon. Rosco can pick us up from here and take us to Scott's, then do it all in reverse once the cattle are loaded. Drop the horses off and drop us back here. All done. We can stay at Scott's tonight. It's closer to the job than this pace." For the first time, a smile cracked Pete's stony face. Not a smug I'll-kill-you smile like Scott often showed, more like a how-easy-was-that smile.

"Aren't the cattle supposed to be tagged?" Seth hoped like hell that part wasn't in the job description. Individually ear tagging one hundred and fifty would take hours.

He wanted this job over *now*. He hated leaving Grace alone for so long.

"Scott's got that organised further along," said Pete. "Hughenden I think. He just wants them out of this area ASAP."

Seth couldn't help himself. "Is the Great Scott getting nervous?"

Pete shot him a you're-bloody-game-or-stupid-asking-that glare without saying a word. Seth couldn't tell if the serious look indicated Pete was in thick with Scott or scared of him.

Jimmy folded the map. "So, that's it then? We all clear? Back here at four o'clock sharp, this arvo."

"Yep." Pete nodded then turned to Seth. "You?"

"Yep. See yous then." Seth walked past the back of Jimmy's utility and out the run-down shed. Staring ahead, his mind on Grace, he stepped in a puddle, splashing water up his jeans leg. "Shit." He yanked open the driver door, jumped in and slammed it shut. He gripped the steering wheel and watched Pete get in his ute. This was bullshit. It all sounded too easy. Nothing he ever had to do for Scott was this easy. Could fate, or whatever the hell it was, be finally on his side?

He doubted it.

He leaned over and opened the glove box. The black pistol was still sitting snug among other contents. Closing the glove box, he nodded. The gun was his security. It just might save his life.

Seth roared his ute into life, reversed around and slid about on the muddy track as he planted his foot on the accelerator. He couldn't wait to get home to see Grace. Beautiful, smiling Grace. The only reason he wanted to keep living. At least *she'd* help take away this heavy feeling of dread that had settled in his stomach.

CHAPTER 33

K ain stopped, dropped his back pack and wiped the moisture from his face with the front of his already damp tee shirt. The rain had lightened – at last. Joe continued pushing on ahead, forty metres to his left while Anthony was roughly the same distance to his right. "Hey Joe." Joe stopped and looked around. "Let's stop for bit of lunch." Kain looked to his right. "Anthony?"

Both men veered toward Kain, who'd now sat on a wet log.

"How far do you think we've come?" Kain asked, perching on a nearby rock and placing his large backpack beside him.

Anthony moved the open front of the yellow raincoat aside and took his phone from his top pocket. He tapped the screen and studied it for a bit. "Hmm, according to this app, we've done about fifteen k's today." His lips upturned and he nodded in satisfaction. "Not bad."

Kain handed a full bottle of water to Anthony. "Thanks again for coming with us, mate."

Anthony pushed back the hood of his raincoat, exposing his curly fair hair. "No worries, Kain. I had to tell a couple of white lies to some of my colleagues. With the cyclone hovering off the coast they wanted us all on deck, filling sandbags and things like that, but if we find Grace it'll be worth it a hundred times over. After everything you've told me so far, I'm glad I'm here to help."

"*When* we find Grace," Joe stated.

Kain was about to say the same thing.

"Sorry." Anthony shook his head and fiddled with his sand-coloured goatee. "I meant to say *when*. For what's it's worth, I do believe you. I'm just a bit worried."

"What about?" Kain's cricket ball of nervousness in his stomach expanded to a basketball.

Joe slid back his raincoat hood and frowned at Anthony.

"I don't mean to put a dampener on things, but we've come all this way, calling and calling to Grace. Either we're barking up the wrong tree, or . . . "

Kain raised his hand in a "*stop*" mode. "Don't say it. I don't want to hear anything negative." He took some apples and muesli bars from his backpack and handed them to Joe and Anthony. "C'mon, eat. We need to keep our strength up." He ripped the paper off his bar and took half in one bite, followed by the rest of the bar.

"Thanks for bringing extra food, Kain," Anthony said between mouthfuls.

"Well, you couldn't very well fit much more in your pack with the tent, sleeping mats and the rifle. I'm so glad you brought that."

"Yeah, me too." Joe unscrewed the top from a water bottle. "Too many bloody wild things out here. Wouldn't be surprised if we find a yowie or two in this scrub."

Kain couldn't help but laugh, easing the nervousness back a little. "Trust you to think of that."

"You're the only yowie in Queensland, Joe." Anthony wore a cheeky smile.

"Get stuffed." Joe grinned and the other two laughed.

Anthony's smile disappeared as did the accompanying eye sparkle. "We have to be bloody careful though. Not really supposed to carry guns in the national park. I'll only use it if it's a matter of life or death."

Kain nodded. "Fair enough." He finished the apple he'd now been munching and had a long drink of water. He looked through a break in the tree tops. "Looks like it might be clearing up."

Anthony tapped his phone screen. "Yeah, could be. According to this the cyclone is moving south now, so we shouldn't see too much more rain."

"Well, that'll be handy if we have to camp the night." Joe stood, rolled his shoulders several times and replaced his back pack. "I just had a thought Kain. Eddy wasn't very happy when I called in sick early this morning, but I doubt they'd be working now anyway. So I don't feel so bad for lying to him."

"Yeah," agreed Kain. "Nothing would dry in this weather."

Anthony continued to stare at and tap his phone screen. "We're about smack bang in the middle of the national park now. The closest road in the direction we are heading is about another ten or so k's away. I think it's called Mountain View Road. We'll have to veer a bit more to the north. It doesn't look like much of a road, but you never know, there might be a house or two on it. In fact, from memory, I think there is."

"I reckon we should spread out a bit more too," suggested Kain. He took out his own phone and tapped the screen. "No bars. Useless. What about you, Joe?"

Joe looked at his phone. "One bar, no wait . . .it's gone. None. How come you can get such good reception, Anthony?"

"Dunno mate." The eye sparkle returned. "Maybe I pay my bill on time."

Joe gave him a playful shove, almost knocking him off his feet.

"Well, we're going to have to stay within shouting distance, but further apart than before." Kain turned away from the others, did a pee and hoisted his back pack. "Let's go and see if we can find that road before dark. Hopefully, the cyclone is moving away. We're stuffed if it does come. My gut tells me we're getting closer to Grace. Then this nightmare will finally be over."

CHAPTER 34

Grace arose from her bed at the sound of Seth's utility approaching and stopping near the house. She was tired, but it was pointless trying to sleep through the day, especially now.

Since discovering the papers with the marked articles of murder and bashings and also Steve's belt, she hadn't been able to eat, sleep or think straight. She'd been lying on her bed for goodness knows how long, pondering the multitude of questions that bombarded her brain, but finding few answers. She just kept returning to the frightening possibility that Seth committed those crimes and also killed Steve.

Fear, dread, shock and loathing thickened and simmered like soup in her stomach. No matter how many times she mulled over how she would approach Seth with her discoveries and assumptions, here she was heading to the kitchen with no idea of what to say. She took several deep, quick breaths, ran her hand through her hair, and wiped her palms on her shorts.

His boots clopped up the stairs. Grace held out her hands. They trembled. She stopped near the table and clasped them together. Seth's outline loomed at the door and he slid off his boots. Grace's heart slammed into her ribcage and her mouth dried to bitterness.

To avoid his face, Grace filled the kettle and turned it on, taking another deep breath. It didn't work. Her nerves still frayed, scattering like dandelion petals on the wind.

Seth dropped his hat on the floor. "G'day Grace. I'm sorry I had to rush out this morning without leaving you a note or saying goodbye. You were sound asleep. I didn't want to wake you."

Grace stared out the window. Unbelievable. He just acted the same. Like nothing was wrong at all. *Maybe because he's innocent.* Okay, maybe he did deserve the benefit of the doubt. She turned to him and forced a smile. Seeing him standing there, only a couple of metres away sent a rush of relief through her. The forced smile retracted and she relaxed enough to allow a natural smile to flow.

His eyes, gentle caring voice, and smile emanating warmth showed he was glad to be home. It was difficult to remain angry with him. Maybe it was best not to ask about the newspapers but Steve's belt niggled at her brain. *If he knows I've got it he'll know I've been in the room.* She had no idea what to do for the best.

"Hi Seth. Would you like a cuppa?"

"Yes please. A good strong one."

She took two mugs from the cupboard and dropped in the teabags. "Where did you go?" May as well be direct. She was sick of tip toeing and playing mind games.

"Just had to take care of something." He headed toward the lounge. "Just going to wash my hands."

Grace poured in the milk and placed the cups on the table before sitting at one. Just this, just that. He made everything seem so blasé when it was far from it.

In no time he was back and sitting opposite Grace. "Thank you." He sipped his tea while staring at the front door.

"Are you expecting someone?"

His body flinched, as if he'd got a fright. "No. Why?"

"You're watching the door."

"Sorry, Grace." He looked at her and for the first time since she'd got over the initial shock of seeing his face, Grace found it difficult keeping eye contact.

"Seth, you seem nervous. What's going on? What have you *really* been doing?" She didn't feel like making small talk and she definitely didn't want to tell him about the pregnancy. The urge to know his secrets was greater than anything else at the moment. It was an avalanche, snowballing toward her, increasing in size that was pushing her to get some answers once and for all.

Seth's eyebrows creased and he straightened up in his chair. "What's wrong? You seem angry at me." His face changed to sad. "Have I done something to upset you?"

"You tell me, Seth." She sipped her tea. Maybe that came out a bit harsh. She couldn't really afford to anger him. He could lock the front door and clear out for good. "If I'm here in your home and we are supposed to be friends, I just wish you'd open up to me a bit more. I feel like the proverbial mushroom. You know, being kept in the dark and fed bullshit."

Seth shook his head. "No, I haven't heard of that." His large chest rose and fell in a deep sigh. "Okay, I'll tell you. I have some work going on. Helping a bloke muster and move a big herd of cattle."

"In *this* weather?"

"Yeah, he's sending them up toward the gulf and already has them booked in, so we just have to do it. I think the weather's clearing up a bit though. Hasn't rained for a while now."

Cattle mustering's not such a big deal, especially with all the cattle properties around the Karisdale area. Some of the thick soup of nervousness dispersed. "Are you hungry?"

"Ah . . . yes actually, I am. But I'll get something after I have a shower." He scraped his chair back and stood. "I have to go back this afternoon and stay the night, then we should finish it all early in the morning. Will you be okay, Grace? Things will be a lot better after tomorrow."

She nodded but her heart and mood sank. "Yes, I'll be fine." She picked up both cups and placed them on the sink. Seth disappeared toward the bathroom and in no time the whirring of the pressure pump began. Why would 'things' be better after tomorrow?

The belt. Should she quickly put it back? Yes. For now, anyway. Grace hurried to her room and reached under the mattress for the precious belt. The pump continued singing. She tiptoed past the bathroom and opened the door of the forbidden room. The musty smell hit her again. She tried not to breathe too deep.

The bathroom door opened. Oh no. Her heart sped a billion miles per hour. She may have *thought* she was through playing mind games with Seth, but there was absolutely no way she dared him find her in this room. She grabbed the door knob and closed the door as quietly as possible.

His bare feet padded down the hall.

Grace held her breath and willed her heart to quieten. That herd of cattle Seth mentioned stampeded through her chest.

His footsteps grew closer. Hopefully he hadn't heard the door. If he had, then this was it. She would have to confront him about the belt and hope for the best. There was no other choice. The round old-fashioned light switch of his room clicked on. Grace bent forward, closed one eye and peered through the key hole, daring not to breathe. Seth stood just inside his doorway, in nothing but jeans. Even his hands were bare as they hung by his sides. Seemed like he'd just stopped dead in his tracks.

Grace stared at his bare back. There was some scarring, but there were also some tattoos. She dropped her gaze to his gloveless hands. Something caught her eye on his left hand. He reached over and pushed the door shut behind him. Damn. Something was odd about that hand. She'd caught a glimpse of his right one by mistake the other night. One finger top was missing.

She had to get out of the room without Seth knowing. With no time to put the belt back in the garbage bag, she clutched it to her chest and opened the door. His closed door could burst open at any second. Slipping through the door, she pulled it closed behind her. A slight noise, but she could only hope and pray he hadn't heard a thing. She ran on tip toes back to her room, leant over and shoved the belt beneath her mattress.

"Are you all right, Grace?"

Grace jumped around and upright. Seth stood in her doorway. Surely he must have seen her drop the mattress down at least. "Yes. Why?"

"You jumped with fright when I came in." His eyes saddened. "You aren't still scared of me are you?"

Here was her chance to ask him about the things in the room. Her mouth opened, but the words just refused to come forth. Something bigger was stopping her. "Ah . . . no, of course not." She forced a smile and glanced down at the side of the bed, hoping no part of the belt showed. All good. "I'm not feeling the best, Seth. I think I might lie down for a while. Do you mind?"

"Of course not. I'll have some lunch then I'll be heading out again soon after. Are you sure you don't want me to make you a sandwich or something? A drink?"

"No thanks." Grace smiled and sat on the bed. "I'm just tired." It wasn't exactly a lie.

"Okay. Well, you get some rest. I'll try to be quiet then I'll go." He stared at her.

His gaze left her feeling exposed, bare and uncomfortable. She looked to the floor. "Seth, why are you staring at me like that?" Slowly her gaze returned to his face.

"Um, sorry Grace. I didn't mean to make you feel uneasy." His eyes darted to the window, to his feet and he placed his gloved hands in his jeans pockets. Now, *he* seemed the uncomfortable one. "Whatever happens Grace, just remember that I . . . I care about you very much and would never ever hurt you." His eyes glassed over, but it wasn't just in sadness. Something else was hidden deep. Something haunting. Fear?

Grace nodded. "I know you wouldn't." *But who else have you hurt?* She lay down and raised her hand in a wave. "I'll see you tomorrow then."

"Yep."

And he was gone. She heard some noises from the kitchen, him walk to his room and back then the ute start up and drive away. She was alone. Again. So much to digest. Something more sinister was going on. She saw it in Seth's face and heard it in his words.

The keyhole image wouldn't leave her brain. Just what was it about his hand and back that jarred her inquisitive mind? Time to snoop in his room again.

Grace went to the front veranda and listened. Listened for the slightest sound of a vehicle. Nothing but a few bird songs, chirping insects and some grateful frogs croaking after the rain.

Satisfied Seth was not returning unexpectedly, she headed to his room. The guilt that hung heavy on the previous snooping session no longer prevailed. He had way too many secrets and she wanted answers once and for all.

His dark room smelled of stuffy mustiness and him. Grace flicked on the light and pulled open the curtains. Now she could see every part of the room. If something suspicious was here, she was determined to find it, no matter how long it took. Seth wasn't due back until the next day and she had nothing better to do. The ticking clock her only companion.

Going through the bedside drawers everything seemed the same as before. She took out the newspapers from the middle drawer and spread one open on the bed. No horrific headlines jumped out at her. There must be *something* significant in them if he kept them by his bed.

Grace scanned every page of each newspaper but found nothing that could incriminate Seth or seemed connected to him in any way. She returned them to the drawer, disheartened but determined to continue searching.

She opened the wardrobe. The guns stood in the corner. Clothes hung on the rack. Nothing appeared different. Several pairs of folded jeans sat on the wardrobe floor, beside a pair of large black boots. She moved the boots aside and slid her hand under the jeans, lifting the pile out. Something small and light-coloured was in the far corner.

Grace reached down and picked up the item. She turned it over as she brought it out to full light. It was a torn piece of a photo containing two children, but only showing their upper bodies. The photo in the wooden box. This *had* to be the missing piece. She rushed to the bathroom and brought the wooden box to her bed. It was still unlocked. Seth mustn't have been back to it.

After listening out again for several seconds and hearing nothing but animals, Grace lifted the lid, grabbed the envelope and pulled out the old photo. Her fingers trembled, placing both pieces together. A perfect fit. She sucked in a breath and smiled through tears. At last she may be able to solve the mystery.

Something in the picture's background disturbed her. She wiped her eyes and brought the new piece up closer to her eyes. The colours were faded, but there was no mistake. What the background showed sent chills hurtling up her spine and icicles snaking through every vein of her body.

CHAPTER 35

Seth turned off the ignition and jumped out of his ute. Pete, Jimmy and Rosco stood by the old shed, overnight bags by their sides. All eyes watched him walking over. All eyes looked worried.

"What's up? Has something else happened?" His gaze moved from one to the other. He didn't like the look of this.

"Nah." Jimmy shrugged and gave a half grin. "It's all good. Well . . ." The grin disappeared. "As good as it can be doing a job for Scott."

Pete slapped him on the shoulder. "We'll be right, mate. This time tomorrow we'll be sitting pretty. A huge wad of cash in our pocket."

"So, are we ready to go?" Seth tilted his hat up a little. He extended his right, gloved hand. "You must be Rosco?"

A fair, freckled hand and arm reached out and returned the shake "Yes. Jesus Christ, what happened to you?" Rosco's green eyes widened among a sea of freckles.

Seth looked into those green eyes. They didn't hold fear or loathing like the people of Karisdale. They didn't hold smart arse attitude like the yobbo at the service station.

They didn't hold anything but genuine curiosity. Seth shook his head. "It's a long story. I'll tell you another day."

"Righto, we've got the horses in the yards over at Scott's," said Pete. "Let's get over there. It's going to be a tight squeeze in the truck, but if we go the back roads and tracks no-one will see us."

"I'll drive my ute over there. I don't see the point in leaving the vehicles here." Seth glanced at the old shed. It was true, he couldn't see any reason for it, but he also wanted to be able to leave as soon as possible in the morning, when their part of the job was done. He couldn't wait to get back to Grace and bask in the knowledge Scott would no longer be running his life.

"The idea of the vehicles staying here was to not have them at Scott's," Pete said. "Easier to disassociate ourselves with him if our cars aren't on his property. If something goes wrong . . ."

"Mother of Mary . . ." Jimmy's face paled.

"I said, '*If* something goes wrong', you idiot." Pete rolled his eyeballs. "All should be good. My source told me that the police got a tip Scott was seen in Brisbane yesterday, so they're hunting around there for him now. Let's go."

"I'll come with you, Seth." Not waiting for an answer, Jimmy picked up his bag and strode to Seth's ute.

"Fair enough." Seth shrugged one shoulder. "See ya's at Scott's." He joined Jimmy in the ute.

The drive to Scott's was quiet. Seth's mind was on Grace and life after tomorrow. Jimmy looked out the window most of the time and hardly uttered a word.

Clouds still hung about even though the rain stayed away. Just as well. The job would be stressful enough without them being drenched to the bone. The cattle would probably play up more in the rain.

Seth jumped out of his utility next to Scott's yards. His eyes darted toward the creek and the makeshift grave. It looked so peaceful but chills of barbed wire buzzed around his body, causing him to shudder.

"You're thinking the same thing as me, aren'tcha?" Jimmy stood beside Seth. "Poor bastard. God rest his soul." Jimmy looked upwards. "God have mercy on us all in the morning."

Seth looked at Jimmy. Pathetic. "You really think God gives a stuff about us after everything we've done? I like your fantasy, Jimmy."

"Hey, it's worth a try." Jimmy sounded hurt. "I promised myself this will be the last ever job for Scott. After this, I'm clean."

"Me too, mate." Seth turned around.

Rosco's blue and white cattle truck rumbled and bumped along the driveway before stopping a little way back from Seth's ute. Pete jumped out, Rosco pulled around to his right and backed the truck up to the loading ramp.

Pete walked past Seth and Jimmy. "Come on." He signalled with his arm. "Let's get the horses loaded."

Seth had been too busy thinking of the dead man and of Jimmy's religious hopes that he hadn't looked at the four horses standing in the yard. Two bays, a grey and the black tornado. His devil eyes met Seth's with a snort. His head lifted and shook about, before his gaze fell back on Seth. He must know something big was going down. He looked more than ready. "Are we going to saddle them here or at the other yards?"

Pete walked through the gate into the largest yard. "From what I've heard about that black rogue you're riding, I think it's best if we run them on to the truck and saddle them over there." He pointed to Seth's mount, which'd now pranced several metres away from the other three. "He'd probably smash the saddle in the truck. Where the hell did Scott get him from? The knackery? He's psycho."

Seth was right behind Pete. "Yep, good idea and I don't know anything about this horse except he's a m-." He stopped himself saying 'murderer'. The less people who knew about what happened, the better.

Pete looked at Seth. "He's a what?"

"A maniac."

Rosco and Jimmy joined the others in the yard. Jimmy walked straight up to his grey mare and rubbed her neck. She clearly enjoyed it, lowering her head for him to scratch around her ears as well. The two bays walked away, unsure of the close human contact. Like a magician, Jimmy pulled a thin rope out of his jeans pocket and wrapped it around the mare's neck. With trepidation etched on his face, he watched the black gelding.

Without hesitation, the grey mare followed Jimmy through the smaller yards and straight up the loading ramp into the truck. The two bays followed but the black monster refused to move. His eyes darted from the other horses to Seth and Pete trying to coax him toward the ramp.

Jimmy continued stroking the mare in the truck. Seth and Pete clapped and raised their hands, gave a few shouts but the horse stood his ground.

"Shit. Come on." Pete's face reddened. "We've *got* to get him on the truck."

The horse reared and pored at the air with his huge black hooves. He neighed, snorted and reared again. The whites of his eyes showed and his ears flattened back. The hooves hit the ground. The horse shook his head high, bared his teeth and charged toward Seth and Pete.

Images of 'Stretch's' death flashed in Seth's mind. Either he or Pete was going to end up the same way. No. No way in hell. Seth spun on his heels and ran for the fence. Amidst expletives, Pete did the same. Thundering hooves followed close behind.

A blood-thickening *neigh* and the approaching nightmare stopped. Dirt flicked up, hitting Seth in the legs as he scaled the wooden fence. Trotting hooves grew quieter. Seth's heart raced louder than the horse's hooves. He looked over his shoulder. The gelding trotted toward the ramp.

Pete dropped to the ground in the yard. "Fuck, that was close." His red face of anger now an ashen face of fear *and* relief.

Jimmy hightailed it over the side of the truck and the gelding settled among the other three horses. Rosco slid the heavy gate across, locking them in.

Seth stepped down from the rails. "Hell, I thought one of us was dead then."

"He's one mean beast all right." Pete placed his hands on his hips and watched the truck. Rosco stood on the end of the ramp, doing up the latch. "Do you think he has a killer instinct?"

Seth looked at Pete but his mind saw the bloodied, crumpled head of the lifeless man lying on this very ground. "Yes I do."

Not wanting to dwell, Seth strode out the yard and to the nearby shed. Hoping to shut out horrible images and memories, he focussed on Grace. With the money from Scott, he planned to buy her something special. But he had no idea what. She didn't seem to want for anything. Anything apart from answers. She certainly wanted answers. One day he'd give her them. Well . . . *some*.

"All the gear we need should be right here."

Seth jumped.

"Geez mate, you're nervous." Pete stood beside him. The truck approached and stopped close to the shed.

"What do you expect? That beast is enough to make anyone nervous, plus I'm not exactly thrilled about doing this job."

"For what it worth, me neither." Pete hoisted a saddle off a round horizontal rail, grabbed the nearby bridle and took them to the truck. The other three men did the same.

"Gunna be a tight squeeze, but we'll do it." Rosco laughed, deep and hearty. "Pile in."

Ten minutes later, the loaded truck pulled up at the gate near Kendall's yards. Seth inhaled deeply, opened the door and almost fell out of the vehicle. The pistol in his pocket bordered on painful. With four men and horse gear squashed into a two-man, albeit large, cabin there was hardly room to breathe, let alone move.

The sun sank low in the west, sending golden pink rays through the parting clouds.

"I'll walk over to the yards," Seth yelled, opening the gate. Rosco nodded.

The truck trundled along the pot-holed track to Kendall's loading ramp. Even after shutting the gate, Seth caught up with it. The horses seemed calm, even the black rogue.

The loading ramp had been dirt-filled, but some dirt had eroded away or compacted down. It would be a slight drop for the horses. Seth scaled the yard fence and stood at the top of the ramp watching Rosco reverse the truck closer. He certainly was adept at this. One go and he was spot on in position.

Seth lifted and turned the heavy pin. He watched the black gelding, which had his rear toward Seth. Satisfied the semi-deranged horse wasn't going to come screaming toward him, he slid he truck gate open and climbed over the ramp fence.

One bay walked out first, followed by the other three. They handled the drop with no problems.

Rosco, Pete and Jimmy approached their horses with ease, putting on the bridles without any fuss from the animals.

Seth approached his mount standing in the far corner, watching him. "Righto, mate, I'm not going to hurt you, so you can forget about hurting me, okay." He kept the bridle by his side and held out the other hand.

The horse's ears flattened back and he threw his head around. One hoof pored at the ground and he let out a high-pitched scream.

Damn Scott and his 'work'. Seth's heart rate cranked up a few gears. He breathed the clean afternoon air in deeply. He must *not* show his fear. He kept his eyes on the black eyes in front of him and moved one foot after the other. His gloved hand touched the gelding's neck. The horse flinched and jumped aside. Seth took another step and rubbed the sleek muscular neck harder. The smell of horse sweat greeted his nostrils. "That's it. Good boy." The horse stood still, only his belly moved in time with his heavy, nervous breathing.

Seth held the top of the bridle near its forehead and pushed the metal bit into its mouth. The gelding threw his head back at the cold hard steel. Seth was tall enough to reach the top of the horse's raised head and pull the bridle over its ears. Hard teeth grinded on the bit. Another toss of the head. Seth lost grip of the neck strap but grabbed it again. "Hold still, boy." Finally, the bridle was on and all done up.

Next the saddle. It was the girth strap that had sent him into a murderous rampage last time. Seth thought of Jimmy and his prayers. Nah, he wouldn't bother. God hadn't helped him before, so he didn't expect help now.

Jimmy had his mare all saddled and hitched to the outer side of the yard fence. He brought Seth's saddle from the truck. "Here you go. Good luck. You'll need it." His negativity matched his grim face.

"Gee, thanks Jimmy." Seth took the saddle. His lips wanted to laugh, but his heart and head were in no joking mood. He trudged back to the gelding, again standing in the far corner. The reins hung over his neck. His head hung low. Seth knew not to take that as submission. This animal was a ticking time bomb.

The horse stood still, a giant mass of muscle and attitude. Seth hung the saddle over his left arm and grabbed the rein with his left hand. While doing so, he placed the saddle cloth over the horse's back. The horse turned his head toward Seth. *Don't you bloody bite me.* A snort came from flared nostrils. Four hooves stomped and pranced a moment before becoming still.

"Need a hand?" called Pete.

Seth looked up and shook his head. He didn't want to call out lest it agitate the horse even more.

Keeping hold of the rein, Seth placed the saddle on the horse. With his left hand he rubbed the sweaty neck. The girth strap dangled down the other side. He continued to stroke the neck while rubbing the shoulder and side with his right hand.

Seth leaned down. The girth was in reach. It was now or never. His hand dived for the end of the girth, bringing it toward him and slipping it through the buckle. The horse snorted again, jumped to the side, but hit against the wooden fence. He kicked out to the side with his back foot. Seth jumped to his left. The hoof scraped the denim of his jeans.

While the horse mucked around, Seth did up the girth and went back to rubbing its neck, harder this time. All good. The horse calmed. Seth also calmed and his pulse rate slowed to a normal pace. He took the reins and lead the gelding to where the others were mounted and waiting outside the yards.

"I take my hat off to you, Seth." Jimmy raised and lowered his cap. "More guts than me, that's for sure."

Seth just nodded. He really didn't feel like talking.

"Right, we've got the gates ready," said Pete in his sergeant-type voice. "I came over earlier and brought the steers some nice lucerne hay and more molasses. I reckon they'll all still be there, ready to camp the night. Let's go round up our cash. Get 'em to Kendall's yards for the night."

Seth placed one foot in the stirrup and, in one mighty effort, pulled himself up and swung his other leg over the horse's back. Adrenaline fired up and charged through his body. The horse pranced and danced, threw his head this way and that, but didn't attempt to throw its rider.

The others had trotted ahead. With a light kick in the sides, he urged the horse into a canter to catch up. Head up, mane flying in the breeze, the horse reared and took off like a fired cannon ball. Seth's arms strained to pull him back to a canter, then a trot. He just wanted to go. Fly like the wind. Race the wind.

This angry machine of energy was possibly going to kill Seth . . . or save him.

CHAPTER 36

Kain sat on a large rock and took a long, much-needed drink of water. The sun had disappeared. Night insects began their incessant chirping, buzzing, biting. "Geez, these mozzies are bad." He slapped his arm. "Joe, pass me the spray when you're finished, please." Joe tossed the aerosol can to Kain "Thanks."

"We'd better get the tent set up before it gets dark." Anthony pulled the tent from his backpack and dropped it beside Kain. "I daresay there won't be any dry wood around, to have a fire."

"Why can't we just keep going with the torchlight?" Kain stood. "I'm not tired. And we could be *this* close to Grace by now." He held his thumb and forefinger several centimetres apart. "How far from that road are we, Anthony?"

Anthony pulled out his phone, tapped the screen and stared. "Shit. Nothing." He walked several metres away and held the phone above his head a moment then down low. "Now I've lost signal too."

"Great." Joe lit a cigarette. "That's all we need."

Anthony walked back to Kain. "Mate, that *hill* we just crossed may as well have been a mountain. It was rugged enough and took us longer than I expected. We wouldn't be far from the road by now, but my back is killing me." He reached around and rubbed his lower back. His face grimaced in pain. "Let's just set up the tent and get some sleep and get out at first light."

"Why didn't you say something, you moron?" Joe shook his head and rolled his eyes. "One of us could have taken the heavier pack. Is it from the fall off the truck last week? Sue mentioned that."

Anthony gave a slight grin. "Yep. Bloody stupid thing to do. It wasn't too bad until about twenty minutes ago." He rubbed some more before bending backwards and to each side.

"Well, I'll take the heavier pack tomorrow." Kain began to open out the tent pack. "C'mon, Joe. You sit down, Anthony." He gestured toward the rock on which he'd been sitting.

Joe and Kain erected the tent and placed the three sleeping mats inside.

"Gunna be a tight squeeze, but if no-one tosses around, we should be right," said Joe. "And if either of you snore I'll stuff my dirty socks in your mouth."

Anthony laughed. "If you fart, Joe Miller, I'll jam this rifle butt right up your coight."

Kain took three tins of baked beans and three forks from his back pack. "Actually, I *am* buggered." He pulled the ring tab on one can. "I wanted to go on. To find Grace tonight, but after what we trekked through this arvie and I haven't had much sleep for days, I'm stuffed." He handed the open can and a fork to Anthony. "Here Joe, you can open your own." He passed a can and fork to Joe.

"Gee, thanks." Joe expressed an exaggerated sad face and accepted the offering. "How come he's privileged?"

Anthony laughed.

Even Kain couldn't help a chuckle. "Because without *him*, you and me would be lost somewhere out there." He pointed back the way they'd come. "And Anthony and his SES mates would be out searching for *us.*"

Joe giggled. "True". He pulled the can open and shovelled a forkful into his mouth.

Kain watched Joe. "Oh shit."

"What?" Joe stopped chewing and looked from Anthony to Kain.

"Are you thinking what I'm thinking, Kain?" Anthony winked.

"I think so, mate." Kain held the grin and shook his head. It sure felt good to laugh.

"Joe Miller. Baked beans. Not a good combination. I might sleep *outside* the tent tonight."

"Me too." Kain opened his own can.

"Ahh, you two." Joe laughed.

Kain's thoughts diverted to Grace. He wondered what she was doing right then. If she was okay, or hurt, or scared, or . . . No. No. No. He looked from Anthony to Joe as daylight faded. "You know, tomorrow's going to be a good day. Going to be the *best* day ever. I *know* we're going to find her."

CHAPTER 37

Grace clutched the two pieces of the old photo in one hand while ensuring Seth's room was exactly the way she'd found it when she began snooping. She returned the wooden box to its drawer in the bathroom and rushed into the kitchen. Night loomed. The long fluorescent tube in the kitchen would give much brighter light than any others in the house. Grace didn't want to miss a single speck of the picture.

She clicked on the light switch and sat at the table directly below the light. Normally it came on in a few seconds, but tonight it took a hundred years. "Come on. Come on". Grace glanced up at the flickering light and drummed her fingers on the table. Finally.

She stared at the picture again. Two little boys. Definitely twins. Same height and almost the same face. She licked dry lips and wiped sweaty palms on her shorts. The house standing behind the boys was *her* family home. The garden bed was her mother's favourite rose bed. A massive kaleidoscope of butterflies swamped her stomach. Afraid to open her mouth lest the butterflies swarm out along with other stomach contents, Grace swallowed hard.

She turned the picture face down on the table. The previously broken words on the back were now complete.

'*Jon and Steven 1985*'

CHAPTER 38

Seth pulled the reins tight, bringing his horse to trot. Two steers had just tried to break loose, but the well-trained gelding had wheeled, galloped after them and turned the rogues back to the mob. This was it. After resting at next door Kendall's yards overnight, the herd headed to the portable yards and waiting trucks.

Seth hardly needed to work the horse, just keep his balance. He had to lean and duck a few times to avoid his knee hitting tree trunks or being totally swiped off by low-hanging branches. The black monster had proved his worth. Seth decided he'd keep him. Scott can get stuffed. With Scott leaving for good, he won't care about the horse. *Don't forget he's taking you too.* Like hell. Seth patted his jeans pocket. The pistol remained, albeit uncomfortable, but *ready* and he wouldn't hesitate to shoot if his life was at stake. He felt the pocket on the opposite side. Bullets were safe.

The herd forged ahead. A couple of swollen creek crossing were a bit dicey, but all steers ambled on to their unknown destination. Most of the herd were Black Angus, their coats sleek and shiny in the early morning sun. Old vehicle tracks on the route were muddy and slippery.

"The yards are just over this next rise," yelled Pete from one side. "There's a couple of fallen trees over the track just ahead too." The lead steers broke into a canter toward the rise. "Slow them down." Pete shouted and urged his bay into a canter, through the bush to head the steers off.

Jimmy galloped his grey mare up the other side to help Pete steady the lead. Seth and Rosco kept up the rear. Like sheep, once the lead steers broke into a run, they all followed. Seth kept his mount steady. The horse snorted and pranced. Even after the ten kilometre trek, he still burst with energy, wanting to take off after the cattle. Seth forearms burned, straining to keep the horse steady.

Pete and Jimmy '*yahhed*' and waved their hats about. Most of the runaways stopped or slowed but half a dozen dived around Pete and galloped on toward their destination. Pete leaned down and spurred his horse after them while Jimmy tried in vain to slow the rest of the mob, who weaved and darted around him.

Bellowing, shouting and confusion reigned. Seth wanted to fly up ahead and help, but he would only stir the cattle more. Best to stay behind, keep calm and hope like hell the portable yards were set up properly and the gate wide open.

Pete and Jimmy disappeared over the rise and more of the cattle broke into a gallop and followed. Birds scattered from the trees. This was turning into one big ugly stampede. Scott will *not* be happy.

Seth and Rosco arrived at the top of the ridge behind the mob. A massive sea of moving black, like tadpoles moving in a mud puddle. Pete and Jimmy rode in front, cutting this way and that, shouting and cursing, still trying to slow the unyielding mob.

Seth's horse jumped clear over a large fallen gum tree. No effort at all. Another smaller tree lay ahead. He let the gelding have his head. Seth leaned forward ready for the exhilarating moment of flying.

"Whoah." He yanked the reins tight. The panting horse stopped. Seth almost landed on its neck. On the ground beside the fallen tree lay a thrashing steer. One front leg bent up below the knee while one back leg lay at an awkward backward angle. Both broken. The terrified steer scrambled to get to its feet but kept falling back to the ground. The whites of its eyes showed, the black tongue curled as it bellowed out its fear and pain long and hard. It needed to be put out of its misery.

Seth looked at the desperate steer and touched his pistol. He leaned back to get his hand into the pocket and brought it out. He reached his forefinger and thumb into the other pocket, took out three bullets and loaded the revolver. Did he dare risk the others, especially Scott, hearing a gunshot? No way did he want Scott knowing he had this gun.

He looked ahead. The yards and trucks were barely visible through the trees. The cattle continued their onward rush. The others would hear him for sure plus it may spook the mob even more. No, too risky. He uncocked the pistol and pushed it back into his pocket. Seth urged the horse ahead, trying to forget about the steer's suffering.

He caught up as the lead steers trotted into the yards. Pete remained on one side of the herd with Jimmy on the other. Rosco urged the last ones in with a shout and wave of one arm. All four riders dismounted. Pete and Jimmy brought both sides of the gate together and secured them with a hook and chain. The men tied their sweaty horses to the rails and walked around the side of the yards.

One red double-decker, B-double already stood ready at the ramps. The gates of its first trailer open at both the higher ramp and lower one directly beneath. A stranger, presumably the driver, stood near the ramp. A similar truck, but dirty brown, waited behind the first.

There he was. The short, arrogant, deranged Scotchman appeared from no-where and approached the men.

"Seth. Pete. Jimmy. Rosco. Good tae to see ye all." He shook each hand in turn.

"Hoo did the horse go, Seth?" The beady eyes squinted and stared deep into Seth's mind.

Seth swallowed a gut full of dread. "Ah, yeah, he went good, Scott."

Scott nodded. "Aye, good." He looked around. "Good mob. Reit, we dornt hae time tae waste. Let's gie them loaded. Pete an' Jimmy wark th' gates an' ramps. Seth an' Rosco brin' them up frae behin'. When they're aw loaded ye dismantle th' panels an' load them back on tae Brian's truck ower there." He pointed to a white, tray-back truck on the opposite side of the yards. "He'll pay ye, awright. Seth, ah want to gab tae ye alone when th'trucks are loaded, awright?" He winked.

Seth nodded. "No worries, Scott." *No worries?* Scott will either force him into the truck or shoot him dead there and then. His belly full of dread swelled like bread in an oven. And what the hell was that wink all about? Jimmy could have been bullshitting about Scott taking Seth with him. Perhaps Scott lied to Jimmy, wanting to keep Seth on his toes. Is it possible Seth was going to give him a bonus and didn't want the others knowing? Ha! Very doubtful.

Seth turned to walk back toward the yards to begin pushing the steers toward the ramps. Rosco was already entering the bigger yard.

"Seth"

Seth gritted his teeth and turned back to Scott, wishing they could just get on with the job. "Yes?" The short, solid Scotchman standing mere metres away with a smug smile needed flattening once and for all.

"Ye dornt fool me." He spun and headed toward the loading ramps.

He was too far away to read Scott's eyes when he spoke, but the undertone definitely contained a threat. But exactly what Scott meant by those words, Seth was unsure.

First trailer was loaded with no problems. The driver moved the truck forward until the gates of the second trailer lined up with the ramps. Gates were opened and the line of steers continued flowing into the semi.

Red and blue flashes stopped Seth in his tracks, herding the last of the mob from the large holding yard to the smaller ones. He dropped the stick he'd been using. More red and blue flashes as another police four-wheel-drive vehicle drove into view and stopped in front of the truck. Yet another. All coming from the direction of the main road, the same way the trucks had entered. Shouts and cursing filled the air as men ran around in panic. The steers raced out of the truck, their solid hooves *clacking* on the wooden truck floor, and back down the metal ramp.

"Police!"

Seth froze to the spot, unsure of who shouted. Through the yard panels he saw numerous uniformed and plain clothes police officers darting about, guns drawn.

"Fuck, I'm outta here." Rosco dived between the two lowest rails and sprinted into the nearby bush.

One uniformed officer raced after him. "Stop. Or I'll shoot."

They both disappeared into the scrub. Two police officers grabbed Pete and Jimmy and placed them in hand-cuffs. The empty truck roared into life, but the engine soon died. They must have got that driver.

Seth looked behind him, heart thumping right up to his temples. His horse was close-by. Alert, head up, ears forward. Ready to fly.

A shot rang out, echoing through the quiet bush. A man was running. It was Scott. Two officers gave chase. Seth bolted toward the back fence. He squeezed his over-sized, agitating belly through the fence and yanked the lightly tied reins from the steel rail.

Scott ran toward him, shouting but making no sense. His short legs almost a blur.

Another shot. More shouting. Seth tossed the reins over the horse's neck, one foot in the stirrup and threw his large frame into the saddle.

More shots.

"*Yah!*" Seth let the gelding have his head, in the direction they'd come. He glanced back. Scott was pointing a pistol at the approaching officers. He turned and pointed it at Seth. The shot split the air and rang passed Seth's head. His pistol was working its way out of his pocket. He took hold, cocked it and fired behind him.

And fired again.

The gunshots spurred the horse on to greater speed. It heaved and spluttered each laboured breath, sending globules of saliva back on the wind. Solid hooves pounded the muddy, but firm, ground. Seth looked back as they entered thicker bush. A man was down. By the clothing, it had to be Scott. Officers gathered around, guns drawn. He *has* to be dead. Scott deserved nothing better and besides, dead men can't talk.

Seth turned away from that scene, leaned forward and let the horse and the wind take him where ever they wished.

CHAPTER 39

Grace flushed morning sickness away, washed her face and rinsed her sour mouth. She turned off the tap to the sound of heavy, rushing footsteps up the front stairs. She headed to the kitchen. Seth ran inside, closed and locked the main door behind him. His face pale, his hands trembling, his chest heaving he leaned back against the door.

"Seth! What's wrong?" She filled a glass of water and took it to him.

"Thank you, Grace." He gulped the water down, strode across the kitchen and clunked the glass on the sink. He stood still and brought both hands to his face. His laboured breath shot out between his hands, reaching Grace's face.

"What happened?" Grace stepped back and pulled out a chair for him. "Sit down."

Seth dropped his hands and glanced at the empty chair. "No . . . thank you."

He grabbed Grace by both shoulders, his dark eyes glistening with . . . with what? She couldn't make out what ran through his mind, but it wasn't good. Sucking in a breath, she pulled her injured shoulder back from Seth's grasp.

"Oh, I'm so sorry, Grace." Seth dropped his left hand and leaned down to eye level with Grace. The fear that bubbled beneath the surface the previous day had errupted. Seth looked terrified. He also looked desperate. "Grace, I need you to come with me. Just pack what things you have and let's go. I'm not going to hurt you . . . *ever*, but you have to trust me, okay." A tear fell from his pleading eyes.

She shook her head. "Seth, I'm not going anywhere until you tell me what happened. Are you in trouble?" She believed he was, but she needed to hear it in his words.

Seth let her shoulder go and stepped back. "Yes, but you gotta understand, none of it is my fault. I've been set up every time. If I didn't do what I was told I'd be killed." More tears slid down his cheeks. He glanced out the sink window then back to Grace. "I'm just going to throw some things together and we'll go. Hurry, Grace." Seth strode down the hallway to his room.

Grace watched him disappear. It was all beginning to make sense now, or was it? As much as she cared about Seth she had no desire or intention of going anywhere with him while he was in this agitated state. Overnight, she'd put two and two together. The answer was shocking. She still couldn't get her head around it, but there was simply no other explanation. She'd intended to confront him when he returned, but she certainly hadn't been expecting this sudden panic and the desperate need to get away.

A vehicle drove in the driveway and stopped.

CHAPTER 40

Kain's phone rang.

"Hey, you got service again," said Joe. "'Bout bloody time."

Kain stopped and pulled out his phone. He really didn't have time for this. They were *so* close to Moutain View Road. "Hello."

"Kain, this is Dr Burns. I've been trying to ring you since yesterday. You missed your appointment. Where are you? Kain, it is *vital* you begin treatment. Your life may depend on it."

Ah, shit. "G'day Doc. Yes, I'm sorry. I'll come in tomorrow. I promise." He cut off the call. Bugger the doctor and the bloody cancer. He'd practically forgotten about it in the past twenty-four hours.

Anthony stopped and held up a hand. "I hear a vehicle. We're close to the road. This way." He pointed a little to the right and pushed on through the bush.

Joe and Kain followed. Kain dodged around several small trees and rocks to run in front of Anthony. If Grace was somewhere along this road, he wanted to be the first to find her. The first to see her beautiful smile and sparkling green eyes and give her the biggest hug ever.

The vehicle noise increased. Kain ran faster, jumping logs and pushing low-hanging branches out the way. The heavier back pack, containing the gun and tent, didn't slow him down. Sweat dripped from his face. His body ached. His mind focussed on only one thing. Grace.

He came to a clearing.

A house stood sixty-odd metres before him. Two four-wheel-drive police vehicles sat at the front of the house. Four policemen alighted from the vehicles. A fifth man got out. Bruce Atkinson.

Kain's heart lurched and dropped. Dropped to the pits at seeing that loathsome man, especially if Grace *was* here. He would surely try and stop Kain from seeing her. On the other hand, if Bruce was here, surely that meant that Grace was too. There could be no other explanation why Bruce would be here with the police.

Anthony and Joe caught up. Kain dragged in a deep breath. "I think we have the right house, but what the hell is *he* doing here?"

"Oh shit." Joe frowned. "And cops too."

"I think we'll just sneak along and try to stay hidden a bit longer, until we can get closer and see what's going on," suggested Kain. "Come on."

His future was in that house.

CHAPTER 41

Grace opened the front door several centimetres. Police officers walked from their cars. She closed and locked the door again and rushed toward Seth's room. He came out carrying a canvas bag.

"It's too late, Seth." She took hold of his forearm. "The police are here."

The life disappeared from Seth's eyes. His shoulders slumped and he dropped the bag. "I knew it would come to this." He sat on the bag and covered his face with his hands. A sob jolted his body.

With a gentle, but shaky hand, Grace took his gloved hands from his face and looked into defeated eyes. "It's okay. I'll stand by you, no matter what you've done." She wanted to hug him, protect him, but took his hand, beckoning him up, and led him to the front door. As much as she needed to tell him what she knew, now was not the time.

A loud speaker hailed, reverberating amidst the surrounds. *"POLICE. PUT YOUR HANDS IN THE AIR AND STEP OUTSIDE. WE KNOW YOU'RE IN THERE. WE HAVE THE HOUSE SURROUNDED."*

Seth clicked the door open and stepped on to the verandah, hands on his head.

CHAPTER 42

The police hailer demanded the occupant come out of the house and Kain looked out from behind a tree trunk. Joe and Anthony stood behind him. Joe's hand rested on Kain's shoulder.

A large man stepped out on to the verandah, his hands behind his head. Kain's gut fell to the ground. His bottom jaw tried to follow. It was the disfigured bloke from the servo that had copped shit from the yobbo.

"What the . . .?"

Two police officers walked toward, then stopped at the bottom of the stairs, arms extended, hands containing a gun. Bruce stood back near one of the vehicles.

"What the hell does *he* have to do with Grace?"

Another person came out the door. Grace. There she was. His beautiful Grace, very much alive. The bush spun into a blur around him. The ground shook below him. Kain leaned over and vomited up the water he'd not long drank.

CHAPTER 43

G race wiped her palms and walked out on to Seth's verandah. She stood beside Seth and placed her hand on his back. His large frame trembled. Yes, he'd done wrong, but she wouldn't let anyone hurt him. Not now. She stepped in front of him. Now the guns pointed toward her. Her heart thudded, threatening to convulse, but they'd have to go through her to get him.

"Gracie." Her father ran toward the stairs. He wore more wrinkles than just a week ago, and he looked so tired. Tears streamed down his cheeks. "Gracie, you're alive!"

One police officer stepped in front of him. "You can't go up there, Sir."

Bruce attempted to duck around the officer, but the man blocked Bruce's path. "She's my daughter. We thought she was dead. Gracieee."

She'd never heard him so distraught. "Dad. I'm-"

"*Grace.*"

Her gaze shot to the right of the driveway. Kain charged toward the house. Another police officer dived forward and grabbed his arm. Kain and her father seemed overtly relieved and surprised to see her. *Too* surprised and relieved.

Grace looked from her father to Kain to Seth. Seth stared at Kain, almost like he knew him. But that just couldn't be possible.

Kain yanked his arm away from the officer, while glaring at Seth. "What the hell have you done to Grace? I helped you at the servo, remember? All this time you've had Grace here when we all thought she was *dead.*"

"Calm down, or I'll put the cuffs on you." The officer beside Kain reached for the handcuffs attached to his belt.

Kain stopped. Anthony and Joe caught up and each took hold of Kain's arm.

"Control your friend, or I will." The officer glared from Joe to Anthony.

Now Joe and a friend had arrived, sweaty and anxious. Grace swallowed down rising confusion and panic.

One of the uniformed officers at the bottom of the stairs looked up and spoke, his hand resting on his gun by his hip. "We are looking for Seth concerning a cattle stealing operation that was busted this morning." His voice deep and hard, the words cutting through the stifling summer air between he and Grace. He took several stairs and stopped, looking passed Grace, directly up at Seth. "Are you Seth?"

Seth didn't move. "Yes." Defeat evident in his voice.

"Can you please come down the stairs." The officer stepped backwards to the ground, his hand still touching his gun handle.

Grace walked down beside Seth, each step brought her heartbeat up a decibel, each step a wretched step closer to losing him. She leaned closer and touched his arm. Maybe it would be for the last time. In a silent prayer, she hoped not. "It'll be okay. I'll help you."

Joe and Anthony let go of Kain. With slow steps he approached the house, wiping both eyes. "I knew you were alive, Grace." He shot Bruce a look that could freeze a wildfire.

Grace and Seth stopped at the bottom step. Grace clutched his hand.

The officer spoke again. "Seth, I am placing you under arrest for cattle stealing and other offences dating back several years. You'll be accompanying us to the station." He took the cuffs from his belt and moved forward.

Seth pulled his hand from Grace's grip and ran to the side of the house yard.

"Seth, come back or they'll shoot." Grace gripped the hand rail. Her heart rode up to her throat. *"Please."*

Seth pulled the pistol out of his pocket and held it up. "No one's taking me anywhere. For as long as I can remember, I've been pushed here, pulled there, forced to do things I don't want to do. Well, no more." He pointed the gun to the side of his head. His faced cleared of any colour. His gaze dropped to the ground. "I'm sorry, Grace. I'm *so* sorry."

"Seth!" Grace screamed, *"no no"*. She ran toward him. Only metres from her, he seemed a hundred miles from her outstretched hand. "Put it down."

Shouts and running. Someone grabbed Grace's arm. She flung the hand off. She'd almost reached Seth. He pushed the pistol into this temple. A shot fired, echoing through the surrounding bush.

"Noooo." Everything blurred in front of Grace.

A grunt pierced the air. Grace turned back. A man was down, blood on his leg. "*Dad*." Kain ran toward Grace, a rifle in his hands. "Kain, did you shoot Dad? What the hell . . .?"

She charged at Kain, who dropped the rifle and held out his open arms. Grace smacked his arm away. All the hurt of the break-up boiled over. She balled her left fist and drove it into his chin. "How *dare* you?" She ran to her father, now in a sitting position, a grimace of pain shrouding his face. "Are you okay, Dad?" An officer standing by called for an ambulance.

"Put it down, or we'll shoot." A police officer's command rang out.

Seth. Her dad's injury didn't seem serious, so she ran back to Seth. He now pointed his pistol at police. Tears streamed down his face. His blank eyes stared straight ahead.

"Let him have it," said one officer to the other.

"Nooo. Don't shoot him." Grace, only metres from Seth, pushed herself harder.

"Get out the way." The order shouted by an officer didn't deter Grace.

She must reach him. Protect him. More shouting, including her name, all jumbled into a cacophony of fear and senselessness. She grabbed Seth's raised hand and pushed with all her strength. The pistol fired to the ground then fell from Seth's hands. The police rushed over, guns drawn and pointed at Seth.

"Move aside, Miss."

Seth remained still, hands hanging by his sides and chin resting on his chest. She stood in front of him, reached back and grabbed both his hands in hers. "No, I won't."

Bruce hobbled over. "Gracie, why are you protecting him? He tried to steal my cattle."

"You don't get it do you, Dad?" She looked around. Kain stood back near the stairs, his pale face in shock. "We can't let them hurt him. He's been hurt enough. Can't you see that? Look at his face." She gripped Seth's gloved hands tighter.

Seth spoke. "He's right, Grace. I deserve everything I get. I did help steal his cattle." His voice quiet but full of resignation. "No point fighting it." He took his hands from hers came out from behind Grace, holding out both clenched hands. "Cuff me."

Grace pushed his hands down. "No, Seth."

Bruce's face reddened. "Grace, get out the way and let the police arrest this . . ." He looked at Seth's face and screwed up his own face. "This . . . disgusting example of a human."

A balloon of anger dropped into Grace's stomach and inflated. Within seconds she was ready to burst. "This *disgusting human* is someone you know."

Bruce's features hardened. "Don't be silly, love. This man is nothing to us. He's a lowdown thief. Come away from him. Now." Bruce reached toward Grace.

Grace ignored her father's hand and turned to Seth.

His mouth dropped open, his forehead creased. "What are you talking about?" He glanced at Bruce. "How could I know him?"

"Seth, take off your shirt." Grace touched his sleeve. "And your gloves."

Seth grimaced and shook his head. "No, Grace, I can't do that."

"If you care about me, you'll do it." This was his final chance, even if she had to stoop to emotional blackmail. "*Please.* Everything depends on this."

"All right." A heavy sigh escaped his lips. "I'll do it for you." With a shrug, Seth pulled off his tight gloves. He put his hands behind his back and glanced from one policeman to another.

"I'll help you with your shirt." Grace undid the buttons.

"Grace, what are you doing?" Kain voice rose to an anxious pitch.

Without a sound, Seth took off his shirt and dropped it near his feet. Grace took his hand and led him closer to Bruce. The policemen moved back several steps and remained quiet but continued to point their guns at Seth.

She held both Seth's hands up to Bruce. "Who do you know that has both ring finger tips missing, Dad?" Bruce leaned forward, squinted and studied Seth's hands with an upturned mouth.

"Show him your back." Grace touched Seth's arm, and with a gentle hand, turned him around. "Look at that tattoo." She pulled her own right shoulder sleeve down and ripped off the dressing. Holding the sleeve down, she turned her back to her father. "It matches mine. Do you remember how angry you were when Steve and I got these, after sneaking out to go to that concert when I was underage?" She held the sleeve down for several seconds before facing her father again. "Well?"

"What are you trying to prove, Gracie?" The corners of his mouth dropped again. Sweat dripped from his face. His tired eyes brimmed with tears. "Are you saying he's . . . he's Steve?" His handsome face whitened and grimaced. Maybe from the leg injury or possibly the shock.

"Yes." It came out a whisper, but she wanted to let the whole state know. "*Yes.*" The tears flowed and she didn't care. She picked up Seth's shirt and handed it to him.

"That's not really enough to prove it. Anyone can get a bloody tattoo. He looks nothing like Steve. Nothing." Bruce straightened his shoulders. The defiant look was back.

"Okay, then wait." Grace ran up the stairs, grabbed the old photo, bottle of black hair dye and Steve's belt and returned downstairs, placing the photo pieces in her shorts pocket.

Seth buttoned up his shirt, staring at Bruce. Kain had come over and stood beside Bruce. Both men watched her descend the stairs. She held out the belt to her father. "Remember when Steve was given this belt from Mandy after winning some events at Mount Isa rodeo?"

Bruce stared at it for several seconds and nodded. "It looks like the same one."

"And this." She held up the black hair dye to Seth. "Seth, do you dye your hair?"

Seth's face reddened. "Um, yeah. What's left was going grey. Scott told me I had to dye it or shave it."

"What colour did it used to be?"

"Ahh . . . brown, I think."

"It still doesn't prove he's Steve." Bruce winced and grunted. A police officer wrapped a bandage around the bullet wound in his leg. "Plenty of people have brown hair. He doesn't look one bit like Steve." He turned away from Seth as if the sight of him made him sick.

Grace's heart cried silent tears. Both for Seth and her father's bull-headed refusal to believe. "Okay, then maybe this will convince you, Dad." She took the two pieces of the old photo out of her pocket, placed them together and held them in front of his face. "Can you see this? Do you need your glasses?"

Bruce squinted and moved Grace's hand back a little.

Grace turned the photo over. "Jon and Steven 1985. Who . . . is Jon?"

Bruce's ashen face turned a sickly yellow. His normally steady hand trembled and reached out for the photo. "Jon." It was barely audible. A croaky whisper. His chin quivered. Silent tears slipped down his cheeks. He aged a hundred years. "My boys."

"Your *boys?*" There was only one answer and she was terrified to ask the question. She placed her hand on Bruce's back. "What happened to Jon?"

"He . . ." Bruce wiped the tears, but more followed. "He died. Not long after this photo was taken."

"H-how?"

Bruce looked at Seth, who stared at the photo in Bruce's hands. "I", he handed the photo back to Grace and his gaze dropped. "I used to believe that Steve caused his death. Pushed him into that water hole where he drowned. Steve had said that he was teaching Jon to swim."

Grace bit her lip and fought back a sob. *I had another brother.* "But Dad they were only little kids. Steve couldn't have known what was going on. Even if that were true."

"I know." He nodded twice. "Jon was . . . was my favourite. I know I shouldn't have had favourites." His body shuddered with a loud sob and his proud shoulders sunk.

Grace wanted to hug him then and there, but needed to hear more. She needed to know more about Jon. A fresh stab of hurt washed over her for the brother she would never know and for the one she had just found, but who still suffered. And she may lose him again. "Go on."

"I blamed Steve for a long time, for Jon's death. Couldn't even hug him or tell him I loved him." His lips and chin trembled. He sniffled and wiped his nose with his hand. "I hated the sight of him."

"Oh dad." Grace's eyes watered, but anger continued to simmer. "How could you hate your own flesh and blood?" Her hand went to her stomach, protecting the life she believed was growing inside. She glanced at Kain and wished she hadn't. His stunned look changed to a frown, his gaze on her hand.

"It wasn't until after Steve left home that your mother confessed to me that she'd been with the boys at the waterhole. Jon had been crying, saying he was thirsty so she ran to the house to get him another drink. The boys had been playing on the bank and she'd believed they wouldn't go back in the water but wasn't too worried because they could swim. All these years she carried that guilt and I'd blamed Steve because of what he'd said. She'd tried to tell me it wasn't his fault, but I didn't believe her." His head lowered and moved from side to side. "Deep down I did, but Jon was gone and Steven was still here. I missed Jon so much. He was so much more . . . I can't . . . say it." He brought his hand to his face, crumpled to the ground and wept. "I drove Steve away. I just couldn't handle him around, even when he grew up and worked for me."

Grace didn't know what to say. A million thoughts and questions flooded her brain. She needed time to process this shocking news. She licked her dry lips and swallowed. A broken man sat before her. As his daughter she longed to reach out and comfort him, take his pain away, but as Steve/Seth's sister she wanted to turn her back. He'd driven Steve away and how much Steve had since suffered was beyond comprehension. His physical scars were obvious and he'd told her some of his torment and past suffering but beneath it all was a tortured soul. A kind, caring tortured soul.

Siren blared and an ambulance arrived with flashing lights, pulling up as close to the front gate as possible with the police cars parked about. Two paramedics got out and strode over to where the police stood.

"Here is the patient." One police officer pointed to Bruce. "Bullet wound to the flesh on his lower leg".

The paramedics helped Bruce up and to the waiting ambulance. He looked back at Grace. An old, worn down man. "I love you, Gracie. Please forgive me."

Grace chewed on her bottom lip a moment to keep it still. "I love you too, Dad. I'll be up to see you soon. Just go with the ambulance for now."

A *thud.*

"He's down." Two police officers ran past Grace.

She turned to the sound. Seth had vanished. Her gaze dropped. Seth lay sprawled on the ground. Her heart sprung to her throat. A jolt of electricity shot through her veins. "Oh no." She rushed to him and felt his neck. He was alive. "Wait," she called to the paramedics.

Two police officers crouched down by Seth. "What happened to him?" one asked Grace.

"I think he fainted. It happened a few days ago too. Maybe the siren scared him." Grace wiped the sweat from his forehead. "I don't know. He needs to get to the hospital." She shielded the sun from his face with one hand while fanning him with the other. "Come on, Seth, I'm not losing you now."

"We don't really have room for him," said one paramedic. "I've called for back-up anyway. They were already on the range road, so won't be long. We'll get this one to hospital." He rushed to the back door of the ambulance, jumped in and closed the doors as the driver roared the motor into life, reversed around and sped off.

"I hope you'll be okay, Seth . . . Steve." She smiled, but it was forced. When she'd realised Seth *hadn't* killed Steve and actually *was* Steve, her whole world turned upside down and inside out, shook about like bingo balls in a barrel. She'd had a bucket of questions before, but now she had even more, plus so many other things to contemplate.

A warm hand touched her arm. "Grace." She spun around. Kain stood before her, his tear-filled eyes a mix of emotions.

"Kain, I don't think I'm ready to deal with you at the moment." She rushed up the steps for a wet washer to wipe Seth's face.

When she descended the stairs, Seth was sitting up, elbow on one raised knee, head resting in hand. Two police officers remained crouching beside him.

"Grace." Kain persisted. "I need to talk to you."

She stopped in front of him, but averted his eyes. "Kain, I told you, *not now*. You *dumped* me. You said we were *over*." She glanced at his face then back to Seth. "Just go home."

Joe stepped forward. "Grace, you really should hear everything he's got to say. He's been through hell this past week. He needs to tell you something."

"Thank you, Joe. Good to see you sticking up for your mate, but in case he hadn't told you, he broke off our relationship in no uncertain terms. Now, please let me help my big brother."

She placed her hand on Seth's shoulder and knelt to wipe his sweaty face.

"What happened, Grace? One second I was standing there then next thing I was on the ground. Did someone shoot me?" Seth's hoarse voice crackled over the words.

"No, you fainted again." She turned to one of the officers. "Please don't arrest him. He needs to see a doctor.
Find out why he's passing out. He's not a bad person."
She looked back at him and a wave of love rolled through
her stomach up to her heart and out her eyes. "He's my
brother, Steve."

Grace threw her arms around his neck and cried, not
caring about the movement hurting her shoulder. The
years of not knowing. The years of wondering if she'd ever
see him again. The years of forcing herself to believe he
was dead and feeling that part of herself had also died, all
poured out. Seth's long arms wrapped around her waist.
His face moulded into her shoulder.

"Grace, I love you."

"I love you too, Steve."

Grace pulled back and wiped her eyes. She laughed,
cried and shook her head. "It really *is* you. Do you remember me or Dad?"

Steve seemed so sad. "No, I don't think so."

"But it's okay. You can have treatment and therapy to
get your memory back."

"Can I get my face back? Can I get you back?"

A second ambulance arrived amidst sirens and lights,
followed by another police car.

Grace held his hand. "I'm not going anywhere, but you
have to go to hospital."

"That's not what I mean, Grace."

She turned to the officers, trying to ignore his comment.
"Please don't arrest him. He doesn't know who he is and
has been through absolute hell. He saved my life last week.

Wild dogs attacked me after the car accident. They would have killed and eaten me, for sure."

The younger of the two officers spoke. "*You're* Grace Atkinson?"

"Yes, why?"

"You were killed in that accident."

Grace looked about. All eyes homed in on her. "Why does everyone keep telling me I'm dead, for goodness sake? Do I look dead? What . . . ? Oh no". Susie or Sally. "The other girl was driving my car. Did she . . . was she killed?"

"There was a deceased person found in the driver's seat of your motor vehicle, Miss Atkinson. She was burned beyond recognition and the only identification located at the scene belonged to you."

Grace raised her outstretched hands. "But couldn't you do DNA testing to identify her or me?" She slapped one hand to her mouth and gulped in a breath. "I remember now. The explosion and flames and the smell . . . oh God." She swallowed the rock forming in her throat. "The poor thing. She'd already been through hell."

Kain stepped forward. "I demanded that, but they told me your father had you, or her, cremated straight away. Typical." Anger flashed over his face.

Two paramedics helped Seth to his feet and toward the waiting ambulance.

"You've been injured Grace," said an approaching older policeman who'd just arrived. "You need to get to hospital."

"Sergeant Rawlings." Kain walked closer and gestured toward Grace. "Believe me now?"

"What's he talking about, Sergeant?" asked Grace. Was she in the middle of some cryptic crossword?

"Oh, he-"

Kain cut in. "He had me thrown in jail because he wouldn't believe you were still alive, Grace. No-one would believe me. No-one. But I didn't give up."

"Come on, we have to get you two to the hospital," urged one of the paramedics.

Kain's handsome face, those gorgeous blue eyes full of love, just like they used to be. Grace placed her hand on her stomach again. Her heart wanted to stay, but her head said to leave. "I'll see you soon, Kain." She walked over to the waiting ambulance without a backward glance. She needed to listen only to her head. One glance back and she would be in his arms, but the pain of the break up still sliced into her heart.

CHAPTER 44

Grace arranged the pillows behind her head so she could sit up. One pillow too hard and the other too soft. The bed not as comfortable as the bed at Seth's but it was clean and everyone was now being taken care of medically.

"Is it all right to come in?" Kain peered around the brightly coloured curtain that surrounded the beds in Emergency. "Only if you're up to it."

His face pleading and hesitant, but Grace's heart lifted and brought a smile to her lips. "Yes, come in."

Kain's face softened and the worry creases disappeared. "At least I smell a bit better than I did out in the bush." He sat on the chair by the bed, unable to take his eyes from her.

"Kain . . . why are you staring at me like that? You're making me a bit uncomfortable. I really don't know what to say to you after everything that's happened."

"Then just let me talk for a while, please." He took hold of her left hand. His hands were warm and clammy, almost sweaty in hers.

"You seem nervous."

"Grace, I feel lots of things at the moment, but mainly relief." His eyes glassed over. "I thought you were dead. Killed in that horrible accident. They thought you'd been texting me while driving. I knew you were angry at me for breaking it off."

Her gaze focussed on the flowery curtain around the end of her cubicle. "Can you blame me?"

"No I don't, but I need to tell you why I ended our relationship."

"You made that clear, Kain. You wanted to go out and be free to *find* yourself. While you were *finding* yourself, doing God knows what, I was lost out in the bush with frigging wild dogs chasing me. They were coming in for the kill when Seth saw them and shot one. I thought I was about to die." She pulled the starchy white cotton blanket up to her chin to try and stop her body trembling.

"I'm so sorry that you went through that. That's not the real reason I broke it off." Silence.

Grace dragged her reluctant gaze to him. "What do you mean? What more can there be?"

"I lied."

Grace's heart picked up, gathered anger and pushed it to her throat. "You tell me all that stuff and now you say you *lied?* Wasn't it enough that you humiliated me and dropped me like a cold stone that meant nothing to you?" Tears stung her eyes. His words stung her heart.

"Grace, no, it wasn't like that."

"Well, what was it like? Did you want a fling? Or had you already had a fling and was feeling too guilty to tell me the truth?" Her mouth bittered at his possible answer but she needed to know. "Well?"

"Grace, I . . . I"

"Just *tell* me, for God's sake. I want to go see Seth, I mean Steve."

"I have cancer."

Grace's breath caught half way in. She froze. Her gaze stopped at a particular flower on the curtain. A rush of thoughts shot through her brain. She shifted her focus from the curtain to Kain. There was no lie in his words or on his worried face. "C-cancer?"

Kain nodded and gripped her hand tighter, his eyes barely blinking the tears away.

"What sort of cancer?"

"Testicular."

"That lump?"

"Yes."

"But why push me away? I don't understand. You must have known how much I loved you. I should have realised that could be serious. I'm sorry, Kain. But you did such a good job of convincing me you no longer loved me." She could barely see him through her watery eyes.

"That was why." He wiped the tears on his tee shirt sleeve. "I didn't want to put you through it all. At best I probably wouldn't be able to have kids. At worst . . ."

"Don't say it." She brushed away her own tears. The thought of Kain dying was too much. Her heart stabbed at her rib cage.

"I never stopped loving you and never will. When I thought you were dead I wanted to die too. I actually tried to do it, but Joe stopped me."

Grace reached for him. Words couldn't get past the rock in her throat. Her eyes couldn't see him for the river of tears. He moved forward and melted into her arms and body. She closed her eyes. No words or pictures were necessary. His warm body fitted hers like they had always melded together. His beating heart totally in sync with her own. Even the beard stubble against her cheek and neck didn't bother her. She held him tight, never wanting to let him go again.

"Ahem." Sergeant Rawlings and another officer that had been at Seth's house stood at the parted curtain. "Can we speak to you both?"

Kain and Grace drew apart, wiped their eyes and beckoned the policemen in with a nod. Words still failed to come forth.

Both officers stepped forward to the end of the bed and Rawlings pulled the curtain closed behind them.

Sergeant Rawlings spoke. "Kain, you first."

Grace looked at Kain. He swallowed hard, watching at the officer. She squeezed his hand.

"You fired the bullet that injured Bruce Atkinson in the leg."

Grace pulled her hand away. "You really did shoot Dad? Kain?"

"I didn't mean to. The gun was loaded and I was worried someone was going to hurt you again. Seth, or Steve, was going crazy with his gun and your father was crazy and-"

"Oh, so you thought you'd shoot him? Just like that? What sort of man have you become, Kain?" She turned her head away from him, unable to look him in the eye.

"Grace, I was in shock too. Deep down I knew there was a chance you could have been dead after days out in the bush. Grace please look at me." He took hold of her hand again.

She expelled a deep breath and turned to him. "But I wasn't lost. I was at Seth's."

"Well, I know that now but your father blamed me for your death. He had you, well, who we thought was you, cremated straight away so I couldn't go to your funeral. Isn't that right, Sarge?"

Rawlings coughed and shifted uncomfortably on his feet.

"He took all your stuff from our place and wrote a horrible note to me on the bathroom mirror in your lipstick. He didn't want me to have even one photo of you. Hell, he threatened to kill me if I went on his property again."

Grace needed a moment to allow her brain to process these accusations. A thousand thoughts and questions flipped and somersaulted through her brain, but nothing wanted to come out her mouth. Surely, her father would have never done those things. Then again, he kept serious secrets that she had absolutely no idea about. Jon!" She shook her head. "I still can't believe I had another brother and he kept it from us, so anything could be possible with Dad."   "Joe knows everything I'm saying. Ask him if you don't believe me."

"I just can't . . ." She covered her face with her hands and rubbed her eyes. "Jon's name was *never* mentioned. It must have been torture for mum. And Steve." A thought struck her like lightning and her incoming breath stuck in her throat. "I bet he ordered Steve not to ever mention Jon."

"Maybe your father is not the bloke we both looked up to." Kain squeezed her forearm. "I'm sorry to say it, Grace."

"Dad does go overboard a bit with his stubbornness and after what happened with Steve . . ." She sighed. "I believe you. But I will need to talk to Dad about it when we get out of here. What about Mum? And Sophie? Are they okay?"

"They're on their way to the hospital now," said Rawlings.

"What else do you need to tell me, Sarge? Am I under arrest?"

"No, Kain. Normally, you would be charged with discharging a firearm without a license and lawfully injuring a man, but we'll waive the charges this time. I will warn Anthony about not carrying guns in the national park. Joe and Anthony told us everything you've been through to find Grace and about your diagnosis. Bruce insisted no charges be laid against you."

Kain sagged in his chair. "Thank you." He smiled at Grace and squeezed her hand with love.

"You're lucky...*this* time." His gaze hardened toward Kain a moment, but relaxed when he looked at Grace. "Now, Grace."

Grace looked at Rawlings, but kept hold of Kain's hand.

"We have to try and identify the woman who was in your car. Do you know who she was and why she had no ID on her?"

"She was crying on the side of the road, when I came along. I can't remember everything. She'd been hitching a ride, but someone had picked her up and then dumped her out with nothing. I'm not sure what her name was. Sally or Susie, or something like that. That's about all I can tell you. Sorry. And I'm so sorry for her." She blinked away fresh tears.

"Why was she driving?"

"I was upset and tired and I wanted to text Kain to tell him I was going away for a while."

"But why let an upset stranger drive your car?"

"I didn't let her drive straight away. We chatted and she brightened up a bit." Grace sat back further in the bed and shrugged one shoulder. "I don't know. I just had an urge to text Kain right then and I was sick of driving."

"So, no mention of where she was from?" asked the second officer.

Grace pressed the sides of her head. A dull ache grew into pounding. "I'm sorry. Wait, I think she might have said 'Brisbane'".

"All right. It seems too much for you now. We'll wait a few days and talk to you about her again. We'll see if we can get a picture from your description of her and send it to Brisbane. She must have family and friends."

"Thank you. It's all getting a bit much for my head." She wiped her forehead.

"Just a bit more." The sergeant folded his arms. "Steve."

Grace's headache lightened at the mention of his name. "How is he? I want to see him. He'll be so scared and confused. You're not going to arrest him are you?"

"We're still deciding what to do with him. He has to be mentally assessed. DNA tests are being done right now to prove if he is Steve or not."

"I *know* he's Steve."

Rawlings held up one hand to stop her saying anymore. "Yes, yes I know you believe he's your brother and all the evidence points to that being correct. But we have to know for sure and your father insisted."

"Ohhh Dad. Why doesn't he give Steve a break?" She let out a loud sigh and dropped her head back on the pillow.

"Grace, your father wants to pay for plastic surgery for Steve. He told the doctor he wants the best plastic surgeon in the country. He'll bring one from overseas if necessary."

Grace looked at Kain, whose eyes almost jumped out of their sockets and mouth had dropped open.

"Wow." She glanced at Rawlings. Her heart ballooned with pride for her father. "He does have a heart of gold after all."

"More like guilt," mumbled Kain.

"I'll just pretend I didn't hear that." Grace resisted a grin, but he was probably right.

"Would you like to see Steve? He's in one of the cubicles around the corner." Rawlings gestured to the right with his thumb.

"Yes please." Grace ignored the hand Kain placed out to her. "It's okay. I'm not hurt that bad."

"How *did* you get these injuries?"

"The shoulder and bump on my head are from the accident – I think - and the others are from being hit by branches of a tree that was struck by lightning. That was just before Seth … *Steve* - that's going to take some getting used to- saved me."

Grace parted her curtains and walked with slow steps toward the cubicle Rawlings was now standing near. She opened the curtain. Steve lay on the bed, eyes closed, chest rising and falling. His upper half elevated by several pillows. He looked at peace. She'd expected him to look frightened and confused. "Seth?"

He opened his eyes. His lips spread horizontal. "Grace. You came?"

"Of course I did. I said I wouldn't leave you alone." She dragged the one plastic chair a little closer to his bed and sat down. Kain had followed and stood beside her with his hand on her shoulder. Rawlings and the other officer waited at the end of the bed, both placing hands in their pockets.

A middle aged bespectacled male doctor entered the cubicle and went to the opposite side of the bed.

"Everyone's here." Seth looked from face to face, but returned his gaze to Kain. "Thanks again for what you did at the servo that day. I had no idea who you were. When you said you had cancer and had just lost the love of your life, I had no idea she was alive and well at my house." Seth held out his hand.

Kain returned the handshake. "It's all right . . . Steve. You couldn't have known. I need to thank *you* for saving Grace and taking such good care of her."

"Righto then." The doctor studied the clipboard in his hand. "We have some results. The DNA tests were rushed through and they come back as a perfect match. You," he looked at Seth, "are Bruce Atkinson's son."

A sob flew from Grace, but left a smile on her face. The monolith on her shoulders lifted and her heart fluttered and danced like a butterfly. Kain's hand rubbed her shoulder and she grabbed Steve's hand, bringing it to her lips. "Hey, big brother." Her face soon ached from grinning and the tears skied down her cheeks, but they were happy tears.

Steve smiled, but seemed sad, staring toward the ceiling.

The doctor continued. "We're still waiting on all the other results, especially the brain scans. As soon as we get them we'll have a better idea of what we're dealing with."

Steve nodded.

"We'll be admitting you, Steve, and having a psychologist assess you in the next day or two as well. Okay, I'll be back shortly." With a swish of the curtain, the doctor vanished.

Steve looked at Rawlings. "Am I being arrested?"

Graced gripped his hand tighter.

"Not at this stage, Steve. Probably not at all. You've committed some terrible crimes, but we know all about James McTaggart and what he did to you."

A deep crease formed in Steve's forehead. "Who's James McTaggart?"

"You know him as Scott, the Scotchman."

Steve's face whitened. "Where is he?"

"Dead. He was shot at the cattle yards. He had several bullet wounds, from back and the front of his body. It wasn't clear which one actually killed him. The autopsy may not even tell for sure. Two bullets went into his torso. Just before he died he said something."

"What?" Steve's chest stopped mid rise.

"He said he made you. Made you his pawn. You were *his* man."

Steve's breath gushed out with a grunt. "He was going to kill me after the cattle were loaded, I'm sure of it. I've always been scared of him and never trusted him, but I had no choice."

Rawlings continued. "We understand he was a commanding, sadistic conman. We'll be interviewing you for more details, when you are feeling up to it. We also know there are other people connected to him and his drug cartel. Did you know about that, Steve?"

Grace gasped. "What a monster. Just as well he's dead."

Steve shook his head. "No. I only did . . ." He pulled the hospital blanket up over his chest and coughed. "I mainly only did the horse and cattle stuff."

"I think he planned to kill you, Pete, Jimmy and the other bloke too." Rawlings shook his head in disgust.

"Where are they?" Seth's brow creased.

"In custody at the moment."

"How did you know where I lived?"

"Jimmy told us. He was in a real fluster. Told us all we needed to know, including whose cattle they were."

Steve rolled his eyes. "That sounds like Jimmy. Go easy on him. Scott treated him badly too. "

Rawlings grunted, but nodded.

Seth took a deep breath. "So, Jimmy used to work for Bruce? I had no idea he was Grace's . . . my father. How did the police find out about the cattle?"

"A member of the public raised suspicions when they saw a truck going into the national park, loaded with fencing panels. We had a few officers go undercover and suss it out. The driver of one of the trucks was one of us." Rawlings grinned and puffed out his chest. "Did a bit of undercover work myself back in the day."

Seth closed his eyes, seemingly not wanting to hear anymore.

Grace looked at Kain then to the officers. "Can I please have a few minutes alone with Steve?"

"Yeah, of course. I have to go and find a phone and make some calls. My phone's flat." Kain kissed Grace's head and left the cubicle.

The policemen nodded and walked away. Their footsteps blended in with the everyday noises of an emergency department.

Grace took Steve's hand again. "So glad we have a bit of time alone. I still can't believe it. After all that time I was at your house, scared of you at first." She laughed at the memory. "Little did I know."

Steve opened his eyes and looked at her. "Yeah, crazy." He smiled for a moment then looked sad again. "Grace . . ."

Grace lowered her voice. "I know what you're thinking." She took a deep breath. "It's going to take a while getting used to calling you Steve."

"I know."

"About what happened at your place." She shifted in her seat. This was not easy. "How we . . . kissed." He looked away. "Seth, we have to forget about that, okay. I'm not going to say a word and I definitely won't be telling anyone, not even Kain and, *especially* not Dad, you held me there against my will. You never have to worry about that."

"Okay."

"But I do need to ask you something."

He looked back to Grace. "What is it?"

"Did you know I was believed dead, too?"

Steve took his hand from Grace's, placed it on his chest and turned away again.

"You did, didn't you? Seth, how could you?" It didn't make sense. He'd assured her over and over that he wouldn't hurt her.

He rubbed his eyes, took a long breath and turned back to Grace. "Yes, but not at first. I was so lonely, Grace and I felt something for you, some sort of con-nection."

"It would have been the family connection."

"Maybe. I don't know. I just wanted someone around. I was so sick of being alone and lonely. I sup-pose you hate me now. I deserve it if you do. You don't have to stay here and feel sorry for me. I'm so sorry for everything, Grace." A drop slid from one eye.

Grace held back her own tears. "I could never hate you and, as I said, I am *not* going to abandon you, *ever.*" She took his hand again.

Kain pushed the curtain aside and entered with a smile. "Just called my doctor and got my treatment organised. Start on Monday."

"That's good." Grace smiled at his relieved face. The final weight lifted from her shoulders. "I haven't even asked what the doctor said about the prognosis."

"He said it's good. Ninety percent chance it'll be treated early enough to clear it."

Laughter, rushing footsteps and crying approached the cubicle. The curtain was reefed aside. Linda and Sophie stood together, mouths agape, eyes red from crying.

"My . . . my babies." Linda dropped, but Sophie grabbed one arm and Kain grabbed the other. Linda lifted her drooped head. "Grace. My girl." Grace stood. Linda fell into her arms. "We thought we'd lost you forever." She clung to Grace and soaked her shoulder with tears. Grace thought she'd have no more tears left to cry, but matched her mother's.

Sophie approached Steve, her hand over her mouth, tears spilling over her bottom eyelids.

With blurred vision, Grace smiled at Sophie and tenderly released her mother's grip. "Mum, you need to save a hug for your son. He's home." More tears.

Linda stared at Steve for several moments. "Oh, my boy. What . . . did they do to you?" She leaned down and softly kissed his cheek, before running the back of her trembling fingers slowly down the side of his face. *Hush little baby don't say a word. Mumma's gonna buy you a mocking-bird.*

Steve closed his eyes.

Linda continued. *"And if that mockingbird don't sing."*

"Mumma's gonna buy you a diamond ring," sang Steve.

Together they sang the next two lines.

"You remember." Linda collapsed against Steve's chest, gasping for air between sobs.

"Sort of." He wrapped his arms around his mum. "I remember an angel singing that song to me."

"Private party or can anyone join?" Bruce poked his head in, sporting a rare smile. He sat in a wheelchair wearing a purple hospital gown, his leg bandaged and an orderly standing behind.

Sophie moved around and embraced Grace. "Oh big Sis, you have no idea how good this feels."

"I think I do." She was ready to burst with love and happiness.

"Grace." The female doctor who'd treated her when she was brought in, beckoned through the open curtains. "I have some results for you."

She let go of Sophie, who then put her arm around her father's shoulders. Grace took hold of Kain's hand and led him out of the cubicle.

The doctor took several steps and spun around, looked at Kain than back to Grace with questioning eyes.

Grace smiled. "It's okay, you can tell us both."

"Well, you have no serious injuries from your ordeal. No broken bones, but I'll send you down for an ultrasound on that shoulder shortly. There could be some ligament damage."

"Okay." Grace nodded, holding her breath for the next information. A kaleidoscope of butterflies *whooshed* through her stomach.

"That's good news." Kain placed his arm around Grace's waist and kissed her cheek.

"The biggest news is . . . your pregnancy test is positive."

Kain teetered on his feet, dropped his arm from Grace's waist and emitted a short, high-pitched grunt.

Sucking in her lips to prevent her cheeks popping with exhilaration, Grace grabbed his hand and looked deep into those gorgeous baby blues, wide open in shock and confusion.

She uttered one word. "Daddy."

What's next?

Will Steve regain his memory and finally be free of Scott's cruel legacy? Can he and Bruce rebuild any sort of father/son relationship while surgeons work to restore his face? His greatest wishes are to look 'normal' and find love.

Can Grace ever truly forgive her father for keeping Jon a secret and ostracising Steve? She must work hard to bring her family back together while welcoming a new life into the world and rebuilding her fragile relationship with Kain. Will Kain beat his cancer?

Find out in "The Winds Of Revenge".

AUTHOR BIO

Julie McCullough enjoys life on her small farm at Rosedale, Qld, where she endeavours to be as self-sufficient as possible. She has two house cows, lots of chooks, three ducks, two cats and a dog plus numerous fruit trees and a huge vegie garden.

Writing has been her passion since high school, and she has had non-fiction articles and short stories published as well as novels, this one being her fourth. She loves to write Aussie Rural Suspense fiction, tapping into some of her own past experiences of life on the land.

You can find out more about Julie and her books or contact her through her website